The OUTLINE

STUDIO
OBSCURUM

The OUTLINE

RORY LONDON

The Outline

Print ISBN: 979-8-9885129-0-5
Ebook ASIN: B0C771TJCX

Cover design and interior formatting by
Stephanie Anderson, Alt 19 Creative
Edited by Angela O'Connell

Published by:

Five Hearts
PRESS

To Nathan,
I wish you'd had more days.

To Shaun,
There will never be enough days.

To My Husbands,
Who taught me that the best time to love is always right now.

Playlist

Good Morning
THE DANDY WARHOLS

The Only Place
BEST COAST

You Look Like Rain
MORPHINE

It's Too Late
CAROLE KING

Sit Next to Me
FOSTER THE PEOPLE

Goodbye
CAGE THE ELEPHANT

Dirty Work
STEELY DAN

Seeing Other People
BELLE AND SEBASTIAN

Feels Like We Only Go Backwards
TAME IMPALA

Soma
THE SMASHING PUMPKINS

Valium Skies
THE VERVE

All I Need
RADIOHEAD

Drive
THE CARS

It Will Come Back
HOZIER

Summer Breeze
SEALS & CROFTS

Your Ghost
KRISTIN HERSH

I'd Die Without You
P.M. DAWN

About Damn Time
LIZZO

All I Want Is You
U2

It Din't Over Til It's Over
LENNY KRAVITZ

A Forest
THE CURE

A Song for the Lovers
RICHARD ASHCROFT

From the Dining Table
HARRY STYLES

PART

One

PROLOGUE

October 31, 2015

A FEW STRAY HAIRS had escaped my braid and were sticking to the back of my neck. I hummed in annoyance as I flicked them away, accidentally brushing elbows with one of three Princess Elsas in the room. Even with the ancient AC cranking valiantly in the window, the heat in the bar had risen to just a few degrees below the surface of the sun. Sweaty bodies slid against me as I maneuvered through the crowd.

Ugh. That better be an arm.

I desperately needed to wipe away the hastily drawn whiskers melting down my cheeks. It was going to be rough making it until closing. Watching customers drink and flirt drained me on my best nights—and that was without disguises and props and inexplicably sexy Sponge Bobs.

Zach had texted this morning to remind me staff costumes were mandatory, clarifying that "harried bartender" didn't count. I'd very elegantly flipped off my phone when that message came through, wondering how he'd guessed my plan. But I knew how stressed he'd been lately, and since he was my best friend, I forgave him for forcing me to play dress-up.

After tugging on a black full-body leotard I used for running in cold weather, I'd swung by the nearest drugstore, intent on finding something to make it costume-worthy. Since it was Halloween night, options were slim. I'd grabbed a black eyeliner pencil and a headband with furry ears. The finished product was ambiguous. The whiskers said "kitty," but the circular ears were more "teddy bear." Whatever.

At nine o'clock, I finally grabbed a bar towel and wiped my face. This smeared the pencil marks but decreased the likelihood I would sweat into someone's drink. At least the customers looked like they were having fun, hopefully in the mood to tip well. Fanning my overheated body with a menu, I resigned myself to dealing with the discomfort.

But as I handed over a drink to a pony-tailed Indiana Jones, I noticed some customers giving me side-eye. A quick check in the mirror behind the bar revealed that my makeup looked beyond terrible. There wasn't enough left to appear as though I was attempting a real costume—it just looked like I had a dirty face. Shaking my hands in the universal *come here* motion beneath the counter, I tried letting Zach know I had to go to the restroom to clean my "whiskers" off properly.

"Zach! Hey, Zach!" Stupid Zach. Making me figure out a stupid costume.

But the customers were relentless and I couldn't catch his eye. We were already down a bartender since one had quit two weeks ago, and Zach had been killing himself every night since. I felt slightly guilty because I'd cut back my shifts, focusing on my schedule-friendly coffee shop gig. I was glad I'd agreed to sub tonight since Zach could never have gotten through it without an extra set of hands. This was the busiest he'd been in months, possibly years.

Annoyed as I was, I had to admit it had been genius of Zach to advertise Hal's as a costumed Halloween party for the night. All we'd had to do was put up a bunch of orange and purple string lights and charge an insane amount at the door, as well as offer one-night-only cocktails of Vampire's Blood—sangria with plastic novelty teeth floating in it—and Ghostly Apparition—white Russian with a color-changing electric ice cube. It was a win for Zach, who had bought the bar earlier this year after being its star employee for a decade.

But my face makeup fiasco was of imminent concern. I didn't want looking like I'd just crawled out of a dumpster to affect my tips. Tuition was due soon. Still failing to catch Zach's eye, I looked up to find the next best option taking a seat on the stool in front of me.

"Busy tonight." Zach's live-in boyfriend, Teddy, exuded elegant calm.

I pounced. "Teddy! Thank God you're here! I need you to tell your man to come over to my side of the bar so I can get a break."

Teddy raised an eyebrow. "He's like thirty feet away. Can't you just ask him?"

"I swear I've tried, but we've been slammed. He can't even hear me when I'm right behind him. I just need two seconds to wipe my fucking face."

"Oh, doll." He tsked at me as he realized my dilemma, and as luck would have it, his pin-striped gangster costume came with a white pocket square, which he dipped in a glass of water and used to mop up around my scowl. I checked his handiwork in the mirror. There was still some smeariness, but it would have to do.

Teddy got up from his stool a few minutes later, immediately replaced by someone else needing an elaborate cocktail or twelve. Couldn't anyone just order a beer anymore?

Around eleven, Zach finally came over to check on me. Of course, his Jack Sparrow costume was in perfect order, including flawless black eyeliner, still evenly applied.

"Teddy said you needed me."

"Dude, that was like two hours ago. I just wanted to use the restroom since my makeup was sweating off my skull."

"Yeah, I see there's something going on here." He raised a hand toward my face and made a circular motion with his wrist. "Good God, woman, haven't you heard of setting spray?"

"I know. I warned you I wasn't a Halloween person. Or a makeup person. On the upside, it doesn't seem to be affecting my tips, or the number of customers asking for my number. Maybe I've been doing it wrong and the reason I'm single is that I haven't been streaking my face with finger paint."

Zach chuckled, but then eyed me seriously. "Sadie, don't come at me with that bullshit. You and I both know that you are *not* single. It's just a fun story you tell yourself because you're afraid of what your heart wants." At that, the traitorous organ constricted powerfully in my chest. The pain must have been apparent because Zach relented. "Don't worry, doll, I'm not going to force you to talk about you-know-who." He winked and added, "Besides, I'd guess the number of customers hitting on you has nothing to do with your face and everything to do with how fantastic you look in that catsuit. All that running...meow."

I smiled, grateful he'd left the messy subject of my love life in favor of my jogging routine. Zach knew better than anyone that me getting back into running these past few years had been more mental therapy than exercise, but it was a nice bonus that my clearer state of mind had resulted in a much higher ass.

"Okay, go away now, Zach. You were too late to save me. Let's just make it through last call."

CLOSING THE BAR took a lot longer than usual. It was almost three a.m. when I finally coaxed the last mermaid and Super Mario outside.

After shutting the door behind them, I leaned against it. I needed to start sweeping and wiping down tables, but I just wanted a minute. I felt every one of my thirty-five years as I closed my eyes and tried to will away the fatigue. Zach had said goodbye to Teddy an hour ago and was in the back office taking care of the registers, retreating after I caught him making some mysterious Twitter posts he wouldn't let me see. I rallied to get started cleaning so we would have a chance of being home before dawn—especially since I'd already told him I'd come back at noon to pull the Sunday shift.

I turned on the overheads and reached into the maintenance closet to grab some rags and cleansers. The ballasts were old, so it took a moment before the bulbs yawned on to reveal the shabbiness of the space. The theme of Hal's Taproom was essentially "old and uninspired." Zach had big plans for the future, but for now, the bar featured mismatched tables and chairs sandwiched between dark-paneled walls lined with neon beer signs.

But no matter how dingy, proximity to UCLA kept Hal's in the black. The students drawn in by convenience and cheap drafts often reminded me why "college kids" was a phrase and "college adults" was not. I envied them their energy and carefree hubris—how confidently they laughed, their certainty of a bright future. I sighed as I rounded up stray pint glasses.

Toward the edge of the bar, I noticed what appeared to be a stack of rumpled blankets propped against the wall, in a space just shadowy enough to be hidden without the overheads on.

Moving closer, I discovered the pile of blankets was actually a cape, a cape being worn by someone passed out and leaning their face against a sticky barstool. What the hell? I reached out hesitantly.

"Hey. You can't be here. It's time to go."

No response. Thankfully, I could see the rise and fall of Blanketcape's chest, reassuring me they were breathing.

"Hey!"

I was louder this time and poked a little. Still nothing. But when I nudged again, a dented silver flask fell out of the cape and clanked onto the floor. Shit! No wonder they were so wasted, if they'd brought their own stuff into the bar. We wouldn't have over-served anyone to this degree, and I couldn't remember seeing Blanketcape here earlier at all.

A low groan reverberated throughout the room as Blanketcape—who I could now see was a woman—stirred and rolled to her side. I guessed her to be in her early forties. Half her stringy bleached hair had escaped the clip at her neck, and she wore no makeup. Dark jeans and a t-shirt under her cape were the extent of her costume. *Jedi? Hobbit? One of Robin Hood's merry men?* I experienced a kindred connection with her lazy attempt at Halloweening.

I shook her gently. "Can I call you a taxi or something?"

She peered at me, dazed and unfocused. After a few moments, she handed me her phone. "Can you call Tommy, please?"

I had been a bartender on and off for much of my adult life, and I'd provided this service more often than I'd have liked. The person who answered, if they picked up at all, was never glad to get this call. I could only hope whoever was at the other end of the line was not a shoot-the-messenger type. I took Blanketcape's ancient iPhone, already unlocked, and found someone in her favorites listed as Tommy.

Pressing the call button, I internally cursed the bar gods for the awkward conversation that was about to ensue. Or the voice mail I was about to leave, being that it was three o'clock in the morning. It rang a few times and I hoped like hell Tommy wasn't one of those responsible people who powered down their phone at night.

"Mom?" a husky voice rasped into my ear. *That voice...*

"Um...no, sorry. Hi. Um...I'm a bartender at Hal's...on Westwood...and I'm here with this woman. She's...um...passed out. Or I guess she's awake now. At least a little. Anyway. She's here and she told me to call you. She gave me her phone. So, I did." Nope. Not awkward at all.

"Did you say Hal's?" *That raspy tenor...*

"Uh-huh." I stuttered. "Do you know it?"

"Um...Yeah...I've...been there." The man on the other end of the line mumbled. *That deep, throaty timbre...*

He'd been to the bar? Tommy? Had I met any Tommys? Awareness pricked at my skin as I replied tightly. "Well, she's here and, uh, needs to get picked up. She said to call you."

"Damn. I can't believe this. Except...of course she went to Hal's... after I told her...Wow." Tommy spoke so quietly it was almost a whisper. I could barely hear him, and the words I could discern made little sense. But then his exhale came through the line. "Okay. I was just heading home so I can be there pretty quick. Give me fifteen?"

God, that voice. He said he knew the bar. *Tommy almost sounded like... No. Just stop it, Sadie.*

"No problem. We're still cleaning up anyway." My tone wavered only slightly.

"Okay. Thanks. I'm on my way. And, um, you'll be there, right?"

"I'll be here."

A KNOCK CAME from the entrance as I was cleaning the icemaker. Since it was the middle of the night, it seemed prudent to be cautious.

"Who is it?" With no peephole, shouting through the wooden door was my only option.

"Hey, it's...uh...Tommy."

I swung open the door to find a grown man in a skeleton costume, complete with full face makeup, looking like one of the

Cobra Kai bullies who beats up Daniel in *The Karate Kid*. I glanced at him briefly—less than a second—before giving him my back and gesturing that he should follow me into the bar.

You didn't need more than a second. He could have been wearing a garbage bag and a mask and you'd still know. Somehow, I kept my voice steady as I spoke, even as my insides shook.

"It was me who called you. She told me to, so I figured it would be okay." I lifted my hand self-consciously toward my dirty, sweaty face, still not looking at Tommy.

You know why, Sadie. You know what you'll see if you look.

"I'm a bit of a mess. We had a big night at the bar. Anyway, I'm so sorry I didn't notice your mom sooner. She was sort of hiding. And we didn't over-serve her. When I tapped her, a flask fell out, so it looks like she brought something in."

He stopped moving, stopped following me. Instead, he stood there waiting patiently for me to meet his gaze. *He knows you. He knows not to push. To let you pretend.* Finally, I peered up. His eyes, large and penny-brown, demanded mine. I staggered back a few steps, and even across the distance, through the makeup covering his face and the coat obscuring his body, his presence filled in more empty space than I'd known was there.

Once he had my eyes, he spoke. "When I heard you on the phone, I thought at first it was wishful thinking. Especially since the last time I tried to contact you, I found out you'd changed your number. But then when you said Hal's, I knew." He shrugged out of his coat.

How had I not recognized that voice immediately? *Hadn't I? Growly and sexy and low.* It had haunted my dreams, along with a decent portion of my waking thoughts, for nearly a year. I drank in the markers of him—his six-foot frame, its lean sinewy lines, the roll of his shoulders, the telltale way he placed weight on his left foot—buried in my consciousness. And as the picture came together, peeling back layers of memory to bring him to the here-and-now, I felt my skin flush. He ran a hand over his black-capped head, and the motion drew my eyes to his long fingers. I could almost feel them on me.

"Sadie," he breathed out.

I had dreamed of those fingers, rubbing on my body, making circles, making lines. So many nights I'd lain awake, wishing they would touch me again.

"Renn."

CHAPTER
One

T HE DISTRESSED METALLIC letters on the entrance read Studio Obscurum. It was ironic that I was trying to make progress in shining a light on my future at a place literally named after the Latin word for darkness. I shook my head and braved the door handle.

It had taken a long time to get here. Ten months since I had made my escape. Ten months on top of eight lost years. I might still be figuring out my next steps, but I was ready for a permanent reminder that my best days were still ahead.

Never having been in a tattoo shop before, my expectations were entirely based on reality shows and the googling I'd done when I'd first dreamed up this idea. Studio Obscurum more than exceeded these imaginings. There were black walls and dim, moody lighting. Mismatched frames displayed gory yet subtly macabre artwork, and decorative creatures preserved in mason jars burdened the shelves. Loud, repetitive death metal music vibrated. Stickers plastered the cabinets and front countertop, advertising everything from gay pride to veganism to the local donut place to Yosemite.

Beyond the gothic aesthetic, this was clearly a well-run and professional workplace. Dark though it was, each workstation had an extensive lighting and magnifying setup. Tattoo recipients were either going to get a kick-ass piece of art or be subjected to an epic interrogation. The two artists I could see had their hands and arms covered in gloves and plastic as they worked. One was shading a pineapple on a woman's ankle while the other concentrated on a man's elbow spiderweb. The antiseptic smell of cleansers permeated the air.

I felt equal parts excited and apprehensive about getting inked. My communications with one of the studio's owners—and potential artist—over the past few months had mostly eased my nerves, but now that I'd arrived, my anxiety roared again beneath the surface.

"Hey, you must be Sadie," a deep voice reached me before my worries could boil over.

I looked away from examining a tiny octopus in a jar as a man came forward to shake my hand. He was wearing a white t-shirt and black Adidas athletic pants, with the three stripes down the side. His light-brown hair was longish, tamed in a loose bun on the crown of his head. The muscles of his forearm corded as he extended it, highlighting a colorful full sleeve. I didn't see other visible ink. I pegged him in his early twenties but didn't catch the dude-bro vibe that radiated from many of the similar-aged students who came into Hal's.

"Yeah. Hi." I shook his hand. "I'm looking for Renn Stoller. We're supposed to talk about my tattoo. My theoretical tattoo."

"That's me." The unfiltered smile on this attractive twenty-something was distracting. I dropped my hand from his before realizing what he'd said.

"Wait...you're Renn?"

"Yep." His grin was the perfect balance of cocky and authentic, highlighting a dimple in his right cheek.

Noticing his smile? A dimple? Jesus, brain. Just stop.

"Um. Okay." I shrugged away my errant observations, stuffing my hands into my back pockets. While the ambience of Studio Obscurum had conformed to my expectations, this man in front of me did not. "Don't take this the wrong way, but the whole time we've been emailing and DMing I somehow thought you'd be a little older, from how you write...and I guess also since you own the place."

He nodded, as though this came up a lot. "It's alright. But I've been doing tattoos for five years, besides being co-owner. I have a big portfolio you can check out if you want to. There's more than what I've got online."

I'd been communicating with Renn for over two months now, after finding his work on Instagram. He was the third artist I'd reached out to, but the only one who seemed genuinely interested in what I wanted to do. I didn't know exactly how I'd pictured him. Definitely older—maybe less Jonas Brother and more Son of Anarchy—but who was I to judge?

"Don't worry, Sadie, you're not the first person to hesitate because I'm young—I'm twenty-three, by the way—especially with the size of the piece you're considering. And it makes sense to be cautious. Ink is permanent and you want your artist to know what they're doing." He reached behind his head and pulled out the elastic holding his bun in place. This lifted his shirt enough to tease a strip of flat, smooth belly, and revealed his hair to be just below chin-length. He twisted it up in the rubber band again before continuing, "And if you really want a more experienced artist, I have someone here with two decades who does great work. But I don't want to abandon the progress we've made with your design. Maybe we can just talk a little and see how it goes?"

His expression was so approachable and open. *That smile.* I was...disarmed.

Forcing myself to shake off the awareness, I exhaled before replying. "Alright."

"Great." He gestured for me to follow him toward the side of the room, where a desk and computer indicated an administrative area. "Did you get a chance to look over the last sketch I sent?"

I had seen it, and it was beautiful. Months ago, I'd asked him to design a tattoo with the themes of strength and renewal, with the caveat that it needed to include a blue lotus. He had sent me a design that had the lotus, but also an ouroboros. I had never heard the word "ouroboros" before, and Renn had explained it was basically a snake eating itself, usually in a circle, and what we now thought of commonly as an infinity symbol evolved from ancient etchings of the ouroboros.

Renn's tattoo sketch was told in four square panels, like a comic book. In the upper left panel, there was a chain-covered brick wall, something pushing it from behind. The upper right panel showed the beginnings of the lotus and ouroboros breaking through the bricks, straining the chains. In the bottom left panel, a vibrantly shaded ouroboros wrapped around a blue lotus busted out from behind the wall. By the fourth and final panel, the snake and lotus had obliterated the wall and chains. It was colorful, and although I'd initially been skeptical of the idea of multiple boxes, the final rendering looked incredible, different from any tattoo I'd seen when I'd searched for ideas.

"I love it," I said. "I appreciate you going back and forth with me so much to get there."

"Like I told you in our *many, many DMs…*" Renn grinned. "It's the first time in a while I can remember truly enjoying the planning. And I'm not just saying that so you'll work with me. No matter what happens, it feels good to be so invested in a project again."

Because my ideas were so abstract, we'd had to work through more on the front end than was typical. We had exchanged *a lot* of messages—so amid solving tattoo dilemmas, there had been many eye-rolling GIFs, surprise face emojis, and stupid dad jokes to break up the impasses. *No, Renn, I didn't want to consider that this tattoo might look better if it took up the entirety of my hip—I hope you weren't being serious about that suggestion!*

Our connection had been immediate. We had volleyed and bantered and negotiated, and I'd reveled in every LOL I'd drawn from him. Even in this moment, confronted with blown expectations of his age and appearance, I still somehow sensed we were in sync.

But I'd also spent the better part of the past ten years being told constantly that I was needy and annoying. Even with months of therapy under my belt, a constant creep of self-doubt remained, so his emphasis on our "many, many DMs" struck me.

Which is why I felt compelled to ask, "Are you sure you didn't mind...all my messages? My questions?"

Renn seemed confused. "Huh? Of course not." His lips flattened as his forehead scrunched up. "Why would I mind? I really enjoyed talking about your tattoo, and I want to get it right just as much as you do. Besides, some of those texts were pretty great." He paused, eyes opening wider and smile returning. "Like, your bullet-pointed list of reasons for not including a wolf or bear pawprint as part of the design was some top-notch entertainment—"

"C'mon. That would have looked stupid on me."

"Agreed. But that doesn't mean your stern DM of 'I'm not Ed Sheeran' wasn't funny."

My jaw ticked. "No offense to Ed. But he's made some questionable choices with his ink—including the pawprint." I looked around as though to ensure the pop music gods weren't nearby to strike me down before adding, "Plus, his music is pretty basic."

Renn chuckled, admiration in his eyes. "See, you're proving my point right now." He looked meaningfully at me. "Nothing about working with you has been difficult."

I couldn't doubt his sincerity as I shook my head. "Thanks. I wasn't trying to make it weird. This is just new territory for me."

"You're fine. I'm about to spend months stabbing you repeatedly with my magic color gun." He lifted his forehead. "It would be strange if you didn't have concerns, especially since this is your first tattoo."

"Okay. But how about *you* make it weird the next time, so I don't feel so bad."

He huffed out a laugh before smoothing out the sketch of his design on the table between us, back in business mode. "Usually, when customers want a symbol of renewal or moving on or whatever, I suggest some kind of phoenix rising. It intrigued me that your wish list beyond the lotus was super vague, except you clearly stated *no phoenix*."

"Yeah. I, um, know someone with a phoenix tattoo and didn't want the reminder. Besides, your design is better."

His cheek lifted at the compliment, dimple on point, not pressing me to elaborate on the phoenix. Instead, he offered, "I'm glad you let me go with the four-panel. It's a bit of a risk, but I think the final product will be something special."

"Well, 'a bit of risk' is what I was going for. Like I said in my messages, I want to symbolize moving forward in my life. I figure inking my intentions on my body permanently will provide some motivation."

"You'd be surprised how many of my clients say something like that. I'm glad when I can help." Renn focused his brown eyes on me. "So, we're good then...we're doing this?" I hesitated only a second before saying yes and shoving my hands back in my pockets. He gave me an encouraging nod and told me he needed to print out some forms.

And even though he'd probably started kindergarten while I was in high school, the decision to move forward felt right. The tattoo was a gamble for me, so it made sense that the artist would be as well.

Renn returned with a stack of paperwork that seemed an appropriate amount to purchase a small city or perhaps adopt one of the

Obama girls. "We're pretty intense about liability here," he joked. "Seriously, look it over. It tells you more than you ever wanted to learn about getting a tattoo and aftercare, all that stuff. Let me know if you have questions. Otherwise, you can sign it and bring it back with you when you come in to do the outline next week."

The outline would be a new beginning. That was what I needed.

THE NEXT DAY, I leaned against the oven in the apartment I shared with my best friend Zach, thinking. After I'd left the shop, my adrenaline-fueled excitement over the decision to go for it eventually became overshadowed by unease over that awareness I'd sensed when Renn had smiled at me.

The whole time we'd been messaging, I hadn't anticipated what it might be like to meet him in person. I'd been lively and free within the buffer zone created by digital distance. All those previous texts and DMs seemed a lot more fraught now that I'd put a face to the name. Now that I'd seen that fucking smile. That dimple. How had I never considered that Renn would eventually be *real*?

I peeled off the outer wrapper and pressed a spoon against the thin cardboard of the canned cinnamon rolls I was holding. *Pop!* The dough started oozing through the seams of the tube and the sight seemed like a metaphor for how I felt now—still raw and doughy, but with that first initial pressure released. I'd come a long way since I'd been back in Los Angeles, but still had so much more to do before I'd be fully baked. Let alone ready for frosting.

And anything beyond a professional relationship with Renn— with anybody—would definitely count as frosting.

It had been ages since I'd felt even a twinge of attraction toward someone. Flirting and dating and romance weren't on my radar. I didn't have a timeline on when those things could be part of my life, but I assumed they should probably come *after* I had an actual career path, and certainly after I'd regained more of my confidence and self-worth.

I'd been bartending at Hal's since January, biding my time while I figured out my next move, working to get past the damage done by my last relationship. I was toying with the idea of going back to school but didn't want to make the commitment until I had a better sense of what I might like to study. I already had a biology degree I wasn't using and I didn't want to risk paying for another bachelor's in a field I was unsure of. I just needed to get in the right headspace to decide.

The energy I'd felt messaging with my at-the-time-faceless tattoo artist had been a bright spot over these past months, but it hadn't yet translated to my everyday life.

I separated out the dough on a cookie sheet and popped the rolls into the oven. Unsurprisingly, the mere presence of pastries in my vicinity brought Henri crashing into my brain. *More sweets, darling? So many empty calories. Didn't anyone ever tell you that self-control is a virtue?* Ugh. I was hearing him less these days, but this predictable appearance was enough to have me removing the cinnamon rolls from the oven and icing them, without daring to take a bite.

Zach came into the kitchen as I stared down at the tray.

"Did the Pillsbury doughboy do something to offend you?"

"No." I looked at him, unfocused, sliding into a chair. "I was just wondering if I'll ever stop hearing Henri in my subconscious, making me feel like shit." Thinking about how ludicrous any sort of romantic attachment would be for me.

Zach frowned like he always did whenever Henri's name came up. Then he leaned over to kiss the top of my head, reaching to snag a roll. "You're getting better every day, doll. It might not feel like it all the time, but you're so much stronger than you were on New Year's."

I hoped Zach was right. But as he attempted to persuade me into taking a bite—his methodology consisting of shoving it in my face to the point I'd probably be sneezing frosting later—I found it difficult to believe.

"Doll, you know what you should do…" He strode around the living room, also the dining room in our tiny space, waving his arms. "You should decorate the place a bit, put your mark on it."

The apartment had originally been Zach's. He'd lived there since before I met him twelve years ago. It was homey, sort of Goodwill chic, crammed with mismatched books and odd mementos he'd collected. Pint glasses from Hal's dotted the space, serving various functions—flower vase, key caddy, coin catcher, M&M's container, toothbrush holder, and occasionally, water glass. When I'd come back to Los Angeles, I thought I'd just be crashing with him for a bit, but we enjoyed being roommates and had made the situation permanent.

"You haven't really done much," he reasoned. "You know I don't mind if you want to display your Vin Diesel figurine collection in the living room or whatever."

"Oh my god!" Zach had a purple throw pillow with "Pretty But Kind of a Bitch" emblazoned on it. I threw it at him. "One time! One time I told you I thought he was hot, and you're never gonna let me live it down!" I laughed.

Zach winked. "Seriously, doll. Feel free to make some changes."

"Yeah. I'll think about it." But I realized in that moment I had no clue where I would even begin. I had spent so long choosing décor and clothing based on styles Henri preferred, I wasn't sure what I liked. Yet another item to add to my mental "Shit to Talk About in Therapy" list.

Zach must have noticed the concentration on my face because he began pulling me toward the door. "C'mon, it's a beautiful day, and I think some fresh air might do you good. Let's take a walk."

Our apartment was small, but the charms of our Silver Lake neighborhood more than compensated, with lots of cute little cafes and busy sidewalks. The walk was slow-going, since Zach had to stop and admire every baby in every stroller we passed, along with kneeling to inform each dog that they were the bestest doggo ever. He could scare the piss out of unruly bar patrons and be the tough guy when needed, but deep down, Zach was a softie. I took a moment to appreciate the sunny day as we meandered to the reservoir.

He eventually asked me how the tattoo appointment had gone, and I told him I'd decided to move ahead with things. I then changed the subject quickly. I wasn't ready to open up yet about the flash of attraction I'd experienced with Renn, and I worried Zach would see it on my face.

I couldn't stop my dumb-idea-loving brain from being drawn to someone. That was just chemistry. Acting on it was obviously out of the question. So I guess I could just...wait it out? After all, Renn was twenty-three and seemed so easygoing. We may have had some great back-and-forth, but what did we really have in common? This weird pull toward him would fade, right? I just needed to stay focused on my tattoo and ignore the rest.

RENN WAS THERE early for my first appointment on a Sunday at nine a.m. Nerves had kept me away from the Cap'n Crunch, but I'd managed coffee. He'd already told me the shop's other artists didn't usually work weekend mornings, so we would have the place to ourselves. The plan was for Renn to do the outline of my tattoo in black today. He'd fill in the rest of the design and add color during later appointments.

I took my sunglasses off as I came inside, grateful for the lack of overhead lights. I'd worked later than planned last night—not enough rideshares immediately available for the number of tipsy coeds who needed them. So I was tired and looked it, rocking a no-makeup face, my long wheat-blonde hair braided in a dull line down my back. I had on a pair of jean shorts and an oversized David Bowie concert tee, since Renn had said to dress for comfort.

"I like that shirt. It looks vintage," Renn remarked as he printed something at the desk.

"It is. I have a box of concert tees from my parents. Mostly from the '70s."

"That's awesome."

"I guess. Although occasionally I'll get someone at my work young enough to look at one of my shirts and ask questions like, 'Who's Carole King?'"

He looked up from the printer. "Wait...who *is* Carole King?"

I frowned before Renn cracked up and started humming—badly—the first verse of "It's Too Late."

With its lack of windows to engage the morning sun, the studio was cool and dim. Renn had a variety of instruments laid out on a rolling metal table alongside squirt bottles of antiseptic and lotion. There were also medical-grade wipes and vials of what I assumed was ink.

Renn showed me the outline, printed out on transfer paper. It was large, taking up almost the entire eight-by-eleven sheet. Reality settled in my stomach, part elation, part dread. I was actually about to get a massive tattoo.

"I'm going to put this on your leg to check the placement. If you like it, I'll go ahead and transfer it to your skin."

Since my tattoo was on the larger side, and wouldn't fit on an ankle or wrist, I'd opted to put it on the back and side of my thigh, so I could easily hide it with clothing if I wanted to. My bravery had its limits.

"I appreciate you scheduling around my weird hours. I always work nights and have been pulling lots of overtime at the bar. It was crazy yesterday since UCLA played. That's the only time we're ever super busy. Because Hal's is kind of rundown, and there are better bars nearby. But it's cheap, so the college kids come. I didn't get home until three in the morning, so excuse me if I'm a bit off."

I was tired. Babbling. In my defense, Renn was on his knees behind me, engaged in an intense examination of my leg. I looked over my shoulder at his coppery hair, pulled back more severely than the first time we'd met. Since I'd known he'd be working on my thigh, the shorts I'd chosen were a skimpy juniors style, but he apparently needed more room to operate.

"I'm going to tape up your hem if that's okay."

"Sure." *Did I squeak a bit when I said that?* Renn grabbed the bottom of my shorts, rolling the hem twice and taping it to my waistband. I definitely ignored the three—no, three and a half— times his long fingers grazed my thigh. I glanced down and saw his face pulled in concentration as he angled the paper toward me. I couldn't help but notice his dimple again. *Nope. Don't go there, Sadie. Not thinking about that today.*

"This good?" He rolled a tall standing mirror toward us so I could see where he was placing the design.

"It looks amazing." I often despaired about the general state of my life and its lack of purpose, but being here made me feel different. I had come so far from the woman I was a year ago. The proof was in the mirror.

However, that didn't mean I was entirely ready to submit to the process. I stood stock still as Renn began rubbing the design onto my thigh. He smoothed the paper in small circles to ensure a successful transfer, working from the outside of my leg inward, fingers pushing against my skin.

Outwardly, it was innocuous. And yet that gentle, intimate touch had the unfortunate effect of stoking my insecurities, my inner critic pleading that no one wanted to touch my imperfect thighs, that all the running and squats in the world couldn't help them.

Darling, are you sure you've been keeping up with your runs? You should consider cross-training so you can firm up more. Unaware I was having a minor mental freak out, Renn slowly peeled away the paper. The purplish outline stood out on my pale skin.

"We'll just wait a few minutes for that to dry," he said.

I exhaled, mini-crisis averted—for now. I could relax much better when his hands weren't on my leg. I went back to the mirror and tried to get a better look.

The death metal playing the first time I'd come to the studio had been replaced by a loop of early 2000s indie anthems. As I stood, the speakers on the surround system crackled, and a Jack White guitar solo cut off mid-wail, followed by the beginning notes of Carole King's *Tapestry* album. I looked up at Renn.

"What?" He shrugged his shoulders. "I figured since you put it in my head, we'd better just play it rather than have it swim around in there all day. No one else is here."

I raised a conspiratorial eyebrow. "So, is this our little secret? Like, I shouldn't tell all your badass, metal-loving employees that Renn listens to '70s soft rock?"

"Go ahead, Sadie. I will own my appreciation for all things Carly Simon, Linda Ronstadt, and The Carpenters." He lifted his eyebrows back at me.

And then he was back to business, gesturing to the portable massage table he'd unfolded in front of him. My nerves came back full force as the reality of the situation hit me once again, just how far outside my usual box I was stepping. But I could do this. It was just like with any hard decision—you had to keep making it over and over again. Second-guessing...and third-guessing...and fourth-guessing...were a natural part of the process.

"Come on, it won't bite." He patted the black vinyl, covered with the thin white paper I associated with visiting my gynecologist. Super. "I'll grab you some little pillows to make you more comfortable."

Laying down gingerly on the table, stomach down, I winced when the paper tore a bit beneath me.

"I'm excited to get started," Renn said warmly.

I appreciated that he was trying to relax me, but there was no way I was going to be at ease when I was ass-up on a table with my shorts taped to expose as much of my leg as possible. When I'd decided to get the tattoo, I'd worked hard not to spend too much time thinking about how vulnerable I'd be while the artist was working. I'd spent the better part of the past ten years being with someone who constantly criticized my body. How it looked. The way it moved. How it felt in his hands. I wanted this tattoo to be a reclamation.

And there would be no hiding from Renn. Not when he had a spotlight and a magnifying glass pulled up next to the table.

"How are you?" He asked. "Comfortable?"

"Um...I guess."

"Seriously. We're going to be at this for at least an hour before I give you a break. Do you want another little pillow or something?"

"Uh...sure." He handed me a round bolster, and I put it under my chin. I was already clammy, plastering quickly to the thin paper.

"I'm also going to put a cushion under your knee so I can work in the best position. We agreed it was *my* turn to make it weird, right? Just sort of move your leg over here a bit." Renn grabbed my calf gently and bent it, then pushed a small pillow underneath, angling my thigh toward him. I tried to breathe through it all but couldn't totally release the rigidity from my limbs. He noticed. "You still seem tense. Nervous about the pain?"

"No." *Only the million unhelpful thoughts brawling in my head.* "It's just odd lying on this table. It's not the pain, more about being out of my element. Feeling awkward."

"Ahh...well, lucky for you, I don't believe in 'awkward.'" He used air quotes.

"What do you mean you don't believe in it?"

"People say that shit all the time, that someone is awkward, when what they really mean is they're doing something a little different or unexpected. I feel like awkward is just the default people use when someone is especially human."

Personal experience kept me from agreeing, having worn the label too many times, but it was a nice thought. And it was clear Renn believed the sentiment, his idealism a reminder of his youth. "I guess that's one way to look at it," I conceded.

"I'm serious, Sadie. You should be comfortable during this process. It inevitably gets a little *awkward*." Air quotes again. "I mean, you're lying on a table, and I have to contort your body into odd positions so I can do my work. I promise to do everything in my power so this experience is manageable—hell, even enjoyable—for you. Stretch breaks...conversation...no conversation...'70s slow jams...whatever helps. We'll be at this over several sessions, so you should tell me anything you need to be okay."

Idealistic or not, he wasn't faking his desire to make things alright for me. And I recognized that I'd been wrong to assume Renn's age and breezy nature somehow translated into a lack of substance. Sure, he was younger, much younger, and he looked different from what I'd pictured, but the fundamentals were the same. We connected. I sensed it. And as he met my eyes and smiled with *that fucking dimple,* changing the music over to Bowie, I knew he did too.

"Okay, Renn, I'm fine now. I can't promise you I'm ever going to be one hundred percent comfortable twisting myself on your table here, but I'll let you know if I need anything."

He grinned. "I promise to keep the Cirque de Soleil level bends to a minimum."

I settled as best I could as Renn's fingers rubbed lotion into my thigh. A moment later, I heard the tattoo gun buzzing, and then the first prick of the needle sunk into my skin.

"Well. You're not a tattoo virgin anymore," he said, keeping his eyes firmly on his work. "How does that feel?"

"Honestly, a bit like getting my eyebrows threaded, if we're talking about a pain scale, so not that bad. I can see why I read on the Internet that some people fall asleep getting tattoos."

"Are you planning to sleep?"

I chuffed. "Um...I couldn't sleep right now even if I'd run a marathon, eaten an entire Thanksgiving turkey, and taken two Ambien."

Renn had to stop working for a moment to laugh. "Don't worry. Lots of first-timers are nervous." He paused before continuing seriously. "I'm just glad you're here. Doing this piece, the faith you put in me to design something with so few limits, it's gotten me excited about my art again. You're like the pop of artistic adrenaline I didn't know I needed. I can't tell you how many tattoos I sleepwalk through these days."

"That's a nice thing to say."

"It's true." Shaking his head, he smiled and added, "I mean, you did say in one of your texts you thought *Parks and Recreation* is a better show than *The Office*. It clued me in that we would click."

I recalled the exchange from a few months ago. In our messages, I'd mentioned that I was finishing up my third re-watch of the series. When he'd texted back with a GIF of Lil' Sebastian, we got extensively sidetracked talking about our shared love for all things *Parks and Rec*. He eventually got us back on course by imploring me, "Treat yo' self...to making some decisions about the sketches I sent you," and I had laughed out loud in the bar at his corniness.

Renn continued with the outline. We talked. About nothing and everything. The superiority of certain Marvel movies, our favorite local restaurants, extracurriculars we'd done in high school. I told him stories from Hal's, including how we were trying to figure out which regular kept stealing all our toilet paper. He told me about some of the weirdest tattoos he'd ever done. I hadn't known that people got the inside of their lips tattooed. There were also tattoos he was sick of doing. No more butterflies, stars, or Deathly Hallows symbols if he could help it.

Ninety minutes passed. Renn let me up to stretch and check out the progress in the mirror. After I walked around a bit and he gulped a Red Bull, I laid back down with much less stress than the first time, even with the tear in the paper. We finished Bowie and started in on Led Zeppelin until two hours later when Renn pronounced himself done for the day, cleansing my thigh, and placing a layer of protective plastic over my skin.

I stood to admire my leg in the mirror while Renn straightened up his workstation.

"Do you have any more clients?"

"Nah...we went for over three hours. That's plenty for today."

He stretched his arms above his head, flexing his biceps and revealing his tight abs. The immediate flash of *want* I felt was enough to steer me toward the door. "Okay. Well, enjoy the rest of your Sunday."

I grabbed my purse, but Renn called out. "Sadie?"

"Yeah?"

I watched as he walked to me, eyes directed at my new ink, before squatting down beside my leg. I couldn't help but notice the sheen of sweat along his neck—tattooing was hard work—and the contour of his chest under his t-shirt. Our eyes met as he slowly reached up and removed the tape from my waistband, rolling my shorts back down.

"Thanks," I replied throatily, feeling warmer than when I'd been cemented to the table.

"It looks good, right?" he asked, tilting his head toward my thigh.

"It does. I already love it." My heart sped up at his continued nearness.

"I know it's technically my job, but...I really enjoyed talking to you, Sadie. I can't remember the last time I thought...the session went by so fast." He appeared almost bewildered, still squatting in front of me, looking at the outline. "It's going to be fun filling this in."

He raised a thumb to my thigh, dragging it along the edge of the plastic covering. "It was peeling up a bit," he explained, talking to my leg, thumb still moving slightly. As he remained in place, the air charged quickly in the silence. His breath skimmed over my hip. He swallowed roughly before peering up at me. Our eyes locked.

I forced myself to turn away.

"I should go, Renn. I'm sure the other artists will be here soon, so you should probably turn on some Hungarian speed metal. I'll see you in three weeks."

Reverie broken, he rose unhurriedly. His smile was genuine when he aimed it at me and told me not to swim or get too much direct sunlight on my leg. I promised him I wouldn't and headed out as he went back to humming Carole King. After a quick gulp of fresh air while leaning against the wall outside the studio, I attempted to assess the situation rationally.

If I had to be unintentionally attracted to someone post-Henri, Renn had certainly demonstrated his worthiness—putting me at ease on the table, laughing at my jokes, making me feel interesting. In another universe, one where I was ready for love, wasn't paying Renn for his services, and he was in his thirties, we might have been a good match. But in this world, the timing was bad, he was off-limits, and an inappropriate age. Still, he was going to leave an indelible mark on me. I looked down at the outline of the lotus and ouroboros taking shape on my leg and smiled.

CHAPTER
Two

B Y THE NIGHT before my second appointment with Renn, the tattoo outline had reddened, crusted, itched like hell, and finally healed over.

The month between the sessions had allowed me to gain a fresh perspective on my attraction to Renn. It was going to be fine. We didn't have to actually *do* anything about the vibe between us. Hell, we didn't even have to acknowledge it. It could just...be there.

Besides, I didn't know Renn's romantic situation. At twenty-three, it was unlikely that he was emerging from a near-decade-long smooshed cow patty of a relationship like I was. He was hot. And an artist. He probably had a line of young women waiting to date him. That heated look he'd given me as he'd kneeled down by my leg—an image I'd been unable to banish from my thoughts—maybe he'd already forgotten it. Or maybe I'd imagined it.

That's what I kept telling myself.

Zach remained unconvinced.

I'd given him the full rundown of the situation after my first ap-pointment. At first, he'd teased me about Renn being twenty-three, calling me a "cradle-robber" and threatening to pull *Moonstruck* off the dusty DVD shelf. As I'd elaborated, he'd grown more serious.

"I don't understand why you're writing this off so quickly, doll. Why just automatically dismiss your feelings?"

We'd been sitting on the couch to that point, talking, and I stood up in exasperation, catching the reflection of my tattoo in the glass door of the balcony slider. "Zach, there are too many reasons to list." I held up my hand as I started ticking them off for him. "I am still getting over an awful eight-year relationship." I put my pointer finger down. "I'm still in therapy dealing with the fallout from said relationship." Middle finger. "I have no idea what I want to do for a career and need to stay focused on finding some actual life goals." Ring finger. "I'm literally paying him to do a job for me, so there's ethical ambiguity there." Pinkie. "He's twenty-three." I curled my thumb in, completing my fist.

Zach came over and closed his hand around it.

"Okay, Sadie, I understand everything you're saying, but I also think you shouldn't just ignore the fact that your tattoo ap-pointment basically sounds like the best first date ever. Amazing conversation with no weird lulls. No discovery of any psychopathic tendencies that had been undetectable through messaging. And a swoony eyes-locking moment at the end—"

"Which was kinda inappropriate, since I'm his client."

"Okay. I'll allow that." He released my fist and pulled me into his arms. "But you won't always be his client, right? And you deserve to be happy."

I didn't argue, and Zach didn't push. He wanted me to be okay, and I wanted that too. I supposed we were both grateful that my desire for Renn proved Henri hadn't broken me completely. But there was an enormous gulf between "not broken" and "ready for a new relationship." Or even just a new possibility.

FOR MY SECOND appointment, I'd been able to schedule on a day I didn't have a shift at Hal's, so Renn and I met at the reasonable hour of four p.m. When I got there, one other person was working. This man embodied more of who I'd imagined when I'd started reaching out to artists. Older than Renn by at least a decade, a leather cord held back his long hair. He wore weathered Doc Martens, along with dark-gray skinny jeans and a black t-shirt emblazoned with the Studio Obscurum logo, a design that looked like a giant heart melting over the earth. He glanced up at me as I entered, tilting his head in hello. I recognized him as the artist who'd been tattooing a pineapple on someone the first time I'd come in.

"That's Archie," Renn said, taping up my shorts. "He's here full time, so you might see him around while we're working." I nodded back at Archie and laid out on the folding table. This time, I knew where to place the pillows, wrangling my body into position with minimal stumbling.

Archie pulled off the gloves and plastic covering his arms, clasping his hands together above his head, inviting his client to take a stretch break as well. He came over to examine my leg. "So, this is the piece Renn was so excited about he was willing to get here before noon on a Sunday. That's looking awesome." I startled at the last bit because it sounded more like *thas-lewkin-ahhsum*. Archie spoke with the fast cadence and distinct accent of a Bostonian. "I mean, it's not as great as my work, but still pretty good."

"Don't mind him." Renn held the buzzing tattoo gun above my leg. "He's lived in Cali since he was ten years old, but still insists on speaking like he's in *Good Will Hunting*."

"Fuck off, Renny. You west coasters wish you sounded this *wicked pissa*." Archie shoved his colleague playfully on the shoulder. He then gave my thigh another once-over, nodding approvingly at me before sticking his middle finger up at Renn and heading back to his own workstation, once again out of earshot.

I grimaced as their teasing exchange dredged up a memory. My mind raced as it recalled an embarrassing dinner party that had begun with everyone offering their opinions on politics and ended with Henri yelling at me for acting like an "ignorant, liberal west-coaster" in front of his co-workers. Good times.

Renn sensed my tension as he began sinking the needle into my skin. "Something up?" he asked. "Is it the pain? I'm working close to the back of the knee and that bothers some people."

"No, no. Just the mention of Boston reminded me of something crappy. No big deal."

"Oh. Sorry. I didn't realize."

"It's fine. How could you have known?" I twisted my neck around to look at him, so he could see in my face I was sincere.

"I'm still sorry you're upset."

"Seriously, it's cool. We all have our shit, right? It just so happens my biggest flaming pile of poo happened in Boston."

He huffed. "That is very...vivid."

"Trust me, it's accurate." I grinned. "I know logically that Boston is a perfectly lovely city, with perfectly lovely historical landmarks and lobsters and crazy baseball fans, and millions of perfectly lovely people who all participate in a mass conspiracy not to teach their children about the letter R." Renn chuckled and I knew I'd never tire of making him laugh. "It just wasn't a lovely place for me."

"Well, I'm sorry for how disappointed you are in one of America's great cities, but it's good you have a sense of humor about it."

"Meh. One person's good humor is another person's ability to deflect difficult emotions using jokes and sarcasm. Semantics."

He chortled again, and I heard the buzzing above my knee as he went back to work.

I appreciated he hadn't pushed for details, but still felt oddly compelled to give him some. Renn had been so accepting of my uncertainty throughout this process, making me feel at ease every time I worried I was acting like a weirdo. I wanted him to understand at least some of where that self-doubt came from. I could convey the basics while leaving out the gnarlier specifics.

I took a deep breath, considering, before finally... "I don't mind telling you a little...if you want to hear."

He nodded at me, expression communicating that he was willing to listen, but also that I had no obligation to tell him anything.

I exhaled. "The short version is that I lived in Boston. It was just after college, and I didn't have real career plans, so I went there on a whim, looking for adventure."

"Why Boston?"

"No real reason. Too many episodes of *Ally McBeal* maybe." I smiled. "I'd been in Los Angeles my whole life, worked at Hal's since I was twenty-one. Figured I'd travel around the country a bit, have some fun, support myself tending bar."

"Apparently that didn't work out?"

I barked a laugh. "Hardly. I seriously underestimated how far my savings would go and sort of got stuck. I was miserable bartending in this sad little townie place where folks came to mind their own business and drink bottom-shelf liquor. It made Hal's seem like a trendy club in comparison. I was trying to save enough to move on, but then some stuff happened, and I ended up just staying in Boston."

Renn motioned for me to face forward again, breaking our eye contact. "I get the sense 'some stuff' might be the biggest part of that story."

"It is." I exhaled as loudly as my stomach-lying position would allow. "But it's same-old, same-old... I met someone...and he, um, turned out to not be a very good guy...and it ended badly."

"Oh…shit." Renn's gloved hand stilled by my side, softly grazing my thigh.

"No. No, it's alright," I said hurriedly. "He wasn't physical with me or anything… Just extra toxic." I rested my chin back on the pillow, but as he stayed quiet, I wondered if I'd said too much. "I'm not trying to barf out my life story on you or anything. I just wanted you to know why the mention of Boston got to me, why sometimes I stress about being *awkward*." My air quotes broke some of the tension.

When he responded a moment later, it became clear I hadn't said too much. Renn was simply treating my admission with the respect it deserved, thoughtful in his reply. "Thank you for telling me, Sadie. I'm sorry you went through something like that. No one should ever have to. But selfishly, I'm glad that—whatever happened in your past—it brought you to me now."

I felt his sincerity, that he sympathized without condescending to pity. *This is what it's supposed to feel like when someone likes you. They're supposed to treat you with care.* He really was an amazing guy. I wasn't prepared to serve up any more details about Henri, but I didn't regret giving him something. "I'm happy I'm here too," I said. "I'm glad you put up with all my quirks."

Renn frowned. "Don't say it like that. I don't 'put up' with you. I enjoy spending time with you. A lot. Like I said, I haven't felt this way about doing a tattoo in a long time. And for the record, there's nothing you could tell me about your past that would change how much I like you." He paused and turned off the tattoo gun. I swung my head around in time to see him gulp hard. He wouldn't meet my eyes, occupied with scrutinizing my thigh.

How was I supposed to ignore our attraction when we were in this zone? Needing to steer us back to neutral ground, I gave him a teasing half-smile. "I don't know, Renn. Some of my flaws are fatal. I can get pretty stabby in traffic—I've flipped off an old lady or two. I've also been known to retaliate against handsy customers at Hal's by making sure their beers were extra warm and foamy."

Renn put his hands up, taking the out. "Hey, you're allowed to look out for yourself at work. And who hasn't been inspired to road rage by someone's grandma? We've all done things we're not proud of."

I laughed. "Even you?"

He smirked. "I once tattooed the lyrics to an entire Taylor Swift song on an eighteen-year-old woman's back."

I shook my head and grinned in reply, turning my neck to rest it on the cushion again as Renn picked up his tattoo gun. Of course, he was correct that everyone had done things they weren't proud of. But there were very few things in my life I *was* proud of. My friendship with Zach was the only stable, longstanding thing I'd ever achieved. Permanently inking T Swift lyrics on impressionable young women aside, Renn was a business owner. He had a passion for his art. I couldn't expect him to understand my angst over my lack of direction.

But that didn't mean he didn't have his own shit. He'd told me twice now that my tattoo had ignited his creativity again. But why had he lost his inspiration in the first place?

Renn was bent over my leg, concentrating on his work, when he began speaking quietly. "Look, I know it's hard to move on from the past when things are...haunting you." He paused, looking faraway for a moment. "But I meant it earlier when I said that whatever happened before won't change my opinion of Sadie-right-now. I may have only known you a few months, but I think I know enough. I know you're humble...and funny...and so damn smart, like, clever, not just in a school way. I know you're the kind of person who answers messages and shows up on time to appointments. I know you have good taste in music. But mostly, I know you're here on my table, outside your comfort zone, because you're looking to symbolize strength and starting over, and that's pretty fucking cool—no matter what went down before. Okay?"

Okay? Okay. Jesus.

I was grateful his "okay" was rhetorical. Closing my eyes, I placed my chin on the pillow and just...revelled in the knowledge that Renn *saw* me. No one besides Zach had seen me in years. The hum of the tattoo gun provided the soundtrack to this revelation. Also, the Metallica on the speakers.

Later, as Renn worked, occasionally loud-talking amiably with Archie across the studio, I thought about my time in Boston. How not-okay I'd been made to feel.

Darling, no one will ever love you as much as I do. You don't need to work in this shithole bar, not when I have plenty of money. I want to take care of you.

I had accepted so little from Henri, confusing control with caring. I'd met him at a low point, directionless and miserable, spinning my wheels at age twenty-five. Henri had been twenty-eight but already had the type of job where a well-cut suit was the expectation. If not for an inopportune flat tire, he'd never have come into my bar. At the time, I'd had roommates I sort of liked in an apartment I sort of hated, but that was about all I had going on. I'd thought Henri was my savior. I was such an idiot. Such a cliché of a girl who got taken in by a pretty face and slick words, missing all the red flags.

WE WERE ALMOST two hours in when Renn thought we should take a break. We'd mostly been exchanging funny childhood stories, staying away from the heaviness of our earlier conversation. Renn now knew about my first kiss in middle school, and I'd gotten an earful about the great bowl haircut of 1998. I got up to check the progress in a long mirror next to my favorite jarred beaver... opossum? Squirrel?

All the filling in so far was in gray-scale, shades of black elevating the outline to a genuine work of art. It was coming along.

"So, when did you get back to California?"

"What?" Engrossed in the mirror, I didn't hear Renn at first.

"How long have you been home in LA? If it's okay to ask." He folded his left arm across his chest and pressed it with his right wrist, momentarily distracting me with the tight flex of his forearms.

"Oh. Sure. You could probably guess. When everything went to hell...with the guy...it just made sense to come back here to figure things out. That was at the beginning of this year. My best friend Zach basically threw me on a plane to LAX and brought me home. I'm not sure I would have made it out of there without him."

"Ah... So, it sounds like you and Zach are...really close—" Renn cringed. "Um...sorry. That just came out. Totally not my business." He suddenly became captivated with arranging his instruments on the silver wheelie cart next to the table.

I chuckled. "Don't worry about it. We're definitely close. But just friends. Friends and roommates." I didn't elaborate, unwilling to out Zach without asking—not that the dude had so much as a pinky toe in the closet. *Why are you clarifying this for Renn at all, Sadie? It's like you want things to stay dangerous.*

"Sounds like a great guy."

"He's certainly done a lot to help me get back on my feet. He was the one that got me hired back at Hal's. That's where we met, when I worked there during college. Zach never left."

Renn turned toward the sink so he could wash his hands before putting his gloves on, waving to show I could lie back down. "Ride or die friends are gold," he said, gesturing across the room at Archie. The blond man was wearing headphones, oblivious to our conversation as he cleaned up his workstation. "That asshole's been in my life as long as I can remember. I don't know what I'd do without him."

I smiled as I pictured the giant muffin and coffee Zach had left for me on the counter that morning, along with a note telling me to have fun getting colored on. "I understand completely."

"It's lucky you got your old job back at least, when you came home."

"Lucky? You don't think it's kind of sad? Like, I'm in the same spot I was in when I was in my early twenties, and the years in between didn't amount to much."

Renn appeared to think that over, but then shook his head as I laid down in front of him. "That's just one perspective. You could think of it as more of a do-over. Like, at least it's better to start back from the same spot rather than ten steps backward."

"Only this time I'm starting with more wrinkles." I laughed and reached my hands to my cheeks, pulling the skin back to my ears tightly.

"Haha. You're not exactly the Crypt Keeper." He glanced at me with obvious appreciation.

"Easy for you to say. You have your whole life ahead of you. It's not really about the wrinkles. Just that it's no small thing to realize you've literally wasted years."

"But you're only in your thirties, right? Like, what, thirty-one?"

"Thirty-four."

"Okay then. You're not even thirty-five, so you still have a lot of good things ahead."

"I hope so, Renn. I love your optimism."

"And I love your sense of humor, even though you use it a lot to poke at yourself." He grabbed my knee to turn it toward him, moving the magnifying glass over as he eyeballed the tattoo from above. "Whatever you've been through, you seem to have come through alright... More than alright." That last part was said in a whisper, and I caught him from the corner of my eye as he dragged his gaze along my body, clearly believing I couldn't see him from my current angle.

The spark between us flared unabated. We seemed unable to stop stretching the boundaries, testing the push and pull. As determined as I was to leave the connection unacknowledged between us, I couldn't deny it.

"It's so crazy, Renn. I never think of myself as being alright. Because of Boston. And even before. But when you say it, I almost believe you."

He smiled in reply before leaning down to get back to work, leaving me to my thoughts.

Most days were still hard. Working through the past in therapy. Struggling to envision and build my future. But with each passing minute I spent with Renn, my insecurities quieted further. He was waking up mental muscles I hadn't flexed in years. With him, I was clever...smart...funny...strong. Desirable. I spent more time contemplating the possibilities of the years ahead of me, instead of focusing on the regrets of the ones in the rearview.

"I can hear how hard you're thinking down there," Renn spoke from above the light.

"Actually, I was just considering what you said earlier..." I recovered with the half-truth. "That you don't think thirty-four is too old to still do things."

"Jesus, again with the age thing, Methuselah. You're still young."

"Tell me that when you're in your thirties."

"You're not that much older than me."

I huffed loudly at that ridiculous statement. I could give him credit for a lot of things, possibly including being wise beyond his years, but he couldn't just wish away the age difference. "Uh-huh... What year were you born?"

I was lying on the table, but he still hadn't started working again. He crossed his gloved hands across his chest defiantly. "1991."

"Yeah?" I thought for a moment. "Well, that was the year I bought my very first CD. I went to Sam Goody Records at the mall on the bus with my best friend from sixth grade."

"What did you buy?" *That was his comeback? Weird, but okay.*

"*Nevermind* by Nirvana."

He startled slightly at that but recovered his game face quickly. "Classic choice...and your point?"

"Obviously, it's a reminder that there is more than a decade between us." *Our easy connection might be undeniable, but those eleven years—they were a* fact.

He uncrossed his arms and sat down on the stool next to the table, so we could face each other, pausing another few beats before continuing. "True...but that doesn't seem to matter, does it? It feels like we get along pretty well." He moved his gloved pointer finger back and forth between us, and his deep voice rumbled. A fissure of awareness ignited in me as he captured my gaze and held it.

"Sure." I breathed out. "We do okay." That was an understatement, especially in light of the things he'd said about me earlier, but I still wasn't prepared to admit anything out loud. I'd come into the studio with that as my hard line, and nothing had changed.

He reached out a latexed finger and ran it thoughtfully over the outline of my lotus. "Look, Sadie. I can't pretend that how we are together is how I am with my other clients. And deep down, I think you know that." His finger detoured to trace the circle of the ouroboros. "There's a lot of other bullshit in my life, but ever since you climbed up on my table, hell, ever since we started talking online, I've felt like myself in a way I haven't in a while. I don't want you to get stuck on the age thing when it's obvious that we—"

Renn stopped himself. He sat up abruptly and dragged his hand through his hair, dislodging the little bun-pony and then cursing because it meant he'd have to wash his hands and change gloves. Doing that before sitting down again, a battle played out in his expression before he ground out, "Sadie...I don't want to cross a line here...but...I can't have you thinking we're not on the same level. Because maybe down the road—"

"I get it," I interrupted him. There was nothing he could say that I was ready to deal with, so I hurried on, "I get it...okay?"

He ran his freshly-gloved fingers over my thigh again, both of us aware he had no legitimate reason to do so other than to touch me. Both of us knowing we desired that touch. "You want to hear something funny?" He asked.

"Hmm?"

"You told me your story about buying *Nevermind* because you wanted to prove how different we are. Like, because I'm too young to have a CD collection, we don't have anything in common."

"I guess that's kind of what I meant. Plus, the reminder that I was busy going to the mall while you were busy being born."

He nodded. "But what's funny is that *Nevermind* is the first album I ever bought, too. I just bought it on iTunes and not at the mall."

"For real?" I shook my head. No wonder he'd smiled when I'd mentioned the title.

"Don't underplay this, Sadie." His deep voice commanded the air as he kept tracing my tattoo with his fingers, pressing them into my skin. "The way we are together is rare, and we shouldn't dismiss it over something as insignificant as age. I don't ever want you to think of me as anything less than your equal."

"Renn—"

"And I don't want to sound unprofessional, but I need to make sure you understand." He leaned down until our faces were level. "I'm a grown man, Sadie."

'HE SAID WHAT NOW?' Zach huffed.

I'd asked Zach to go for a run because I needed to debrief my tattoo session from three days ago. I'd kept the details to myself that long, trying to make sense of Renn's words before calling in reinforcements. Midday sun hovered pleasantly over the dirt trails, and the Los Angeles skyline gleamed postcard-perfect in the distance, but I barely noticed my surroundings.

"He said 'I'm a grown man, Sadie.' But he said it sort of low and growly, like Batman. I've been so used to thinking of Renn as all sunshine and rainbows and approachable hotness, but all of a sudden he was...I dunno...a *man*."

"That actually sounds...kind of sexy?"

"I know." I sighed.

I stopped running and pulled off to the side to escape the crowds. A woman in full makeup and lashes jogged by wearing a "Stop the Turkey Holocaust" t-shirt. Gotta love Thanksgiving time in LA. I was happy to be home, but it was a dumb idea to come to Griffith Trails on a sunny weekend.

"So, what happened next?"

"What?" I took a long swig from my water bottle as we settled onto a bench.

"After he used his Batman voice to declare his manhood. Then what?"

"Oh...well, nothing really. We'd already had enough serious conversation that appointment for, like, thirty tattoo sessions. There was some tension in the air for a minute, but he just put his head down and got back to work. We made small talk. He finished up this section after a few hours and I left." I pointed out the shading on my leg.

"Well...that's kind of a letdown."

"Sorry I can't entertain you with Real Housewives of the Tattoo Parlor or whatever, but I'm sure Renn and I are on the same page. We don't want to say anything we can't come back from."

"Honestly, that's too bad, doll. I'm really thinking he might be good for you."

"Zach, we've been over this. I've told you I'm not ready. Sure, it feels good in the moment, but once I'm away from Renn and can look at things from a distance—the situation is just so fucked. And he's still twenty-three."

"Yes, but...*he's a man*." Zach did his best attempt at a Batman voice, but he sounded more like Tom Waits.

"Shut up, dork. I brought you here to make sure I stayed sensible, not to talk me into doing something I definitely should not do. I admit I'm attracted to him. I'll even admit that I enjoy it a little. But I know myself. I'm not prepared for more."

"I'm just saying, you seem...I guess more awake would be the way to describe it...than I've seen you since you got back. And it sounds like you and Renn have already crossed a line. You're more than artist and client, based on everything you've said."

"Zach, as my friend, if you truly want what's best for me, I'm asking you not to push it. Please."

"Fine." Zach went back to openly ogling the runners passing by before continuing a minute later. "Doll, I just don't think you should write the idea off completely. Take the time you have left on this tattoo to decide. Maybe you can start something after you're no longer his client, when there's less ambiguity. Maybe you'll be ready then."

"It's not gonna happen. Even if he is a grown man...I'm still a disaster."

CHAPTER

Three

"I HAD TO PULL a ten-hour at the bar last night. And I've had a headache all day." I slumped in the passenger seat of Zach's car. "Maybe we should do this another time?" He had asked me a few days ago to attend this party, and I'd reluctantly agreed, but now I was second-guessing myself.

Zach sighed in exasperation, turning to give me a *look*, but not saying anything. He had driven us into the bowels of the Holly-wood Hills, insisting I wear the slinky eggplant-hued cocktail dress I'd hidden in the back of my closet. The gunmetal-gray stilettos already causing my toes to go numb were the first heels I'd put on since Boston.

"I can't believe you talked me into this outfit," I said nervously as he pulled up to the curb. The closest street parking he could find was a quarter mile from our destination, so we were walking the rest of the way.

"Think of it as your armor, since you're finally venturing out into the land of the living." Zach waved his arm around the nondescript rich-people-live-here street, as though to point out the wonders of overly manicured hedges and decorative streetlamps.

"I don't want armor. I want to be able to feel my feet."

"Well, sacrifices must be made for beauty." We arrived in front of a beige stucco mansion as Zach continued his pep talk. "Just try, doll. You barely get out of our apartment. I didn't drag your ass across the country to watch you tend bar or sit at home every night. Plus, you look super-hot, thanks to your genius stylist."

I knew Zach wanted me to own my look, but I just wasn't comfortable with this yet. I didn't feel like a hot girl at a party. More like a toddler playing dress-up. But I supposed I had to start somewhere.

"I appreciate the kick in the ass, Zach. I guess I've gotten so used to standing still that it's hard to move forward toward whatever's next."

"Well, what's next right now is this party. Let's see how it goes. Also, you *know* why I want to be here."

"Yeah." I knew. It was the main reason I'd agreed to come.

We followed some other guests on an illuminated pathway to the backyard. "Don't think of it as coming to a party," Zach reasoned. "Think of it as doing a solid for me. I need my wing woman. Anyway, this place is lit."

"Don't say 'lit.' You sound like a jackass."

"I think you mispronounced badass."

I grinned. "Sure."

"Well, then not lit. It just looks like fun."

It looked like misery. The last time I'd been to a party had been New Year's Eve, and thoughts of *that night* felt like slow vivisection. But I'd promised my best friend.

Zach pulled me by my wrist, and we passed through the archway of a stone fence into a large mission style courtyard. Strung Edison bulbs idled in the breeze, reflecting in the enormous pool. It was warm, even by December standards, but some people still congregated next to the freestanding heat lamps. Others milled around the massive firepit table, or by the glass bar filled with enough booze to restock Hal's for a week. There was a low hum from the six dozen twenty-and-thirty-something guests laughing and making conversation. I registered that this wasn't a keg and red cup kind of party. This was posh, although in a casual way.

"I see Teddy." Zach pointed to a wooden bench on the other side of the courtyard.

Teddy. The reason for this excursion. One of our regulars had introduced him to Zach and they'd hit it off instantly. I wasn't sure what Teddy did for a living, but it was enough to get him on the guest list to this party, and to invite his own guests, apparently.

With his optimistic charisma and mischievous smile, Zach never had trouble pulling men. But this was the first time he'd shown interest in doing more than just hooking up. Until he'd started getting all love-hearts-coming-out-of-his-eyeballs over Teddy, I wasn't sure if he'd ever thought of having an actual relationship.

Zach led me over to a tall, muscular but lanky man, with short dark hair, sporting a two-day beard. He was dressed casually in a patterned short-sleeved button-up and dark jeans with black Vans slip-ons, an outfit appropriate for a college student, but somehow this fortyish-year-old guy wore it well. Zach had mentioned that Teddy had money, a fact only evident from the ginormous silver watch he wore that would have looked at home on the wrist of Tony Soprano. He was attractive by any objective standard, but Zach had dated good-looking guys before. I wanted to know what made him *special*.

Teddy gave me an enthusiastic handshake. "Sadie, it's so nice to finally meet you. Zach told me big parties aren't your thing, so I appreciate you coming out tonight." He smiled with warmth that reached his eyes and my bullshit meter stayed quiet. I waited for a tingle of skepticism to crawl up my spine, but there was nothing.

After Teddy dropped my hand, Zach leaned in to give him a hug and Teddy held him at the waist, tapping their foreheads together. "I'm so glad you made it."

"Yeah?"

"Yeah. I wasn't sure when I asked that you'd accept the invite, and I just really want to spend time with you."

Okay then. No coded messages or secret handshakes from Teddy. For someone who had only known Zach two weeks, he certainly seemed all in already. I couldn't help but find his directness charming.

"Besides," Teddy continued, "These things can be boring, so it's nice to have you here to make it a better night."

"By 'these things' do you mean parties in general, or just the ones where you are having the awkward introduction to your new boyfriend's best friend?" I chimed in jokingly, noting that neither man flinched at my use of the B-word.

"Oh, this isn't just a party. This is a House Party of Hope..." Teddy used air quotes. "Which is a fancy way of saying it's a casual fundraiser someone hosts in their home, mostly for younger donors. This event is benefiting the LA Teen Suicide Prevention Coalition. That's why you see a microphone set up over there. At some point, the hosts will get up to make a speech and ask folks to donate." I looked over and saw the microphone, sending up a silent prayer of thanks that it wasn't for karaoke.

"And are you here because you support this coalition thing?" Zach was clearly learning about this for the first time.

"I support several non-profits, but I'm here mainly because a company I've invested in specializes in event planning for charity. They help coordinate these parties and find folks willing to host. So I go to a lot of them—"

"Shit, does that mean we'll need to make a donation?" Zach interrupted.

"No, of course not!" Teddy appeared taken aback. "I already pledged my support, and it was more than generous enough to account for all three of us. You're here as my guests."

I wasn't sure how to feel about that, Teddy shelling out what essentially amounted to a cover charge for us to attend this party. Zach also seemed uncomfortable with Teddy paying our way, reaching behind his head to palm his neck, glancing around warily.

"Damn, did I majorly fuck up?" Teddy ran his hand over his face. "I'm so sorry. I just wanted you to be here because this philanthropy is such a big part of my life, and I thought it would be a great opportunity to show you...and I didn't think about it being weird for you that I'd donate on your behalf."

It didn't take a genius to deduce this might be the first hiccup in Zach and Teddy's budding relationship. They looked like they wanted to hash it out, so I did something that seemed necessary, even though it made me slightly nauseous. I walked away to wander on my own.

I FOLLOWED A few other people into the home's lower-level interiors. Most of the guests were outside, so I felt less on-display in these uncrowded rooms and alcoves.

Small tables ribboned the hallways, dotted with baskets every few feet, and I realized this was a silent auction. Dozens of displays encouraged bids on things like restaurant gift cards and home décor items. At the end of one long hall, I saw a basket with a Seattle Seahawks jersey and a football signed by a player I'd never heard of, but knowing Zach was a superfan of the team—having been born and raised in Seattle—he'd appreciate it. Bidding on it could be a win-win, too, a way for Zach to give to the cause without having to make a massive donation. I needed to let him know it was here.

I turned around to head back outside, but I rounded the corner blindly and ran right into a wall. A wall in the form of a man who looked to be a few years older than me, solidly built and cute in a typical, unremarkable way, like a mid-to-late-thirties Ken doll. He smiled as I stumbled back, grabbing my arm gently to prevent me from falling on my ass.

"Thanks." I slapped imaginary dust off my hip with my free hand.

"No problem. The corner needs a warning sign."

I extracted my arm from his light grip. "Or at least a speed bump."

"It's funny running into you—literally—because I noticed you outside."

"Oh?" I'd been only marginally mentally prepared to attend a party tonight. I wasn't sure I could handle flirting. Although, this guy seemed fairly harmless.

"Uh-huh. I saw you standing off to the side of the pool, ducking around all these beautiful, fabulous people, working like a champ not to make eye contact." He grinned.

"I mean...you're not wrong." My cheek lifted.

"Then I can't help but wonder..." He raised his eyebrows. "Who brought you here and how much do you hate them?"

Disarmed, I laughed as I replied, "My best friend in the world and so, so much."

I didn't immediately remove myself from the conversation, so he pressed on, "I'm Pete."

"Sadie."

"Nice to meet you." Huh. This guy was really trying to make conversation. I guess things like that could happen when you stuck your toe back in the real world. "You're here to support the Coalition?" he asked.

This was something I could do—make small talk. I just needed to channel my inner bartender. Deep breath. "I believe in the cause, but someone actually brought me here under false pretenses."

"False pretenses?"

"Yep. I came to meet my best friend's new guy, but it turns out I accidentally got invited to their first fight."

"Ahh...so you're giving them some space? Hiding?"

"Hiding and admiring this genuinely hideous wallpaper...unless, of course, this is your house, in which case the wallpaper is bold and interesting."

"Not my house. And I agree the Brady Bunch would love this wallpaper."

I was good with this type of nothing banter. Anything beyond, and I was back to being awkward and uncomfortable.

"What about you?" I asked. "Are you here to support the cause?"

"In a way. I'm part owner of a business that donated an item. The hosts extended an invite to say thanks. And I don't turn down free food and drinks...and the chance to meet new people."

Bold. I wasn't interested, but I could still recognize a clear shot when it came my way. "That's cool. I mean, that you donated."

"I can't take full credit for it. My business partner's the one who's always looking for causes to support." Pete ran his hands through his hair and the gesture reminded me of Renn.

Jesus. Now he was just materializing in my thoughts out of nowhere? Get a grip, Sadie!

"Our basket is over here." He led me to a table I hadn't noticed before. "Oh, there's my partner." Pointing toward a dimly lit hallway, Pete gestured at a man facing the opposite direction.

No.

The odds.

It simply could not be.

Somehow, thinking about him had conjured him up. I observed the long line of his beautiful, sinewy body as he leaned to examine a basket of puppy items. The fingers lifting a bejeweled collar were so familiar I could practically feel them. He was most definitely a *grown man*.

"Renn—" Pete called to him.

"Oh, hey, man. I had to give the hosts another copy of our business license. They said you forgot to—"

His words died as he glanced up, startled when he saw me. His eyes drank me in, lingering on my face before falling like silk down my body, slowly, all the way to my metallic heels. I watched his throat work as he took in a breath.

"Sadie?" It was a question and a statement.

We locked gazes, both of us unwittingly intense for a moment before he broke the stalemate with a smile. He looked even better than I remembered in his usual Studio Obscurum t-shirt and jeans, hair undone and curling over his shoulders.

I'd been wondering how it would go the next time we saw each other. And I had assumed that would be at my next appointment, but of course, it was at this random party. At least we were in a semi-private area.

But his quick smile faded as he again noticed the man standing by my side, too close to be a stranger. "So...uh...are you, like, here...with Pete?"

Pete cast his eyes between Renn and me curiously. He paused a beat before stepping in to answer. "No. We just met a few minutes ago. I was bringing her over to see our basket."

Renn's tight features eased. "Wow. Small world." He gave the other man an indecipherable look before turning to me. "Well, it's great to see you." He grinned. "But I admit I'm surprised. Based on everything we talked about, it doesn't seem like this would be your scene?"

My shock at our unexpected encounter abating, I recovered enough to answer. "It's not. I came with a friend. I was heading back to find him when I ran into Pete."

Renn nodded, eyeballing Pete's hand, which was hovering close to my lower back.

"How do you two know each other?" Pete asked, dropping his arm under the weight of the other man's glare.

"The studio." Renn angled closer to me. "I'm in the process of giving Sadie one of my favorite pieces I've ever done." He glanced meaningfully toward my thigh, covered by my knee-length dress. Our eyes fixed together again as he lifted his head up.

"That's awesome," Pete said hesitantly, eyeing Renn as though expecting the younger man to say more, but Renn flattened his lips. I couldn't diagnose the emotions playing out on either of their faces. The words were pleasant enough, but there was a strange undercurrent, something hiding behind the outward placidity of their features—tense, but also just...odd. *Were they acrimonious business partners?* Pete pushed on. "Renn is crazy talented," he told me. "I only handle the paperwork side of things at the studio. He brings all the creativity."

"Uh...thanks, Pete."

In theory, the other man had just complimented him, but judging by Renn's I-just-drank-chunky-milk-from-the-carton grimace, which morphed into an I-don't-need-your-approval-eyeroll, it was obvious he did not appreciate the praise. Pete wore a less contentious expression, almost...expectant? Hopeful? These guys were definitely on different pages, air growing thicker by the moment.

Confused by the strange vibe, I attempted levity. "Well, I'm glad he's so good at what he does—because if he messes up, I'll have to wear pants the rest of my life." I turned to Renn and punched him teasingly on the shoulder. "No pressure."

Renn's face softened, and he chuckled as he blew on his fingertips, then brushed them back and forth across his chest. "Oh, I can take the heat." He winked at me. "You will not be disappointed."

I grinned. No matter how serious, or how much of a *grown man* Renn was, he would always be someone that could make me smile.

Pete kept glancing between us. His still-unreadable expression took on a hint of caution as he continued. "Renn, you seem... different. I haven't seen this side of you in a while." He executed his fingers-through-the-hair maneuver again before venturing further. "You've been so...matter-of-fact...about the clients. But this is great." He peered up, almost daringly. "I'd forgotten what it's like to see you so engaged in the work. Not since—"

"Well, it's easy to be creative when Sadie has given me free rein to be an artist," Renn interrupted abruptly and crossed his arms. Evidently he'd known what Pete had been about to say and wanted to shut it down. "Besides, I haven't seen much of you these days, so it's not like you'd have noticed anyway."

Yikes. Harsh. At Renn's hostile tone, my head whipped in his direction. I imagined he thought his aggressive comment would put an end to this conversation, but rather than back off, Pete nodded his head. "You're right. I haven't been around enough lately, and it seems like I might have missed something important here." He looked at me again.

"Pete..." Renn clenched his jaw and glared, sending an unmistakable signal that he wanted the other man to stop talking.

But Pete didn't take the hint, instead growing even more animated, continuing to swing his eyes between the two of us as he spoke. "I guess I owe Sadie and her tattoo a thank-you. Because you finally seem kind of like your old self. I mean, it was bound to happen, right?"

"Seriously, man, you need to—"

"And it's really great to see because your dad would have wanted—"

"Dude, can you please just drop—"

"For you to be happy—"

"Pete—"

"And feel creative again—"

"Fuck!" Renn hissed, throwing his fists against his hips. "Stop! Can you stop!"

Pete ceased talking, finally registering Renn's pained countenance. Renn reached up to pinch the bridge of his nose, inhaling and exhaling loudly, the way they tell people to do when they're hyperventilating. Was he having a panic attack?

I was so confused, too stunned to move or do anything. I waited for Renn to say something, perhaps yell at Pete for talking over him, but when he finally raised his chin, it wasn't anger, but anguish, that ruled his features. He looked wrecked.

Renn blinked rapidly, giving every sign of needing to regroup. "Just give me a sec, Sadie," he said, retreating. I watched as he stumbled down the hallway and began low-key pacing back and forth, not in a way that would draw attention, but enough that I could tell he was working to get hold of his emotions.

"Shit," Pete muttered under his breath, pressing his fingers to his forehead. "I guess I read that all fucking wrong."

WTF? It was so bizarre. Renn was clearly struggling right now, but why? He'd seemed fine at first, up until they'd started interrupting each other—annoyed, but fine. I hadn't even imbibed what had been said. Something about Renn's dad? Luckily, none of the other guests seemed to notice Renn's distress. The low buzz of conversation among the few folks nearby continued unperturbed.

I turned to Pete, perplexed and incredulous. "I know I just met you, but can you please explain what the hell just happened?" This wasn't really my business, but seeing Renn's distress brought out my protective instincts. No matter what other confusing shit was going on between us, he was my friend.

Pete exhaled heavily, leaning back against the wall. Tapping his fist against it several times, he mumbled soft curses under his breath before kicking at the baseboard and replying. "It's because I mentioned his dad. Since Thomas died, Renn doesn't like to talk about him." Tap. Kick. "He doesn't like anyone else to talk about him, either."

I replayed the exchange in my head, applying the new information that Renn's dad had passed away. In all the hours we'd spent together, Renn had never mentioned his father, or really anything about his family.

I sympathized with not wanting to talk about your dead parents.

"If you're aware Renn doesn't like it, why'd you do it? Kind of a dick move."

"I didn't mean it like that. I've always been terrible at talking to Renn. I guess I got confused by how he was acting with you. I haven't seen him much these past few months, and I mistook his enthusiasm for your project." Pete tilted his head toward me. "It's cool how you're defending him, though. That must be some ink he's giving you." He raised his eyebrows in question.

I hmphed. "You pretty much forced me into this position. I wouldn't have chosen to watch you argue."

This type of exchange was the exact reason I'd been avoiding parties since Boston—too much potential for shit-stirring. But I cared about Renn so I wasn't sorry to have this opportunity to stick up for him. He was still out of earshot but appeared more collected as he pretended to examine the baskets.

"Sadie, I meant what I said. I'm glad whatever you have with Renn is...*special*. He hasn't seemed so happy doing a tattoo since his dad..." Pete stopped for a moment, and as he collected himself, I got a sense of his own grief, less raw than Renn's but still there. "You know, his dad was also an artist. He taught him. Renn was only nineteen when Thomas died, but the kid had already learned so much. They were close..."

Pete trailed off and his features clouded. He looked the way customers at the bar sometimes did, like he needed to say this to someone—anyone—so badly, that it didn't matter who it was. Talking to strangers offered a clean slate, no past history to color the conversation.

I had sympathy for Pete, but Renn was ultimately the one I wanted to stick up for.

"So why push? Why not let him grieve in his own way, let him decide when he's ready to talk?" I had good reasons for getting my hackles up when people decided how children *should* grieve their dead parents.

"Because it's been four years!" Pete whisper-shouted. "Thomas isn't Voldemort. Or Candyman. Fight Club. We should be able to say his name, talk about him, tell funny stories without having to worry Renn's going to go apeshit, or shut down and walk away." He gestured his hand in Renn's direction. "I mean, fuck, Thomas was my big brother. I miss him too. But I also worry I'm letting him down because his son..." He exhaled. "Forget it."

Holdupnow. What? "His dad was your brother? Wait—you're Renn's uncle?"

"It's how we're partners. Thomas and I started the studio together when Renn was a toddler." Pete seemed defeated as he leaned against the loud wallpaper, eventually dropping onto his haunches, hands covering his face. It was curious that he'd referred to Renn as his business partner when we'd initially met, rather than his nephew. I also thought about how Renn had recoiled from his uncle's praise.

"You know, even before you mentioned his dad, there was a weird vibe between you two," I ventured.

"Caught that, huh?" Pete released a staccato laugh. "We generally do a better job masking the *weird vibe*." Still crouching, he rested his hands on his knees. "It's been difficult between us since Thomas passed, but he's usually more easygoing." Pete eyed me intently. "Although, I have an idea why he acted so defensive tonight."

I didn't pretend to misunderstand his insinuation. But I also wasn't going to respond to it.

"I'm sorry, Pete. That you lost your brother. That it's so difficult with your nephew. I still think you should have been less oblivious with Renn just now—" I stopped, reining in my judgment before exhaling resignedly. "But I get I don't have all the history here."

"No, I'm the one who's sorry. Four years later, and I still can't seem to get it right. It's like walking around a minefield blindfolded. Always setting off bombs. I understand Renn's an adult, but in my mind, he's always going to be that kid drawing tattoos on his arms with Sharpies and getting his head stuck in his dad's boot."

"He's not a kid, Pete." The irony of my defense was not lost on me.

"I know." Pete straightened and rubbed his forearms, rolling up the already-rolled-up sleeves on his plain white button-down shirt another notch. "And I can see why Renn likes you." He chuckled, shaking his head. "I can't believe I thought I was just talking to a girl at a party, and then all this." He waved his hand around absently. "Some game I've got."

"Just so we're clear, you and I won't be playing any games."

He laughed again, glancing significantly at his nephew. "I'm clear." He leaned closer. "But it would be nice to be friends. Maybe I'll see you around the shop."

"Maybe."

I looked over to catch Renn frowning at us. He appeared to have his emotions fully in control as he made his way back to my side, pointing toward the end of the table.

"Hey, check it out. Our donation is going for more than five hundred dollars." Studio Obscurum had a basket on display with two logoed t-shirts, but the real prize was the offer of a small flash piece.

"That's great, way beyond the value of the tattoo. Have you decided who'll do it?" Pete's question sought a truce.

"I guess it depends on who buys it and what they want. Either me or Archie. I'm happy to donate it, to support suicide prevention." They shared a look before Renn turned back to me.

"Sorry, I had to step away."

"Don't worry about it. We all need a minute sometimes."

"Yeah, but I'm still embarrassed."

"Um…I'm pretty sure that was you in the room when I got all weird about laying down for my tattoo."

He smiled. "Point taken."

Pete chose that moment to chime in. "If it helps, Sadie informed me I was being a bit of a dick. Sorry, by the way."

At that, Renn's smile grew, and I saw the first glimpse of some nugget of affection between him and his uncle. A minuscule glimpse.

"Thanks for defending my honor." Renn reached out and ran his pointer finger along the back of my hand, pausing it on the tip of my pinkie.

"Thanks for saying how much you love my tattoo." I started to curl my finger.

Just another half an inch and our fingertips would hook together. *Closer...closer...*

"Hey, doll." Zach pulled up beside me, breaking the moment like a record scratch. "Did you see there's a Seahawks basket? I put in a bid."

The appearance of my best friend quickly broke me out of whatever spell I'd been under, and I stumbled slightly before replying.

"Oh, great. I'm glad you found it. I was on my way to tell you about that when I got sidetracked by these guys."

Zach raised an eyebrow at me. "Well, it's good to see you making *friends*." Yep, he'd definitely seen Renn and me practically holding hands. "And are you going to introduce me?"

I blinked. "Sorry. This is Pete...and Renn. This is my best friend, Zach."

"Renn, as in, your tattoo artist?" Zach appeared almost gleeful as I glared at him. He met my stare with one of his own, reaffirming that he'd just caught me getting friendly with the man he thought I should give a chance to.

Renn grinned at me and reached out his hand to my friend. "I take it Sadie has mentioned me. I think I've heard a bit about you as well."

"Yes. She may have mentioned your name a time or two. And I have to say that the partially done piece she has now is gorgeous."

"I'm gonna take that as high praise," Renn said.

"Oh, you should. My praise is rare and very valuable," Zach said solemnly. I rolled my eyes.

Renn chuckled before leaning toward me again like a magnet. "It's going to be fantastic when it's completed."

I glanced at him, feeling his nearness. Our gazes met and held as his laughter trailed into a warm smile. I watched as his tongue poked out to lick his lower lip. He really did have nice lips. *Jesus. Stop it already!*

Pete and Zach looked back and forth between us before Zach finally spoke. "Well, I came to find Sadie, to see if she wanted to hang out with me and my new man, but if you're in the middle of something I can—"

"No." I shook my head. The threat of Zach's departure brought me to my senses. It had already been an *eventful* night. I'd been having enough trouble keeping Renn at a distance even before this party. I didn't want to stay here and blur the lines even further. "I'll come with you. I do want to get to know Teddy." I turned to Renn. "I'll see you soon, at my next appointment."

"Can't wait." He reached out and sort of squeezed my arm, pulling his hand away slowly. "It was great running into you."

"Yeah, for sure... Nice to meet you, Pete."

"You too. Thanks."

Zach draped his arm across my shoulders, steering me toward the other hallway. "What the hell was that?" he asked.

I explained to Zach about Studio Obscurum having an auction item and running into them by accident.

"Okay, yeah, that's an insane coincidence," Zach said. "But I was talking about that next-level sexual tension between you and Renn."

"What?! There was no tension, dummy. You're imagining things."

Zach barked a laugh. "Who do you think you're fooling, doll? I know you said there was something there, but damn, you way undersold that. The air was practically nuclear."

I snorted delicately but didn't argue. And as we stepped toward the patio, something compelled me to look back over my shoulder.

I sucked in a breath as my eyes met Renn's, my body instantly captured in the headlights of his blatant stare. He regarded me, brazenly, as I walked away. There were at least twenty people between us, but his hot gaze reached me easily, and I shivered as the immediate sensation of *want* caused a million different thoughts to barrel through my brain—none of them helpful. I wanted to stay in this moment. I wanted to keep reveling in the awareness of him *looking* at me. I wanted to go over and lift the bottom of my dress, to place my palm over his hand as he ran a fingertip over the place where he'd inked my thigh. I wanted to touch him back.

I walked away.

AN HOUR LATER, Zach and I were crawling on the 101. He and Teddy had hashed out the money thing to mutual satisfaction, and much as I'd suspected, Zach had made himself feel better by placing the winning bid on the football basket. He'd mercifully dropped the subject of Renn, recognizing my need to process, and instead distracted me with inane stories about some of the "rich fucks" he'd met at the party as we drove home.

"You want to stop for a burger or something?" Zach reached over to pat my knee.

I wasn't interested in hitting up a drive-through, but I was absolutely looking forward to my stress-eating combo of choice.

"Do we have Diet Dr. Pepper and Fig Newtons at the apartment?"

"I've got you, doll." Best friend code dictated Zach knew all my favorite coping mechanisms. "After you told me about your hot tattoo guy growling at you about being a grown man, I stocked up. I figured you'd need it eventually."

Zach mumbled an occasional obscenity as he navigated the late-night traffic. I was grateful he drove since I was exhausted.

The evening had been a revelation.

I'd told Renn a little about Boston, but he'd only hinted at his own past. Tonight, I'd gotten more of the story. I'd seen him vulnerable. There was no way I could keep pretending he was just the cool, articulate artist I had fun talking to. Now he had *depth*. And the more layers he peeled back, however unintentional, the more drawn in I became. *Fuck!*

It was hard to turn away. So. Hard. I'd never been as instantly affected by anyone as I'd been with Renn. And that thing Pete had said—that I'd brought out something in his nephew that'd been missing for years, basically confirming Renn's own assertion—it had to mean something. *Dammit, why now? Why him?* Our connection was undeniable, but I had things I needed to reconcile in my life before I could think about romance. Figuring out a career, feeling comfortable in my skin again—these were my priorities. And, of course, I needed to be sure that the damage from the years of Henri's cruel words had healed, or at least scarred over.

I woke up the next morning determined to regroup, going for a long run around the neighborhood, close to eight miles in perfectly cool and overcast weather. Zach had encouraged me to start running again a few weeks after I'd come back to LA. Initially, I'd been reluctant. I'd done cross-country in high school and even run a few marathons during college. I'd kept up the habit when I'd lived in Boston but had developed a complicated relationship with it when Henri had taken an interest. *If you ran a little smarter, you might get more tone on your inner thighs. Why'd you cut that run short?* But eventually, I'd realized I was running for myself again. It kept me sane, and reclaiming its association away from Henri was a huge win.

Clarity about the events at the party came with every footfall of my shoes on the pavement. I'd come away relatively unscathed—even though there had been drama. I'd engaged. I'd advocated. For myself and Renn. After the time I'd spent with Henri cowering in the background of my own life, that felt like momentum.

I was researching course catalogs online and having my second cup of coffee when Zach woke up. He made a face when he saw I was still in my running gear because it offended his personal ethos of showering right after working out.

But he didn't comment on my sweaty sports bra, instead leading with, "Do you want to talk about last night?"

"What do you mean?" I kept my eyes fixed on my laptop.

"Don't play dumb." The weight of Zach's inquiry pressed me into the tiny two-person IKEA table I sat at. "What was going on before I rolled up? Not just you and Renn. Who was that Pete guy?"

I gave Zach the longer version of what I'd already started telling him last night. Pete flirting with me. Running into Renn. Me calling Pete a dick. I hesitated a moment before talking about Renn's dad, but since I was sure Zach wouldn't say anything, I figured it was okay to share. I concluded by explaining that, according to Pete, Renn hadn't been passionate about his work since Thomas died—not until my tattoo.

Zach looked at me sternly.

I blanched. "This is the first time in forever where an eventful night didn't make me feel like I wanted to crawl back into my shell. Please don't stare at me like something's wrong."

"Doll," he exhaled slowly. "This is not my 'something's wrong' face. Something is obviously very right. But you keep dancing around what that is exactly."

Fun Zach had left the building. The serious motherfucker who had once knocked out an unruly bar patron with a single punch stared back at me.

"You're talking about Renn?" I ground out slowly.

"Renn—as in the smoking-hot guy who eye-fucked you for ten minutes as we left the party last night—yeah, I'm talking about him."

"I don't think we need to revisit that. Nothing has changed. I'm not in a place to think about relationships right now."

"Doll, last I heard, you were going to just crush on Batman and give yourself some time to see what happens while he finishes up your tattoo."

"And?"

"Well, that was before I saw you two together. Nothing ambiguous. The way he was looking at you...you're lucky the hallway didn't catch fire."

"Zach—"

"No. Hear me out. Just keep your mind open, truly open, to this possibility. You deserve to have someone who looks at you like that, Sades."

We both started getting ready for work. My morning clarity continued through my shift at Hal's. As I mixed drinks and wiped down glasses, I finally had the certainty that this gig was just one stop on a longer, more fulfilling road. I was a bartender today, but I was also someone seeking to be not-a-bartender as well. The little voice inside me that had been providing a constant negative commentary for almost a decade had been quiet during the party. Sure, the self-doubt remained, hovering at the edges, and I still heard it on the regular, but if last night had proven anything, it was that I'd finally developed at least some ability to tell Henri-in-my-head to just shut the hell up.

Maybe Zach was right. All signs pointed to the fact that I was healing more every day. Even if I wasn't ready now, maybe I would be soon.

CHAPTER

Four

ZACH HAD TO run some errands near Studio Obscurum the same Sunday as my next appointment, so he offered to drive me and pick me up. I happily agreed because this plan served the dual purposes of access to the carpool lanes and distraction from overthinking about how this was the first time I'd be seeing Renn since the fundraiser two weeks ago. I had assumed Zach would entertain me with stories about whatever shenanigans he'd gotten up to this week, but he seemed uncharacteristically serious from the outset. That he had his own reasons for wanting us to ride together became clear fifteen minutes into the drive, when he turned down KROQ and angled his head toward me.

"Sadie, I need to get your opinion on something, but I'd like it if you don't ask too many questions or try to dissect why I'm asking."

I was intrigued. "Okaaaaaaaay."

"Seriously, just because I mention an idea or want your thoughts on it doesn't mean anything definitive is happening." He exhaled a deep breath. "It's only talking, you know?"

I veered quickly from intrigued into concerned territory. "Zach, what's going on?"

"Don't worry. Nothing's wrong. I've been contemplating certain things, and it's time to get the best friend opinion."

"Alright, if no one's dying and there's nothing to worry about, you should just tell me."

"You're probably gonna think this is coming out of left field, especially since you've heard every dumb thing that's come out of my mouth for over a decade, so I want to remind you that people can and do change." He emphasized this point with the slow removal of his sunglasses, using the opportunity of a red light to look me in the eye.

"I know that. Of course *I* do, after this past year. Now what's up?"

Zach gripped the steering wheel and returned his gaze to the road, tapping his left foot against the car floor nervously. He opened his mouth and closed it a few times, looking like an intoxicated goldfish, before words started coming out. "Well, ever since Larry and I talked about me buying the bar, I've been thinking a lot about the future—"

My phone buzzing in my hand interrupted us. I looked down to see several texts come through in quick succession.

RENN: I am so sorry but I need to push back our appointment by an hour.

RENN: I hate being unprofessional, but I have a conflict that will keep me from getting to the studio on time.

RENN: I promise I tried to avoid it. I hope I'm not letting you down.

RENN: So I'll see you at 11 instead of 10. I know I said we'd finish close to 2, but it might need to be 3. If that's a problem we can figure it out the next appt.

> **RENN:** Again, I'm so sorry. *sad face emoji*

Zach glanced at me. "What's up?"

"Nothing really. Renn needs to push our appointment back by an hour. No big deal, but he seems super worried I'm upset by it."

"Are you?"

"Course not. Stuff happens. How many times have I been late for a shift? He just takes a lot of pride in his work and doing things right." I'd only known Renn a matter of months, but it was long enough to ascertain he was hard on himself. "Are you okay with picking me up closer to three?" Zach nodded.

> **ME:** Don't worry about it. I don't work until tonight so can stay if we need to. See you at 11.

> **RENN:** Thanks. Sorry for all the texts, for being weird about it. You're the best. *smiley face emoji*

> **ME:** Totally fine about meeting later. That's not weird. But texting in full sentences, complete with punctuation, that's a little weird.

> **RENN:** LOL srry SYL8R

I chuckled at Renn's text and replied with a smiley emoji before putting my phone away. "Well, Zach, this delay may be a good thing because it's clear you really need to talk to me about something. And you better actually fucking tell me as opposed to giving me a bunch of hints and codes of conduct related to how I should react to whatever it is you have to say."

He smiled at me and put two fingers to his forehead in a mock salute. "You're right, doll. This conversation deserves a latte and a sit-down."

Twenty minutes later we tucked into a corner table at Starbucks. Zach had magic coffeeshop karma whereby, whenever he walked in, the best and most comfortable chairs would suddenly become available. Meanwhile, I was lucky if I got the lid back on properly after dumping two stevias in my cup.

I had only been sitting a nanosecond before he started talking.

"Do you ever see yourself having kids?"

I nearly spit out my coffee. "Jesus, Zach." Recovering, I set my cup down on the table. "Let a girl get comfortable and figure out the least disgusting patch of floor to put her purse down on before you ask her to contemplate her biological clock."

"What are you, an animal? Hang it on the back of the chair."

"Can't. The shoulder strap snapped and the short handles aren't big enough. And before you tell me to balance it on my lap, just shut your face and don't worry about it. I regularly shove it behind the bar at Hal's. I have no hope that my purse bottom isn't covered by all manner of bodily fluids, rotting food particles, and illicit chemicals. That's why I buy them cheap."

"Delightful."

"It's what you get for reminding me of my womb before noon." I shook my head at him. "This is what you wanted to discuss? That you think I should have kids? Or was it that you think I *shouldn't* have kids?"

As a woman living in the world, of course I'd imagined the prospect of motherhood. I had never pictured a future without some murky idea of children in it. Henri and I had always talked about it as something we'd consider seriously after I turned thirty, but we never did. Yet another casualty of those wasted years. *Darling, I'm not ready to be a father now. You wouldn't want to give up our freedom too soon, would you?*

"I wasn't trying to start anything, doll. It kinda came out because...well—not to shock you—but I've been thinking lately that I'm ready to be a parent."

Waitholdupwhat? I was floored. Zach had never once mentioned wanting kids. I guess this explained why he'd been so interested in making googly eyes at every baby in Silver Lake on our walk a few months ago.

"Wow," I said dumbly, understanding why he'd been trying to manage my reaction in the car earlier.

"I never really thought of myself as the husband and family type of gay, but now that I've met Teddy, and honestly even before that, I'm reevaluating lots of things."

"Of course you are, silly." I recovered my voice. "It makes sense you're starting to think of it, since we're getting older. Hell, you're pretty close to joining AARP, aren't you?"

"I'm only thirty-seven, *fuckyouverymuch*." His cheek ticked up and he sipped his drink absently. "But I've gone most of my life without contemplating parenthood, and now all of a sudden it's on my mind constantly. Do you think that's strange?"

I offered a slight smile. "I mean, it would be concerning if you were already interviewing daycares and collecting Thomas the Train toys, but I think a general evolution of your thought process is okay."

"Truly?" He looked at me searchingly, so foreign from his usual self-assuredness. I felt a bit unglued. He was the sherpa, I was the ill-prepared hiker. That was our dynamic. But I stepped up as best I could.

"Honestly, Zach, I doubt these thoughts are out of the blue. Things just sort of...change sometimes, and you don't even realize it. Like, ten years ago you were a bartender at Hal's and now you're a few months away from owning the place. And as long as I've known you, you've been an unapologetic little fuckboy..." I raised an eyebrow, daring him to disagree, but he merely grinned at me, recovering some of his swagger as he shrugged. "But since meeting Teddy you've done a one-eighty."

"Your point?"

"That people change...goals change...dreams change...you can't map your entire life at age twenty-five. You're not locked into whatever dumb shit you said five years out of high school." I placed my hand on top of his across the table. "And I'm so glad you asked my opinion on this, because I know for a fact, you'd make a wonderful father. I mean, you've been taking care of me for ages."

He nodded but kept nervously circling the straw in his iced latte, so I knew there must be something more he had to say.

"God..." he began. "I'd really like to think I could have a kid, but...how does that even work?"

I chortled. "How does it work? Ah...I can see it's time for *the talk*." Dramatically steepling my fingers in front of me, I cleared my throat with a delicate cough. "Well...ahem...Zach...when a man and another man love each other very much, they give each other a special kind of hug. It's special because they touch each other, even with their bathing suit parts—"

"Fucker." He took his straw out of the cup and flicked it toward me, drops of coffee narrowly missing my t-shirt, vintage MC5 from my collection.

"No, seriously." I dabbed at the table with a napkin. "I realize you'll need to consider the logistics, but you guys have been together what—two months? The first step is probably to decide if it's something you both want...I mean, assuming you're considering doing this as a couple?"

"Definitely a couple. Being with Teddy is what made me start imagining white picket fence shit. But he's also forty-one years old, so, once we decide, things are probably gonna move quickly."

"Do you know how he feels?"

"We've mostly talked in theoreticals, but he wants a family."

"I can't believe you guys are already discussing this stuff."

"I get it. It sounds crazy fast. But I've been with a lot of people and there's just something about him. It's like that old cliché— when you know, you know."

"Wow. That's amazing." Even though it meant losing my most favored nation status in Zach's life, I couldn't help but be happy for him. I was grateful I got such a good vibe from Teddy. It would have sucked if my best friend found his soulmate and we hated each other.

I had sudden sympathy for what it must have been like for Zach to watch me fall under Henri's spell. I recoiled at the memories of late-night, time-difference-challenged calls where Zach had tried to help me see the light. He would always stop short of badmouthing Henri so much I'd cut him off completely, but his aversion had been unmistakable.

When he'd visited me in Boston, he and Henri had been combative enough that Zach had always checked into a hotel rather than stay in our spare room. In the eight years we'd been a couple, Henri had never insisted I end my friendship with Zach entirely, but I could recall many derogatory comments. Henri had often pitted himself against Zach and forced me to choose sides—from serious things—*Oh I see how it is darling, your precious friend thinks it's a bad idea for us to move in together and you value his opinion more than mine*—to less serious things—*Darling, you can't still be rooting for the Seahawks because they're Zach's team. This is Patriots country.*

Two summers before the New Year's incident that ended my relationship with Henri for good, Zach had come to Boston for a long weekend. Henri generally saved his more cutting verbal assaults for when we were alone, but the regularity of Zach's visits caused him to lower his façade. That weekend, Henri had been vile to me while the three of us were out at a bar. He'd accused me of "slutting it up" and putting my "big soft titties" on display for the bartender. Angrily demanding Henri treat me with more respect, Zach had almost thrown a punch before insisting he and I go outside for fresh air. On the sidewalk, he'd begged me to come back to his hotel, to get some distance. But Henri had followed us, sheepish and all apologies, reasoning that he was only jealous because he loved me so much. Zach had nodded sadly as I'd made excuses for Henri's behavior and gone home with him.

I was nowhere near where I'd been before meeting Henri—even if that girl had been lost and directionless, at least she'd been young and vibrant—but I was getting there, feeling spicier every day.

"Hey, doll..."

Oh right, I was still in Starbucks, not actually living in my head. "Yeah?"

"I need to confess something to you, because I have to tell somebody, but I don't want to come off like a total asshole." Ah... here was part two, whatever had Zach taking his nerves out on a defenseless straw.

"Babe, there is literally nothing you can say that would make me think that."

He nodded, more to himself than me. "Alright...you know how I said I wanted kids but wasn't sure of the logistics?"

"Um hmm."

"Well...jokes about special hugs aside...and again, please don't judge me for this...but I don't think I want to adopt an older child."

"Okay." I scrunched my face in confusion.

"A lot of guys—hell, a lot of my friends or friends of friends— they make families by being foster parents and then adopting older kids, or even straight to the adopting part. But that's not what I envision."

"Alright, Zach, but I'm still not sure how that makes you an asshole?"

"Maybe because I want a baby—an actual peeing, pooping, burping, giggling baby that I raise all the way up from the day it's born. If I'm gonna be a dad, I'd like the complete experience."

"*That* makes you an asshole?"

"I mean, it seems greedy to want that when so many kids out there could benefit from having a good foster situation or being adopted. Like the liquor guy from Hal's. He and his partner just adopted a twelve-year-old."

"Just so I'm clear—your thesis is that it's greedy to want a baby and not an older child?"

Zach sort of shrugged his shoulders and looked at me. "Yes?"

"So, by that rationale, every heterosexual couple that has a kid are greedy assholes."

"I mean, obviously it's a double standard, but—"

"Zach, it's okay for you to want a baby. It's actually good that you understand that about yourself. So, if you decide to start this with Teddy, whenever the time is right, you can articulate exactly what you want."

"It might limit our options."

"Look, based on what I saw at the *House Party of Hope...*" I borrowed Teddy's air quotes. "Teddy has enough money to make this process a little easier for you than it might otherwise be, assuming it's something you decide to pursue."

"Well, now I do feel like an asshole. As in, Teddy's loaded so we can get a baby. Like, sorry, working-class gays, sucks to be you."

"That's ridiculous. You can play that game all day. Everyone has their own shit. Just because money isn't your obstacle doesn't mean you won't have other issues. Isn't that what this entire conversation has been about? None of this is easy. It's all a jump into the unknown."

"I guess."

"You can't predict it, Zach. You and Teddy might want different things. Or you might want the same thing, but it doesn't go the way you imagine. Or you might start down one path and realize it's the wrong one and switch courses. That's just how it goes."

He sat there thoughtfully, maybe digesting what I was saying, maybe just contemplating the five-thousand varying shades of beige providing the Starbucks décor. "You know, doll, for someone who claims to be directionless, you sure have clarity when it comes to sorting out my life."

"That's because I love you, dummy." I scooted my chair around the table to give him a quick side hug. "I've got your back, whatever happens."

"Same, doll. Same."

ZACH HAD TO leave earlier than me so he could get across town to pick up some new signage he'd ordered for Hal's. He'd been managing the bar for over five years, and Larry, the owner, was getting ready to retire and sell it to him.

I still had a few minutes before I needed to head to Studio Obscurum. Customers drifted in and out of Starbucks. I was looking down and scrolling through my phone when the barista called out rather loudly, "I've got two grande hot chocolates for Turtle and Sloth..." This elicited subdued chuckles from nearby customers. "...and a black coffee for Renn."

My head flew up as an annoyed preteen voice whined, "Oh my god. You are so embarrassing. Did you tip the barista to make her write those names on our cups? So lame."

A giant espresso machine obscured his sightline, so Renn hadn't noticed me. But I could see him on the other side of the counter, standing stiffly in charcoal Dickies shorts with his arms folded across a Studio Obscurum t-shirt. Loose hair framed his disapproving face as he spoke to the boy in front of him, a kid of about twelve whose appearance I'd describe most effectively as mini-Renn. "It's the least you two deserve after this morning. If you're going to act like slow-moving animals, that's what I'm going to call you. Also, when you get home, I want you to clean your bathroom and finish up the laundry you should have done yesterday." Renn looked sternly at the sullen tween, as well as another younger boy, standing quietly to the side.

"C'mon, bro. We were just a little late."

"Don't backtalk me, Robbie. You made me push back a client. You're lucky I'm not putting you on restriction. And your bathroom is currently a hellscape that smells like marinating body parts, so you'll thank me once it's done." Renn uncrossed his arms and grabbed the cups off the counter, handing "Sloth" to the older kid and "Turtle" to the younger one. "Plus, I'm buying you hot chocolate. That either makes me a saint or a sucker, so I don't want any more complaining."

I sat mesmerized. I had no idea who these kids were, likely family based on the resemblance. Another side to Renn I'd never seen. He was spectacular in full-on dad mode. I hoped he never found out I often left my clean laundry folded in the basket because, seriously, who has time to put things in drawers? I held my breath as Renn exuded calm control, masterfully staring down his adolescent counterpart.

The older boy huffed but stopped arguing. As their group turned, Renn finally looked my way.

Just as at the party, seeing me so unexpectedly, he evinced an immediate flash of happiness. For a too-brief moment, we forgot ourselves as our eyes met, everything else falling away while our bond flared unapologetically.

"Sadie, hey." He approached, raising his hand in tentative hello. "It's so weird how we keep running into each other outside of the studio."

"Nah. Seeing you at the party *was* random. But since I was already heading in when you texted this morning, you probably had a fifty-fifty shot of running into me at Starbucks, right? Unless I was going to hang out at the dry-cleaning place or get a spray tan," I reasoned teasingly.

He winced. "I'm so sorry I had to do that. As you can see..." He pointed to the kids next to him. "I had my hands full." Both boys stared at me curiously. I smiled at them as Renn continued. "These are my brothers, Robbie and Gage. Guys, this is Sadie."

"Nice to meet you both."

They smile-stared back and mumbled hellos.

"They're why I needed an extra hour. When I stopped by to pick these two up after a sleepover, they weren't even awake yet, let alone dressed—even though I told them to be ready by 8:30 so I would have time to drop them home and get back for our appointment."

"We're sorry, Renn. We stayed up late and when Ryder's mom knocked on his door this morning we sort of...lied, I guess, and said we were already up and...sorry." This from Gage, and I'd never heard anything cuter than his sleepy, shaky little voice.

Renn huffed and explained to me, "When I got there, Lydia— that's their friends' mom—was like 'oh yeah, they're upstairs, I'll get them.' Of course, they're still snoring. She's a single mom so I'm not trying to rag on her, especially since she did me a solid keeping them last night when I had to stay late working on a guy's back piece." He looked harshly at Robbie and Gage. "But it's not Lydia's job to make sure you guys get up. I gave you that phone specifically so you could set the alarm. That's your responsibility."

Big brother Renn. I was into it.

The three of them sat down at my table. Seated on my right, Renn pointed at the partially shaded tattoo visible on my thigh. "I'm excited to get back to work today."

I tilted my chin in agreement as Robbie, following Renn's finger, blurted, "Oh! I get it. You're one of his customers."

Renn blinked hard before nodding.

Robbie looked at me. "Makes sense now. I couldn't figure out at first why he was just, like, staring at you."

"Robbie!" Renn cried, embarrassed.

"What?" Robbie stared challengingly at his brother. "You were." He took a triumphant sip from his cup while Renn just shook his head. Gage snickered and tried not to smile.

I didn't have the full picture of Renn's relationship with his brothers, but knowing that his father had died, and based on what

I'd just seen, I had to assume it went beyond birthday cards and the occasional ballgame.

A minute later, I watched as Pete came into Starbucks and made a beeline for the boys.

"Thanks for coming to pick them up," Renn spoke to his uncle in a stilted voice.

"No problem, kid. Happy to hel—Sadie?"

"Hey, Pete."

"What are you doing here?" He looked questioningly from me to his nephew.

"I'm Renn's morning appointment." I wanted to make sure there was no lingering weirdness between me and Pete. "I guess I have you to thank for the fact that Renn didn't need to cancel altogether."

"Yeah...appears so."

Renn gathered up the boys' backpacks. Giving them hugs, he ushered his brothers to the door with instructions to wait outside for their uncle. Once they were off, Renn sat back down and angled his chair toward mine, knees touching, making sure Pete had a clear view of it. Renn gripped the back of my chair behind my neck and leaned in near my ear—much closer than necessary—before asking if I was ready to leave.

Pete gave him one last look, and then glanced at me. He puffed his cheeks up and blew the air out slowly as he stepped away. "Alright, guess I'll get the boys home. See you later."

Well. Renn hadn't exactly pissed on my leg, but he'd certainly added fuel to Pete's assumption that there was more between us than just a client-artist relationship. I wondered again about their tenuous bond, and where Robbie and Gage fit in. There was so much about Renn I still didn't know, so many more potential obstacles to face if we tried to make anything happen post-tattoo. I'd promised Zach I would keep an open mind, but when I thought about Henri-in-my-head, the question mark where my career plans should be—not to mention the age difference—my mind spun. And those were just deterrents on my side. As this morning proved, Renn had concerns of his own.

Were a strong connection and undeniable chemistry enough to offset all the other hurdles? I had two more months to figure it out. For now, Renn and I needed to head across the street so he could add some color to my tattoo.

December 31, 2013

'SADIE, WHY DO you have to be so fucking dramatic all the time? It's New Year's Eve, and it didn't seem like too much of a stretch that we'd want to spend it with our friends." Henri stomped around the apartment, yanking his two-hundred-dollar tie off his neck and tossing it angrily across the room before going to work on his shirt buttons.

Great. He'd only been home five minutes and was already in a *mood*. I braced for a verbal offensive while remembering the promise I'd made myself that I would try harder. It was a new year, after all. I had to believe the Henri I'd met eight years ago was in there somewhere behind this feral beast always finding reasons to snap. I just had to reach him.

I tried to placate. "I'm not being dramatic, I'm just surprised. They're *your* friends, not mine. It's been months since you've brought me along on one of your after-work things."

Almost all of Henri's friends were his co-workers at the firm, finance bros with their model girlfriends I had nothing in common with. My ability to make dive bar small talk never worked with his people. After a few years of begging for scraps of conversation from Henri's crowd, I'd given up. I'd merely smiled and nodded, sticking to the sidelines. Eventually, Henri had stopped insisting I join him, other than when absolutely necessary. Like tonight, apparently.

"And whose fault is that? The last time I brought you, you just sat there like a statue making people uncomfortable. Everyone else's girlfriend can drink and laugh and have fun, but mine has to be the fucking wet blanket."

I took a deep breath and looked at Henri across the room. Back to me, he removed his undershirt. I stared at the phoenix rising between his shoulder blades and thought again of how surprising it was that my polished, fussy boyfriend had a tattoo. No one would ever guess. No one would ever guess a lot of things about Henri.

Still, I had loved him for a long time. It had been almost a decade since he'd found me in Dorchester, working at some shithole-in-the-wall. And he loved me, based on his willingness to put up with how different I was from all his friends' wives and girlfriends.

But some days took more effort than others.

"You're really being insane right now, Sadie," he complained as he continued to undress. "You can't have it both ways—you can't be embarrassing when we go out together and then get mad when I don't want to be with you in front of my friends. I let you stay home most nights because you seem to like it that way. But people are aware we live together, so it'd be weird if you didn't come with me tonight, since it's a holiday. You can't keep expecting me to make excuses for you. I really hope you can just...try a little."

Was he right? Was I being crazy? Should I have tried harder with his friends? It seemed like he'd been happy when I'd stopped going out, but now I wasn't sure. Making him happy was like playing whack-a-mole. Every time I'd hit one, some other grievance would pop up to keep him pissed.

I sighed. "I'm sorry, Henri. It's just that I'd planned something special for us at home." I thought of the elaborate meal I'd ordered and the bottle of champagne chilling in the fridge. I'd had a mental image of a romantic dinner, kissing at midnight. Henri coming home and informing me we were going to a bar to celebrate with his work friends hadn't been part of the picture.

He seemed to relent a little. "Look, darling, at least I'm inviting you along this time. That earns me boyfriend points, right? Even if you are the most awkward, least talkative girlfriend on the planet, I'm not asking you to stay home."

I didn't think he meant it when he said things like that. He had a stressful job and reminded me all the time that he needed to be "on" at work all day, so I had to accept his rougher edges at home. Lately, I'd been the recipient of *a lot* of rough edges. I missed the softer moments we used to share. The kinder words. There'd been so few of them lately, and every attempt I'd made to please Henri had seemed less effective and more desperate than the last.

CHAPTER
Five

SIGNS OF THE holidays were popping up all over the city, in the usual way of sunglasses-wearing Santas and decorated palm trees. I'd been back almost a year and California was finally feeling like home again.

Renn and I passed the five-minute walk from Starbucks to the studio in companionable silence. There was a lot for my brain to unpack from the previous hour. The wall provided by our working relationship was crumbling, becoming closer to dust each time we interacted.

I smiled as we reached the entrance. Studio Obscurum had made a nod to the season with a black wreath on the door, wrapped in silver ribbon with tiny white skull ornaments adorning it.

"I'm not sure who would enjoy that wreath more—the Addams family or The Cure."

Renn smirked. "Honestly, if I'd had my way, we would have a bunch of red and green twinkle lights around the door next to a four-foot Santa, but Archie said we should keep it pretty chill, kind of dark, so we didn't—let me see if I remember his exact phrase—'give people the impression that we're not total badasses.'"

"Ahhh. You wouldn't want people to find out what a big ol' Santa-loving marshmallow you are." I playfully punched him on the shoulder as we walked into the space and he grabbed his arm like I had just gone Hulk smash on him.

"Ow...us marshmallows are delicate flowers." I stood in the entryway while Renn woke up the lights, fans, and sound system and began preparing his station, the familiarity of these tasks evident in his seamless movements. "Seriously, the success of the studio is my priority, and if that takes a certain aesthetic, then it's fine with me."

"Well, if you're ever jonesing for some disgustingly traditional and over-the-top Christmas kitsch, you should stop by Hal's. Zach's in charge of decorating and he goes crazy every year."

"I remember Zach from the fundraiser. That's your friend who... uh...helped get you back to LA, right?" I appreciated Renn being careful, not saying explicitly he remembered Zach was the person who'd rescued me from Boston.

"Um hmm. He'll be Hal's official owner in a few weeks. Anyway, he loves the holidays so always goes overboard. I've basically been tending bar in Santa's workshop since Thanksgiving. Feel free to check it out whenever." Renn's eyes snapped up. I hadn't meant it to seem like I was asking him out. It was one thing to run into him by chance, or exchange a few—okay, more than a few—non-tattoo-related texts and DMs, but we'd never made a firm plan to see each other outside the studio. Still, the idea of him visiting me at Hal's, seeing me in my other life, was undeniably appealing.

Renn eyed me levelly, deep voice replying slowly. "I just might stop by."

"Okay...cool."

I felt intoxicated by the draw of him. And just like the other times I'd been near him, I let myself revel in the pull between us as his admiring gaze swept over me. But there was also a teensy part of me that found the sensation worrying, reminiscent of the drug-like hold Henri had had on me when I'd confused attraction with willing suffocation. Henri's voice may have been relegated to the fringes of my mind these days, but I still heard it often enough to know it was there, like a scorpion waiting to strike.

As though sensing my inner conflict, Renn blinked away our stare-down and switched topics casually. "So, you've met my brothers. Sorry Robbie was rude."

I huffed. "You do realize I'm a bartender? I handle rude douche-canoes all the time. Except those frat boy idiots don't have Robbie's excuse of being an actual child. He was fine. Besides, I really like kids, even though I don't get the chance to be around them much."

"Yeah, that makes sense, working in a bar. What about siblings? Nieces or nephews?" Renn was engaged in the pseudo-yoga routine I'd seen him do several times before and during our sessions. Pre-tattoo warm-ups or whatever. That was why he missed me flinching at his benign question.

"Um...none of the above. Only child." I plastered on a neutral smile.

"Well, that's probably why you like kids. Because you don't have to be around them often enough to be driven slowly insane." He grinned and stretched an arm across his chest.

"Do Robbie and Gage drive you crazy?" Renn had been so precious with little Sloth and Turtle.

"I mean, sometimes. Like, Gage is obsessed with the movie *Cars*. He literally will watch it five times in a row. When I tell him goodnight, he always wants me to say it using my 'Mater voice.' And Robbie is just getting to that age where he's straight-up disgusting, so his room always reeks like I imagine the inside of a bag of stale farts and chopped onions would. I've been thinking of hunting for mushrooms in there."

I chuckled as he scrunched his nose like he was smelling something foul.

"Honestly, Sadie, they can be challenging, but I wouldn't want you to think I don't love the little monsters. It's a fairly good balance between love and insanity." He switched arms, stretching his left one over the melting heart logo on his Studio Obscurum tee.

I had wondered in the coffee shop about the relationship between the brothers, and with Renn's mention of bedtime, as well as the regular assault of a stank tween bedroom, the picture was becoming less hazy. "So you live with your brothers? And you're… in charge?"

Renn looked taken aback for a moment, and I knew I'd stumbled on a delicate subject. "Uh…Pete is around. He helps sometimes, like you saw him pick them up earlier. But the boys live with me, and it's mostly me who takes care of them."

Interesting. I knew Thomas had passed away, but what about their mom? There was certainly more to the story, but Renn didn't offer it, and I didn't push. I understood not wanting to expose yourself. That was why I hadn't told him the real reason I liked being around kids so much.

I shuffled my feet as Renn fluttered around the studio, grabbing a folding table and rearranging some things on the shelves. As he prepped, my mind replayed the scene from earlier, the love clear between the brothers. That was what all children deserved.

My grandma had tried. But even as a preschooler, I could sense her simmering resentment. As an adult looking back, I almost sympathized. I mean, one minute, she's a year past retirement, finally getting to socialize and travel, pursue her hobbies after a thankless career as an executive secretary to some real estate fuckwit. The next minute, she's saddled with raising her only granddaughter.

I thought about Renn scolding Robbie and Gage that morning. I would never have found myself in the boys' situation because I had never slept over at friends' houses. Never joined a scout troop or attended backyard birthday parties. I'd known better than to ask for things that required extra effort on Grandma's part. From a young age, I'd understood that the way to make Grandma happy was to inconvenience her as little as possible, and as I got older, she remained as absent from my life as I'd tried to be from hers. She hadn't hassled me about grades or made me do chores. Never cheered me at a track meet or asked about dates. There'd always been food, and birthday presents, and money to buy shoes or go to the movies, but never more than the basics. Just enough to keep things copesetic. When I'd left for college, her relief had been palpable.

I didn't understand what I'd been missing. I just thought that, with Henri, I'd found it.

Poor, sweet Sadie. All alone in the world. I can be your family, darling.

Eleven months of therapy had helped clarify things. Henri hadn't physically abused me, but he'd played on every insecurity. He'd filled the void where Grandma's unconditional love should have been. And he'd filled it with judgment, criticism, and the withholding of affection.

As I watched Renn move adeptly around the studio, humming as he set up his instruments, I knew rationally that he wasn't Henri, that he was "good," but I couldn't trust whether our connection was genuine, or if I was just trying to fill in the empty places again.

I punctured the silence. "No one else is working today?"

He patted his table and gestured for me to tape up my shorts. "I think Archie might come in later, but it's like I told you. Morning on a Sunday is an unusual time."

"This whole no-one-works-in-the-mornings thing is a little suspicious." I brought my pointer finger to my lips. "You know…I can keep a secret. So tell the truth—are you all secretly vampires?" He laughed as I tapped against my mouth. "Be honest with me. Does the sun burn?"

"I mean, tattoos really don't like direct sunlight, so…"

"Yes. I read that in the tree-murdering amount of paperwork you gave me the first day." I smirked before continuing, "Hey, Renn?"

"Yeah?"

"Will you do the 'Mater voice?'"

I didn't really think he'd accept my dare, but he raised an eyebrow as if to show he was more than up for the challenge. He picked up the tattoo gun and held it up and out to his side, *Texas-Chainsaw-Massacre*-style, and gave me his best impression. "Whooweee. C'mon, Sadie, let's git-r-done!"

Oh God. Oh God, it was awful. The worst Larry the Cable Guy I'd ever heard. I held my fist to my mouth as I attempted unsuccessfully to muffle my instant burst of laughter.

"I never said it was good," Renn muttered, smiling the whole time as he beckoned me with his instrument.

I laid down on the table as Renn re-taped my shorts—I never went as high as he needed me to—and bent my leg the way he liked it. The tattoo gun buzzed. Its hum, so recognizable by now, stilled my restless thoughts.

I DOZED A bit. Yep, it turned out I was one of the people who could do this while getting inked. When I opened my eyes again, Renn had changed positions. His stool was pulled right next to my torso as he worked. This was the first time I'd seen him in shorts, and at this angle, I noticed the tattoos on his calves. There were many small ones—animated characters, flowers, something that looked like a box of crayons. But the one that stood out most was what appeared to be a giant heart melting over the earth, identical to the Studio Obscurum logo I'd seen on t-shirts and at the shop.

"Renn?" He was loading ink onto his gun and had turned toward his instrument table, face in profile.

"Hmm?"

"How come all your tattoos are so colorful, but you have that big one on your left calf that's just an outline? The one that looks like the studio logo. It's so different from the others."

For a moment, his shoulders tensed, and *something* flashed behind his eyes. An unreadable expression quickly replaced it. "We've been at this for more than an hour. Let's take a break to stretch before we start back up again." There was an aggressive snap of rubber as he pulled his gloves off.

Startled by his abruptness, I rolled over to face him fully, leaning back on my elbows to sit up a bit. "Shit. I'm sorry. I didn't think it'd be weird to ask an artist about his tattoos."

He exhaled loudly and ran his hands over his hair, taking care not to disturb the bun-pony. "No, you're fine." He laughed a little, mumbling to himself, "I should have worn pants today." He fiddled with his phone and a moment later the speakers switched from *Simon and Garfunkel's Greatest Hits* to Radiohead's *In Rainbows*. Even in that taut moment, my brain could appreciate that Renn's taste in music was as eclectic as mine. I doubted he even liked the studio's typical death metal playlist.

I waited patiently until he finally continued. "I...uh...it's really hard to talk about. I don't want to be unprofessional or lay my shit on you."

"Renn, we've never had a problem talking to each other. I think we can both agree that our issue is more like we've said too much," I chuffed. "Pretty sure we passed the 'clear professional distance' exit a few miles back."

"I know you're right. You're just so easy to talk to that it almost makes me feel guilty. Like, I never really say anything real to Archie, and I've known him my whole life. I'm not the person who likes to dwell on heavy stuff."

"Listen, Renn, I've given you the bullet points of my epic relationship fail in Boston. I've also told you some deep philosophical shit about how I need to find purpose and direction in my life," I joked, raising my eyebrows. "Pretty sure we've moved past the point where we need to stick to the weather or your favorite type of donut or what you watched on TV or whatever. Don't think you're being unprofessional or that I can't take it, okay? That being said, you don't *have* to talk about something you don't want to."

He nodded once and looked down at his tools, reaching for the antiseptic. I let the silence linger, putting our conversation in Renn's hands, ready to defend my preference for maple bars if that's what it came to. Uncurling my stiff body to a standing position, I moved across the room and did some deep-knee bends to work out the kinks. Laying stock still for over an hour was not for the faint of heart. I had felt silly stretching on the first day, but Renn had encouraged me, saying it would really help us go longer in these sessions. I linked my fingers together in front of me and reached my arms above my head, rolling my neck in circles—

"It was my dad's."

Huh? I turned toward Renn, ten feet away, who looked away as he continued. "It was my dad's work. He did the outline. It was right before his vacation to Costa Rica. And he would have done the color, too, but...he...uh...he died. Drowned. In a riptide there."

I'd known Thomas had died. But somehow, hearing this detail from Renn made it so much more heartbreaking. Without thought, I rushed toward where he sat and grasped one of his hands in mine. I stood in front of him as he sat up tall on his stool, locked in place. He looked down at our joined hands and ran his thumb back and forth over my palm. "Thank you," he whispered, squeezing my fingers.

His voice broke and his eyes were glassy. He was so good at playing a part. The happy, unaffected artist. But as his thumb traveled a path from my palm to the inside of my wrist, I knew his mask was off.

"We were close, my dad and me. Like, really close. He had me young and my mom cut out, so I grew up around the shop with him. It was just the two of us for a long time, and Pete of course." Renn inched his chair closer to me and I inhaled his unique scent—tea tree oil, which I guessed was from his shampoo, along with the lemony clean smell of the studio. He spoke fast, as though the words might dry in his throat if he didn't get them into the air quick enough. "Eventually Dad met Mary, Robbie and Gage's mom... After...Costa Rica, I went a little crazy. Drank, smoked, drugs, girls, you name it. I'd never been much of a partier, but I was only nineteen and I missed my dad, ya know? Maybe it was just blowing off steam. Maybe I was on my way to developing a real problem. Except it never got that far because shit got even worse, and I had to stop."

"Worse than your dad?" I asked gently.

"Mary died."

It took me a beat to process what he'd said. "Wait...What? The boys' mom died too?"

"Six months after my dad. It was unexpected, and I realized how fucking sad Dad would have been if he could see how I was behaving. So, I got myself together. Worked my ass off to keep the shop from going under. Stepped up for my brothers. Tried to stay cool with Pete, even though the dude can be a real asshole sometimes." His breath whooshed out.

"Wow, Renn, that all sounds...really hard." No wonder he seemed so much older than he was.

The black wash and macabre artwork on the walls enveloped us in the type of subtle darkness that allows vision but no sense of time. Not even a streak of daylight in our temporary fortress. Renn took a moment to compose himself, still gently gripping my forearm.

"That was four years ago. And don't get me wrong—I might not want to talk about my dad—but that doesn't mean I don't think he'd be proud. I like to think he's up there on some cloud, sipping a Corona with a lime in it, loving the afterlife and watching me run the studio. I never wanted to do anything else but be an artist." Renn's thumb on my skin continued its indiscriminate dance, and I shivered as he tickled me with circles and plus signs and random letters. "Pretty sure he bought me my first sketchbook when I was still in diapers, and he was always displaying my scribbles, showing them off to customers like they were masterpieces."

"He sounds like a great dad." Not that I would know from personal experience, but Thomas seemed like the type of father any kid would want.

"He really was. The first tattoo I ever did was on him. He didn't have much real estate left on his body by the time I was sixteen, so he asked me to wedge in Gage's name on this sliver of skin on his side. I was so nervous, I did a blowout."

"Blowout?"

"It's when you put the ink too deep under the skin, into the fatty tissue. It makes things look sort of spready and splotchy, so when it happens with letters, they're hard to read."

"Yikes."

"I was so pissed at myself. But my dad just said, 'that's how you learn,' and he walked me through doing a cover-up of my mistake, and that tattoo—shaded dice—turned out great."

As Renn progressed from relaying the details of his dad's death to being sparked by the happier memories he had, the atmosphere in the studio shifted.

He looked down at our entwined fingers, creating a language of touch. The barely-there graze of a pinkie to a palm. A rough pointer finger to the veined center of a soft wrist. Thumbs pressed together until the pads turned reddish-pink. An intimate exploration of lifelines and knuckle indents and pen calluses.

Renn looked up, his stare growing bolder as he captured my gaze. Quietly, "You're so easy to talk to."

One of his hands crawled up my forearm while the other reached out to rest lightly on my hip. He seemed to know intrinsically to be cautious, go slow, test.

I gasped softly as Renn tugged me closer until I was standing with my legs against the stool, wedged between his spread thighs. He kept his features even, but the spotlight above his workstation caught the nervous bob of his Adam's apple and the beads of moisture at his temples. I could feel the wiry hair on his calves scratching against my smooth legs.

We were abruptly bathed in silence as the album ended, amplifying the distinct hammer of my heartbeat in my ears. I placed a steadying palm on his shoulder as my throat went dry and my breathing stuttered. My tongue snaked out to wet my bottom lip—drawing Renn's intense gaze to my mouth. His own lips parted, and I couldn't help but imagine them pressed against mine, against my skin. The mental picture of Renn moving his mouth along my body sent an immediate spike of heat to every part of me.

God, I wanted him, so warm and solid beneath my hand. I had forgotten how good it felt to want someone.

That was why, for one blissful and heady moment, I allowed myself to drown in the sensation of being possessed by this wanting. Every atom in my body felt lit up. I longed to melt into Renn, craved more of his touch.

But then, slowly, his palm on my hip grew more insistent, his grip on my forearm firmer—as though preparing to pull me close.

My trance broke as these languid movements began to feel familiar.

Familiar in all the wrong ways.

Every touch unlocked a memory, every puff of breath a reminder. Henri running his fingers up my side, coarsely palming my breasts. Henri staring at my lips, before gripping them between thumb and pointer finger, claiming a harsh kiss. What Renn sought softly, Henri had made hard and brittle.

I was unprepared for this flood, this strike from the buried edges of my consciousness, unsure if my racing heart signaled passion or terror.

"Oh God," I moaned faintly.

Renn stilled his movements.

I felt his warm breath on my face just before he inhaled it raggedly back into his chest, eyes still shining with unmistakable desire.

And understanding.

He looked resignedly at my mouth before removing his hand from my hip. He dropped his other arm from mine but joined our fingers again, lifting them to his face. Closing his eyes for a moment, he gave me a chaste kiss on the back of my hand before unlinking our fingers and rolling his stool away to put a few feet of distance between us. I shuddered as I came to myself.

Renn had almost kissed me. Almost. He'd seen the conflict. My fear. I didn't regret our near miss because that raw feeling of arousal I'd had—however brief—was a token of what could be, in time. Silence existed between us again, claiming the things we could not speak of. Henri. Renn's father. Our almost-kiss lingered in the space for a few moments, but eventually, the silence claimed it too.

DECEMBER 31, 2013

HENRI WAS SLIPPING a tan button-down over his perfectly gym-honed torso when the doorbell rang. We weren't expecting guests, so I walked to the living room ready to redirect someone to one of the neighboring apartments.

I wasn't prepared for the handful of confetti thrown in my face as soon as I opened the door.

"Surprise! Happy New Year, doll!" Another handful, again right in my face.

"What the hell?" I stammered and spat out stray bits of paper as I struggled to reconcile the sight in front of me.

Zach stood on my doorstep grinning like a kid on Christmas morning. He leaned on a small rolling luggage bag with a stars-and-moon pattern. I recognized it. I remembered when he'd found it in the little charity thrift store in the strip mall across the street from the bar. Hal's. Just thinking of California had a lump forming in my throat.

"Zach. Oh my God…What are you doing here?"

His grin died as he registered my face. Confronted with the burst of my friend's brightness, I couldn't stop the moisture from gathering in my eyes, and I reached out to make sure he wasn't a mirage as the tears escaped. Zach gathered me up in familiar arms and I buried my face in his shoulder. He embraced me fiercely, placing a hand on my head.

"Don't cry, doll. I'm here now." He whispered the last part solemnly in my ear. Then he stiffened. Henri had come out of the bedroom.

"What the hell…Zach?" It had been a few years since they'd been in the same room, and to say they weren't each other's biggest fans would be a colossal understatement. "What the fuck are you doing here?"

Zach pulled away from me and walked over to Henri, arm outstretched in greeting. "Nice to see you too, man." Zach had completed a minor degree in passive-aggressive sarcasm masquerading as polite manners.

Henri shook his hand grudgingly. "Seriously, why are you here? Sadie didn't say anything. We have plans for tonight. You can't just expect us to drop everything."

"Henri! Don't be so rude. I didn't know. It's a wonderful surprise." Henri squinted his eyes at me, clearly displeased by my admonishment. There had been a time when he'd hidden his nature from Zach, showing him the same charming face the rest of the world saw. As it became clear Zach's loyalty would always be to me, Henri had abandoned the effort. Over the years, he'd succeeded in fraying the bonds of our friendship. But Zach standing in my living room was proof of its ultimate durability. And as I continued to lean heavily into my best friend, I could only thank God for that.

"Sorry to interrupt your plans. I hope I didn't intrude on anything important. I wanted to surprise my best friend for the holiday." Zach tried to keep a cheerful tone, but I could see his pulse thudding in his neck. Henri, meanwhile, became engrossed by whatever text messages had just come through his phone and turned his back on us.

When I asked my boyfriend a minute later if he wanted to hang out with me and Zach before meeting his work friends, Henri acted like I'd asked if he wanted to drink bleach. He kept looking down at his phone, the constant barrage of incoming messages clearly bothering him. He had one of those twenty-four-seven jobs, so lots of texts weren't unusual, but he seemed particularly annoyed by whatever he was seeing. I didn't care. I was grateful they were distracting him, since it meant he was too busy to sulk about Zach's sudden appearance.

Henri pointed his finger at his device, indicating he needed to deal with whatever situation was happening. He took the phone into the bedroom, gripping it aggressively as he frantically texted, seeming relieved when Zach and I headed to the bar early for some best friend time.

CHAPTER

Six

December 21, 2014

AFTER OUR ALMOST-KISS, which we both seemed content to pretend hadn't happened—or at least pretend that Renn had been going for a chaste back-of-the-hand kiss the whole time—I busied myself at the mirror looking at the progress on the tattoo. A lot of the shading was complete, the detail on the busted-through chains particularly popping. And even though the air had been so thick mere minutes ago, the heaviness didn't linger, quickly surrendering itself to the natural ease that had always existed between Renn and me. He spoke again after a few minutes.

"Thank you, Sadie, for listening. About my dad. It's been four years and sometimes it seems much longer, but then there are still days it feels fresh. I guess that's why I never had anyone else fill in that tattoo. It would be too final."

He put on his gloves and arm coverings, motioning that I could lie back down.

I positioned myself the way I knew worked best, hooking my

leg in an L shape. "In some ways, it has to be comforting that you have a piece of him on your body, right?"

"That's usually how I see it. Except it's also a marker of how young he died. He was only thirty-nine." I tried to wrap my head around the fact that Renn's dad was only five years older than I was now when he passed away. "The tat on my calf is a constant reminder of my dad's unfinished life."

Renn seemed inclined to end the conversation there, but between what he'd shared and the intensity of our almost-kiss, I couldn't help but want to give him something more.

I hadn't given him the goriest details about Boston, the embarrassing specifics about how Henri had forced my hand. And I hadn't been able to kiss him, to bring myself to take that step, despite my body aching to. But I could give him something else.

"Hey, Renn." He paused in the process of rubbing cream into my thigh and raised an eyebrow. "There's really not a good way to talk about this, and it feels weird to just say it out of nowhere, but then it feels worse to keep it to myself now that you've told me about your dad."

"Okay..." He stopped what he was doing and his jaw ticked. "I'm listening."

"Look, not to just blurt it out, but I want you to know that I understand at least a little of what you feel because my parents are also gone...passed away. They died when I was a kid. Normally, I wouldn't just bust out with that, but...since you told me about your dad. And it's not like there's a way it was going to come up naturally or casually. So...there it is."

"Wow. Uh...I'm sorry." He didn't go back to work, looking nonplussed. "Thank you for telling me...I, uh, I don't know what to say."

"There's nothing. I mean, is there anything people say that feels right when they find out about your dad?"

"If there is, I haven't heard it yet. The grief is so raw, it's just easier not to talk about it."

"And that's the thing, Renn. My big confession, if you want to call it that, is that the type of grief you have—I don't feel it."

He put down his instruments, and I had his full attention. "What do you mean?" An adorable wrinkle appeared between his eyes as he scrunched his forehead.

"It's hard to explain, but I don't experience the sadness the way you do. Partly because they died when I was young. I don't even remember them. And partly because they weren't really interested in me even before they were gone. They died when I was six, but even before then, I had been living with my grandma. They'd dumped me off with her when I was a toddler, so when they died, I was just like, 'okay.' I feel guilty that I don't mourn them the way the world expects me to. I mean, I'm not totally indifferent. I wish they were here and that I knew them, but I don't truly grieve them as people." It was a testament to my comfort level with Renn that I could spit out these truths without stammering and staring at the ground.

"But that makes sense, if you weren't close, even before they died."

"You'd think so. Except sometimes things can 'make sense' and still be completely fucked up and confusing. My parents were missionaries. They died while working with a migrant camp in Mexico. By all accounts, it was a flu, likely treatable, but they couldn't get to a proper hospital. They died two weeks apart. All my life, people have told me they were heroes, that they died serving humanity, or doing God's work, stuff like that. But to me—they are just the people that had a kid and then left me with grandma to go off and save the world. Like, how are they heroes if they were such bad parents?"

"Damn."

"I always ask myself why they bothered to have a kid in the first place if they didn't want to raise one. My grandma never said much about it, wouldn't talk about them. She wasn't exactly thrilled to have the task of raising me, and she died while I was in college. I don't have any aunts or uncles, so there's really no one left to ask. I have concert t-shirts and their record collection, but mostly I just kind of live with not knowing. I try not to think about it too much." I'd learned in therapy the past few months that I was a champion compartmentalizer.

"That sucks, Sadie. It sounds sort of lame to say I'm sorry again, but I really am."

"I told you because I figured you'd understand. I don't know what to do with it, other than just live with it." I rolled my neck in a circle. Unburdening myself to Renn *had* made me feel better. I didn't fear him judging me.

"Well, we have that in common—figuring out how to live with it—me with the certainty of what I've lost and you with the certainty that you'll never exactly know."

I recalled Renn's theory of awkwardness as humanness from my first appointment. I hoped life never beat him down so much that he stopped being an amateur philosopher. His simple acceptance of my story had made me lighter, so I couldn't help but smile at his words. "That was deep, Renn."

He grinned back. "This is a full-service tattoo studio. Comes complete with armchair psychology."

We left it there. I spared a last glance at the unfinished outline on his leg before closing my eyes, barely registering the pain as Renn worked on filling in my lotus. Sirius XM was playing now, set to a station that specialized in easy-listening rock of the '70s—James Taylor, Carly Simon, Jim Croce, and the like. I loved how Renn and I shared a taste for music released before we were both born, the age gap between us seeming more irrelevant with each moment we shared. But while our bond was undeniable, and Renn seemed solid, our almost-kiss had been a reminder that I was still basically made of wet paper.

RENN SUGGESTED WE break for lunch just after one o'clock.

"I'm feeling pretty fancy right now, Sadie, so I was thinking... Taco Bell?"

I huffed. "I hope you're not thinking you're making a joke, because I am totally fine with that."

He wasn't kidding. As we walked three blocks toward the siren call of processed and sodium-enhanced goodness, we discovered a shared loathing of high-end restaurants. We also had a healthy appreciation for all varieties of fast food, especially late at night. Since we both worked strange hours, there was a mutual understanding of the euphoric delights of a three a.m. cheeseburger after a long shift. Proof of our culinary compatibility was further revealed at Taco Bell, where we shared the same order—basic bean burritos, with plenty of mild sauce packets.

Heading back to the studio with our food, still shuddering over the prospect of white tablecloth venues, I relayed the horror story of a bad date I'd gone on in college where the guy had cut it short because he said my accent was appalling when ordering at a French restaurant.

"He ended the date because of that?"

"Uh-huh. He told me he was going to be working at his parents' law firm one day and while it might be fine to date a bartender, he couldn't really see it going anywhere because he needed a girlfriend that could be an 'acceptable plus-one at elegant functions'—those were his exact words—and he didn't think I fit the bill."

"What an asshole."

"True. But also, he wasn't wrong. I really hate fancy parties and stuff like that."

"Yeah, but what a dickwad that guy was. Any guy would be lucky to have you with him." Renn's voice was rising and he used his non-bag-holding hand to sort of wave around in my general direction. "I mean, look at you. You're, like, you know..." At this point, his waving evolved to more of an up-and-down motion. "Beautiful...especially now I've gotten to know you. Any guy would be lucky..." He trailed off, looking only slightly abashed.

My face flushed instantaneously. I was grateful to be outside in the cool air, and for the two greasy bags of burritos keeping Renn at a safe distance. "Um...thanks. That's really nice." What else could I say?

He didn't speak again until we were back in the studio. Once we got inside and he had cranked the '70s yacht rock up again, Renn pulled two Cokes out of a mini fridge hiding behind the admin desk, and we sat down in the studio's small waiting area to eat.

"Sadie?"

"Um hmm?" I was busy unwrapping a tortilla. I was firmly in the camp of unwrap-the-burrito-and-put-the-sauce-packet-on-the-whole-thing-before-you-start-eating-it, as opposed to the murderer way of put-a-dollop-on-each-individual-bite-as-you-go type of burrito eating.

He took a deep breath and I saw at least five million different emotions fly across his face before he steeled himself and spoke. "About before, after I told you about...my dad...I really wanted to kiss you." Another big inhale. "I'm not so sure that I actually would have, because of you being my client, but I really fucking wanted to."

I couldn't pretend. The words just came. "I know you did."

"Is it okay I admit that?"

"As long as it's okay for me to admit that I probably would have let you, except for the fact I couldn't get out of my own head in that moment."

"I got that. I saw it in your face, heard it in your voice." He took a moment before asking the question I'd been expecting. "It's because of…him, right? The Boston guy?"

I nodded slowly. "Yeah. I realize I haven't told you details other than it was bad. But I'm working through things. And it was almost good when you were…touching me."

"Almost good? You really know how to turn a boy's head, Sadie." He grinned.

"Shut up. You know what I mean. Before my stupid brain got involved, I really liked it."

"I thought so."

"Don't get cocky."

He smirked at me. "I guess it's a smart idea that we don't worry about that now, since you're still technically my boss." I gave him side-eye at that comment as he continued to grin. After everything we'd shared, and especially after today, the idea that we weren't something more was laughable.

"Look, Sadie, I get the timing is bad. But it's never been this effortless for me, being around someone. I'd like to explore what there could be between us. I won't push, but when you're ready…I'm here."

"I don't know what to say."

"You don't have to say anything. I realize it's not as simple as I like you and you like me. You've got your past, and I come pre-packaged with a third grader whose hands are always inexplicably sticky and a grouchy almost-teen whose sole peanut butter eating method is spoon-in-jar-double-dipping. I'd just like the opportunity to spend some time together, to get to know each other better. Without expectations. If you're down with that."

Backwashed peanut butter seemed a small price to pay for the chance to spend time with Renn without the pressure to define what we were.

I was suddenly not feeling my burrito. I wanted to tell him how happy he made me. I wanted to tell him how scared I was.

When I spoke, it was barely audible. "Seriously, Renn, I was not... expecting this. Expecting you."

He stood, reaching out hesitantly and drawing me toward him, giving me plenty of time to signal if I was unwilling, before pulling me into a hug.

Renn's arms circled my torso, and I reached around him, tentatively at first, finally clasping my hands together above his waist as I leaned into his embrace. "This okay?" He whispered, and I nodded.

One of Renn's arms stayed around my middle while the other wrapped around my shoulders. His fingers splayed across my back, anchoring me to his solid frame. I felt the slide of his hands steal through every part of my body, overwhelming my senses like an intruder. His lemony tea tree oil scent surrounded me. I moved to lay my cheek against his chest as he rested his chin on top of my head, swaying to the soft music while permitting no space between us.

My legs turned to jelly as I surrendered to his embrace. He was keeping himself carefully in check, but the errant finger I felt hooking into my center back belt loop was a sign his equilibrium did not come easy. He exhaled hotly, and the touch of his breath against my ear sent shivers to my feet. I squeezed my thighs together.

As far as hugs went, this one was off the charts. After a minute, Renn leaned back, still holding me around the waist.

He was reaching one hand toward my face, about to say something, when the door opened abruptly, and Archie came in.

"Hey, did you get Taco Bell, or did we decide to move the dumpster into the main room?" Archie was talking and laughing at his own joke as he entered, and although Renn and I separated quickly, I couldn't be entirely sure of what he'd seen.

My face flushed and I jumped away from Renn, as though he'd suddenly been covered in dogshit. *Smooth, Sadie. Real smooth.*

Renn recovered quicker and asked Archie if he'd like a burrito. Archie looked back and forth between the two of us before shaking his head and declaring he'd sooner eat a dirty sock.

"Don't mind him," Renn said to me. "Archie had a bad Taco Bell experience a few years ago. I won't go into the gory details, but let's just say it involved a seven-layer burrito that he swears included an extra layer and resulted in him needing a two-day vacation from the studio."

Archie visibly convulsed. "Hand to God, Renn, it's like I said—that guy definitely spit in my food. He'd come in for a flash piece the week before and was mad I didn't give him a deal."

"Sure, Arch. I'm sure that was it. And not the three pot brownies you'd had the day before."

"It was the burrito, man."

"If you say so."

Archie was still mumbling under his breath. I couldn't make it out entirely, but I definitely heard the words "motherfucker," "two days in the bathroom," and "burrito conspiracy" in there. Archie was certainly a character, and Renn looked at him with unapologetic fondness.

I imagined the other artist had worked at the shop for a while. And even though Archie seemed in good humor, I caught his keen eyes staring at me later when I laid back down on the table. As Renn got in the zone, hands moving confidently above my thigh, I turned my head and caught Archie's gaze directly.

He stared at me, and I knew. He had seen me in Renn's embrace. And he was wondering what was going on between us.

Join the fucking club, Archie.

December 31, 2013

'ZACH, OBVIOUSLY I'M thrilled to see you, but this is crazy. You realize that, right? I mean, why are you here? Did something happen?" I looked around at the raucous New Year's crowd. Luckily, we'd snagged a corner table so we could hear each other.

"Hell, yes, something happened!" Zach whisper-hissed. "We were on the phone the day after Christmas, and you sounded fucking miserable. I've heard you like that before, but something in your voice got me worried enough to hop on a plane. It just took a few days to make arrangements for Hal's."

"What are you talking about?" I was racking my brain, trying to remember.

"Are you kidding me right now?" Zach shook his head, face turned to stone as he leaned across the finely polished wood of the tabletop. The bar we were meeting Henri's work colleagues in was definitely a few steps above Hal's in the class department. "Doll, you called me crying because Henri—your fucking boyfriend that you live with and is therefore supposed to be your biggest fan—got you a Fitbit, a fat-measuring bathroom scale, and a motivational weight loss journal for Christmas... You're a size six for Christ's sake!"

I remembered. It had been an awful morning. Henri said he'd done it out of love, pointing out that he'd also purchased a Fitbit for himself. I'd asked him point-blank if he thought I was too fat, and he'd been quick to reply, "Of course not, darling, but you have to pay attention, especially now that you're in your thirties." That had almost made sense until he followed with, "God bless men who say this, but I am not one of those boyfriends who can say I'd love you at any size. I can't have a fat girlfriend. I want you to stay cute. Because you are adorable, darling. And because I love you."

Yep. Merry Christmas. I'd gone out jogging then, pushing until my new Fitbit hit twenty thousand steps. The next day, still smarting, I did something I'd stopped myself from doing every other time Henri had made similar remarks. Every other time he'd made me feel like I should be grateful just to have him, I'd stayed quiet. But that day, in my humiliated stupor, I'd called Zach and told him exactly what Henri had done.

At the time, Zach had listened and made me feel better, said all the right things. I'd thought it was done. But now, here he was.

"You scared me, Sades. I didn't want to say anything against Henri on the phone because you'd just change the subject or get mad at me. I can't stand listening to you defend him anymore."

"He also got me a Starbucks card," I mumbled. "And some perfume."

"Sadie! I need you to listen." The bar was getting more crowded, and Zach was practically in my lap as he spoke urgently. "This is *not* normal. Do you hear me? This is not how a loving partner behaves. Maybe Henri was different before, but whatever has gone on in the past—and I'm guessing there is a lot of messed up shit you haven't told me—what's happening now is not okay."

"Zach, I know you mean well. I really do. So—I say this with love—stay the fuck out of my relationship. You live in California. I'm sorry I scared you on the phone. I was having a bad day. But one bad day is not a reason to throw away eight years."

"Sadie, it's not one bad day. I didn't fly three thousand miles for one bad day. It's because, little by little, you've been disappearing."

I scoffed. "That's a bit much, don't you think?"

"Not at all. I'll admit that when you first left for Boston, I was worried. You didn't really have a coherent plan. But hey, you got here and started working, and I thought you'd figure things out. Back then, I recognized you. I mean, you hadn't found that *purpose* you were looking for, but you were still Sadie—"

"I'm still me."

"No. No, you're fucking not. You're like a Sadie shell, a husk. When you met Henri, I thought, okay, she's met someone. Good.

She's always wanted love, a family or whatever. But then you stopped calling as much. You moved from that apartment you had, away from the roommates you considered friends, in with Henri. A year later, you don't work anymore. And every time we talk, it's like your life gets smaller and smaller."

"I'm a homebody. Big deal."

But Zach was far from done. "And Henri is always picking at you. Tiny paper cuts, but they are adding up. The past few years, it's been hard to get you on the phone at all. I get one-word answers to my texts, and you only want to talk about me, never yourself. Do you even realize it's been almost two years since I've seen you in person? Did you even notice that your life is passing you by?"

Had it been two years? The days were bleeding together. Ever since Henri had effectively banished me from hanging out with him in his post-work happy hours, I'd mostly just left the house for my daily jogs and errands. I watched TV. I read. I tried to cook and clean the apartment, not that my efforts ever satisfied Henri. But there were good parts too. Henri could be very sweet. He occasionally brought me flowers or small gifts. He told me about his day. And sometimes, even when he was being beastly, I liked the fact that I was the only one he let his mask fall for. It was twisted, but somehow, being the recipient of Henri's harshness made me feel special, since I was the only one who saw it.

"Earth to Sadie." Zach snapped his fingers in front of my nose to grab my attention. "I can see you making excuses in your head. That's why I got my sweet ass on a plane and came all this way, and why I didn't tell you I was coming. I didn't want to give you any time to prepare a façade of bullshit. None of this is okay. Henri doesn't treat you right."

My hackles rose. Henri and I were building something. I was sure of it. I mean, it wasn't perfect, but we were still together. We were making it work. So what if he commented on my thighs? Or didn't think I made great conversation? He was probably right.

My thighs could be a little tighter, and I could try harder with his friends. What did Zach even know about anything? He went through men like water.

"Zach, I'm sorry to tell you that you wasted a trip. I'm fine. I really am. I shouldn't have worried you on Christmas. It was just a bad day."

Zach looked at the table in defeat. "Well, I'm not sorry you called, doll. I'll never be sorry you call when you need me. I'm just sorry I can't get you to see it my way."

"You didn't really think you were going to come here, throw some confetti in my face, and get me to give up on Henri, did you?"

He exhaled heavily. "No. But I had to try. And hopefully, even me trying will make you think about it."

"Okay, Zach. I can see how it might look from your perspective, but you're wrong. Let it go, okay?" I placed my hand on his across the table, noticing the atmosphere livening up as evening moved into late night.

He gave me a bleak smile but still nodded, putting his arm around me as he ordered us two cocktails, ready to ring in the new year.

CHAPTER

Seven

I WAS STILL LAYING down at three o'clock when Zach arrived to pick me up. It occurred to me it had been less than five hours since we were at Starbucks talking about his desire to be a father. When I got out of bed this morning, my best friend was a happy-go-lucky single dude, and I had been determined to keep my attraction to Renn in the shall-not-be-spoken-aloud category. Now, Zach was headed toward parenthood, and Renn had stated unambiguously that he was interested in exploring a relationship with me post-tattoo. I made a mental note to pick up a few lotto tickets on my way to Hal's.

Renn greeted Zach enthusiastically, waving a gloved hand. He gestured toward Archie, who'd been stood up by his client, and introduced the two men. "We're just finishing up, so I'll have Sadie to you in five minutes, as soon as I get the plastic on."

"It's fine." Zach wandered around Studio Obscurum, giving each object and piece of art a discerning glance. He meandered to a shelf near Archie's station. "I'm grateful for the extra chance to examine this unique décor. Perhaps I should get a taxidermy bat or a painting of the devil sitting on a throne of skulls for Hal's."

"Don't be an ass, Zach." I frowned at him.

Renn laughed, unoffended. "Or you could just try a fresh coat of paint."

After our eventful day, Renn saw me and Zach out of the studio with a nod and a wave, along with a casual, "See you soon."

I was halfway to the car when I realized I'd forgotten my sweater. Zach headed to the parking lot while I went back to grab it. Renn must not have closed the studio's front door fully because it was partially ajar, and I stopped short of the entrance upon hearing Archie's distinct New England accent.

"...You can't tell me there's not something there. I see how you look at her."

"Archie, back off. I don't need your help here."

I froze just outside the doorway. Were they talking about me?

The studio was in one of those ancient strip malls dotting the area. Far enough from the street that it was easy to hear over the traffic noise. And because the two other businesses in this complex, a dry cleaners and a spray tan place, were both closed, there wasn't anyone nearby to wonder about the crazy woman crouched near the entrance.

"Don't play around, Renn. Every time I see you two together, you're flirting."

"Flirting? We were just talking. As you are well aware, I talk to all my clients."

"C'mon," Archie cajoled. "You don't normally talk to your clients like that. Laughing and joking... You need to level with me. Are you sleeping with her?"

"What? No! Jesus."

"Well, that's good at least."

"Dammit, Archie." Renn exhaled loudly and seemed to gather himself. "Do you want me to admit that I'd like her to be more than just my client? Because I will totally fucking own that. The girl is amazing."

Archie hmphed. "Look, Renn. I get it. She's a cool chick. She's funny and sarcastic and a knockout to boot. And that new tattoo you inked on her is sexy as hell. But...I think you should be careful...go slow."

I knew how close he was with Archie, so both the annoyance and the hurt were plain in Renn's voice. "Why?"

"The boys. The shop. Your fucking uncle. I've known you a long time—you were just a little squirt when I started apprenticing with your dad—and you've got a lot on your plate right now. I'm only looking out for you." I heard Renn's intake of breath at Archie's casual mention of Thomas, but the other man continued undeterred. "Obviously, getting involved with a client is a bad idea, too, but I won't pretend I haven't done it. I just want to make sure you've considered everything."

"Everything?"

"Yeah, like, she's a bit older than you, right?"

"She's thirty-four, man, not exactly ancient."

"Okay, I get that. But still...an older woman comes with baggage."

"No offense, Arch, but that's crap. Yeah, Sadie's thirty-four, but not the kind of thirty-four-year-old with, like, two divorces and a bunch of kids."

Wait...what? My crouch next to the doorway became a full-on squat as I rested my forehead against my hands. Did Renn honestly see my lack of adult markers as a positive?

Because he doesn't know everything. How could he understand? The impression of a tight red dress and tangled hair came unbidden to my mind. The smack of plastic on the bar. Humiliation, enveloping and suffocating. Henri's eyes on me. And finally, shame.

"That doesn't mean she hasn't lived, Renn. It's a lot of life experience between you two when someone's as young as you are.

Think of it this way—she's only one year younger than me and four years younger than Pete."

Even I hadn't done that math. It was funny how I'd basically dismissed the age thing from my mind, but that didn't mean other people would. It was probably past time for me to announce my presence and grab my sweater, but my feet remained rooted to the concrete.

"Archie, trust me when I tell you that the age thing doesn't matter. When we're together, it's so obvious we're on the same level. I don't want to sound like some corny motherfucker, but she seriously brings out the best in me." I couldn't help but smile when I heard that, but alarms were ringing in my head. *Be honest. Renn's lack of caution is concerning.*

Renn was unfazed by my age, but plenty irritated by the other piece of Archie's argument.

"Besides," Renn grumped. "You really shouldn't compare anyone to Pete. He's not exactly the model of a mature thirty-eight-year-old."

Archie chuckled. "Hey, kid, you don't have to convince me. There's no love lost between me and your uncle, but you realize that at some point you're going to have to deal with this shit with Pete."

"What shit?"

"Don't play dumb. You're pissed because he doesn't do more for the boys." *Thank you, Archie. I'd been curious about that.*

"What the fuck do you want me to do, Arch? I can't exactly force him to do his part. I don't know why he sucks so hard, why he insists on keeping his distance."

"So you're just gonna stick with the low-key anger, passive-aggressive guilt trips, and underlying tension that's been going on since..." Archie took a deep breath. "...since Costa Rica?"

Renn sighed heavily. "At least Pete picked them up from the coffee shop earlier. I don't want to jinx it, but it seems like he's been trying more lately. I didn't even have to ask him twice."

"Nice that he throws you a bone now and then," Archie grouched.

"Look, Arch, I can't claim to understand Pete's actions. I don't know why he doesn't want to help Gage with his spelling or listen to Robbie practice guitar. If it makes him sad. Or maybe he's just not interested. But nothing's changed in four years, and I'm done hoping it will."

"That fucking prick," Archie whispered, so vehemently I couldn't help but wonder if he knew more about Pete's behavior than he was letting on.

"Archie...another thing...about Sadie..."

"Yeah?" Archie spoke gently.

"I told her about my tattoo. Dad. Mary."

"That's... You don't talk about...wow."

Renn's voice was soft. "It's like I said. There's something there."

"Okay. You get I want you to be happy, right? And it's great Sadie gives that to you. I just want you to be prepared, so trust me when I say being with her is gonna be a lot more complicated than you think."

I heard Renn's distinct exhale. I was one hundred percent positive he was running his fingers through his hair. "Have you even met me, Archie? You're so stuck on the baggage Sadie *might* have, but let's be real here—I'm also carrying a metric fuckton of it. Do you think with my life I could date some airhead sorority girl or some shit like that? Do you think there's a young woman out there just waiting for me to take her to dinner and a movie, while we hold hands, and I talk about the shop getting audited, or how I picked Gage up from school early because he had explosive diarrhea? Honestly, dating someone my age seems almost insane. Not many twenty-three-year-old women out there that would want to deal with that."

"And Sadie would? It's something she's ready for?"

"For fuck's sake, Archie, we're nowhere near that conversation. The only thing I know for sure is that nothing I get into is gonna be easy." Renn's voice grew agitated, and I heard the sounds of him breaking down his table as he spoke. "And I'm okay that this might take some time to figure out. I don't want some lame hookup. I think she's worth waiting for."

I wanted to be thrilled at everything Renn was saying, except deep down inside, all I felt was uneasy. Renn was naïve about our obstacles because he didn't understand the significance of my past. He didn't have the full story about Henri, what had happened to me. Apparently, my visceral reaction to our almost-kiss hadn't provided enough of a clue. He'd said we could take our time, but did he mean it? I wasn't ready for him to come at me full-throttle. I was barely ready for him to approach walking-heel-toe-carrying-fifty-pound-kettlebells.

I knew I should stop eavesdropping, but it was so hard when it was me being discussed. Zach almost took the decision away from me when he came walking swiftly toward the studio and caught me crouching near the doorway. "Doll, what the hell are you—"

"Shh. Hush!" I mouthed the words at him, flailing my hand up and down at my side to motion he should come stand against the wall with me. Thankfully, I didn't hear any sign from inside that they'd picked up on his arrival.

"What are we doing, Sades?" Zach took my cue and soundlessly over-enunciated his question so I could read his lips. Once he was close enough that only I could hear his whispers, he asked, "Why are we playing secret agent outside the tattoo studio?"

"Shut up, you. This is serious." It was the barest whisper, mostly soundless miming. "When I came back to get my sweater, I heard Archie and Renn talking about me."

Zach's expression grew concerned and I recognized my friend from our last day in Boston. "Do you need me to go in and punch someone?"

"No. Just hush." I made big eyes at Zach and implored him with a glance to stand down.

Zach leaned in behind me as we continued listening, tacitly in agreement that hearing what they had to say was a higher value than not eavesdropping.

"...Renn, no matter what happens, I'll always be here for you."

"Then stop worrying. I'm okay with not having things all tidy right now. When I'm with her... Just trust me, whatever the obstacles, she's worth it."

Zach squeezed my shoulder and whispered in my ear, "It sounds like he really likes you, doll. I think you found a good one." I closed my eyes, going cold. I knew Zach just wanted the best for me. Inside the shop, only Archie seemed to share my own concerns.

"Renn, if this is what you want, I support it—"

"Sadie's been pretty honest about her past, Archie." *Clearly, I haven't been sufficiently honest, if you think you have enough of the story to decide all I need is a little time and patience.* "I won't tell you because it's not my place. I understand what you're saying, and I love you for it. But with how she makes me feel—I'd be crazy not to try."

Archie didn't reply. I imagined him nodding or something similar, and a few seconds later I heard the distinctive sound of the two men slapping each other's backs. A conversation-ending bro hug.

I crumpled against the brick wall and put my head between my knees, more than a little afraid I'd pass out. Zach held me from the side, so I didn't fall all the way over.

"Alright, doll, I don't know what's happening right now, but I'm gonna go in and grab your sweater really fast and then I'm taking you out of here."

I held myself against the cold exterior as I heard Zach enter the studio, casually locating my sweater. Renn said it had been nice seeing him again, totally unaware I was falling apart just beyond the doorway. Zach gathered me up after he exited and practically threw me into his car.

"Okay, Sadie, what's going on? All I heard was that gorgeous man tell his friend how much he liked you, but you're acting like you just watched *Marley and Me*."

I dragged in my breath and gave Zach a tortured stare. "I don't think he gets it."

"Renn? Gets what?"

"Me."

"What do you mean?"

I replayed Renn and Archie's conversation in my mind. "Well, for starters, I've told him where I'm at in life, that I need to make certain things a priority. Even if the timing was better, there's still where my head is after all the shit with Henri. I've explained to Renn some of that, about Boston, but obviously not enough."

Zach still hadn't started the car yet. He reached out to put a hand on mine before asking, "Why would you think that?"

"Because Renn fundamentally does not understand that I'm in this place in my life because I spent years being dragged down and feeling like a piece of garbage."

Memories assaulted me. Henri introducing me as his girlfriend and talking about the future. Telling me he loved me, that I was special, that he couldn't live without me. Doing just enough to convince me we were fine, all while trying to dictate every aspect of my life. Discouraging me from working and controlling my finances. Telling me what to wear, what to eat, when to work out, and then critiquing every aspect of my appearance.

"...I lapped up scraps, any sign I had pleased him. By the time you helped me leave, I'd surrendered all my own desires in the service of being molded into Henri's idea of the perfect girlfriend."

"I know, doll. But I think you're missing the key fact—*I* was there, but Renn wasn't. The Sadie he knows is not that girl you just described. You realize that, right?"

Did I? I *had* left. But I still experienced that shame deep in my bones. It wasn't just a terrible memory I'd learned to live with. Every day, it felt fresh. Every day, I was still a little bit...humiliated.

It had been almost a year. I was in therapy. I'd reclaimed my running. I worked. I laughed and joked around. I was looking into school and getting excited about planning career goals. And after talking with Renn about my childhood today, plus seeing him with his brothers, I was getting a glimmer of an idea about what that future could be.

There were long stretches—during movie marathons or coffee dates with Zach, in the middle of an entertaining shift at Hal's—where I felt normal. But the idea that I wasn't still sporting an open wound was laughable. If Renn thought I was anywhere close to fully healed, then he didn't grasp the situation nearly as well as he needed to.

The irony was that Renn himself provided the most balm for my bruises. It wasn't the therapy or the running, the times with Zach, or the shifts at Hal's that had penetrated my walls the deepest. It was the warmth that pooled in my belly when I was around Renn. Renn putting me at ease, Renn singing for me, Renn declaring himself my equal, Renn looking past whatever icky parts I had on display, Renn bringing his smile and his light into my world, unreservedly.

The timing was a beast. I couldn't force my recovery. I couldn't be whole for Renn just because he thought I was. I couldn't squish myself into another box for another man, even someone as amazing as him.

"Zach, how can I make him understand?" I gulped hard as I thought about the moments in the studio. "He almost kissed me today." Zach looked giddy and started to make a clapping gesture, but I shut him down with a shake of my head. "I said *almost*. He pulled me close and we were holding hands. But it wasn't just holding hands. It was so...much. Touching him feels...I can't explain it. And it seemed so right for him to be close." I took a beat, angrily squeezing a fist into my palm. "And I wanted it...I really did...until I didn't...because I couldn't get Henri out of my mind!" I groaned and leaned my head back, bending my neck as far as it would go against the headrest of Zach's sedan.

"Sadie, I really need you to hear me here." Zach put his finger under my chin and forced me to meet his gaze. "There's nothing you need to make Renn understand. You don't need to be whole and perfect for someone to love you. You're one hundred percent lovable just the way you are."

I sighed, bringing my head upright. "You don't think it's unfair to him, to explore something I might not be ready for?"

"You'll never know if you don't try. Renn is a big boy who can make up his own mind. If there is even such a thing as a stable, well-adjusted adult—and the jury is still out on that—but if they exist, I bet those people have shit relationships too. Just like the rest of us plebes. Nothing's guaranteed, doll. Isn't that what you said to me at Starbucks a few hours ago? But from what I heard in there, he seems like a solid guy."

"He is pretty great."

Zach nodded. "Then how about you just take your time and see how things go? You need to trust that everything he's telling you is true, especially the part about him being willing to wait. I am saying this as your friend who loves you so much. Get. Out. Of. Your. Own. Head."

We stayed parked. Clearly, Zach wasn't going to put the key in the ignition until he was sure I was okay. I thought about our talk this morning. *How was it just this morning*? He was going to make a fantastic father someday.

"Zach?"

"Hmm?"

"I know I've said this before, but I just wanted to thank you again for being there, in Boston."

"No thanks needed, doll." He winked.

"No, really. That day was...so dark. You were like the one tiny sliver of light in all that. Just enough light for me to find my way out."

Zach grabbed my left hand with his right, bringing our joined fingers to his lips. He brushed a soft peck on my knuckles before resting our laced fingers on the center console. "Sadie, you don't need to keep thanking me. I'm glad I was there. And I'd do it again in a heartbeat. You know I'd do anything for you."

"Me too."

Today had been a day. Jesus. So much to think about. But I could handle it. I wasn't in Boston anymore. I wasn't spending my life in the fruitless pursuit of Henri's happiness. I could survive an almost-kiss with Renn. And a hot hug. I could listen to him talk to Archie, knowing everything would be far from easy. And, looking at Zach in the driver's seat, I was sure I could be the friend I wanted to be.

December 31, 2013

AS HENRI'S WORK friends had arrived, it became evident that the reason for my compulsory attendance was to help him paint the picture of blissful domesticity for a senior partner who was visiting the Boston office from San Francisco. Upon introducing me to Jim and his lovely wife, Helena, Henri had played the doting boyfriend so well it had been startling. Zach stood off to the side, scowling like he'd found a roach in his soup. Helena was unlike most of Henri's friends' wives and girlfriends. She was older and looked less like a model and more like someone who played the wife in a detergent commercial. I relaxed and made conversation, admiring pictures of her two sons playing soccer and vacationing in Florida. Jim looked pleased to see our connection, and Henri beamed at me from where he and Jim were drinking by the bar.

The older couple left well before midnight, at which point my boyfriend made a beeline for me.

"Sadie, that was amazing! I knew they would love you, how you're just, like, a regular girl. Jim wants the company to feel like a family, and now that he's met you and seen us together, I know he'll consider me for the regional vice president position. I can't wait to tell my dad." Henri, tipsy, pulled me to his chest and kissed my cheek, hard and wet. I froze. It had been so long since he'd offered me unchecked praise. "Well done, darling. I love you."

With that, Henri sneered at Zach and left our table to go over to the bar with his friends. His movements were exaggerated and effusive, as though he'd won the lottery and not merely impressed one of his bosses. Come to think of it, he'd been sort of off all night.

"That was, um, something," Zach offered.

I raised my hand to my cheek where Henri had kissed it. "I can't think of the last time he said that to me."

Zach frowned. "Well, it's good at least that he can occasionally appreciate you."

Good? It was weird.

Henri's praise and declaration of love coursed through my body. Except I wasn't elated the way I thought I should be. I felt like I wanted to throw up.

I watched Henri across the bar, doing shots with someone named Freddie, who I had mentally nicknamed "Hands" based on the number of times his palm had *accidentally* contacted my backside over the past few hours. His other friend, Bill, had his hand straight up a woman's skirt, fingers working underneath the bar top as she giggled and half-heartedly pulled at his wrist. Henri stood between them, an arm thrown over each of their shoulders. When I'd met Henri, I'd been so dazzled by this side of his world. The assuredness of these men. Masters of the Universe. But what had once been intoxicating was now revealed as simply toxic. And maybe it was watching Henri's red eyes as he took another shot, or maybe it was Zach's frowning presence, but for the first time I could see things clearly. *These guys were dickheads.*

No. That was disloyal. And Henri had just told me he loved me, something I'd actually been hoping to hear tonight, even if the script I'd written in my mind had involved privacy and candlelight. Not a sloppy thank-you in an overheated bar.

Those conflicting thoughts were the ones rolling through my mind when the woman in the red dress walked in. She came through the door like a tornado, uncaring of the attention her entrance drew, and I watched her in slow motion as she headed straight for Henri. She looked young, early to mid-twenties at most, long ashen hair haphazard down her back. Her rosy cheeks flushed with anger as she stalked bitterly toward my boyfriend.

"You asshole!" That was her opener, and I envied her ability to not cower under the glare Henri gave her, as though she was hot garbage come to life. He removed his hands from his buddies' shoulders, making them into fists at his sides, the happy daze he'd been in mere moments ago blown completely aside. The woman was undiscouraged. "Ignoring my texts won't make me go away!"

I stood far enough away to disengage almost completely, even as I felt Zach fold me into his side. It was simply a movie playing out in front of me. Theatre. Something I was watching from a distance. Watching as she slapped Henri across the face. Watching as she called him a "fucking liar" and a "sleazy used car salesman" and the "worst fucking thing to ever happen to" her. Watching as Freddie and Bill glanced over for my reaction, unsurprised by this unfolding drama, confirming that the woman in the red dress was not unknown to them. Watching as Henri looked urgently toward me, seeking the gaze I had the strength to deny him. Watching when the woman smashed a six-inch white stick down on the counter in front of Henri.

A pregnancy test.

How lucky that I was standing across the room, and not next to Henri. How fortuitous that this happened only minutes after my epiphany that Henri was honestly kind of a dipshit. If not for those things, I don't know that I could have given the right answer when Zach turned to me and asked gravely,

"Will you come back with me to Los Angeles? We can leave right now."

CHAPTER

Eight

HAI'S WAS MERCIFULLY dead when I made it in around six o'clock for my shift.

The week after Christmas seemed to come with a different playbook for everyone. Some got a jump on returning to the ordinary, hauling dried-up noble firs to the curb and putting lights and decorations back in storage. Others reveled in an extended seven-day holiday that didn't end until the last football game on New Year's Day. I was just trying to get from one end of it to the other without acknowledging the occasion.

Not that I was anti-holiday as a rule. I had a few fleeting fond memories from my childhood. My love for pop-top cinnamon rolls began with Grandma's tradition of having them for "special breakfast" on Christmas, and she always made sure there were presents beside the small plastic tree she put on the coffee table, even if I never quite got whatever I'd been hoping for. The season had taken on a certain glamour during my time in Boston, weeks marked by the black-tie parties Henri was required to attend for work. But this New Year's Eve would be one year since my return to Los Angeles. Ignoring the day altogether seemed like the safest way to avoid summoning any demons.

However, my best friend put a damper on those intentions by insisting on seasonal cheer. Zach's exact words were, "Fuck that. Henri had you for eight years, doll. He can't have our first Christmas back together, too."

Besides the abundance of red and green—and plaid, *so much plaid*—regalia saturating Hal's, Zach had gone full Martha Stewart in our apartment. There was a kitschy snow globe collection on the windowsill and special candy cane potholders hung from the oven door. A six-foot blue spruce shedding needles in the middle of our living room made it impossible to evade even the smell of the season.

I understood Zach's desire to make merry. He was in the throes of a serious relationship, and the holidays were more fun when you had someone to curl up with to drink hot chocolate and watch Bing Crosby movies. I had also never seen him so excited about exchanging gifts. Teddy had given him a stunning watch inscribed with *All love is sweet, Given or received*, and Zach had given Teddy—with my blessing—a key to our apartment.

They made sure to include me wherever possible and never made me feel like a third wheel. Zach and I had plenty of best friend time at work and we kept a standing date to watch every Seahawks game together, since football wasn't Teddy's thing. Teddy had also started reaching out to me on his own. He'd cemented the final selection of the watch he'd given Zach only after multiple texts, getting my opinion on everything from size and style to inscription. I had given him the hint of choosing Percy Shelley, Zach's favorite poet. "That's why I love you, doll," he'd said to me then. "You know everything." Teddy's easy adoption of the nickname Zach had been using on me for more than a decade had been natural.

Teddy was becoming a genuine friend in his own right. Which made the conversation I'd been putting off feel more urgent.

Zach was changing out the tills and grimacing at the ancient register when I arrived. Larry insisted on running the business side of things like it was 1975. The bar's stubborn owner had barely consented to the laptop in the back office, so getting him to purchase computerized machines for the front end had been a lost cause. Just before I'd left for Boston, Zach had convinced him to let Hal's accept credit cards, but there hadn't been many improvements since that epic struggle. The good news was that Larry would officially retire in the new year and Zach had finalized his purchase of Hal's. Another reason we needed to talk.

I was tying my apron when I noticed Teddy at the end of the bar. He'd been coming in now and then to keep Zach company during his shifts. Zach finished wedging the last till back in the register, slamming it shut with a flourish. He picked up his phone and, with a few flicks of his fingers, the music coming out of the scratchy sound system switched from the frat boy anthems of early Beastie Boys to the sad dad music of the Dave Matthews Band.

I looked up at the speakers and frowned at Zach. "Dude, are you sure you're even gay?"

Teddy leaned across the bar to plant a kiss on Zach's lips before turning to me with a wink. "I assure you that he is very, very gay."

I laughed. "Calm down, tiger. You're giving those sorority girls... *ideas*." I gestured toward a pack of tittering students at a nearby table.

"I was on my way out, anyway," Teddy said. "Gotta head back to the office."

"At this hour?" It was just past six, starting time for me and Zach, but to most of the working world, it was time to Netflix and chill. Or in my usual case, Netflix and snack.

"I can set my schedule, so I've been trying to align more with Zach. At least sometimes. I'd miss this guy too much if I worked a straight nine-to-five every day." He put his hand over his heart, sighing dramatically. "The things you do for love."

Teddy gave Zach one more quick, hard kiss—cue the giggling coeds—then grabbed his coat and offered me a hug before exiting toward the parking lot. I waited until I could hear his footsteps echoing across the asphalt before speaking.

"So it's love then?" I asked Zach, who was still looking at the door.

"It's been love, doll. From the minute we met."

Zach and I really needed to talk.

BY TEN O'CLOCK there were no patrons in the bar other than Gary, a mid-sixties, gray ponytail type who came in several times per week to spend two hours drinking exactly three beers while reading a book.

"Hey Gary, are you good for a minute? I need to talk to Zach, but I don't want to leave you hanging."

"I'm good, Sadie girl. I've got my pint and a book. Don't worry about me."

"Thanks." He buried his nose in a beat-up paperback. The title was obscured, but there was a black-and-white photograph of a military helicopter on the cover.

I found Zach hunched against the counter, scrunching his face as he examined the bar's "books," shaking his head as he tried to connect whatever was on the paper to what he could see on the shelves. Good old Larry. I imagined him as the type of person who went to his accountant and dropped a ratty shoebox full of receipts at tax time. He did keep a Mesozoic-era version of QuickBooks on the laptop, which ensured employees got paid correctly and we observed the barest legalities regarding money handling, but the rest of the record-keeping system was a mess. What passed for inventory was basically a collection of handwritten spiral notebooks.

Zach had made a lot of improvements as manager, but he would still have a mess to untangle when he took the reins for good.

"Can I help with anything?"

"Nah." He started putting things away beneath the bar. "I can't do any more right now. I'm getting weird." He looked at me and crossed his eyeballs.

I chuckled. "Alright, since we have a few minutes here—Gary's cool—I'd like to talk to you. I've been thinking about something for a while, but I wanted to get through Christmas."

Zach laughed back. "And you didn't think we could chat at home? Like, in the mutual space where we cohabitate and see each other constantly?" He arranged bottles along the shelves as he teased me.

"Shut up. I've had a ton on my mind. Besides, Teddy has been over a lot lately, and as much as this involves him, I thought we should discuss it privately first."

"What do you have to talk about that involves Teddy? Is everything alright?"

"Yes, yes. Nothing's wrong." I dragged in a big breath. "I just want to return to the conversation we had at Starbucks a few weeks ago." Zach startled in the middle of turning the labels out on the bourbon shelf, and I couldn't have asked for clearer confirmation that he knew exactly what I was referring to.

"Oh, that. Well, I thought we'd sort of left it at I needed to make sure things were on that path with Teddy, before I dropped the I-wanna-be-a-dad-and-not-just-theoretically-and-probably-really-soon bomb."

"Um...Zach. The man changed his entire schedule to revolve around your life. He declared his love for you in front of drunk sorority girls, not to mention Gary, a few hours ago. He must have texted me fifteen Shelley quotes before he was satisfied that he had the perfect one for your watch. When I got home yesterday, he was emptying *our* dishwasher. Like, he knows where the forks go and about the ridiculous 'Pet My Pussy' cat mug you got me. So, yeah, dude, pretty sure you're good to have that conversation."

Zach nodded and the most ginormous grin took over his face. "I think he's it for me, Sadie. It freaks me the fuck out to say so, but it's true."

"I know I don't get a vote, but duh. Teddy's fantastic."

"He really is."

"And he'd make a great father."

"He really would."

I put my hands on either side of Zach's face and spoke in the slowest, most enunciated voice I could muster. "So you should have that conversation."

"You're right." Zach chuckled and stepped away from my steady gaze. "I know you're right. I promise I'll do it soon."

I dragged his eyes back to mine. "Don't worry. Like I said, Teddy's clearly all in. But before you talk, I want to make sure you have all the information."

"Information?"

"I'm sorry I didn't say this to you sooner, and I should have offered the minute you told me you wanted a baby, but I was sort of in my head that day, and it didn't register, and then I had that intense appointment with Renn right after, remember the one I told you he almost kissed me, but I couldn't kiss him back because of goddamn Henri, and we got Taco Bell, and hugged, then overhearing him and Archie, and after that I didn't have any space in my brain left to think about it, but then, once I did, I realized—"

"Doll, what was that you were saying about none of us getting any younger?"

"Sorry." I fidgeted with a loose string on my apron and centered my thoughts before pulling Zach to lean against the bar. "I just wanted to make it clear that if you decide to have a baby, of course I am totally down to help you out."

"Help me out?"

"Don't be obtuse, Zach. I could…you know…assist. Carry the baby, or I dunno, be an egg donor, or whatever, if you're not afraid of my DNA."

"Sadie…" Zach did a slow nod, and I could tell he was gearing up for some careful words. "I realize that, since I want the whole new baby experience, surrogacy or adopting a newborn are essentially my options. And you're my best friend. So, obviously, the thought has crossed my mind. But I'm nowhere near ready to get in the weeds or think through specifics."

I smiled at his admission that he'd considered me in this capacity already. "Totally understand that. I'm just saying that whenever you are ready, my offer is on the table."

"Doll, there was a point you made that day—Teddy has money. Assuming he's on board to do this with me, we'd be able to afford another surrogate if we decided to go that route."

"But no one else is your best friend. And besides the fact that I'd help you out for free, you'd be doing me a favor. I would love to do this."

"You would?"

"Absolutely. I'm one hundred percent volunteering for morning sickness and stretch marks and whateverthefuck else comes with growing a human being. You get how much I love you, right?"

"I do, but it's a big ask. And this has been a tough year for you."

"You're not asking. I'm offering." I pulled the bar rag he was twisting into knots out of his hands and rested my palms on his shoulders. "Zach, we both know I owe you everything. When you brought me home a year ago, I was a wreck. You helped me put myself together and I'm getting stronger every day. But that's not why I'm offering. I want to do this because it's something I *can* do. Something I *can choose* to do. I was numb for so long, but I'm feeling things again. It's like with the running. I'm starting to get in touch with my body, without hearing Henri in my head telling me I need to tighten up or lose a few—"

"He was such an asshole," Zach muttered.

"And you shouldn't have to rely on some stranger. C'mon, Zach. I have a uterus just hanging out in my body, doing nothing other than supporting the Tampax corporation. It's probably riddled with cobwebs and getting dustier by the second. Let me put it to good use before I'm completely geriatric."

Zach guffawed. "How can I resist the allure of your old-ass, dusty uterus?"

"You can't. And Teddy won't be able to, either."

"And you don't think you might want to—you know—keep your uterus available for your own babies?"

I barked a laugh. "Zach, come off it. Even if I met *the one* tomorrow, and started a relationship that was headed in that direction, I'd still be years away from having babies. Trust me, I've thought about this. Since you told me you wanted a baby sooner than later, the timing is perfect."

I wasn't trying to lie to myself. In the back of my mind, I couldn't help but question if Renn might be *the one,* assuming I was ever able to actually date him. But even if that miracle happened, we were still in the maybe-we'll-try phase, not the planning-for-forever phase. I could do this for Zach now. Zach understood where things stood between me and Renn, so I was sure he was making the same calculation, why he appeared to seriously be considering my words.

"Alright, doll. How about this—I'll keep it in mind. And if and when Teddy and I start considering how to build our family, we might take you up on your offer, which is incredible, by the way."

"I'd be honored to help, Zach."

We went back to completing the bar's closing tasks, which were all muscle memory at this point. Even though I was ostensibly listening to Gary tell me about his book, mostly I was in my own thoughts. I'd been in stasis so long that the low buzz of possibility I felt after conversing with Zach had the blood thrumming in my veins.

And that slight euphoria wasn't just about Zach and Teddy. These past few months, other things had become clear. I was almost afraid to say it out loud, too cautious to hope that I had found my path, but I was pretty sure I finally had an answer to what was next with my career.

You know why you don't have a job right now, darling? I take care of you, and you like that. You like that I make all the decisions. Isn't it easier to just let me take the lead? Fuck off, Henri. *I wasn't just going to spend my life sitting.*

I'd made a lot of progress dealing with the negative voices in my head—sometimes mine, sometimes Henri's—and I was learning to reflect on my time with him without the ensuing sense of defeat, the shame of those years.

I had done a decent job being Henri's ornament. But that differed from feeling like I'd meant something to him. I had known Renn for less than six months, and he'd already told me I had inspired his creativity and helped him talk about his dad. Henri and I were together for eight years and I didn't think I'd ever given him such a gift. *Look, darling, I told you I had a bad day at work. What I need is for you to do the dishes, then go put on the green dress I bought you, and smile and be charming for the exec team tonight.*

Henri had taken and taken and taken from me. Yet somehow, I'd given him nothing.

But now...now I could envision myself doing something amazing for Zach and Teddy. I could see myself having a fulfilling job. And although I still hadn't mustered the courage to share my career plans with anyone, I knew I wanted to make a difference in people's lives. And after my last conversation with Renn, I had figured out how I wanted to do that.

Early January 2015

NEW YEAR'S DAY had brought tons of customers into Hal's to watch bowl games and celebrate the last gasp of the holidays. They'd been rowdy and impatient for drinks, so I'd found myself commemorating the anniversary of my exit from Boston with a pitcher of margaritas dumped down my shirt, courtesy of an unruly elbow. Serving the steady crowds had helped the day pass, and I'd ended it on the dull note of falling asleep in front of the TV watching a repeat broadcast of the Rose Parade.

But when I arrived for my shift on the second, things were quiet. Half the tables were empty and the only person at the counter was Gary, still reading the helicopter book.

I loved when the bar was this sleepy, but to be successful, it needed more big-number days like yesterday. This was an enormous concern for Zach, since he was now the official owner. If there was a discordant note in his relationship with Teddy, it was their differing financial statuses. Zach had confided that a big reason he wanted Hal's to be profitable was to feel like more of an equal partner in their relationship. He had plenty of ideas about how to reinvent the place and attract a good crowd, but most of those would require money, and as cash wasn't abundant, change would be slow. I figured it was my duty as his best friend to distract him from the empty barstools.

"I noticed you didn't come home last night."

"We were at one of Teddy's fundraisers. It was for an animal charity, and we had a total blast." Zach pulled out his phone and showed me a picture of the two of them in tuxedos. Zach's was a rental, a basic black tie suit tux. Teddy's was more unique, navy blue velvet with a black button-down and bow tie, perfectly tailored to his tall, lean physique.

"Dude, your boyfriend is smokin'."

"Yeah, he is. Do you know he owns that tuxedo? Matter of

fact, he owns three of them. That's how many of these things he goes to."

"But that's okay, right?"

Zach hesitated only a moment. "It is. I never thought I was one for those types of events, but Teddy makes them fun. I'll never love it the way he does, but he also doesn't love Hal's like I do—yet he sits at the bar and keeps me company all the time."

The smile on my friend's face spoke volumes. He and Teddy were different, but they were solid. Zach had finally spoken to him about wanting a baby. I was zero percent surprised Teddy had wholeheartedly embraced Zach's vision, excited to talk more about having kids when the time was right. And it appeared likely that would be in the very near future.

"Sadie, honestly, it's been so good with Teddy. Sometimes I worry it's too perfect."

"Really?" I could remember living with Henri and experiencing the opposite, trying to convince myself things were perfect, but never truly feeling like they were.

Zach sighed and started wiping the bar top with a towel. "I just keep thinking there has to be something wrong. Like, is he balding? Way too into *Star Wars*? Spends all his money collecting vintage sneakers? Puts ketchup on his eggs? Unacceptably high number of sex toys hidden in a drawer?"

"Is there an unacceptable number?"

"Fourteen, doll. Fourteen is the cut-off."

I laughed and was about to reassure Zach that Teddy was definitely the type of guy who put hot sauce on his eggs when I heard the creak of the door. I looked up, expecting to greet a customer. To my shock, Renn walked in.

He was wearing close-fitting dark jeans, cinched with a thick brown leather belt at his hips. His long-sleeved gray Henley was turned up to the elbows, and his exposed forearms—one with the colorful full-sleeve—had bracelets at the wrists. His hair hung loose around his chin, tamed by an olive-green beanie. If the sexiest parts of '90s grunge had a baby with a sunny day, and that baby paid particular attention to arms day at the gym, it would be Renn. He looked up at me and smiled, looking amazing. I wasn't the only one that noticed.

"Hi Reeeeennnn," Zach sing-songed. He turned his back to Renn as he mouthed to me, "He's so hot. What's he doing here?" I shrugged and glared at Zach as he returned his attention to Renn. "Fancy seeing you here."

"Oh, hey, Zach. I forgot you worked here too. Cool. Sadie has talked so much about Hal's, I figured I'd come by and see it for myself."

"Well, luckily you came just in time to settle the debate. Sades and I were discussing what an acceptable number of sex toys is. Thoughts?"

I hissed at Zach, "Shut up, you monster. Stop causing trouble." Zach made kiss-lips at me as I turned to Renn. "You do not need to answer that."

Renn held his hands up like we were robbing his register. "I plead the fifth."

Chuckling, Zach drifted away, leaving us alone. I hadn't seen Renn since my last appointment. Since our almost-kiss. Since I'd overheard him talking to Archie. Since Zach told me to get the hell over myself and just see where things went.

Renn had texted me quite a few times since that day, signaling that something had elevated between us. Some were all busi-ness—confirming our upcoming session or sending me a receipt. Thank God for online payment portals, so we never had to address that awkward elephant out loud. Some were for fun—a *Parks and Recreation* GIF wishing me Happy Holidays or links to songs and videos he thought I would like. And there were the undefinable others—thanking me for talking, telling me how much he enjoyed spending time together.

Standing in front of him now, I couldn't help but remember the feel of his hand gripping my hip. If he tried to lean into me again, what would I do? Would I panic and have another flashback to Henri? Just wondering made my heart beat faster and I knew I wasn't ready to test the waters. *Your body always comes alive under my hands, darling. It's like it was meant for my touch and no one else's.*

Ugh. I didn't want to believe Henri had ruined me forever. I wasn't ready now, but that didn't mean I wouldn't be someday. And in the meantime, I was going to enjoy the way Renn was smiling at me across the bar as if I was the best thing he'd ever seen.

"Sadie, I wanted to see Hal's, but I also had another reason for coming," Renn said.

"What's that?"

"You told me you run as a hobby. I help on the PTSA at Robbie's middle school. I'm the events chair, and we organize a 5K race to raise money for the school. I was wondering if you'd like to participate? It's next Saturday morning, the tenth."

I powered through the ovary-bursting information that Renn volunteered for his brother's PTSA and mustered a reply. "For sure. I usually take long runs on Saturdays, so it works out."

I appreciated Renn had come up with a plausible reason for visiting me outside of work. After all, I'd invited him to see Hal's, and the garish decorations were still up so he could get his red and green—and plaid!—fix. I asked him what he liked best, and he said the enormous stuffed Rudolph Zach had rigged through the ceiling to hang above the bar. He expressed faux outrage when I informed him that the red-nosed reindeer was my least favorite of all the tacky items on display.

"Why's that?" Renn asked.

"Because it looks like a piñata up there. I want to cheer Rudolph on his magical journey, not beat him with a stick."

Renn grinned. "Which one do you like then?"

"She likes the mistletoe," Zach piped in from where he was eavesdropping across the room. "It's over the hallway leading to the office. You should go check it out. Both of you. At the same time."

"Subtle," I mumbled. Renn just laughed and smiled at me again, making no move toward the mistletoe.

He stayed for another half hour, ordered a Diet Coke, and we talked about how we spent our holidays. He'd been able to score a sweet new bike for Robbie, and Gage was stoked about his Teenage Mutant Ninja Turtles Sewer Lair. I didn't elaborate on my Boston anniversary. I just told him I'd worked through the holidays and left it at that. Renn made a point to include Zach in our conversation. They were both small business owners and had quite a few boring-ass things to talk about related to local taxes and regulations.

As Renn got up to leave, he whispered something in Zach's ear. Zach pulled back and nodded, smiling mischievously. At that, Renn walked over to where the mistletoe was hanging. He reached up to pluck it from the doorframe and brought it over to me. *He's walking over to me with the mistletoe. Am I going to freak out? Am I about to ruin this whole good night we just had?*

But I should have known Renn would never let me down. He stood in front of me and held the mistletoe above my head. He leaned in toward my cheek, coming in close to my ear.

"May I?"

I nodded, and Renn placed a chaste, closed-mouth kiss on my cheek. I felt the brief peck to my core, mesmerized. Then he pulled back, smiled at me, placed the mistletoe on the bar top, winked at Zach, and walked out the door. I put my hand to my face, mouth open in a small O.

Zach grinned and started fanning himself with a menu. "Doll, you are in so much trouble."

CHAPTER
Nine

T HE SKY WAS the color of soupy cement on the Saturday of the 5K—terrible weather if you were hoping for a winter tan but fantastic for running. I had been jogging consistently for a year and was fitter and stronger than I'd ever been. I might have the beginnings of forehead lines and my pores weren't what they used to be, but damn if I wasn't proud of my quads. Having picked my outfit with an eye toward showing off Renn's handiwork, I had on little purple jogging shorts and a navy-blue running tank, finishing the look with blue-striped athletic knee socks.

When I arrived, I realized just how remarkable it was for Renn to be overseeing the event. Robbie's wealthy middle school in Pasadena was insanely crowded, rivaling the large charity runs I'd done in Boston. Massive white-stucco buildings came together like a palace complex among the manicured grounds. The abundant event signage looked professional.

I parked in the designated overflow lot, a deserted-on-the-weekends office park nearby. When Renn had described this as a school fundraiser, I'd envisioned something more low-key, but this was serious business. I received an official logoed t-shirt at registration when I picked up my racing bib. I was almost certain it was Renn's handiwork on the design.

I still had another month to run in the women ages thirty to thirty-four category, as my birthday wasn't until February. Renn's group, men ages eighteen to twenty-four, had already completed their race. A large screen projected the results. Out of seventy runners, they displayed only the top twenty-five finishers. Renn's name wasn't there. But I'd already known it wouldn't be.

6:30 a.m.

RENN: I'm at the school. We've been setting up since 5. I wanted to check in and make sure you're still coming. *smiley face emoji*

7:56 a.m.

RENN: I guess you're not up yet? You know your group runs at 10, right? I probably should have confirmed with you yesterday.

7:58 a.m.

RENN: I'm texting in full sentences again. Adding superfluous hashtags to soften it. Also using five-dollar words like superfluous. #cantstopwontstop

8:11 a.m.

RENN: I hope you're okay.

8:50 a.m.

RENN: My group runs in ten. I'm glad we opened it up to the community because we're making four times the amount of money as when it was just for school families.

8:52 a.m.

RENN: But some of these guys look serious. I'm afraid. There are some very short shorts going on. And so many pairs of long, skinny runner legs. Pretty sure some of them are bird people. I better get to the start line. Hope to see you soon!

9:15 a.m.

ME: I'm here! Sorry I didn't get home until close to 3 after my shift and forgot to plug it in so I woke up with a dead phone. Charged it in the car so just now seeing your texts.

9:17 a.m.

ME: You know, for someone who claims to be busy you sure had the time to text me.

9:18 a.m.

ME: I'm heading over from the overflow parking. I'll try to catch you coming across the finish.

9:34 a.m.

RENN: Well at least I didn't come in last. Just under 28 minutes. What can I say...I'm not a runner.

9:35 a.m.

RENN: I'll have you know that I'm an excellent multi-tasker and I can text you and tell people where the water table is at the same time

9:37 a.m.

ME: Glad you didn't totally embarrass yourself. I tried to pick you out from where I was standing but there were a shocking number of men with longish brown hair and tattoos. So I couldn't find yours among the stork legs. Sorry.

9:40 a.m.

> **ME:** I picked up my bib and am waiting near the start line. I know you're busy so I won't try to find you, but I'm here if you want to say hello.

Based on the enthusiasm with which Renn had been messaging me all morning, I half expected him to materialize as soon as I sent the text. But he didn't. I looked around at the rest of the runners in my category. Most of the women wore expensive designer gear. While I didn't aspire to owning overpriced yoga pants, I still felt somewhat out of place, so I focused on my pre-running routine. I set my Garmin to help pace me and began warming up, bending over for a hamstring stretch when I felt a tap on my shoulder.

I turned around, happy to see Renn, but ended up giving my bright smile to Pete.

"Sadie, I thought that was you."

I hadn't seen him since the day at Starbucks, and only twice in total, but the content of our interactions made him feel like more than a passing acquaintance.

"Oh, hey, Pete."

"You were expecting someone else?" He smiled knowingly.

"Yeah. Renn asked me to come, and he's been texting all morning. I didn't realize you'd be here."

His smile fell. "You do know Robbie is my nephew, right?"

I startled at his dickish tone.

"Damn...Sorry, Sadie. I didn't mean to sound like an ass." He rubbed his eyes and ran both hands through his hair, shuffling his weight from one foot to the other before releasing a long breath. "I've just been trying to make more of an effort with the boys lately and not always succeeding."

Since I'd overheard Renn talking to Archie, I had more insight into what Pete was admitting than he realized. "All good. Apology accepted."

"Thanks." He was quiet for a moment, then sounded proud when he asked, "Did you know Renn organized this entire thing?"

"Uh-huh. He told me when he invited me."

Pete glanced around at the proceedings—banners hung everywhere, t-shirt and registration tables, screens and loudspeakers announcing results, volunteers coming and going with water, Band-Aids, and whatever else might be needed. He shook his head before stating, "It's impressive. Renn's so good at everything he does…He's just like his dad in that way." Pete's features softened, bemusement showing he'd lost himself in a memory.

I supported Renn's right to avoid discussing his dad, but his uncle's desire to remember Thomas seemed reasonable as well. And since I was one of the few people who understood this push-and-pull between them, Pete must have felt emboldened, because he kept on light-heartedly. "Thomas also excelled at anything he tried, but you couldn't even be annoyed because he was such a great guy."

I huffed playfully. "Well, then you're wrong about him being exactly like his dad because there are definitely times I'm annoyed by how perfect Renn is." I moved into a squat, checking for soreness in my left ankle. I'd bruised it the day before in a kick fight with my longstanding nemesis, the icemaker at Hal's.

Pete grinned. "Totally relate." Stuffing his hands in his pockets, he looked down before speaking again. "So…uh…you and Renn?"

I blanched, breaking the stretch I'd just begun. "What do you mean…*me and Renn*?"

"You know, you're a thing, or whatever. I thought maybe after how he acted at Starbucks, but he hasn't said anything definitive. But, since you're here and all, I figure…"

My mood sobered in an instant. "Look, Pete, don't make assumptions. My relationship with Renn—however *we* define it—is not your business."

He held up his hands. "Of course. Sorry…just…like I said at the fundraiser, he's different since he met you. It's good, I guess."

I laughed bitingly before starting on some reverse lunges. "Gee, thanks for that ringing endorsement. But the key point remains..." I made a quick circular motion with my wrist to prompt him.

He smirked. "That this is none of my business?"

"Bingo." My tone was light, but my message was clear.

"Okay, I get it. You want me to stay out of your...whatever it is with Renn. Shouldn't be hard. It's not like he tells me anything, anyway." Pete didn't sound bitter, just sad. What I'd overheard Archie say to Renn had been accurate. There was something in the way of the uncle-nephew dynamic.

What had brought them to this point where they seemingly loved each other but still circled like wary cats? Renn had given me the basic rundown of their situation at our last appointment, but no details on how or why they'd arrived there. I knew Renn had primary custody of Robbie and Gage, that he'd moved back into their Pasadena home after Thomas and Mary had died, trying to provide some sense of continuity and normalcy for the boys. Pete had a room at the house, but still spent most of his time at the downtown apartment he shared with a roommate. It seemed strange that the boys' nineteen-year-old brother had taken on that burden when they'd had an uncle in his mid-thirties. Why had Pete insisted on keeping his distance back then? How had Renn ended up in the master bedroom with Pete part-time down the hall?

It was almost time for my race to start. I was about to say good-bye to Pete when we both spotted Robbie across the field, carrying a large jug to the water table. Pete called out and raised his hand in a wave. Robbie looked over and scowled at his uncle before going back to his task.

"He hates me." Pete frowned.

I laughed. "He doesn't hate you. And even if he did, he's twelve, it's his job to hate everything."

"Sure."

"Hey, at least he didn't flip you off."

"No, but he probably wanted to," Pete said. "And, honestly, he'd be justified. Like I mentioned, I've been attempting to do more for the boys, but I'm not sure they know what to make of me yet."

"I'm sure if you keep trying, Robbie will come around. And Gage?"

"That little dude. He's always cool. Easy."

"Well, that's a start."

Pete sighed. "I guess."

"Look, whatever your reasons were for staying away from your nephews before, you're trying now, and that has to count for something."

"I hope you're right." He nodded and straightened up before switching gears. "Thanks for listening. I'm glad you and Renn are doing...whatever you're doing. It's good to see him smile."

I let out a wary groan and my tone held a warning, "Pete."

"Got it. I won't bring it up again." Pete mimed zipping his lips and throwing the key over his shoulder.

Static came through the loudspeakers, followed by an announcement that my race was about to begin. Pete gave me a wave and jogged away. For all their sakes, I hoped he could figure things out with his nephews. Based on personal experience, I believed people could change. Pete wouldn't be the first person to do things the wrong way before eventually getting it right.

20:53. It wasn't the fastest 5K time I'd ever gotten, but it was better than the races I'd run in Boston. I could remember coming across those finish lines, Henri looking bored on the sidelines. He had a regular gym routine that included the treadmill but wasn't one for working out in the fresh air. *I like the atmosphere in the gym, darling. If you're just running outside, it's too easy to let yourself*

be lazy. It seemed insane looking back—he'd made me question if I was running enough when I was averaging three to four miles per day. Fucking gaslighter.

But when I crossed the finish line at Robbie's school fundraiser, I still reflexively looked for Henri. I grimaced, disgusted with myself at the instinct. *Dammit. Are you ever going to stop waiting for Henri to clap for you, Sadie?*

The results went up on the screen a few minutes later. I was swigging from a water bottle when I looked up and confirmed I'd placed third. Not too shabby.

I was half-expecting some sort of congratulatory message or appearance from Renn, but none came. Between the conversation with Pete making me wonder if we were being too obvious, along with instinctively seeking my ex's face at the finish, my insecurities were threatening to get the better of me. I spiraled further as I worried Renn's lack of communication meant he didn't *actually* want me there. I wondered if I should just leave.

But a sticky hand tugging my wrist took the decision away from me. I looked down to see Gage at my side. Renn's youngest brother gave me a gap-toothed grin, and I smiled back, spiral averted in the face of this adorableness. His longish hair grazed the top of the overlarge event t-shirt he wore.

"I remember you. You're Renn's friend. I remember your flower." Gage pointed a stubby finger at my thigh.

"Hi, Gage." I squatted down so I could speak to him eye-to-eye. "Yes, I'm Renn's friend, Sadie. I came here today to support Robbie's school."

"Did you run?"

"I did. My race just finished." I pointed at the screen nearby. "See that name by the number three? That's me."

"The one that's S-A-D-I-E?"

"Yep. Now, can I ask you something?"

"Yep." He popped the P and grinned up at me.

"Does someone know where you are? Are you supposed to be with your brothers? Or your Uncle Pete?"

Gage's smile grew wider and his voice lisped a little. "Archie said I was big enough now that I could walk around as long as I stayed on the inside of the track." Hmm. Apparently, the other tattoo artist was somewhere around the event, too.

"Ah, so you're good if you stay on the football field. Got it. Hey, it looks like you've lost a tooth, Gage. One of the important ones right up front."

"Uh-huh. Two days ago. The tooth fairy left me five dollars. When I lost one of the side ones, it was only one dollar. Renn said she left more this time because it was a big one."

"Renn is right. Front teeth should definitely be worth more."

"You want to know something, though?" Gage whispered conspiratorially.

"Of course."

He bent in close to my face and spoke in a hushed voice. "Robbie said that Renn was...it was a bad word." He tilted back to look at me, and I could only hope I was making the right decision when I nodded at him encouragingly to continue. "Robbie said...he said that Renn was full of shit...that the tooth fairy isn't real."

"He said that?"

"He likes to say bad words now. Since he started middle school. Renn took away his iPad for a week because he said the F-word three times when he was playing a video game."

"Well, I wouldn't worry too much about it. Middle school sometimes makes you want to try out using bad words. Sounds like Renn is handling Robbie."

"Yeah." He shuffled his feet.

"Hey, Gage, I'm really glad you came over to me, and that you like my tattoo flower, but I'd feel better if I brought you back to Archie, or someone in your family." I certainly wasn't looking for an excuse to walk around searching for Renn.

"Okay, come on then." Gage led me to the bleachers on one end of the football field. Underneath them, there was a table housing the AV equipment used for the projectors.

There were four women clustered around the table, looking down. I surmised they were PTSA members because they had that look of wealthy LA moms—enough money to stay plumped, waxed, threaded, tanned, toned, and clothed in the latest—moving into their late thirties and early forties with axe-sharpening precision. One woman glanced up at me and smiled while the others kept gawking at something under the table.

"Do you need help?" The smiling woman asked me at the same moment she noticed my companion. "Gage?" I could tell she was trying to puzzle out who I was, since she clearly knew the little boy beside me, but her gaze was merely curious and not unkind.

"Hi, Lydia. This is Sadie. She's someone Renn did a tattoo on." Gage turned to me. "Lydia is Ryder and Benji's mom. They're our friends."

"Sadie!"

I startled as the coven of moms parted from what they'd been staring at—Renn working underneath the table, evidently making some kind of repair. He'd been laying on his back and popped up, tugging down his event t-shirt over a pair of running shorts. Holding a screwdriver in one hand and a ring of duct tape in the other, he swiped an arm over his brow to wipe off the sheen of sweat. This motion emphasized the tight fit of the shirt across his chest and brought it up enough to reveal the low rise of his shorts, which hung loose and emphasized his perfect, round backside—admired not only by myself but also the other women.

Renn spoke quickly. "I'm so sorry I didn't see you before your race or after. It's just been one thing after another. During the men's thirty-to-thirty-four-year-old slot, there was a problem with the timekeeping device. Right after we solved that, the whole AV system could have collapsed because some genius—and by genius, I mean me—put all the heavy equipment on this one stupid folding table, so one leg started to buckle, and all the stuff almost came crashing down, and no one could find the janitor to let us into the storage closet to get another table, so I have been struggling to hold the fool thing up and fix it for fifteen minutes, seeing if I could get it to balance, until Lydia remembered we had duct tape at the registration desk, and I was just now able to repair it, to at least get it through the event, but anyway...I'm sorry I missed your race."

He was breathless from his frantic recitation, chest rising and falling.

"It's fine, Renn. That sounds like...a lot." Lydia and the other women started to crowd around us. "Well, I just wanted to bring Gage back, and my race is over, so I guess I can get out of your hair—"

"No—wait!" Renn reached out and grabbed my wrist. He slid his hand down to squeeze my fingertips before putting his arm at his side. One of the women, who had a confident "don't fuck with me" posture to go with her shiny dark hair, noticed the intimacy of this gesture and squinted her eyes at us.

"How'd you do?" Renn asked me, uncaring of our onlookers.

"Oh. I came in third, so pretty good. 20:53."

"You beat my time by almost eight minutes." Renn laughed, and I was hyperaware of the women's eyes on us. "I'm sorry I wasn't there to cheer your epic finish."

"No worries. I was only alone a few minutes until this one found me." I gestured back to Gage. "We had an excellent discussion about tooth fairy economics."

At that, Renn smiled, and the ladies were done being spectators.

"Great job with the table, Renn," Lydia said. "I'm sure it will hold." She placed her palm on the edge and pushed down a bit, proving its integrity. "And I wouldn't worry about the other stuff. There's always nonsense that happens during these events. I remember chairing the school auction during Ryder and Robbie's kindergarten year. What a nightmare. The auctioneer arrived an hour late, drunk off his ass. One of the dads had to fill in for him. Actually, I think it was Robbie's—" Lydia put her hand to her mouth, looking stricken as she realized too late where her memory was taking her. "Shit, Renn, I'm sorry. I know you don't like to talk about him."

One of the other three women looked puzzled. The cool brunette leaned over to whisper in the confused woman's ear, causing her to push her cat-eyed sunglasses against her nose and nod discreetly in understanding.

Renn squeezed his eyes shut, and his body froze. After a few beats, he rolled his neck and turned to me, reaching out to grasp my hand. "It's alright, Lydia," he ground out, blinking rapidly and swallowing hard, clearly fighting off *bigger* emotions.

I hoped Renn could recover quicker than he had at the fundraiser when he'd walked away from Pete mentioning Thomas. Gripping my fingers, he didn't appear to be contemplating an escape route, but he didn't seem in full control yet either. It was wild how just the mention of his dad could cause this reaction. One of the women tentatively put her hand on his shoulder as the silence grew sharp.

Something poked my hip and I looked down to see Gage making his eyeballs big, willing me to help ease the tension.

I stuttered a moment before coming up with, "Uh...hey...Lydia, did you want to see the piece Renn is working on for me?" The last thing I wanted to do was display myself for these women, but I needed to draw their attention away so Renn could gather himself without their eyes on him.

Lydia shot me a look of gratitude as I pulled my hand out of Renn's grip and twisted my leg so they could view the tattoo. Gage looked at me and smiled, tilting his head like a puppy.

One woman—not Lydia, not Icy Brunette, not Designer Sunglasses, but the one with her hand grazing Renn's shoulder—leaned down and squinted at my thigh. Her exquisite size two physique was encased in expensive all-black apparel, complemented by a perfect high blonde ponytail.

"It's cute," she said, straightening up. She ran her long French manicured fingernails up and down Renn's arm. "I always forget that this one has such an interesting day job. He does so much volunteer work at the school. I think of him as just one of the parents."

"Oh." I had no response to that. It seemed unimaginable that Renn could ever blend into this crowd. Besides being covered in ink, he was much younger than the dozen or so other guys wearing PTSA VOLUNTEER badges. Not that the men walking around were schlubs or anything. They were as ego-driven as their wives, and most fell firmly into the DILF category. Even so, they weren't Renn.

"Well, we appreciate you coming and supporting the cause. I'm Hannah." PTSA Athletic Apparel Barbie extended the hand that wasn't currently occupied grazing Renn's bicep, and I shook it. "What a great idea for Renn to invite his clients."

Given the minute to compose himself, Renn's breathing and demeanor had mostly returned to normal. He tactfully moved himself away from Hannah's touch. "I didn't invite all my clients. I only invited Sadie because she and I are...friends."

He said that last word with just enough inflection that all four women took notice. And their slight notice turned to outright gawking when Renn joined our hands again and laced his fingers through mine.

High ponytail Hannah cast a glare at them before scrutinizing me from head to sneakers and asking cattily, "What category did you run in Sadie?"

"Uh...thirty to thirty-four." Did she think Renn didn't know how old I was? Sadie from a year ago might have withered under her rude stare, but Sadie right-now would not allow this woman to age-shame her. "I just got it in under the wire, too, because my thirty-fifth is next month."

Renn's response to this was a squeeze of our joined hands. He turned to the women. "I'm gonna take a break since I held that table a while. I want to walk Sadie to her car." Lydia grinned, giving me a wink. Hannah looked taken aback, and the other two appeared bored as Renn and I stepped away.

As we headed toward my car, still hand-in-hand, Renn told Gage to find Archie and tell him they didn't need another table anymore. Appreciative of being given such an important task, Gage took off like a bolt.

"WHAT WAS THAT back there?" I smiled at Renn as soon as we were past the crowd.

"What was what?"

"With those ladies, your PTSA brethren. You basically implied we're more than friends."

"We *are* more than friends." He ran his thumb along mine. "I wasn't playing around when I said I wanted to know you better. But for now, I'm just glad you came."

Today had provided a solid taste of what our relationship could be like outside the bubble of Studio Obscurum. I didn't fit in with the PTSA moms, but then again, neither did Renn. And if Hannah wanted to imply I was too old for Renn—let her. I had way fewer fucks to give lately about those eleven years and what the world thought of them. It was progress that I'd felt the other woman's judgement and it hadn't caused me to roll up in a ball.

But thinking of my healing journey brought someone else's to mind.

"Hey, Renn, about earlier..." I hesitated to spoil the moment, but it seemed wrong to pretend he hadn't almost completely shut down before.

"Earlier?"

"Yeah...um...when Lydia mentioned...you know. You seemed pretty upset. I hope you're okay."

His jaw tightened and he stumbled. Taking a few moments to gather his thoughts, he was gentle when he eventually replied, "I'm so grateful you listened to me talk about my dad and Mary at the shop... You know it's tough for me." He gripped my hand tighter, nodding his head for emphasis as his pace slowed. "And I can imagine how it looked back there. But I'm not, like, depressed, or wallowing in sadness or anything. It is harder when my dad gets mentioned out of the blue, like at the AV table. And the fundraiser. But I promise you, those moments are rare and not a big factor in my life at all. It's just a fluke that you've seen it twice."

"Lucky me." I wondered if he realized those times were probably infrequent because his friends and family intentionally avoided them.

He huffed. "Hopefully, it hasn't given you a distorted picture. Sadie, I'm fine. The grief is there, in the background where it belongs, but you've been around me enough to see I'm a fully functional person, and generally a happy guy." He gave me a maniacal grin for emphasis.

I pushed on his cheek. "Stop smiling at me like a demented Pennywise."

"I was going for *Donnie Darko* vibes, but okay."

I thought about what I'd seen, first at the House Party of Hope and just now, in front of those women. "Renn, joking aside, I'd be doing you a disservice if I didn't at least mention how much therapy has helped me since Boston."

He stopped mid-stride and dropped my hand, turning to face me directly. "Sadie, Archie and Pete have suggested it too, but it's just not for me, okay? I don't think it would help to spill my guts to a stranger. I promise I'm fine." He crossed his pointer finger over his heart.

He'd made a valid argument. Or at least, an argument. Maybe he was fine. People had terrible moments. And while his grief was tangible, it hadn't exactly inhibited his life. On the contrary, he displayed a shocking degree of having-his-shit-togetherness.

"Alright, Renn. I just wanted you to know I'm here for you."

We started walking again as the murky sky darkened, threatening rain and giving the sidewalk a bluish pallor. The cool air on my heated skin was welcome. Our silence companionable, Renn reached for my hand again.

I understood where he was coming from, at least a little. I knew what it was like when those feelings, the ones you had to work to hold back, came at you unexpectedly. Like an assault.

"Can I tell you something that happened to me today?" I asked.

"Of course."

I felt the familiar knot of shame wash over me as I thought about earlier. "At the finish line of my race, I looked around for Henri." Contemplating my ex's hold on me always made me a little sick. "I hate that it happened, but for a moment, my brain reflexively thought he might be there. Because there's a part of me, a part I wish didn't exist, that still seeks Henri's approval."

"Henri, that's the guy you left in Boston?"

"Yes." Had I really never said his name to Renn?

"Damn, that sucks. I'm sorry you still feel like that sometimes."

"Yeah, well, making me work extra hard for his love and affection was kind of his MO. It's a tough habit to break." I stopped us again so I could look Renn in the eye. "The reason I'm telling you is that it's something that still affects me, even if I don't like to talk about it."

Renn connected the dots. "Like me with my dad?"

I nodded. "I understand not wanting to speak about things you'd rather leave in the past."

He reached out to grab a tendril of hair that had escaped my ponytail, worrying it between his fingers before wrapping it around the rubber band. "I'm glad you get it."

"Renn, I think part of the reason our connection is so strong is because we both have these things underneath the surface other people can't see. My grandma always used to say, 'like recognizes like.'"

We reached my sedan, and I dug in my zipper pocket to retrieve my keys. Renn stood a foot away at first, before slowly inching closer. I leaned back against the door as he brought his arms up on either side of my head to rest along the roof of the car, effectively penning me in.

He felt unbearably close, even though no part of us was touching. He leaned toward my neck as he spoke, hot breath making me shiver. "Thank you for telling me about Henri. But for the record, I don't believe our connection is forged by some hidden-beneath-the-surface pain. It exists because standing right in front of me, very much above-the-surface, is one of the most amazing women I've ever met." His lips skirted my jawline and the rough traces of his stubble grazed my skin as his deep voice whispered in my ear. "I don't have to look too hard to find reasons to want to be with you. And I know we're taking our time, and I'm not trying to push you...but you should know that much, at least."

I'd grown comfortable in situations with Renn where we spoke and acted more like friends, but whenever things took this turn, I still got all tied up inside.

His gaze was so intense I had to turn my head away. He held himself in place, maybe hoping I'd respond with words, perhaps just enjoying our closeness. Finally, he brushed his lips in the hint of a kiss on my shoulder before leaning back, running one hand along my side, ending the caress by tugging the keys from my hand. He unlocked the door and opened it for me. I fell into the seat like a lifeline, still avoiding his eyes.

"Thanks. See you at my next appointment," I said breathlessly as I clicked my seatbelt in place. I reversed out of the spot, waving as I drove off.

Renn was all in on exploring a relationship, but what I'd said to Pete an hour ago was still true. Nothing was definitive. There was so much about me Renn didn't know. *How could he be so sure?* Boston had left me with too many scars to share his unfailing optimism.

I gripped the steering wheel. I almost wished Renn hadn't expressed his feelings so freely. They scared me. His willingness to put himself out there scared me. His blind faith that we'd find a way to make things work scared me.

The fact that I hadn't mentioned Henri's name to him before today scared me.

CHAPTER

Ten

I ARRIVED TWENTY MINUTES before my scheduled appointment at Studio Obscurum. It was a Friday and my paycheck had deposited into my account that morning. I'd been stoked when I saw my bank balance—large enough that I could register for some online courses. My biology degree only came with so many basic education credits, and I had some work to do to get another bachelor's in a field I was legitimately excited about.

When I'd initially entered college at nineteen, I'd had no idea what I wanted to do as a career. My primary objective had been escaping my grandma's house, so a full-time job had been a necessity to afford both school and dorm life. Biology had been the major of both my parents. I'd been told they'd met while doing their undergraduate study at UCSF and that they'd gone on to earn master's degrees, which led to their humanitarian work setting up sanitation projects abroad. I'd picked biology in an impulse of wanting to feel like my parents were somehow part of my college experience, but toward the beginning of my senior year, I'd admitted to myself I had no actual interest. However, without an alternative I was passionate about, I completed the degree rather than stick around for an extra year or two racking up more loans.

But now I knew. The events of the past few months had revealed my calling, and I couldn't wait to get started. Come spring quarter, I'd be an undergrad again. After registering, I'd ordered books, gone for a run, and cleaned the apartment. *Fuck you, Henri, I was back.*

My restless energy was what had brought me early to the shop. Renn had told me he'd finish most of the work during this session. The final one in a few weeks would just be to confirm it had healed properly, ensure no touch-ups were needed, and take final pictures.

When I arrived, Renn wasn't there yet, but since it was two p.m. on a Friday, there were two other artists working, including Archie. He gave me a tentative smile and a wave, saying I could wait in the chair by Renn's station. I had been sitting there ten minutes when Pete walked in from the back. Even though I'd known he co-owned the business, it was the first time I'd seen him there.

"Hey, Pete."

"Sadie. I didn't realize you were coming today. It's great to see you." Pete sat down next to me, waving goodbye to the artist whose name I didn't know as she left the building. "How did you end up doing Saturday?"

"Good. I came in third in my division."

Archie interjected from across the room. "I'm just glad you made it. Renn was stressing out a bit in the early part, wondering why you weren't responding to his messages. Hope everything was okay?"

I recalled the flurry of texts that had come through once I'd turned my phone on. "Oh...yeah. My cell was dead when I got up that morning. I did text him as soon as I could, and I caught up with him after my race."

"Stop busting her chops, Archie." Pete frowned at him. "Renn's a big boy and he can deal with waiting for his texts."

Archie glared back. "I wasn't busting her chops. I'm just saying Renn was happy to see her." He motioned to me. "Little dude Gage was excited too. Something about the tooth fairy."

"Yeah. He's a cool kid." This was a point we could all agree on. "And I was glad I made it. It's been great getting more into running since I've been back in Los Angeles."

Pete looked like he was about to ask me to elaborate, but we were saved from making more small talk by the groan of the door as Renn walked in.

"Sadie—hey! You're early." He came over and leaned down, giving me an eager hug, and I smiled with the realization that I welcomed it. But from Pete and Archie's faces, I deduced he did not greet most clients with an embrace.

Renn pulled back and his adoring look melted me, despite the expressions of the other men. Any lingering unease I'd had about not responding more fully to his assertion of my above-the-surface appeal after the 5K evaporated. I should have known everything was okay since he'd been sending me sometimes-banal-sometimes-hilarious-sometimes-both texts and memes most days since then.

He looked down. "Is that a concert t-shirt for The Doors? 1970?"

"Oh, yeah. This one my grandma could tell me about. My parents went to their concert in San Diego, just before Christmas that year."

"Wow. That's cool." He reached out to finger the thin tan material. "I feel like you should have all these shirts framed."

"Nah. They sat in a box the whole time I was in Boston. They deserve to be seen, right? Besides, they complement my new kick-ass tattoo."

Renn grinned at me but then noticed Pete. He looked annoyed as he spoke to his uncle.

"I thought you were picking the boys up after school." He stuffed his thumbs in his pockets. "Weren't you going to take them bowling?"

"Sorry. I got caught up with some things. Lydia asked if Robbie could come stay at their house tonight to keep Ryder from climbing the walls, and she volunteered to pick up Gage too, since he sometimes hangs with Ryder's younger brother."

I remembered Lydia had been the friendly one of the PTSA gaggle at the 5K. But Renn did not seem pleased.

"Wait...you told Lydia the boys could stay overnight?"

"Yeah. Why wouldn't I? I'm sure Robbie will be thrilled. They can stay up and play *Super Smash Bros.* until their eyes bleed." Pete seemed perplexed by Renn's reaction.

"You could have said no, Pete. Gage has swimming super early in the morning, and I need to be at the shop. The reason I agreed you could pick them up in the first place was because I figured you wanted to spend time with your nephews. You can't just make plans like that and not run it by me."

"Jesus, kid. I'm sorry, but you can't have it both ways. You can't get mad at me for not being around more in one breath and then remind me you're the boss in another. I get it—I'm just a visitor in my nephews' lives. Message received." I rolled my eyes when Pete said this as I recalled our conversation at the race. Did he think this counted as making an effort?

Renn's body stiffened and he breathed through his nose like a bull. I watched his face go red as he pressed his fingers against his forehead before gritting out to Pete, "That's not fair, and you know it—" He stopped and exhaled loudly, looking from me to Archie before turning back to his uncle. "I'd rather not fight with you. But you just can't make decisions that affect our family schedule without asking me. Being a visitor in their lives—that wasn't something I asked you to do. That was a choice you made."

I couldn't help but think about how few twenty-three-year-olds had to worry about swim lessons and sleepovers. It was like Renn had gone to bed one day and woken up a middle-aged soccer mom.

The morning that Renn had been late to our appointment, it was because of confusion picking up the boys. Before meeting Renn, I'd not known how much parenthood was just making sure your kids were in whatever place they needed to be in and supervised at least well enough to prevent most fires, injuries, and other disasters. Renn was not only a good parent—he was a good *single* parent. At twenty-three. Jesus.

My grandma had been fine letting reruns of *Good Times* be my babysitter. We'd had fast food for dinner two or three times per week. The idea that she would have planned an event for the PTSA or signed me up for sports lessons was laughable. Come to think of it, Grandma and Pete would have gotten along, laden as they both were with good intentions. The difference was that my grandma's deficiency lay in believing doing the bare minimum was enough. His was in not knowing what to do at all.

Pete looked like he wanted to protest his nephew's summation at first, but then he dropped his chin.

"Sorry, Renn," he said sincerely. "I should have asked you. I honestly didn't think it was a big deal. You know how much I appreciate...everything you do. I really have been trying...I wish... fuck...I wish I could do better. Do more."

"Well, maybe someday you'll explain it to me why you can't." Renn sounded resigned, as though this was a discussion they'd had before. Pete being unable or unwilling to be a parental figure to the boys was something everyone had long since accepted. Even Archie seemed unsurprised by this turn of the conversation. Renn looked at Pete as though his uncle was going to give him an answer, but the man remained stubbornly silent.

Renn sighed. "You know what, Pete, don't even worry about it. Being with the boys—I wouldn't have it any other way. Whatever your fucked up reasons are for sticking with the fun uncle routine."

"I'm your uncle too, Renn, and I love you."

Archie gave Pete a death glare. Renn just shook his head. "It's cool, Pete. I'll call Lydia and make sure the boys are good for the night. Thanks."

"Sure. And, um, maybe next week I'll take them bowling?" Pete headed toward the exit.

"Yeah. Maybe next week."

Pete stumbled out the studio door and the ensuing silence was choking. Renn was a few feet away, back to me, but when he spoke, I heard him. "I'm sorry you had to see that, Sadie. You've caught me and him in a few difficult moments."

I stood up and went to him, waffling my arm awkwardly for a few seconds before putting a hand on his back. Renn leaned into my touch as I reassured him. "Don't worry about it. If Pete isn't embarrassed to air things out in front of me, I don't see why you should be." I squeezed his upper arm. "If you don't mind me asking...what's the deal with you guys, anyway?

"Honestly, I can't say. He's just sort of always been this way. After my dad's accident, it was obvious Mary was drowning trying to grieve and take care of the boys. I already told you I acted a little crazy then. I remember Pete tried to help at first, but after Mary died, he just stayed away. It's like, he's been around, but never really *here*, if you know what I mean."

Did I know what he meant by someone being a ghost in their own family? Did I understand how a person could fade into the background? Renn didn't realize how loaded that question was. The treatment I'd received during my childhood and later from Henri had allowed me to perfect my technique of being *there but not there*. I wondered what had triggered it for Pete. He clearly loved his nephews, enough to keep clumsily dipping a toe in, but something kept him away.

Archie had a more succinct way of putting it.

"What do you mean you don't know, Renn? Bottom line is, your uncle is a massive prick, and that's the end. Your dad was a saint, bringing Pete into the business and looking out for him. Thomas always made excuses for him the same way you do now. But there's no good reason Pete never stepped up for Robbie and Gage. He's a selfish bastard, plain and simple. Not much more to it than that."

I was stunned by Archie's sudden vehemence. Renn was not. "Don't be so hard on him, Arch. He can be unreliable, sure, but there are moments when he's okay. He *has* been making more of an effort lately. Besides, Dad loved him."

Renn leaned heavier into my side, seeking support since Archie had brought Thomas into the discussion.

"Your dad was a great man, and he loved his brother way more than Pete deserved," Archie said this with such fierce finality that Renn and I were both taken aback.

I looked at Archie—his arms crossed, eyes and countenance blazing with sympathy and indignation on Renn's behalf. And in that moment, I would have bet a month's worth of tips at Hal's that the mysterious *something* that had kept Pete away from his nephews was not a mystery to Archie.

A FEW HOURS later, the tension preceding Pete's exit was swallowed by the elation I felt at seeing my almost finished tattoo. In the final panel, the vibrant lotus appeared as though it had a hundred degrees of blue in it, all bursting off my skin. The ouroboros looked powerful as well, intertwined with the flower and announcing itself triumphantly. Most of the ouroboroses—ourobori?—I'd seen online were black and gray, but mine was a riot of greens, browns, and oranges. That description sounded horrible when I said it in my head, like some awful 1970s rec room, but what was tacky coloring for shag carpeting and artificial wood panels made for beautiful ink on my thigh.

"Man, I am proud of this one." Renn was examining my leg, checking for any imperfections. "You'll need to come back in a few weeks for one last check, and I'd like to take pictures for my portfolio, but I can't see any immediate need for touch-ups."

I was still laying stomach down on the table but doing my best to admire the tattoo over my shoulder. I couldn't believe we were almost at the end of this journey. Throughout my early twenties, I'd secretly wanted a tattoo but had hesitated because it was just so damn permanent. After a childhood spent not calling attention to myself, risk-taking was not in my repertoire of common behaviors. When other girls in college had been getting cute little butterflies on their bellies and inspirational words on their wrists, the most I'd ever ventured was henna that lasted two weeks. In Boston, I'd brought up the topic with Henri once, early in our relationship while I'd still been dictating most of my appearance, floating the idea of getting a small piece on my ankle. He'd looked at me with such disgust I'd felt ridiculous for even asking. *Seriously, Sadie, do I look like a man who dates a woman with tattoos? Can you imagine if I brought a tattoo girl home to my parents?* The irony, of course, was that Henri himself had his phoenix tattoo, but he'd explained to me he'd done it in a fit of rebellion at eighteen and regretted it.

But now I realized I'd had it all backward. Immovable though it may be, my tattoo was a constant reminder I could grow in my life, and it symbolized the strength I wanted to project. Keeping my rosy-hued skin untouched would have been more permanent, my unadorned thigh a lifetime nod to my inability to take risks or change. Renn's masterpiece wasn't the blemish snobs like Henri thought it was. It was a monument to my ability to shift, to heal.

Archie inspected my tattoo. He'd said goodbye to his client an hour ago and had been lingering around cleaning up his station, staying to support Renn to this finish line. Like Pete, Archie had made several comments about how enthusiastic Renn seemed about my project. I knew he had reservations about how close I was to his friend, but I also knew it pleased him to see Renn so lively, and that his concern stemmed from love.

"That looks wicked." Archie leaned over me and lifted a small magnifying glass. "I like what you did with the navy color on the leaves. Must have been a bitch to get that detail in."

"Thanks, Arch. Leave it to you to pick out the hardest shit right off the bat. I totally thought those chains would get me, but you're right, it was the navy tips on that lotus."

Archie hummed in reply and moved back toward his station as Renn put the protective plastic on my thigh. I was not looking forward to a few days from now, when my leg would be itching so badly I'd want to claw my skin off, but for now, feeling the way I did and seeing the pride in Renn's face—it was all worth it.

Renn helped me to my feet. And as he stood smiling at me, both of us radiating satisfaction from our joint venture, it seemed the most natural thing in the world for him to pull me into his arms, rocking us back and forth. As I rested my cheek on his shoulder, it wasn't passion that had my blood pumping faster in my veins. It was confidence.

My car had been making some strange noises earlier that day, so I'd played it safe and taken an Uber to my appointment. I was about to request my ride home when Pete came back to the shop. He looked sheepish, holding a brown carrier tray of Starbucks cups as he set a grande black coffee in front of Renn. A peace offering. He shuffled over to Archie and handed him a Venti cold cup that looked like something a teenager would order. I wasn't sure what it was, but there were chocolate swirls visible along the sides and whipped cream spilling from the domed lid. Archie seemed like he still wanted to give Pete the finger, but the sugar must have been too enticing because he settled for an acknowledging grunt.

Pete came my way next. "Sadie, I didn't know what you like, so I got an iced soy latte and a hot mocha. Hopefully, one of them works."

I wasn't in the mood for either, but didn't want to detract from Pete's overture. I grabbed the latte with a thanks. Pete stepped back to admire my tattoo. He wasn't an artist, but he knew enough to comment on the intricacy of the lotus's shading.

Our peaceful interlude was interrupted when the entrance to Studio Obscurum crashed open a minute later, followed by a furious Robbie. He slammed the door shut so hard it rattled the little statue of a skeleton holding a black rose on the nearest shelf.

"Robbie! What the hell?" Renn took a moment to process his brother's presence in the space. "I thought you were supposed to be at Ryder's."

"We were going there." The twelve-year-old practically spat. "But Lydia said we could stop by the house to grab my bathing suit."

"Okay...and?"

"And that little asshole got into my shit again!" Robbie's chest heaved and he looked glassy-eyed. I remembered how big everything seemed at his age. But if I would have talked to my grandma the way Robbie just spoke to Renn, she would have...actually, I had no idea what she would have done because there is no way in hell I would have ever talked to her like that. Robbie held no deep-seated fear that acting like a belligerent pain in the butt would make Renn stop loving him.

Renn took a deep breath and crossed his arms. "First, you need to calm down and check your language. I can tell you're upset, so I'll let what you've said pass, but the next curse word puts you on restriction for a week." Robbie grumbled but didn't say more, so Renn continued. "I'm assuming you're talking about Gage?"

"Of course I'm talking about Gage!" Robbie wailed, waving his arms in frustration. "It was so obvious when I opened the drawer with the bathing suits he'd been in my room."

"Are you sure? Is it possible you just forgot the last time you moved things?"

"No." Robbie's face turned red. "I have a...um...picture...in that drawer. I know I put it under my swim stuff, and it was definitely on the wrong side."

"What kind of picture, Robbie?" Renn questioned gently.

"Just...a picture. It's not bad or anything. It's a comic, but there's... uh...it's some women and they're drawn with...um...you know."

I appreciated the unwanted latte keeping my hands and mouth busy. As I put the green straw to my lips, I tried not to smile. I'd never been part of a *loving* family, and watching Renn deal with Robbie's struggle to hide pornographic anime in his room provided the chance to experience one from the periphery.

Renn put his hand on Robbie's shoulder. "There is so much for us to talk about here, and I want to have a longer discussion about you looking at pictures like that. It's natural to be curious, but I think we should have a conversation." Robbie glanced up at the fans forever circling on the ceiling, looking like he wanted the earth to swallow him whole. "Later," Renn clarified. "But soon. A question for right now is how you got here."

"Oh...um...Lydia dropped me off. She knew something was wrong because I kinda socked Gage in the car, but I wouldn't tell her why. I told her I needed to talk to you, so she said you could drop me off at her house later, but she still has Gage. She texted you."

Renn reached for his phone, scrolling quickly through his messages before turning back to Robbie. "Okay. I get you're mad. And I'll help you have a conversation with Gage about respecting your privacy. But you also just admitted that you hit your brother. That's not the way to handle things."

"It wasn't hard," Robbie protested. "You've gotta tell Gage he needs to stay out of my room."

"You didn't ask him about seeing the picture?"

"No. I didn't want to say anything in front of Lydia or Ryder, but he knew why I was mad. He was acting weird when I asked to stop off for the suits, like he knew I'd notice. Little shit."

"That's a week, Robbie."

Robbie groaned and hurled himself into a chair. Archie went over and sat next to him, speaking softly so no one else could hear, but whatever he was saying seemed to calm the boy down. Pete stood off to the side, surveying the scene in contemplation. When Robbie finally noticed me, he offered a questioning glance but wasn't openly hostile.

Renn chuffed as he came my way. "At least we had five minutes to enjoy finishing up the major work on your tattoo before Hurricane Robbie came in."

"I'm also enjoying Pete's guilt coffee." I raised the straw to my lips again.

Renn laughed. "Never a dull moment around here."

He wasn't kidding. They were lucky Archie's customer had already left, because the scene with Robbie probably wasn't the kind of thing clients expected in a tattoo studio. Never mind wondering whether Renn had space for me in his life. I wasn't even sure he had space for me in this day.

Still, I wanted to offer comfort if I could. I motioned toward Robbie. "He'll come around. Don't worry. Everything's hard at his age." *Did that sound helpful? I knew nothing about parenting a teenager.*

Renn ran his hands through his hair and spoke quietly to me. "I keep reminding myself that none of this is easy for Robbie. I don't blame him, but God, he's tough to handle these days."

"Sorry. You're doing the best you can."

"It's so not fair to him, what happened to his parents. But I don't want to play that card, you know? I don't want to remind him how much more time I had with our dad than he did. Or make his whole life about that tragedy... Like, hey, Robbie, your grades suck. Our *dead father* would hate that. Robbie, you never do your chores. Our *dead father* would be so disappointed. Robbie, your language sucks and so do all your rude little friends. Our *dead father* would not approve. I don't want to say it, so I don't. But in this case, it is really, really true. Robbie being so at odds with Gage? Our dead father would absolutely hate that."

Renn gripped the back of a stool with the heavy effort of speaking about his dad for the second time that day, closing his eyelids forcefully before opening them again. Although what he'd explained after the 5K was true—he did seem to manage it a little easier when it was his choice, as opposed to when others brought up Thomas out of the blue.

"Maybe I can help," Pete interjected from where he'd been leaning against a table, a thoughtful look on his face. Archie grimaced and Renn eyed him with skepticism, but Pete pressed on. "You're right, Renn. Thomas was the world's greatest brother and he would hate that his boys weren't getting along. Not just Robbie and Gage, but you and Robbie, too."

"What are you thinking?" Renn asked grudgingly. I imagined he was at his breaking point to be considering anything Pete had to say.

"Hey, Rob?" Pete spoke to his younger nephew.

"Yeah?" Robbie's sullen expression remained.

"You know how to take the bus to my apartment, right?" Robbie nodded. "Well, how about I give you a key and then you can go there whenever you want? Just to chill. My roommate is almost always gone, or in his room playing video games with a headset on, so there's plenty of privacy if you need it."

Robbie still looked suspicious, but the worst of his surliness had abated. "Why?"

"So you can just get away for awhile. Have time to yourself. I think that's preferable to murdering Gage."

"For real? You'd let me just go there?"

"Renn has to agree. And you can't just show up whenever you want without letting us know. You need to text before you go, and it can't be after dark, so no one worries." Pete looked at Renn, who dipped his chin in agreement.

Robbie almost smiled. "What about Gage?"

"This would be just for you. I might offer when Gage is a teenager, but I don't think he's old enough to take the bus by himself right now. I mean, Gage will still come to my apartment if we're doing something together, but the key and the coming and going privilege will just be yours."

"It's okay, Renn, right?" Robbie asked hopefully.

"Yeah. I think it's a good idea."

Robbie lit up. He didn't even complain when Renn asked him to take out all the garbage cans in the studio in exchange for reducing his restriction to three days. Once the tween was out of earshot, Renn turned to his uncle. "Did you just come up with this, Pete?"

"Honestly, yes. I want to help. And I'd like to spend more time with the boys. I'm serious about that."

"Well then, I'll take you up on it. I think it would be good for Robbie to have something apart from Gage. He's just so angry all the time, and I'm willing to try anything at this point. Hopefully, getting a little space will help."

Pete smiled at Renn as though he'd won the lottery and I stood there while they discussed logistics for this new privilege of Robbie's. Renn warned Pete to hide anything inappropriate or embarrassing because there was no way a twelve-year-old wouldn't snoop around if he found himself alone in the apartment. Also, he'd need to lock down the controls on the Wi-Fi and the cable. Pete agreed to all of it and said he'd have a key cut the next day.

"Just don't forget he's a teenager," Renn warned. "I appreciate you doing this, but prepare yourself that he'll probably only last a month before he does something you don't like."

As it turned out, it took less than a month.

CHAPTER
Eleven

S O FAR, IT had been a pretty shitty thirty-fifth birthday. Despite positive momentum in some areas of my life, I couldn't seem to stop finding roadblocks in others. In particular, my goal of being an excellent best friend seemed doomed to failure. Zach had been my rock for years, but instead of returning the favor, I had nothing but disappointments to offer him.

My proposal to be his surrogate had hit a wall. Although he and Teddy hadn't started making firm plans yet, I couldn't resist some preliminary fact-finding—all to discover that no reputable agency would permit someone to be a surrogate if they hadn't carried at least one pregnancy successfully to term. I was pretty sure Zach had done no comprehensive research yet, focused as he was on his purchase of the bar these past few months, so I was not looking forward to admitting how naïve I'd been in offering my services. I was determined to help him pursue his dream of fatherhood, but how? Was there even a way to be more than just a shoulder to lean on?

I also needed to quit Hal's, or at least severely cut back my hours. Once school started up in the spring, I wouldn't be able to manage late work nights and early classes. I needed a day gig. And while Zach didn't expect me to stay there forever, and he'd been nothing but encouraging of me finding career direction, I knew he relied on me at the bar.

Adding to the birthday shitstorm was the reality that my forced interactions with Renn were ending. This would be my last day coming into the studio for the tattoo because as far as I could tell, no touch-ups were needed, and he was just going to take final pictures. Whatever came next between us would need to be a choice, not a circumstance.

There was so much to consider. The weight of my future sat like lead in my belly, the question mark of how I could help Zach a blinking light in my brain. Not to mention my therapy, starting classes, looking for a new job, and keeping up with my runs. I was all but certain Renn wanted to be with me, but I still wasn't sure what *I* wanted. What I was capable of.

I'd put off thinking about it too much because I could. I'd been enjoying all these interludes we'd had in large part because they'd been guaranteed. It was one thing to text regularly and have monthly appointments on the calendar, but another to choose to make space for someone in my day-to-day life.

Renn and I were already aware of each other's most intense baggage, heavily invested in each other's lives, but had done none of the usual dinner-and-a-movie-a-few-times-a-week routine to get there. Did we even have a foundation?

I was still contemplating that question when I arrived for my appointment. Once inside, I noticed Renn bent down in the corner, frowning at a trash can collecting dripping water from the ceiling tiles. Another artist, a woman with a rockabilly vibe, was tattooing her client's ankle on the other side of the room.

Renn must have heard the door open but didn't look up. "Dammit, Arch. I think it's getting worse. That's all we need is another fucking leak!"

"Well, I wish I could help you, but I'm afraid my plumbing experience is limited exclusively to bleeding the air out of the kegs at Hal's."

"Oh, Sadie. Sorry. I didn't realize it was you." Renn stood up and gestured toward the corner. "I didn't mean to sound so pissed, but this stuff can be frustrating. I'm sure my dad and Pete thought they were doing the right thing when they bought the property back in the day when things didn't cost you your first-born child, but between the mortgage and the constant maintenance... Shit. Sometimes I wish I just had a landlord to yell at."

"No, I can relate. Zach and I do have a landlord to yell at, and believe me, we take advantage. I think Zach gets an actual high out of asking George to change outdoor fluorescents at midnight. It's his passive-aggressive way of dealing with yearly rent hikes. Along with dumping our recycling into George's bin and starting a change.org petition to have the pool open twenty-four-seven."

"Have I mentioned lately how much I like your friend Zach?" He smiled and brushed his hands against his thighs. "Ah, well. Hopefully, this setup will hold for a day or two until I can get someone out here."

Done worrying for now, he asked me the usual questions about how the tattoo was healing. I told him everything was great, but when Renn inspected my thigh, he decided to touch up part of the last panel.

"I want it to be perfect," he said. "It's just a small line, and I'll still take the pictures before I put the plastic on, but I want to make sure I've done as good of a job as I can for you."

Even though I already thought it looked amazing, I wasn't going to argue with the artist, so I taped up my shorts, finally going high enough that Renn didn't need to help.

IT WAS DONE. For sure this time. He'd already taken photos, and I felt Renn smooth the protective film over my leg as I stood next to the table. Two stations away, Archie was talking to his client as he bent over the man's forearm, detailing an intricate puzzle of skulls. The two men were animatedly discussing possible plotlines for the next season of *Vikings*. Rockabilly was cleaning up after her appointment. She pushed a button on her phone and I grinned as the speakers switched from death metal to different death metal—only faster and in Spanish.

Renn walked me over to the table that functioned as the makeshift admin area and handed me a pamphlet.

"Seriously? After all the trees we've murdered, you have more paper for me."

"This is it, Sadie, the final aftercare reminder. Read it cover to cover. There's a test later."

"I'll keep that in mind." I gave him a shaky laugh as I pulled out my phone. A few flicks of my pointer finger and our working relationship would be done. "I just Venmoed you the balance."

"Thanks."

I kept Renn's gaze as I put the phone in my back pocket.

"So I guess you're not my client anymore."

"Guess not."

His left cheek pulled up in half a smile. He took a breath, and I thought he was about to say something else, but...he didn't. Exhaling, he ran his hands through his hair, taking out the rubber band. As he shifted his weight from one foot to the other, he just...looked at me.

There was everything in that look, a shared understanding. The House Party of Hope. The almost-kiss. Hal's. The 5K. Hours in this studio. Knowing Pete. And Zach. His brothers. So much between us, none of it clear. Was it all hitting him then, too?

The pace of the water dripping from the ceiling tiles intensified, a hollow bubble bursting noise echoing in the metal can. Archie's laughter across the room faded to a buzzing in my ears.

Five or ten seconds went by, but it felt like millennia. Why was Renn just fixed in place? After everything we'd been through together, everything he'd said—why the hell was he just standing there? The plastic covering my thigh grew clammy and my pulse jumped. I watched, mesmerized, as Renn swallowed thickly.

I couldn't be wrong about what he wanted, could I? I'd heard him tell Archie. He'd been pretty unambiguous with me as well. *Had he changed his mind?* He just kept standing there, silently. Like a sexy mannequin. A sensation of inadequacy, the one I had *finally* relegated from constant companion to infrequent visitor, rolled over me in a wave.

And crashed.

Oh God.

My insecurities rioted inside my brain. *He's come to his senses! You're too old! You don't have a real job! You've got cellulite!* I had no business trying to make something happen with anyone right now. The weight of the silence was collapsing me.

I didn't realize until that moment how much I'd been counting on Renn to take the lead, to do what he'd been doing for months—somehow inspiring me to be the strongest version of myself. And even though it wasn't fair, I couldn't help feeling like he was letting me down.

You always want too much, Sadie.

Shut the fuck up, Henri. I'm busy freaking out.

"I guess I'll...see you around?" I stammered. Excruciating. I turned toward the exit.

But the reality of my imminent departure broke Renn's stupor. I saw the moment my leaving registered, and he finally moved. It was achingly slow, his inked arm reaching out in the space between us, the space that was so much larger and more fragile than Renn realized. I was still reeling, but when he finally touched me, the sensation broke through.

"Sadie—wait."

I looked down at his hand wrapped around my forearm. "Renn?"

He glanced over his shoulder at the two other artists, both busy and oblivious to our exchange. "Damn...Sadie." He used his thumb to rub a faint circle over the inside of my wrist before letting go. "Shit...I'm sorry...I just..."

He took a step back and looked at me, toying with the rubber band between his fingers before flicking it onto the table. There was a waver to his smile, an uncharacteristic jitter in the way he held himself. It was disorienting. This person in front of me, someone unmoored and unsure—he was new. His hesitancy continued to unleash my doubts.

"Sadie, please, I'm sorry I lost my voice for a second there. I've imagined this a few times, where you weren't my client anymore. I'm sorry...I'm...ah...damn..." He shifted his weight again, looking up toward the ceiling as though help would come from that direction. Then finally, almost inaudibly, "...I'm nervous."

I wasn't sure what I'd been expecting, but not...that. "Nervous?"

"Yeah. Yeah, I am."

He was nervous? About starting something? Why was he picking this moment to have an uncharacteristic lack of surety? One of us had to be sure! I looked longingly at the door. I supposed therapy had helped me upgrade my conflict avoidance game. With Henri, I cowered and tried to placate. At least with Renn, my instinct was to run away with my dignity intact.

Renn gave another glance upward, to the three ever-circling fans. He also spared a glare for the water collecting in the trash can. "Sadie...please. I'm nervous for the same reason you look like you're about to bolt. Because it's scary that we can be *more* now...after everything. Not just talk about it, but be it." He twisted his hands together. "And I want that. But I understand you're hesitant. So I'm nervous I'll say the wrong thing and scare you off."

Nervous about saying the wrong thing? Did he think saying nothing was preferable?

"More." I didn't say the word out loud, simply mouthing it with my lips.

Sensing I had one foot out the door seemed to have inspired his revival. He hinted at a grin, confidence returning. "I know. It's a lot."

I wasn't back with him yet. Maybe it was good to be reminded of my fragility, because I was still stuck in a minute ago, feeling ugly and unsure. Henri in my head. Faced with an unfamiliar side of Renn, wondering what else I was missing. He may have moved on from that awkward minute—ten seconds?—of nervous silence, but for me, that was gonna leave a mark.

I felt the buzz of a text come through. Renn heard too and glanced toward the impression of the phone in my pocket to indicate I could look. I shook my head slightly.

"Sadie, hey, come over here with me."

He led me over to the full-length mirror. Thanks to the L-shape of the studio, we were out of eyeshot of the others. He turned me around so my back faced the glass, reflecting the shiny, still-slightly-raised tattoo. Renn stood before me but kept his focus on the mirror. I turned my head over my shoulder to meet his eyes there.

The intensity of the moment reminded me of the day he'd done the outline, the first day I'd known the two of us were...connecting. My earlier hesitancy faded as I grew warm under his steady, watchful gaze. Then, before I realized it was happening, Renn squatted down in front of me. Just like that day.

His face now level with the tattoo on my leg, he grazed the edge of the plastic with two gentle fingers as he spoke to the Sadie In The Mirror. "I fucked things up just now by not saying this immediately. I never want to make you feel uncertain. So let me be clear." His breath felt hot on my thigh, thick and heavy against me. "You should know how important this piece is to me. I've told you how much I love it as an artist, how it brought out something in my work that's been missing for a long time."

"I remember." It was a whisper, all I could manage with his lips an inch from my skin.

"Sadie, these hours we've spent together." Renn's gentle fingers continued to graze my thigh over the plastic, just lightly on the outside. "I didn't realize how much I needed them until you gave them to me. I wasn't looking for someone, but I'm so grateful we met. I don't want to stop knowing you."

He stayed in a squat, his other hand hovering near my calf as he stared at me in the mirror, seeking permission. I nodded subtly and he curled that hand around my leg, palming it slowly to the back of my knee.

I closed my eyes so I would sense nothing but his fingers on me. So many times during the tattoo process I had forced myself to *not* notice those fingers, touching me so intimately. Indulging in the sensation now was heady, consuming enough that I ignored the buzz of another text in my pocket.

I opened my eyes and looked down at Renn, who was still focusing on the mirror. I placed a hand gently on Renn's shoulder and rested my thumb against his cheek, capturing his gaze with my own.

A few minutes ago, I'd been completely spooked, ready to run. Did I have enough to offer him? I knew from his conversation with

Archie that Renn didn't realize how much of a work in progress I was. I'd made strides, but not the kind that would allow me to meet him even halfway. Would it be fair to ask him to do all the heavy lifting? Knowing I'd always be looking for the exit. Still—

"I don't want to stop knowing you either, Renn."

He tilted his head to rest it against my thigh and his grip on my knee tightened.

"Does this mean we're friends now?"

I huffed. "I don't know about you, Batman, but my *friends* don't rub my thighs and calves."

He raised an eyebrow. "Batman?"

"I'll explain it to you someday, but for now just take it, m'kay?"

"You got it." His easy laughter, so welcome, was back. "So, more than friends?"

"Yes," I squeaked. "I mean…I want that…maybe…" I couldn't stay coherent with his breath tickling my thigh and his hands all over my leg. "I just…oh my God, I can't even think…Renn, you need to stand up."

He pressed one gentle kiss to the back of my knee and another to the edge of the plastic on my thigh before rising to his full height.

My phone buzzed again in my pocket. Neither of us acknowledged it.

Standing face-to-face with Renn, or as close as we could, considering he had about four inches on me, I was at peace. I could live with ambiguity about what was *exactly* next. Propelling myself forward while being unsure about the future was basically my life philosophy at this point. It was enough for now to know that this wasn't the end for us.

Renn reached for my hands. He laced our fingers together and leaned in to speak cheek-to-cheek. No one on the other side of the room could see or hear us, but it was as though he wanted to be sure I knew his next words were just for me.

"You bring out something in me, Sadie. I didn't know it could be so easy to be with someone. I want you in my life. Whatever that looks like. But I hope…"

Our bodies were pressing against each other now, Renn locking our joined hands from fingers to wrists to forearms, and the fear I'd felt the day of our almost-kiss was gone. My breasts pushed against his chest and my breathing stuttered as I felt the outline of his cock against my hip. He squeezed my hands. Looking at his face from this distance, I noticed for the first time that the perfection of his radiant smile was actually slightly imperfect—his two front teeth sort of angled in together. How had I never noticed before? There was so much left to discover.

Renn leaned down to rest our foreheads together for a few slow seconds, and I closed my lids as he began placing leisurely, closed-mouth kisses on the corner of my eye. My cheek. My jaw. I shivered as he caught the bottom of my earlobe lightly between his teeth before kissing there too. He untwined our hands, resting his on my hips as his mouth continued its lazy exploration of my shoulder. Of the sensitive place where it met my nape. The force of the pleasure worked like a current, heating me from the inside.

He was inching his kisses from my neck to my chin, toward my mouth, when my pocket buzzed again.

He pulled away languidly. "Sadie, by my count, that's four in a row. You'd better check it." I sighed regretfully as he squeezed my waist and I turned away from him. I reached for my pocket, annoyed that Zach had picked a terrible time to send me his annual mildly amusing, slightly dirty happy birthday GIFs.

BANG!

Before I could pull my phone out, someone crashing into the studio claimed our attention. The loud noise brought Renn and me rushing into the main area in time to see Robbie tear through the entrance. Did this kid ever come in without slamming the door?

Rockabilly took that as her cue to leave, hastily grabbing her bag and slinking out the back.

"Robbie! What the hell?" Renn exclaimed.

Shaking with fury and struggling to calm down, Robbie bent over and rested his fists against his knees, as though he'd just run to the studio. As he attempted to catch his breath, I saw he was clutching a piece of red paper in one of his hands. No, not paper. An envelope. Although faded and worn, it had once been brightly hued. On the front, waning but still visible enough, I could make out block letters. PETE.

Renn noticed it too. "What's that?"

Robbie straightened and stomped toward his brother, slapping the card against his chest. "Read it."

Renn looked like he might argue for a moment, but then nodded once and did as Robbie asked, pulling a card from the envelope that had a picture of a cake on it. I watched as he read it silently, his expression ping-ponging between sadness and anger.

"Well!?" Robbie asked Renn. "Did you know?"

Renn shook his head, handing the card wordlessly to Archie, who read it with a grim look on his face. When he was done, he gave it back to Renn and made a gesture toward the corner. "That drip looks like it's getting worse. Coming faster. I'm gonna go in the back and try the plumber again."

Clearly, Archie thought the brothers needed to hash this out on their own. I took the hint and picked up my purse, debating whether to go near Robbie to grab my coat, or wait until later. The tween was lit by a halo of anger, and I didn't want to get too close.

"Sadie, no." Renn saw I was preparing my escape.

"It's fine. We can finish our conversation later." Or not. It seemed like other discussions in our lives should be the priority right now. Renn and Robbie needed to talk about whatever was on that card, and I hadn't forgotten that I had important things to discuss with Zach.

"No!" Renn spoke emphatically and reached his hand out to me. "No...I want you to stay. Please...don't leave."

Robbie huffed and eyed his brother warily. "So, is she, like, your girlfriend now?"

"No," I said at the same time Renn said, "Maybe."

"You know what...I don't even care." Robbie flailed his arms around. "You can tell her. It's not like she doesn't already know Pete is a total douche."

I wasn't sure why Renn wanted me to stay, but it was hard to deny him. Had his lips been on my neck only minutes ago? It seemed like every time we got close, things got harder. Any minute we claimed for just the two of us seemed stolen.

Renn handed me the card, motioning to show I should read it.

Dear Pete,

Happy 30th. You said we shouldn't talk for a while, but it is your birthday, so I figured—why not? I understand you want me to make it work with Thomas. For the boys' sake, I'm going to try. But I think you're wrong. I think Thomas would have understood if we explained it to him.

You really hurt me last week. I've never been so kicked in the teeth. But if your intention was to convince me that there truly is no hope for us—mission accomplished. You want to forget this ever happened. Fine. But I want you to know that I will always believe

you are the love of my life, and that we are meant
to be together, even if you're pushing me away right
now. I won't wait for you, because you asked me not
to, but in a way, I'll always be waiting. I love you now
and always.

Happy Birthday.

Mary

Pete and Mary? The boys' mother? Stunned, I looked up just as Renn asked Robbie, "Where did you get this?"

Robbie was more composed than when he'd entered. "From Pete's apartment. I've been going there, you remember, ever since he gave me the key." Robbie leaned against the wall and slowly slid down, landing with his legs straight in front of him on the floor. "He has this picture, on the bookshelf, of him with my mom and our dad." *My mom and our dad.* I'd gotten the impression before that Renn hadn't had a close relationship with his stepmom, and this was further evidence. "I picked it up to look closer and that card just sort of slid out."

"And you decided to read a card addressed to Pete?"

"C'mon, Renn. I know my mom's handwriting. Wouldn't you have read it?"

"Yeah...yeah I would have." Renn crouched down in front of his brother while I stayed rooted in place, hoping to be unobtrusive. The only sound was the water dripping from the ceiling, and I agreed with Archie that the trickling seemed to be getting faster.

"What are we gonna do, Renn?" Robbie implored. "I'm so mad right now. I wanna punch him. But then I also have, like, a million questions." Robbie ran his hands through his hair in a gesture I'd seen Renn make many times. The boy appeared to be growing his matching brown locks out.

"I don't know, Rob. I'm still processing this myself." That was an understatement. Renn looked like he'd been hit by a truck, but he was keeping his focus on his brother.

"This means they were together, right? Like, during the time my parents were married?" Robbie popped up from the floor and radiated with anger all over again. "Fuck!" He shouted to the general room. "Fuck him!"

"Robbie—"

"I need to take a leak," Robbie practically shouted, swiping his face with his sleeve and avoiding our sympathetic expressions as he headed toward the hallway leading to the back office and restroom.

CHAPTER
Twelve

I LAID MY HAND on Renn's. He was clutching the card. It didn't look like a grenade, and yet, here we were. With his main reason for keeping calm currently in the bathroom down the hall, Renn's features clouded with rage.

I thought about the conversations I'd had with Pete at the fundraiser and the 5K, the ones I'd witnessed him have with Renn. This explained so much. Did Pete regret staying away? Had he done it for the boys, because he'd been worried they'd find out? Had he wanted to protect their mother's memory? Or did he just hate the reminder that he'd been involved with his brother's wife? No wonder he was so all over the place.

Even though I empathized with Renn's anger, I also had compassion for Pete's guilt. Because it had cost him his nephews, all he had left of his brother. When it came to blood relations, I was alone in the world. I couldn't imagine the loneliness of having family within touching distance and feeling like you couldn't be a part of it.

I spoke as carefully as I could. "Does it matter, Renn, after all this time?"

"How can you even ask that?"

I moved my palm to his shoulder, gently placating. "Because whatever happened, it was between them. Pete and Mary, and your dad. People make choices, sometimes bad ones. You're such an amazing guy. You're not used to disappointing people. Pete's not good like that."

"She was his brother's wife!" Renn pulled out of my grip, expression furious as he clenched the card.

"I'm aware. And I understand why you and Robbie are so upset. But maybe talk to Pete before you go flying off half-cocked."

"Why? What could he possibly say to make this better?"

"I don't know. I can't speak for your uncle. But I think he knows he fucked up. He basically admitted that to me, even if I didn't understand what he meant. He's...trying."

Renn's energy was as red as I'd ever seen it. He was practically shooting lasers from his eyeballs, and I realized this was the second time today I'd seen a new side of him.

"Fuck him! And fuck his trying. Why the hell are you defending him!?" I flinched as he yelled at me, chest heaving with angry breaths. Stunned by his vehemence, I took two steps backward.

Renn saw me startle and realized his mistake right away. "Shit... Sorry, Sadie. I didn't mean to shout at you." Finally releasing his hold on the card, he ran his hands roughly through his hair. "I know you only want to help."

The chaos of his emotions was palpable. He'd never directed anything resembling anger toward me before. And for the first time, I really imbibed what a relationship with him might be like. With any man. Because any man wasn't necessarily going to be like Henri, but they were going to be a human being. With human failings. And as Renn stood before me, eyes burning, I wondered if I would be able to handle his.

Perfect, beautiful, caring Renn already scared the shit out of me, as much as I wanted him—but flawed, yelling-at-me, human Renn? Could I even imagine being with him?

"I understand you're upset," I said carefully. "But you can't raise your voice and take it out on me."

"I'm sorry. I'm just so pissed at Pete right now. I don't even know what I'm saying."

He appeared untethered, perhaps still in shock. My eyes landed on the card, which Renn put down on the admin table. Although faded, the blue cake with purple candles was still distinct. "You want to hear something funny?" I asked, gesturing toward it.

"What's that?"

"Today's my birthday."

"What?" Renn seemed confused for a moment as my statement sank in, before exclaiming, "It's your birthday!? Jesus, happy birthday. How did I not know this?"

"Meh. I think I mentioned it, but I didn't exactly drive home the date. I don't want to make a big deal about it." Shoving my hands in my pockets, I stood tall. "The thing is, I'm thirty-five today and in a much better place than I was at thirty-four, and definitely better than thirty-three. When I was with Henri, I never could have told him not to yell at me. With you, I feel safe enough to do so. Wanna know why?"

He gazed at me as he shook his head. "Why?"

"Partly because I'm getting my act together, but partly because of meeting you, seeing you exist in the world. Because you're a good man. And I needed to know there were people out there like you. Even if you yell sometimes and aren't perfect. I think you can figure this out with Pete. You're good at taking care of people. You're reeling now, but I know you can get through this, make it okay for you and your brothers."

Renn reached for my hand and kissed the back of it. "I hope I'm worthy of your faith."

"You are."

"The thing is, my dad and Mary went to Costa Rica to work on their marriage. Things were hard between them at the end. Frankly, things were pretty rough the whole time."

"You're saying it's Pete's fault Thomas died because he caused problems in their marriage?"

"I mean, maybe?" Renn drew out that last word, seeming to have calmed. "It's just hard not to blame him, seeing this note."

"It's a crappy thing to find out, for sure. But you need to talk to him. He told me at the race he wants to make amends. I think he stayed away because of this." I was sensitive to the situation, especially considering my history with Henri, but everything I knew about Pete led me to believe he was genuinely remorseful, not a narcissistic asshole.

"That seems obvious now. I just don't know if I can forgive him."

"I understand. But he is your uncle. If you decide not to forgive him because of something that happened, what—almost a decade ago—that's a big deal. Take it from me. I don't have any family left, no one to cut off. Not an aunt or an uncle, a sibling or a cousin."

"God, Sadie. You've told me that before, but I didn't really get it, not truly, until just now. I mean, Robbie and Gage can be a handful, but I'm grateful for them every day. Hell, I even see my mom every few months."

"You do?" He nodded but didn't elaborate, and I figured we'd unearthed enough family secrets for one day.

Renn's face softened, and he sighed with relief as I allowed him to wrap his arms around my shoulders. He twined his fingers together in a crown behind my neck.

"What are you going to do?" I asked.

He leaned his forehead against mine and his warm breath caressed my skin like velvet. "Well, first I'm going to take Robbie home, try to calm him down. I don't think Gage needs to know about this. And then I guess I'll call Pete, tell him what happened, find out if he wants to talk things out."

That sounded like a good plan. Renn's quick return to reason was encouraging, but it called to mind the conversation I'd overheard him have with Archie last month.

"Renn, do you think Archie knew?"

He considered the question a few moments before replying. "I do. I remember when I was young that he and Pete were cool, but they've been low-key angry with each other for a long time, basically since Mary came into our lives, so he must have known."

"Well, I'd imagine it's been hard for him to keep it to himself, but I respect that he kept his nose out of your business. He'll probably be glad to get things aired out."

Renn laughed. "Maybe. Archie's a chill guy. But I'm pretty sure he enjoys having free rein to unleash any dickish parts of himself on my uncle. I can relate. I'm not sure I know what to say to Pete now."

"Hey." I pulled back and forced him to look at me. "Just make the call. Talk to your uncle, see where it goes from there. No need to write out a whole script just yet."

Renn moved to link his hands behind my waist as he spoke. "Oh, and how did you get so wise?"

I grinned. "A full year of therapy and thirty-three years before that being a stupid idiot."

"Don't call one of my favorite people an idiot." He pecked my forehead.

"Fine. I'm just saying I have a lot of experience making poor decisions. Now you can learn from my mistakes so you don't have to repeat them. Lesson number one—don't take your family for granted."

"Alright, Obi-Wan. I'll keep it in mind." He kissed the side of my neck again before wrapping me in a tight embrace and whispering in my ear. "Happy birthday, beautiful. I'm sorry for how it's gone down, and that your special day got lost in all this, but I'm really glad you were born."

In the mirror, I looked at the blue tips of the lotus, the ouroboros making a meal of its tail, the broken-down wall and chains of my tattoo. Renn would be with me no matter what. He pulled away and gestured that he was going to check on Robbie, frowning at the almost-full waterline in the trash can as he passed it.

RENN APPEARED COMPOSED when he and Robbie re-emerged. The knifepoints of the earlier tension still reverberated off the black walls of the studio, but time dulled them as Renn coaxed his brother to grab his things. He told me he'd call later, promising to do something special for my birthday. I hoped the drive home would give them a chance to decompress, and I was eager to get back to my apartment to talk with Zach.

But an oblivious Pete walking into the studio annihilated the tenuous calm.

He entered with the sunlight barreling in on his back, pulling off blue-mirrored aviators as he shut the door behind himself.

It was instantly clear the others hadn't been ready to see him yet.

Archie, who had returned to his station, sat back on his stool, crossing his arms as he cemented his lips in a grim line. Renn put a firm hand on Robbie's shoulder in front of him and the pink tinge of his fingers revealed he was applying pressure, holding the boy back. I did my best to plaster my back against the wall, head down and body still.

There was no diminishing the friction his entrance caused, silence hanging heavy in the air, punctuated only by the drip of the leaky ceiling. Pete registered the tense faces of Archie and his nephews, asking tentatively, "Hey everyone. What's up?"

"You fucking asshole!" Robbie screamed, shrugging out of Renn's grip but making no move toward his uncle.

Pete looked stunned as he took in the tween's infuriated expression. "Robbie? What the fuck?"

"Robbie, stop," Renn interjected. "That's not helping."

"Well, he is an asshole." Robbie had tears in his eyes and looked like he wanted to wreck Pete, as much as someone frozen in place could look that way.

Pete took in the room again, more insistent when he asked, "Does someone want to tell me what the fuck is going on? Why am I an asshole?"

Oh, Pete.

"Robbie, I need you to stay in the car while I talk to your uncle." Renn's voice was flat.

"What? No way, Renn. I don't want to leave just so you guys can invent some bullshit story to sell me on later. You can't just make this better!" Robbie swiped his tears away viciously with the arm of his hoodie.

Pete leaned toward his nephews, looking like he was going to say something, but Archie stood and glared at him, shaking his head to signify that any words Pete tried to utter would be met with a quick tattoo gun to the neck.

Renn reached out to his brother and spun him around, bending so they were speaking eye-to-eye. "Hey listen." He put both hands on Robbie's shoulders. "I need to talk to your uncle. Alone. I think you understand why. But you have my word I won't lie to you or keep things from you, okay? I can't pretend you didn't see the card, and I'm not going to sugarcoat it. But I have to find out what's going on. This is all news to me, too."

"Really?"

"I promise." Renn tried to muster a laugh as he continued. "Besides, it will be better this way. If I decide to murder our uncle, you won't have to testify against me." Renn looked my way. "Sadie can watch, since she seems to witness all my finer moments these days." He glanced at me with an earnest expression that encompassed everything from "I'm sorry" to "Holy shit."

"And you'll tell me? Whatever he says?" Robbie persisted.

"Absolutely. Please, just go in the car. You can listen to music or whatever. I need you to give me a few minutes with Pete."

Robbie nodded and headed toward the door, keeping his head down and deliberately knocking Pete with his elbow as he passed him.

After Robbie left, I grabbed my purse. "Since this is a family thing, I'm gonna take off." Archie tilted his chin at me, but Renn was immediately on his feet.

"Fuck that," Renn said. "Sadie, you basically already know everything and if there's more, I'll just repeat it to you later, so please—" He caught my hand and gripped it tighter than he had before. "I want you to stay."

I looked at our joined fingers. I wanted to leave because this felt so heavy, that slap of the card on the table so evocative of a plastic stick slapped down on a bar in Boston just over a year ago. Renn was taking it for granted that I was going to support him and I just...didn't know if I had it in me.

"Archie, you should stay too," Renn stated. "You're family. Besides, I have a suspicion this isn't new information for you."

Renn peered at Archie and the other man met his eyes coolly. "It wasn't my place, Renn. Your dad confided in me because we were friends, and that's where my loyalty will always be. I still don't think it's my place, but I'll stay if you want me to."

"Dad knew?"

"Jesus Christ! Thomas knew what!?" Pete was coming unglued,

still standing near the entry. "I need someone to tell me what the fuck is going on!"

Renn sighed loudly and glared at Pete before grabbing the card and putting it in his uncle's hands with a staccato, "Robbie found this."

Pete stared at the envelope, recognition dawning. He looked at his nephew, then me, then Archie, then back to the envelope again. A guttural noise—something between a hiccup and a groan—escaped his throat. Both horror and relief clouded his face, as though he'd known this reckoning was coming, before his expression finally settled into one of resignation. He dropped into a chair.

Turning to Renn, he asked, "What do you want to know?"

"All of it. I don't need the dirty details, but the rest." Renn dropped my hand but moved it to pull me loosely to his side. "You can thank Sadie for me giving you a chance to explain, instead of me just punching you out. I'd encourage you to not waste the opportunity."

Renn's acknowledgment of my influence in this situation made me queasy. I really, really wasn't ready to be involved in this level of drama. But I did my best to stay stoic, not wanting to draw attention to myself at this critical moment.

"I'll tell you everything." Pete began. "I thought I was doing everyone a favor keeping this secret, but really, it just poisoned the well."

"That's real poetic, Pete. Now talk."

"I'm getting there. If you've read that card, you can already guess the gist of it. Mary and I had a thing. You understand that your dad and Mary only stayed together because she got pregnant with Robbie. It was never smooth. After he was born, Thomas put everything into the shop and making it a success. He worked a lot, took care of you. You know your mom was the love of your dad's life, and that never changed. If he could have convinced her to give up the bottle, your parents would have stayed together, no doubt." He inhaled deeply, running his palms back and forth across his thighs. "Mary sensed that. She told me she always felt like second choice. She hoped it might get better when they moved to Pasadena, but it didn't. She was isolated, had a toddler, no friends in the neighborhood. Your dad was so busy with the studio, he asked me to check on her. So, I did. We were friends, and eventually…it changed."

I closed my eyes, shielding myself from the current as the heavy waves of Pete's regret rolled across the room. Archie folded his arms over his chest and looked down at the floor. Renn's body stiffened, but he said nothing as Pete continued.

"Don't ask me why I did it, Renn. I wouldn't be able to tell you. She was there, we were close, and on some level, I was jealous of your dad and how he was so successful and everybody loved him. Technically, we owned the shop together, but he was the driving force. There was something about Mary that made me feel good, as if her liking me more meant I could finally be better than Thomas at something."

Archie hmphed grumpily at the same time Renn offered, "That's fucked up."

"Completely fucked up," Pete agreed. "And it didn't last very long. When it became clear that Mary was way more invested than I was, I stopped it. She thought we were destiny or something, that she was in love with me. I was never there with her. Never." He sat up taller in his chair before breathing out slowly through his nose.

"So, I ended it. I said some terrible things, trying to convince her what we were doing was wrong and Thomas should never find out. She finally accepted what I was saying and agreed not to tell him. A few months later, I got that card."

"And you kept it?"

"I can't explain exactly, Renn. I was still dealing with everything when I put it in the picture frame, and I wasn't ready to throw it away. Eventually, I just forgot it was there."

"Archie said my dad knew?"

"He figured it out. I'm not sure how. Mary swore she wouldn't tell him, but I guess it was how we acted around each other, or because I stayed away after that. But right before they went to Costa Rica, he told me he knew, and that he didn't want to discuss it with me, ever."

At that, Archie stood up from where he'd been leaning against the wall.

"She lied." Archie sighed heavily and rubbed his forehead with tatted fingers. "If Mary said she didn't tell him, then she lied. They were fighting viciously one night and she told him, threw it in his face. After a few days on my couch, he decided to go home and work it out. He said he felt responsible in a way because he'd always loved Renn's mom the most, so he owed Mary a pass. He thought they could salvage things, since Pete and Mary had ended the affair years before. Thomas told me the thing he wanted most was to just put it in the rearview and not bring it up again."

Renn looked like he was doing complex equations in his head. He stepped away from me and reached his arm behind him, placing a palm against his neck as he paced the floor. "Alright, Pete. I think I get the basics of what happened. But that brief affair you had with Mary was enough to keep you from your family? Just the guilt from that? All this time?"

"No. Not from that."

"Then why?"

"I felt guilty about the affair. It never should have happened. But that wouldn't have been enough to keep me away."

"Okay..."

"Renn, I know you promised to tell Robbie the truth, and I'm going to give it to you. But I want to say that I think this is something he and Gage don't need to hear. They deserve to remember their mom the right way."

"Just tell me."

Pete nodded and straightened his shoulders. "After your dad died, Mary waited a few months and then came to me. She wanted to try. To be together. The idea was horrifying, of course. I was so raw from missing Thomas. If you remember, during that time right after he died, I was around. You were busy going off half-wild, but for those six months, I was the one helping Mary with the boys and keeping the shop going."

"If you say so."

"I was trying to do the right thing, but me being around so much, it must have made her think... She kept coming on to me, at first just little comments, but then one night she crawled into my bed. I'm still not sure she knew what she was doing, and of course I shut her down. She was really upset, had been drinking, and started crying about how I was the love of her life and we should be together. I tried to let her down gently. I promise you, I tried! Tried to explain that I never felt like that about her. But she just wouldn't accept it. We went in circles for a while and finally, I got angry. I said some terrible things because I needed her to give it up."

"What things?"

"I don't remember it word for word, but I'm pretty sure I accused her of being a shitty mother and a terrible wife to Thomas, not grieving him properly. I told her I could never love someone like her." I had been staring at the floor as Pete's story unfolded. But I looked up at that last part, as the raw emotion in Pete's voice blanketed the space.

"Jesus." Renn and Archie jinxed each other with the sentiment.

Pete rubbed his eyes and blinked rapidly, and I realized in bewilderment he was weeping. "The next day, Renn. The next day was…" Pete practically choked on his words. "The next day was the day she took the pills."

Pete snuffled and his nails made crescents in his palms as he squeezed his hands. He was no longer trying to stem the tears. He wouldn't have been able to, as furiously as they were coming. And he summed up his confession in a breath between sobs. "I stayed away because it's my fault the boys' mom killed herself."

CHAPTER
Thirteen

THE NEXT TEN minutes were somehow both predictable and fraught. I knew before he said so that Renn would not blame Pete for Mary's suicide. People cheat and people grieve, but they don't all kill themselves. By the end, Renn didn't exactly embrace his uncle, but he said he understood Pete's reasoning for staying away. It was plain that Pete regretted his actions, that the burden of his secret had cost him dearly, but with everything now out in the open, they might finally be able to move past it. Renn also conceded that, deep down, he understood Thomas had died in an accidental drowning which wasn't Pete's fault.

As to the affair, Renn told his uncle Robbie would have a tough time getting over it, but Renn himself came around to my way of thinking—that the affair was between Pete, Mary, and Thomas, and it made little sense for Pete to keep trying to make amends with people who weren't alive to forgive him.

I knew Renn hadn't let go of all his anger, but at least he was saying the right things and attempting to improve the situation.

Renn reached for me as he and his uncle quietly conversed, once again putting his hand in mine. He squeezed my palm gratefully, and it appeared the worst had passed. I hoped Renn's family could heal. Perhaps even grow closer.

Or not.

I looked over and noticed Archie standing stiffly in front of his station. He hadn't said a word since giving his account of Thomas's perspective and seemed unmoved by Renn's capacity to forgive his uncle.

"Tell him the rest," Archie's voice commanded as he looked at Pete, still seated by the door.

Pete appeared confused at first, but then turned his tear-stained face to the blond man. "Archie—"

"The rest?" Renn directed an accusatory glare at Pete. "What more is there?" He bounced his eyes between the two older men and implored, "Haven't we had enough secrets? I want everything out on the table. Now."

"Tell him, Pete."

Pete ran a hand over his forehead and blinked, squeezing the bridge of his nose. Archie assaulted him with his unrelenting gaze as the air thickened.

"Tell me what?" Pete and Archie continued their silent stand-off. Renn grew impatient and I realized that, even though he'd returned to rationality, he was still very much on edge. "Seriously, what is it?"

Pete opened and closed his mouth twice before murmuring the barest whisper. "Gage."

"Gage? What about Ga—"

Renn put it together at the same moment I did. Pete was thir-ty-eight. The card was for his thirtieth birthday. Archie looked at us before lifting his chin to the sky, mouthing inaudible words—to Thomas, I assumed. Renn's grip on my hand moved from strong to viselike as he pulled me over with him, stalking his uncle until they were nose to nose. White-hot anger radiated through his features.

"Is Gage yours?" Renn didn't soften it.

Pete looked like he was about to launch into some sort of speech, but his nephew was having none of it, cutting him off before he could begin with a wave of his palm.

"It's a simple question."

"Renn, I—"

"Is...He...Yours?" The words were quiet, but spoken with such hostility, it took me aback.

Renn's arm lifted menacingly. I blanched, thinking he was about to slap Pete, but he merely reached to grab the decorative octopus-in-a-jar from a shelf behind his uncle's head, as though this moment would be easier if he had something to hold on to.

Something other than my hand, since he chose that moment to let it go.

Renn fondled the container, calmly running his fingers along the smooth glass, jostling the sea creature suspended inside. His body was taut, breathing even as he rolled the mason jar back and forth, twisting it in his palms, rage seemingly contained by the repetitive motion.

Until it wasn't.

"*Is. He. Yours!?*" The raw fury oozing from his pores unleashed itself as he hurled the jar across the studio, glass shattering as the octopus landed on the wall, sliming its way down to the floor. Renn glared unblinkingly at his uncle.

"I don't know," Pete whispered.

"What?"

"I don't know," Pete spoke more firmly. "It's a possibility...Mary thought so. But we never did a test."

Renn nodded, as though to himself, exhaling from the deepest part of his belly. Time passed in a fog as uncle and nephew faced this life-altering revelation.

As every emotion played out across Renn's face—anger, hurt, shock, sadness, grief, and finally, acceptance—my head went light. I hadn't been in a room this tense since the woman in the red dress had walked into the bar in Boston. *What the actual fuck was I doing here? I couldn't take this on.* I had just watched Renn hurl an inanimate object against the wall. No matter how good it felt with him, the reality of that shattered glass had brought me instantly to my senses. And as I descended into my own fog, unwilling and unable to be present in the moment, I couldn't deny it anymore.

Maybe someday I could be with Renn, but not now.

I had been focusing for months on whether Renn could handle Messy Sadie. But somehow, I'd missed one of the more salient points—could I handle Messy Renn?

I could picture it in my mind. Over the next few months, Renn and Pete would dance around each other, talking about the past, working toward a resolution, consoling a traumatized Robbie. And the whole time, I'd be worrying about it. How was Renn? How could I help? How could I fix it? As much as I'd progressed since Henri, the instinct to fix things, to please my man, was there and strong and vibrant. If I stayed with Renn, I'd fall into that role and everything I'd planned for myself would get lost. I wasn't in the place where I could balance things yet. No matter that I was stronger than I'd ever been, I was still fragile.

But I also didn't want to hurt him. I had to make him understand.

Through the haze, I heard him engaged in hushed conversation with Pete. Renn was no longer yelling, although the residue of fury remained in the hard set of his jaw. I stayed focused on my own thoughts but caught the men's resolution—that the possibility of Gage being Pete's son didn't need to be explored. No one else knew, and no one needed to know. Renn was still pissed, but in typical fashion, he returned to necessary calm as the minutes ticked by.

Pete looked destroyed. Tears and snot soaked his t-shirt.

Finally, Renn released a leaden sigh. "Give me a few days, Pete. I need to talk to Robbie and make sure he won't say anything about the card to Gage. But no more fuckups and no more secrets."

"Renn, all I want is a chance to make it right." Pete reached out his arm. Renn looked at the outstretched offering long enough that I worried he wouldn't take it, but he finally grasped his uncle's hand in a quick shake and left it at that.

"Pete, why don't you head out the rear exit. I'm not sure what you were planning on doing here today, but you'd better just go back to your apartment. I'll call in a few days."

Pete nodded and mouthed "thank you" to me on his way out. Archie spared him a head nod, and I regained my earlier belief that the Stollers would be okay.

"I'm gonna try another plumber." Archie looked between me and Renn knowingly as he gave us privacy. "I don't think that ceiling will last the night."

After Archie left, Renn stood silent for a few moments near his station. He glanced in the mirror, which triggered me to look there too. Our eyes met, and he came over slowly, creeping up behind me cautiously.

"Well, this kind of ruined our moment, didn't it?" He gripped my hip and wrapped his arms around my waist, pressing his solid chest against my back. After this mindfuck of a day, I felt instantly soothed, allowing my hands to drift along his powerful forearms as I gave myself a few seconds to revel in the feel of him. But when he leaned down and touched his nose to my shoulder, I pulled away.

"Renn, maybe that's a good thing."

"What?"

"Yeah." I paused. "I think we need to put the brakes on...whatever we were doing." I turned around to face him, putting a few feet of distance between us.

"Wait. Why? Because of what Pete said about him and Mary?"

"No. Not exactly."

Then his eyes went big, as though something had just entered his mind. "Is this because I yelled? Or threw that jar? Shit! I am so sorry. Sadie, I promise that is really, really unusual for me. I'm not, like, a yeller. Or a rager. Usually."

I huffed. "I know that, Renn."

"Then why?" He ran his hands through his hair before waving one of them toward the red envelope. "I mean, I realize it's been totally insane since Robbie came in, but I thought we were headed toward a different place...before that. Now you're saying you don't want to be with me? Like, at all?"

"It's not that. I absolutely want to be with you. Every time I look at you, I can't decide what I want to do more—talk to you, or squeeze you, or just crawl all over you. That has never been our problem." I gave him the hottest of hot looks to emphasize my point. "The problem is that I *can't* be with you right now. I can't be with anyone. Seeing this today, I realized I'm not able to take on anyone else's stuff."

"I'd never ask you to do that."

"I know you say that, but that's not okay, either, is it? I don't want to be in a relationship with someone I can't fully support when they need me."

"It's not like that, Sadie. Just because I wanted to hold your hand doesn't mean I expect you to prop me up, or whatever it is you're thinking. I like having you with me, knowing that I have something good in my life, but I'm capable of dealing with hard things on my own." He folded his arms across his chest.

Renn would need more from a relationship than he was ready to acknowledge. As he'd said to me after the 5K, he thought he was "fine," that he wasn't someone who needed help with any deeper issues—the octopus stuck to the floor would beg to differ. Being with Renn would mean taking on pain he wasn't even willing to admit existed.

He started pacing and shaking his head. When he looked at me, his beautiful eyes were glassy. "Don't do this, Sadie. Please." He reached out, and I backed away, almost faltering when I saw his expression, how much hurt that movement caused him.

"I'm not in the right place now, Renn. Think of it like this, if you were trying to make spaghetti, no matter how much you liked it and how much you wanted to make it, no matter how good you were at mastering the recipe, you couldn't do it if you didn't have any pots, or a kitchen. A solid base to build from."

"And you're saying this is a world where you couldn't just drive to Olive Garden? There's always a workaround, Sadie. I can be patient. But I don't want to be apart."

I put my hand on his shoulder. "Renn, I'm not ready. If we do this now, we will fail. Do you want a relationship with someone who is always waiting for the other shoe to drop? I was ready to walk out that door earlier today when you were just understandably nervous. How I am now, I always assume the worst. Give me time, and when I come back to you, I'll be better."

Renn stopped pacing and rubbed his hands aggressively over his face, pulling his fingers down his cheeks. "When?"

"I'm not sure. Not too long. But if you want to move on in the meantime, I'll understand."

"What?! Fuck no! Do you have any idea how long I've waited to feel this way about someone?" He reached for me and pulled my hands to his chest. "I'll tell you how long, Sadie. Forever. That's how long. Because I have never had this kind of connection with anyone. Never even came close."

"I'm sorry," I stuttered. *I feel the same way.* His earnest plea had me reconsidering, but I knew I was doing the right thing.

"What are the rules here, Sadie? Can I text you? Email you?"

"Maybe give it a few weeks, and then, yes?" It sounded arbitrary even to my own ears, but I hadn't exactly had time to create a rulebook once I'd made this decision. "I haven't got all the answers right now. I'm just saying I need space to figure it out. And it seems like you have plenty to deal with."

"Sadie, I want you to know that I don't agree with this. Not even a little bit. I wish you could see us the way I do." He stepped back. "When you can, I'll be waiting."

"That was such a perfect thing to say, Renn."

"But it didn't change your mind?"

I smiled sadly at him before answering, "No."

He groaned in resignation. "Every part of me wants to convince you to stay right now. But I also don't want to be like Henri the prick. I want to respect that you've decided."

"Thank you." I started gathering my things for the third time that day, knowing I'd actually be making it out the door. "I'll see you soon, Renn."

"Sadie?"

"Yeah?"

He walked over to me and reached out a hand, tucking a strand of hair behind my ear. I closed my eyes and angled my face into his touch. Renn stared at me, running his thumb back and forth across my cheek. Finally, he whispered, "Can I kiss you before you go?" His thumb swept from my cheek to brush across my lips. "Just once."

I didn't have the resolve to deny him. Or myself. "Yes."

Renn moved his left hand against my lower back, pressing me into his thighs. His right hand moved from the side of my face to my neck, the light scratch of his fingernails causing goosebumps as he twined his fingers in the hair at my nape. He held my chin at an angle, and I surrendered to his embrace. Thankfully, no memories came forward to ruin the moment. As Renn's eager mouth came down on mine, I experienced only its voracious inquiry, so soft yet so demanding against my own.

His tongue ran against the seam of my lips, and I opened for his sensual assault. He moaned into my mouth with a sound of sheer carnality. The kiss was long and deep, tongues tangling in a delicious give and take. I brought my hands up against Renn's chest, twisting at his shirt as I pulled our lower halves together. The outline of his erection pressed firmly against my belly, and my heart hammered at the sensation. I felt sweet relief when Renn nudged his knee between my legs, allowing me to press against his thigh. We held like that for a few minutes, enjoying the taste and feel of one another as we explored the way our bodies fit together.

Eventually, Renn gentled the grasp of his palm on my neck and brought it back to my cheek. His other hand explored every notch of my spine as he worked it upward until he was holding my face on both sides. He continued to ravage my mouth, gradually less frantic, before slowing our kiss and breaking away completely. I blinked as we broke contact, panting and bringing a finger to my swollen lips, already missing him.

He kept our hands joined but stepped away. "Sadie. That was..." He didn't even try to hide it when he pushed a palm against his cock and breathed out. "Damn."

Words weren't needed. We both knew. I grabbed my things as I headed to the exit. "I have to go. Robbie's probably wondering where you are. We'll talk soon. Promise."

I practically hurled myself out the exit, not giving him a moment to say anything else, because after that voodoo he just did with his tongue, he might've been able to convince me. I was so glad I hadn't been afraid, that I'd finally experienced Renn's kiss.

I allowed myself a glance back as the door yawned, my view of the shop's interior closing like the shutter of a lens. Just as the latch snicked shut, a loud cracking sound broke the placidity of the moment, followed by Renn's exclamation of "Oh fuck!"

The telltale whoosh of the water almost brought me back inside. Was I a monster for leaving when he had so much to deal with? I had to believe I was doing the right thing. I sent a silent prayer for the plumber to arrive quickly at Studio Obscurum and kept walking.

"Sadie!"

I stopped by the side of the used Ford Escort I'd purchased a few months prior as Renn called out. His soaked white t-shirt displayed the outline of his chest, and he squeezed his damp hair as he ran over. Stopping in front of me, he reached out to put a hand on my wrist. He was breathing raggedly, though he'd only jogged a hundred feet.

"I know, Sadie. I know I need to let you go. But watching you walk out..."

He brought his hand to the back of my neck while fisting the other one at my hip. I closed my eyes and leaned into his touch before waving my arm up and down in front of him. "I'm so sorry about the ceiling. You have so much going on—"

"Don't worry about that right now. It's not important... This is." He moved his other hand until he was cradling my face on both sides, and I shuddered as he brought his mouth to mine. This kiss differed from the other. Whereas before it had been all heat, this time was more reverential as Renn pressed his lips firmly against mine, not invading, but showing me how much he cared. "I'm sorry. I couldn't let you walk away without—"

"I'm not changing my mind, Renn," I said gently, disentangling us. "But I'm also not sorry you kissed me."

"I just..." He pulled his clinging t-shirt away from his chest as he stepped back. "When you were leaving, I suddenly got terrified I'd never see you again."

"I meant what I said. Give me a chance to work through some things. I feel what you feel...the rightness of this. It's the timing that sucks. But I'm pretty sure the universe has plans for us, plans that don't include being strangers."

"You sound sure."

And in that moment, I was. "I am, Renn. And like I said, you can text me or send me funny memes or whatever. I just think we should avoid seeing each other or getting too heavy until I sort some things out."

He nodded in defeat. "I'll miss you."

I smiled at him, reassuring myself as much as the man I was probably falling in love with. "Don't miss me too much because I'll be back. Someday you'll pick up the phone, and I'll be on the other end. And I'll ask you to come to me."

Those words to Renn, I honestly meant them. I thought I understood our obstacles. I hadn't been lying when I'd said I believed we'd be together soon.

I wasn't a liar.

No. Not a liar.

I was an idiot.

I should have remembered that fate and circumstance don't always play nice in the sandbox. As I got into my car, still thrumming from Renn's kiss on my lips, I remembered I never checked those texts. Preparing for some inanity from Zach, I unlocked my phone.

CHAPTER

Fourteen

I **WANDERED DOWN THE** hallway of the apartment in search of coffee and some sort of painkiller. Every muscle in my body was sore. My knees were reminding me I was, as of today, thirty-four years old—and so were my joints. When Zach had encouraged me to go out running yesterday, I'd went ahead and done eight miles—a supremely dumb idea when it had been close to four months since I'd hit the pavement. But it felt good to run just for myself. I'd still heard Henri's critique in my head. *You need to pick up your feet, darling, you don't run as much as you lumber.* But I'd just kept going, until finally, he got quiet, and I believed for the first time since I'd left Boston six weeks ago that I had outrun him.

The euphoria hadn't lasted long. I'd gone back to the apartment and by the time I'd finished showering, the soreness had set in, Henri's monologues about the deficiencies of my thighs invading my thoughts.

That was to be expected, I guessed. Rome wasn't built in a day and all that bullshit. I'd seen a therapist yesterday and we'd clicked, so I was pretty sure I would start seeing her regularly. That was something. I'd also picked up a few shifts at Hal's this week and even had some fun there. My drinks had been slightly off at first, but eventually, I had sunk back into that bartender role like it was a favorite old sweater I'd rediscovered in the back of a drawer—a little dated, but still suitable.

When I got to the kitchen, Zach was already there, handing me a cup of coffee. "Happy birthday, doll!" He'd tied balloons to the dining chairs and a giant cardboard "34" was taped to the glass of the slider. Less cheerful was the scorched earth smell hanging in the air, its source being our kitchen garbage. I glanced at the offending object, not daring to raise the lid to investigate.

Zach shrugged. "What can I say? I thought you might want pancakes for your birthday breakfast. Then I remembered I don't know how to make them. Then YouTube failed me. So blame the 3-Minute Chef tutorials for your birthday bowl of cereal."

I kissed him on the cheek. "I love cereal. And it's the thought that counts. This day is already head and shoulders above my birthday last year." The one Henri forgot.

As I hunted down the Cap'n Crunch, Zach grew serious when he noticed the object in my grip.

"Did you turn it on yet today?"

I tightened my fingers around the iPhone I was clutching and shook my head. Zach looked at me sternly. "It might be time, doll. Your birthday seems like a good day to do it."

I considered my best friend's words as I glanced at my hand again. "He's been quiet the past few days. He probably doesn't even remember it's my birthday."

"Does it matter?"

I put the phone down on the counter, cereal forgotten, and started opening cupboards, looking for ibuprofen. "I guess not."

Did it matter if Henri remembered the day? With Zach's help, I'd managed to avoid replying to any of the hundreds of texts he'd sent me over the last six weeks. Part of my methodology was to keep my phone turned off whenever I was home or with Zach. My world had gotten so small there was no one else who might need to contact me urgently—hence, no definite need to have the phone on. The downside was that almost every time I'd powered it up, I'd had messages waiting from Henri.

In the beginning, there were unavoidable logistics to go through. Henri and I had been meshing our lives for almost a decade, after all. But I had stayed strong, handing the phone to Zach, who would reply from his own number, freeing me from having to communicate with Henri directly as we separated our accounts and organized having some of my things shipped from Boston. There wasn't much. Eight years, and I was down to only four suitcases of clothes, old photos and yearbooks, a few boxes of childhood mementos, and my parents' vinyl and concert tee collections.

But Henri had kept texting me. There were the "I'm sorry" texts, and the "Please let me explain" texts, and my personal favorite, the "You're the only girl I've ever loved" texts. But he also had other modes. There were bitter "You owe me a conversation" texts, and "It was just one fucking mistake" texts, "It meant nothing" texts, and the startlingly honest refrain of "I never meant for you to find out." Well, duh. *But I did find out, asshole. I did find out, and now I have red dress woman haunting my dreams.*

Since we'd sorted through the fundamentals, Zach had been after me to block Henri's number. He thought it was promising that I'd been able to keep myself from replying, but he didn't get why I still felt compelled to read them. I didn't fully understand it myself, except there was a part of me that kept expecting Henri would eventually stumble upon words that would somehow make it better, some magical text that would make it less humiliating that my boyfriend had knocked up another girl while we were together.

I kept rummaging around, still not finding something to cut the pain. "Zach, I didn't see any Tylenol or Excedrin or anything in the bathroom and I'm coming up blank here." I started opening drawers more aggressively, the ache in my knees intensifying. "Where the fuck do you keep the meds in this place?"

Zach came up behind me and reached over my head to a small cigar box on top of the cupboards. He pulled out a bottle of Aleve and handed it to me. "Thanks," I muttered, opening the bottle and swallowing a pill with a sip of coffee.

"You're welcome." He walked over to my cell phone on the counter and poked it gingerly with his index finger, as though it might detonate. "How about a change of subject?" He leaned against the sink. "I got you something for your birthday."

I watched him as he turned toward the fridge. "Please don't tell me you got a cake, Zach."

"Doll, c'mon. I would never. I'm your best friend, so I know about your irrational prejudice against cake."

"It's not irrational at all. The cake industry has scammed the world. What's not to hate? A dry, crumbly slab that's not sweet enough covered by a layer of thick paste that's way too sweet." I shuddered. "Cake is trash."

Zach smiled at me. I returned the gesture because it was in moments like these that we both realized it was possible for me to gain back my feistier pre-Henri self. I just needed to figure out who my post-Henri self was.

"Well, then you'll be happy it's not cake. I bought you five different flavors of Ben & Jerry's, and we can stick a candle in one of those whenever you want." He opened the freezer and pointed at the colorful pints. "However, what I was going to grab was this."

He reached past the fridge to the small desk next to it and produced a shiny gold gift bag from a drawer. He handed it to me and I peeked inside, eventually pulling out what I'd initially mistaken for a live flower, but upon closer inspection realized was a delicate wood carving. It was just larger than my fist, with a yellow center so vibrant it almost glowed. Each of the delicate petals was narrowly oblong, coming to sharpish points, and painted in a palette of deep blues, with the color saturated at the tips.

"What is it?" I asked.

"It's a lotus. There was an artist selling these at the Farmer's Market last week and it reminded me of you. It's supposed to symbolize strength, or something like that. And she said each of these carvings is one of a kind."

I held the lotus closer to my face and inspected all its intricate nooks and folds. It seemed fragile, but once in my hand, I realized it had some weight to it. My eyes filled with tears and gratitude for Zach's gesture. I walked into his embrace, and he held me loosely as I breathed out. "Thank you so much. For this flower. But mostly for believing in me."

Zach leaned back, and I imagined he was about to say something equally sentimental, but the loud bang of a door slamming on the other side of the apartment saved us from getting too maudlin.

I raised an eyebrow. "Zachy, did you forget to send your hookup home last night?"

"What?" He held up his hands. "It was late and it seemed rude to make him grab an Uber. I don't mind a sleepover as long as he understands it's a one-off."

"Does he?"

"Definitely." Zach winked at me. "A very flexible one-off."

"Gross."

One-off came out of the bedroom at that moment and walked into the kitchen. Apparently Zach's hospitality didn't extend to loaning his shower because this guy still had makeup smudged around his eyes and had tossed on the same rumpled crop top and slashed jeans ensemble he'd worn yesterday, confirming my suspicion that Zach had met him out clubbing. One-off looked at me standing practically in Zach's arms and his face flushed.

I stepped away from my friend, pushing him against the counter. "Don't worry," I said. "I'm just the roommate."

One-off nodded at me and gave Zach a kiss on the lips, slapping his butt as he made his way out the door, evidently not seeing the necessity of actual words. I grinned at Zach. "Someday, you're going to find someone that you want a two-off with, or god forbid, a three-off."

"Someday, doll."

Zach and I had Ben & Jerry's for breakfast, and he did put a candle in the Cherry Garcia. But I had no special wish for my birthday. I asked the universe for the same thing I'd been hoping for since New Year's—to get over Henri and figure out what the heck I wanted to do with my life. I was sitting on a biology degree, but one of the few things I felt certain about was that I had no desire to do anything with it. I also knew I didn't want to be a bartender forever. Beyond that, career goals eluded me. I was just starting to recognize how catastrophic my family's and Henri's mistreatment had been to my well-being, and this had led to the vague thought that I'd like to somehow help people for a living, but I hadn't narrowed it further than that.

There was also another idea that had been on my mind, something that seemed more manageable than mapping out a whole life plan. It wouldn't radically alter the trajectory of my existence, but it was a small thing I could do now that Henri wasn't exerting control over every facet of my life.

"Zach?"

"Hmm?"

"I've been considering getting a tattoo."

Zach had been delivering a bite of mint chip to his mouth but paused mid-arm raise. "A tattoo? That's a little out of left field, isn't it?"

"Not exactly. I've always kind of wanted one, even when I was in college. I just never pulled the trigger. It was a 'someday' sort of thing. Then, when I was with Henri, he completely vetoed the idea, so I gave up even thinking about it."

"Okay." Zach steepled his fingers. "I'm not a tattoo guy, but hey, it's your skin if you want to get one."

"You say that so lightly, but you have no idea how hard it has been to take back my body. Henri would *hate* me getting a tattoo."

"I don't think that's a good reason to permanently disfigure yourself."

"It's not disfigurement." I laughed. "I'm not gonna get a winky emoji or something stupid like that. It'll be something beautiful. Meaningful. And it's not about Henri. Knowing he wouldn't approve is just a pleasant bonus."

"Like I said, it's your body, doll. The more you imbibe that, the better you'll be. Do you have any ideas about a design?"

"No. I haven't thought that far ahead." Then I looked at the wooden lotus sitting proudly on the table. "But I'm starting to feel inspired."

ZACH HAD LEFT for Hal's by the time I snatched my phone off the counter. I took it into my room and sat on the bed, moving the pillows to create a wall behind my back to lean against. I palmed the device, flipping it nervously several times before pressing my thumb against the power button and bracing for whatever might come. As it fired up, I heard the familiar pings alerting me there were texts waiting. Pushing aside the knot of dread in my stomach, I was pleasantly surprised to see happy birthday messages from a few old college acquaintances, as well as one from Larry, Hal's grumpy owner.

But, of course, Henri's name also popped up. And there were more than a few messages.

FEBRUARY 12, 2014

8:01 p.m.

HENRI: Darling I really hope you'll call and let me wish you a happy birthday for real. I miss your beautiful voice. I'm so sorry about everything.

8:04 p.m.

HENRI: Remember your 29th birthday? I took you to Hawaii. Bought you that silver necklace. I hope you'll remember things like that and call me back.

10:58 p.m.

HENRI: How long are you going to keep punishing me? I miss you so much. We belong together. I'm never going to love anyone like I love you, and I don't think you're ever going to love anyone as much as me either. Why are you just throwing us away?

11:31 p.m.

HENRI: I've gotta be honest. I am impressed at how long you've gone without talking to me. But I think it's time, don't you? You owe me a conversation, Sadie. We were together a long time. I deserve a conversation.

FEBRUARY 13, 2014

5:06 a.m.

HENRI: Sorry about that last one. I am trying to give you space. But it's hard. We belong together. It was just one fucking mistake. Do I deserve to be punished forever because of one fucking mistake?

6:52 a.m.

HENRI: *Happy Birthday GIF of Michael Scott at his desk*

7:22 a.m.

HENRI: I love you so much. I'm never gonna stop. I wish I was there for your birthday. I want to be with you so badly. I miss you.

I looked down at my phone. I read the messages. Then I read them again. And again. After that, I indulged in one of my favorite recent hobbies—responding to Henri's texts in my mind. I put my phone down, so I wouldn't be tempted to let any of my feelings come out of my fingertips, but goddamn, did I get murderous with my thoughts.

Miss my beautiful voice? When did you even once tell me you liked my voice? My twenty-ninth birthday? You mean the one in Hawaii where you worked the whole time and bought me the world's ugliest necklace, telling me I had "lowbrow" taste for preferring the cool beaded one sold by the beach? Punishing you? Seriously? I'm the one who got humiliated. I'm the one who was lied to! And I didn't throw us away, asshole. You did that all on your own when you got your dick wet outside the house. And apparently forgot a condom. How about the three days I spent sweating, waiting for test results to make sure you hadn't given me some terrible STI? Owe you a conversation? I don't owe you shit. One fucking mistake? No. Just no. Letting the car run out of gas on the highway. That's a mistake. Putting sour cream on your bagel because you grab the wrong container from the fridge. That's a mistake. Having a celebratory fuck with the HR intern after closing a big deal because your girlfriend has her period isn't a mistake. It's a fucking fork in the road. For all of us.

As angry as I was, Henri could still set me back. Despite everything, there was a part of me that responded to his entreaties, that craved his happiness. Did I owe him a conversation? Did I owe him a chance? I understood objectively that the answer was a hard no, but if I kept going this way, I knew his sorries would eventually supersede my anger. My rage would fade, and when it turned to loneliness, or boredom, or fatigue—how vulnerable would I be to him?

It was something I understood deep down. Henri could wreck me. I had been strong until now, but someday he might find the right words. The words that would have me overlooking all his transgressions, all the poison he'd unleashed into my life.

I went into the kitchen and grabbed my lotus, placing it on the bed next to my phone. I paced and fidgeted, huffing and internally cursing at how difficult this was. And it was *hard*. It took ten minutes. But, finally, with one glance at the wooden flower, I picked up the phone and gave myself the best birthday present I could.

He had put it plainly in his last text. He would never stop. So, I had to stop.

I blocked Henri.

FEBRUARY 13, 2015

4:01 p.m.

UNKNOWN: Darling it's Henri. When I figured out you'd blocked my number I was angry, but I finally got it through my head that you were done with us for a while. It impressed me. I didn't think you had it in you. But it's time. I've screwed around enough and it's been fun this past year but mostly it reminded me that I want to be with you. That hasn't changed. It's hard for me to imagine that you don't want to be with me too.

4:04 p.m.

UNKNOWN: I'll be in Los Angeles for work next month and I want to see you. I need to see you. You owe me more than this silence. We have things to say to one another.

4:08 p.m.

UNKNOWN: I'll apologize again and again if that's what it takes. I know I screwed up. But I can't say I'm sorry for my son. I want you to meet him. I want us to be a family. I want to tell you I'm sorry, but then I want to tell you how much I love you and how much I want us to be together. I want us to move on from this mistake. We were good before darling. We can be good again.

4:11 p.m.

UNKNOWN: Happy Birthday Sadie. You can't pretend we didn't happen. I'm never going to stop loving you. Never. What do I have to do to make you understand? What do I have to do to get you back? We belong together

PART

Two

CHAPTER
Fifteen

"**S**ADIE."

"Renn."

I blinked and he came into focus. Even in a skeleton uni-tard and full-face makeup, I knew. He was my Renn. I reached behind myself to grab a table, worried I might crumple under the weight of my shock. He raised his arm as though to steady me, but pulled back at the last second, pushing the hood off his head. He ran his fingers through his hair in a gesture so familiar it made my breath hitch.

"You said that someday..." Renn closed his eyes and slowly opened them. "You said that someday I'd pick up the phone, and you'd be on the other end...and you'd ask me to come to you."

"I remember." I surprised myself by getting the words out, whispered as they were. It felt like I'd lost the ability to speak.

"Somehow I wasn't picturing this." He waved his hand back and forth between us and then was silent for a few moments before beginning to pace. "I wasn't picturing it would be eight months until I heard your voice again."

His tone rose at the end of that statement, and I could see he was working hard to maintain equilibrium. He dragged a hand across his face. I digested the evidence of his pain, his ragged breaths and ice-laden words. The accusatory gleam in his eyes. I gripped the table harder.

He ceased pacing and waving, turning to face me. "Sadie, I've had fifteen minutes in the car to get myself together, to think of what I wanted to say to you...but...I've got nothing...I just need to know..." He pushed one balled-up fist into his other hand. "...you...ghosted me...just...why?"

Hurt etched across his tight jaw, naked on his face. He deserved answers. And more. A low moan across the room interrupted us. *Shit! Blanketcape.*

"Your...mom...is over there." I was still in disbelief, processing. He'd had fifteen minutes. I'd had zero. Renn was here. And Blanketcape was somehow his mother, passed out on the floor at Hal's. I walked him to her. "I told her she could sit up in a chair, and I offered the couch in the office, but she just wanted to stay there. She seems okay. Not totally blacked out or anything. It doesn't look like she got sick either, so that's good."

I kept babbling as he gently lifted the woman from her slump. Getting tugged upright revived her. She stood on her own as he led her, stumbling toward the door.

"Car's outside?" she slurred, and Renn nodded.

"Can you make it there, Mom? I just need a minute."

She bobbed her head in lethargic reply and reached her palm up to pat Renn's cheek. "You're a good boy, Tom. I knew you'd come."

"Yeah, Ma. I'll be out in a sec. Door's open." She tottered toward an SUV parked near the entrance as Renn and I watched from the doorway.

"What's your mom's name?" I asked as I stepped away and busied myself collecting pool cues. It seemed disrespectful to keep thinking of Renn's mother as Blanketcape.

"Sheryl."

"I hope Sheryl is okay."

Renn came over to stand in front of me, stern expression communicating he wasn't about to be distracted. I shivered. He was so close.

So close, and so fucking beautiful I wanted to cry. God, I'd missed him.

"My mom will be fine. I should have known she'd come here." His tone sharpened.

I twisted my hands together, leaning back against a pool table. "What do you mean?"

His already level gaze became laser focused. "I asked you why you disappeared—"

"I know you did, Renn, and I absolutely want to tell you—" He raised his hand up.

"I think it would be easier to have that conversation if I answer your question first."

"My question?"

"About why I should have realized my mother would come here."

"Um...okay."

"Because, Sadie..." He wasn't touching me, but I sensed the heat of his breath as he gritted out, "I've been feeling like a chump for almost a year, so confused, and sometimes I try to talk things out with my mom, if I can catch her when she's sober."

He stepped away, reaching behind himself to rest his hands where back pockets would be, eyeing me warily. His face looked harder than it had in February. Still, that glow he had, the inner light that had drawn me in from the first moment, shone through resolutely. I owed him an explanation, but I hadn't been prepared to give him one today. Keeping my knees from buckling was all I could manage.

Renn opened and closed his mouth a few times, hands still clenched above his hips. Eventually, he resumed.

"I told my mom the story of how I met a beautiful girl. How I thought this girl and I had something pretty fucking great, and that, even with everything going on in my life, she made me believe things would be okay. So, I finally worked up the courage to tell this girl, and she said she felt the same, that I made her feel okay too, but she needed time to figure things out. And she said she'd talk to me in a little while. I was expecting a few weeks, maybe a few months. But that isn't what happened. I sent some texts. An email. Waiting for her reply. And guess what? Nothing...no communication at all. So...I swallowed my pride and reached out again. One text. And another. All unread. On the last try I got a 'new phone, who dis?' and I realized that my beautiful, perfect girl had changed her number."

He took a breath and strode a few lengths of the pool table, again struggling to contain his emotions, and I froze at the evidence of my miscalculation. I'd looked at the situation sideways for so long that I'd missed what had been in front of me the whole time. Renn. Hurting. I'd been waiting for the right time to talk to him, waiting to feel brave and worthy, while he had just been...waiting.

Renn got himself in check and stopped pacing, finishing his story. "I told my mom how I finally had to give up and move on. Because I can take a fucking hint. But I also told her that sometimes I wonder if I should just come to Hal's on Westwood, where this girl is a bartender, and ask her what happened. And I guess my mom decided to come see for herself who twisted up her son so bad."

Renn's shoulders heaved as he met my eyes, sadness and distress tangling in his face. But between his hurt and his anger, it was clear which sentiment dominated his tender heart.

He deserved answers. But where to start?

"Renn, I..." I whispered, stopping to gather my words.

"Before you say anything," Renn spoke tentatively. "I just need you to admit that what we had was real. If you're about to tell me I imagined how special we were to each other, then you can just save it. I won't believe you. Whatever your reasons for ghosting me...I wasn't making it all up in my head."

I wanted to pull him into my arms. But I didn't have the right. His doubts. His anguish...however inadvertently, I'd caused them.

"Renn, I would never try to convince you what we had wasn't real. Never. Because it would be a lie. I know I did things. Pushed you into a corner. Stopped communicating. But I wouldn't lie to you." He was upset, but I knew he wanted it to make sense. I approached cautiously, testing his instinct to retreat. When he remained in place, I hoped it meant there was an opening for him to understand my actions. I reached out to grab his hand and held our palms together, meeting no resistance, aching at our first touch in eight months.

He looked down at our joined hands before I forced his gaze back to mine. "Please hear me when I tell you it was real." I took a deep breath because I owed him the full truth. "I was falling in love with you. Since the day we met, it's only ever been you."

He blinked and a strangled sound came out of his throat—a cry of relief muted by the release of a long, pent-up breath. I answered him with a nod and a silent tear, after which the wheels came off. He tugged me to him and crushed my torso to his, our twin black bodysuits turning us into one mass in the dark. His warm breath skimmed my ear as he folded me in his embrace, rocking us. "I know I should be mad, but I can't not touch you. Not when you're finally close to me. Why? Why did you shut me out?"

I whispered back against his cheek, "It's a long story, but to be honest, all the reasons that made so much sense at the time seem insignificant right now."

A horn blaring from the parking lot broke the spell.

"Shit. I need to get my mom home." Renn glanced toward the door and then back at me. "Can I have your number?" I pulled away from him to find a pen. I gave him my new cell number, written on a napkin like it was the '90s. No room for a bulky phone in my catsuit. He smiled. "I'm going to text you later tonight. Okay?"

"More than okay. I do want to explain everything."

Renn stood and faced me, fully collected as he spoke in that deep voice I'd missed so much. "And I want to hear it. I need to hear it. You hurt me these past months—"

"I'm so sor—"

"Nope, let me finish. I don't need an apology. And you know I'm not big on hashing out my feelings. I'm not saying I'm over it, or that I'll forgive you instantly, but I want to hear you out. I want to get there. The reason it hurt so damn much is that we were amazing together. I've missed having you in my life."

With that, Renn grabbed both of my cheeks and kissed me on the lips. Closed mouth, possessive, a possible promise of things to come, before he headed out into the parking lot. And I felt like Sleeping Beauty waking up from a hundred years of sleep.

The sound of a throat clearing in the hallway to the back room startled me from my reverie. Zach stood there, leaning in the doorway, munching on popcorn. He grinned at me before putting the bag down and doing a few slow claps. "That was quite the scene, doll. He looks even more delicious than before. And what do you know—he's just as interested in you as he ever was. Thank God. Maybe you can stop being such an Eeyore now."

"I'll stop being Eeyore when you stop being the judgmental baby from *Family Guy*." I threw a bar towel at him. "Also, where the fuck did you get popcorn?"

November 1, 2015

I WENT HOME for what amounted to a quick shower and a cat nap since I had to be at Hal's before noon. When I arrived, Zach was already there, getting set up for the day. I couldn't believe the Halloween party had been last night, and I was back just six hours later. I was tired but running off the adrenaline high I'd gotten seeing Renn again so unexpectedly. He'd texted, asking to come by and see me later tonight. I'd replied that I was off around nine and would love to hang out after.

I was locking my purse up in the safe behind the bar when I noticed Zach using the electric air pump to blow up a large balloon-like decoration. He was cursing with his efforts as the mammoth inflatable kept collapsing on itself, different sections creasing and folding to prevent success. Finally, it rose, and I found myself face to face with some sort of giant, irritated-looking bird.

"What the heck is this?" I bopped its hooked beak.

"It's Blitz."

"It's what now?"

"Blitz. You know—the Seahawks mascot."

I groaned. Would the madness never end? Must we have a giant bird balloon in the middle of the bar?

I gave Blitz a poke in the nose.

"Okay—so angry bird here is the Seahawks mascot, but why exactly is he in the bar?"

"Well, I think I have my big idea for Hal's."

"Your amazing idea is to have a giant blow-up Blitz?"

"No. Hear me out. There is a massive Seahawks fan base in LA, lots of folks that live here and travel. People like me. There are bars all over Southern California for certain fandoms. I want us to be a Seahawks bar."

I hadn't been working at Hal's too often lately, so this was the first I'd heard of this. "You want people to come to the bar from Seattle?"

"No, you're not listening. There are plenty of local fans, and if we tell them this is the place where they can be with other Hawks fans—they're called 12s by the way—they'll make a special effort to watch the games here."

"And you think that will work?"

"Yep. You're aware I've been trying to figure out ways to make Hal's more profitable." Zach picked up the fully-inflated Blitz and walked to the front, placing the frowning fowl decisively by the door. "The Halloween party last night was successful—we just need stuff like that, specific reasons for folks to be here. I don't have the money right now to really do up the bar, but if we can just get Seahawks fans here every Sunday to fill the place, that will go a long way."

It wasn't the worst idea I'd ever heard, and as Zach started droning on and on about how he'd already put out on social media that Hal's was the official SoCal bar of Seahawks fans, while he ran around covering the bar in three-by-five neon green and navy flags with giant logos on them, it was impossible not to be charmed by his enthusiasm. It couldn't hurt to try. And as I pulled on the snug-fitting number twelve jersey he gave me, I hoped it would work.

It worked.

The game started around 1:30. The Seahawks were playing the Cowboys in Dallas and customers started rolling into Hal's just after opening to find a spot. Thank goodness Zach had invested in several large flat screens. I knew those TVs were the reason Hal's was still dealing with peeling paint in the ladies' restroom and HVAC issues in the office, but as dozens of folks swarmed into the bar, all dressed in Seattle jerseys, I began to see Zach's vision.

Toward the end of the game, Teddy came in. He gave Zach a huge congratulatory kiss across the bar and greeted me as I rinsed glasses in a moment between customers.

"Hey, doll. What do you think of all this? Pretty great, right?"

"Well, it seems like a hit, so that's good. Other than it's crazy how less than twenty-four hours ago this was a Halloween party and I hadn't even heard of this idea."

"Yeah, he's been sitting on it for a while, ever since finalizing the purchase. He came home early this morning and was basically like, 'I'm going for it.' Stayed up all night making posts on Facebook and Twitter in Seahawks groups and whatnot."

A cheer among the patrons marked the end of the game as Seattle secured a thirteen to twelve victory.

"What a relief for Zach to have a firm plan for Hal's. Especially now that you two have something so exciting to look forward to." I winked at Teddy, thinking of the news they'd shared with me a few days ago.

Watching Zach's dreams come to fruition was surprisingly emotional. He was the closest thing I had to family, and our friendship would always be a priority in my life. Now that I was standing taller on my own, it was nice to flip our dynamic. I loved being his support system for a change.

I paused a few hours later in my post-game cleaning to congratulate him. "Hey genius—I'll admit this was a good idea, but you're definitely gonna need more help."

"Yeah. I'll hire someone this week. You liked that woman, Cyd, right? For now, we'll stick with being closed Mondays and Tuesdays, unless the Hawks are on *Monday Night Football*."

"Wow. Okay, then. I guess you're really doing this. Are you going to paint the bar that hideous neon green color?"

Zach shrugged and came up behind me, wrapping my arms in a hug and speaking earnestly into my hair, "Thanks so much for today, doll, and last night, even with the costume fail. I couldn't have done it without you."

"You know I'd do anything for you, babe." I turned in his embrace to tell him directly, "Even though I'm moving on from bartending—minus the occasional hellacious Halloween party—working here these past few years really helped me regain my sense of self. I'll never forget it. I'm so glad it's going well for you at Hal's. And with Teddy. You deserve all of this...happiness."

"You deserve to be happy too, doll."

I sighed, pulling away.

"Seriously, Sadie. I know you've gotten busier with school these days. Working, running, therapy. But you deserve love in your life, too. I saw the way you-know-who looked at you this morning. It was total fire. And it's tough to look sexy in skeleton makeup and a unitard. But your man was doing it."

"He's not my man."

"Don't kid yourself, doll. That's exactly what he wants to be. And I think he'll understand if you tell him what happened."

"Don't jinx it, okay, Zach? We're supposed to talk tonight and then we'll see."

"Alright. But you can't stop me from rooting for you two."

"I'd expect nothing less than your nosy ass all up in my business...but, Zach?"

"Yeah?"

"Can you explain to me one thing?"

"What's that?"

"Why the hell is Blitz so pissed off?"

I WAS DEAD on my feet by eight o'clock, and Zach told me to knock off early since our crowd had thinned out. Gary came in with paperback in hand and took his usual seat at the bar, glaring at nearby football fans. I pulled him a pint of his usual as my last act of service before texting Renn.

Nine o'clock rolled around and I hadn't received a text back. A low knot formed in my stomach when 9:30 passed, still with no word, and then ten o'clock arrived with more silence. I worried Renn had changed his mind. Maybe he'd decided I didn't warrant forgiveness, or even a conversation.

The instinct to throw my hands up and head home to Fig Newtons and Diet Dr. Pepper was strong. But this time, I wanted to do better. I'd rather hurt my pride than hurt Renn.

10:14 p.m.

ME: Hey Renn, I thought we were meeting up after my shift? I'm still here at the bar.

10:58 p.m.

ME: I'm really sorry I didn't get to see you tonight. I hope everything is okay. I'm going to head home. Please text me when you can.

11:49 p.m.

RENN: I'm so sorry. Robbie isn't here and I've been trying to find him. He should have been home for dinner. I'm sorry I didn't get to see you as well.

ME: Oh no that's terrible. I hope he's okay!

RENN: I'm sure his friend Ryder knows where he is but I can't get a hold of his mom.

ME: Fingers crossed you find him.

MONDAY

1:33 a.m.

ME: I just wanted to let you know I'm heading to bed. Please text me once you know Robbie is fine, no matter how late. Thinking about you.

2:11 a.m.

RENN: We found him.

RENN: When Lydia got home Robbie was in their basement. I'm going to pick him up now.

8:30 a.m.

ME: Just woke up. I'm so happy he's okay.

RENN: Dropped him off at school. I am so angry but he's having a rough time right now. It's hard to know what to do.

ME: I'm sure you're doing the best you can.

RENN: Thanks for saying that. And I appreciate you texting with me tonight. It helped.

RENN: I don't want to scare you away again. There's a lot going on in my life (obviously). But I still want to see you.

ME: I don't scare as easily now. I want to see you too.

RENN: Can't wait.

CHAPTER
Sixteen

DRIVING TO RENN'S neighborhood in an older area of Pasadena was a bit like going back in time. I'd grown up in the San Fernando Valley, and this looked similar, mainly ranch-style family homes with manicured lawns and cars pushed out to the driveway by overstuffed garages.

The Stollers' house was single-story, painted dusky cream, with rust-colored trim and shutters. A brick walkway led to oak-paneled double front doors. The well-kept yard was simple, just a lawn and some decorative rocks in the built-in planter boxes—no trees, flowers, or hedges—as though aesthetics had been abandoned in favor of utility.

I pulled into the driveway, per Renn's instructions, and steeled myself as I headed toward the entrance, ringing the doorbell with more than a little trepidation.

My tension deflated at being greeted by an enthusiastic Gage, who swung the door open wide and pulled me inside, heedless of the fact we hadn't seen each other for months.

"Sadie, Sadie, I lost two more teeth since you saw me last time!" He pointed to his wide grin, minus two incisors.

I'd expected Renn and was happily surprised to see this kid again instead. "Awesome, Gage! Those look like some big tooth gaps. I hope you got your money's worth."

He was about to answer me when Renn came up behind him, out of breath. "He has definitely used the business of losing his baby teeth to practice his negotiation skills...or should I say, extortion skills." Renn ruffled his brother's head. "He beat me to the door. I was trying to tidy the house a little and I guess I didn't hear the bell."

"That's okay. Also, don't worry about cleaning up for me."

Renn looked down at Gage. "Hey, buddy. There's pizza for dinner in the den. You can go wash up and grab some. Your brother will be home soon. I need to talk to Sadie."

Gage nodded and traipsed off as I came further into the space. Whereas the outside gave an impression of austerity, the inside revealed the opposite.

The kitchen was to the side of the entry, its almond-colored appliances old but chic in a retro sort of way, complementing the decorative baskets tacked up to the walls. There were at least a dozen child's drawings of different sizes on every available wall and cupboard surface, stuck up haphazardly with blue painter's tape at Gage's eye-level. Renn saw me noticing and shrugged. "Gage found the tape and put them all up himself one day. He was very proud."

I examined the papers and smiled. "He should be. These are some impressive renderings of the Ninja Turtles." One drawing was tacked on the refrigerator with a magnet, next to school photos of the boys, and a few spelling tests with "100%" marked in red pen at the top.

Past the kitchen was a living and dining room area. The home was too old to be an open concept, but at some point, an owner had hacked away at it, leaving only a half wall between the two spaces. On the worn dining room table was a camo backpack crammed with books and papers, overflowing onto the chipped wood. An electric pencil sharpener sat atop mismatched placemats as the centerpiece, along with a mason jar half full of cloudy water and paint brushes. A cheap plastic shelf sagged in one corner, weighed down with papers, art supplies, and comics. The other corner housed an easel, complete with a drop cloth-covered canvass. Like the kitchen, the dining area had many drawings taped up pell-mell. The artistic chaos belied the white walls, and I sensed the distinct flow of creative energy. I'd had the same feeling the first time I'd walked into Studio Obscurum.

Renn put his hand behind his head, almost apologetically. "We don't eat in this room. Usually in the den. But Gage loves to draw and paint, so we do that in here a lot. Robbie used to...but not so much anymore."

We already had things we needed to talk about without opening another potentially hot topic in Robbie. I settled on, "You paint?"

"Occasionally. I usually draw, but sometimes paints and canvas are more appropriate for my ideas."

This became clear when we reached the living room, the one area that appeared as though they'd put some care into the décor. Framed paintings stood out beautifully tetrised along the walls, divergent themes and styles made coherent through matching black frames. Books crammed a shelf on one wall—everything from old leather-bound heirlooms to newer paperbacks—and a checkerboard table in the corner housed a half-done *Star Wars* Lego set.

Sandwiched among the books were photographs in dollar store picture frames. There were many of the boys, most recent, but my curiosity drew me to the older-looking pictures, where I got my first glimpse of Renn's father. There was Thomas standing next to a '90s version of Pete, holding toddler Renn beside an A-board sign that read "Studio Obscurum, Now Open." Another one of Thomas had him leaning his head near a woman lying in a hospital bed holding a newborn. Since a young Robbie and a teenage Renn were also in the picture, I surmised this was the day Gage was born. I blanched a bit when I thought it might have been Pete who'd taken the picture.

My musings must have been evident on my face because Renn volunteered, "I wish I could say it's gotten easier, but it hasn't. I meant what I said that day about trying to understand where Pete was coming from, but it's been difficult."

Renn was so reluctant to acknowledge when he was hurting. That seemingly hadn't changed. I wanted to offer my support, but we weren't there yet.

One side of the living room led to a long hallway with five doors. At the end of the hall was another open room, and I heard Gage laughing at the TV in there. All the doors were ajar except one. Renn pointed to it. "That's Pete's room. He's been coming by more, like he said he would, but hardly ever sleeps here. Robbie still can't stand to be around him, and I don't push since he's having such a tough time with it all."

Poor Robbie. He was such a sensitive kid, just a little lost. I again had the instinct to help. I wanted Renn to lean on me, now that I believed I could handle it.

Renn gestured toward the couch and I lowered myself to the edge. He sat down next to me, leaving a half foot between us. It felt a lot more stilted than it had on Halloween, and at first, I couldn't think of how to begin. But I owed it to him to try.

"Renn, I just want to start by saying that, when I left on my birthday, I fully intended to get back in touch with you sooner..." I tapped on the armrest with my pointer finger. There was no good way to explain the next part. My insufficient words caught in my throat.

"What happened, Sadie? Just tell me."

I nodded. "In my car, I unlocked my phone and saw that I'd gotten some texts from Henri—" I closed my eyes briefly, thinking about those four awful messages from UNKNOWN.

"Oh."

"Um hmm. And...they leveled me in a way I couldn't have predicted."

He leaned forward, resting his elbows on his knees. "What do you mean?"

"I mean, I thought I was getting past most of the pain Henri had inflicted on me, but his texts pulled the one hurt lever I hadn't insulated myself from."

As I told Renn about Henri's words, and specifically about the son he mentioned, the nauseating twist of shame in my belly resonated as I attempted to explain my actions. After coming to Los Angeles, I'd spent a year working through my pain and anger in therapy. I'd been able to acknowledge that Henri had treated me poorly, gaslit me, cheated on me, and even that he'd gotten someone else pregnant while we were together. But, for reasons I was still discovering—most likely rooted in my own unhappy childhood—I hadn't allowed myself to consider the fact Henri would have a child out there, that the man who supposedly loved me went out and made a family with someone else. I couldn't deal with it, so I'd buried it. Refused to discuss it, even in therapy, at least not until recently. In the months after leaving Boston, while working through breakup logistics, I'd never permitted Zach to inquire about the baby. If I'd ever had a stray thought wondering whether it had been born, or if Henri was part of its life, I'd evicted that question ruthlessly from my brain. So, when those texts had come through, I'd been unprepared. He'd had a son. A son he apparently loved. And I'd felt more insignificant and taken advantage of than ever before. I'd been gutted.

"I felt dirty, Renn. It's not rational, but somehow the reality of that baby made me feel unlovable to a degree I can't even explain. The shame was unbearable. That anyone could want me after that, after I'd been made such a stupid fool, was too much to contemplate. I didn't feel whole. I just felt used. And I needed time to recover from that."

I watched him intently as I finished my recitation, leaning in and scooting my hips closer. His face grew pensive, and he ran his hand through his hair, falling back against the couch. His shoulders tensed and relaxed in turn as his thoughts wrestled across his features.

"I'm sorry, Sadie. I wish I could have been there to tell you just how amazing and loveable you are." He breathed out thickly, sitting up and grabbing both my hands. "But I have to ask, once you started to come back from this, why didn't you call me? It doesn't seem like you're in the same dark place now."

I nodded and squeezed his hands, so grateful he had reached for mine first. "Make no mistake, Renn. That dark place still comes to grab me sometimes, and it probably always will. Henri's texts absolutely savaged me. I had to stay focused to avoid derailing completely. I began school online. I got a day job and cut back my hours at Hal's to focus on my education. For months, I was in a semi-lifeless state, just going through the motions. I stayed busy with things I could do on autopilot to keep from spiraling again—school, work, running—better than hiding, but not really living, either. Time doesn't have a lot of meaning when you're in survival mode. In the back of my hazy mind, I vaguely knew I should call you, but I kept putting it off because I could never be sure if I was ready. I was just Henri's fool. Even these past few months, where I've started feeling more like myself again, I was worried you'd see me and instantly reject me. But I realized on Halloween that being rejected by you isn't the worst thing that could happen. Missing out on what we could have together is."

Renn frowned as something occurred to him. "Shit. And you didn't really call me this time, did you? Not on purpose."

"I suppose. But I'm glad things worked out this way." I ran my thumbs along the sides of his palms as we faced each other on the couch. "I'm grateful that your mom came into Hal's, that she gave us that push. Honestly, Renn, I thought about you every day. I'd look at my tattoo and think about being with you, all the times we laughed and talked. Those memories helped keep me sane."

He leaned down and rested his forehead against mine before replying. "I thought of you all the time, too. At first, it was fine, but then, after so long, thinking about you, instead of being with you, was... hard. I don't want just thoughts. I want you. Even if you're...dark."

He didn't sound angry, more like reconciled, and it seemed the most natural thing in the world then to lean into his arms. I nestled myself sideways in the crook of his shoulder. "I always thought I'd see you again. Even on Halloween, just a few hours before you showed up, Zach made a comment about how I needed to stop being scared of wanting you. I'm sorry I was afraid and waited too long. But you always had my heart."

"And you're ready now?"

I nodded. "I'm still scared, and I'm starting to accept I always will be, but if you'll have me, I'd like to try."

Renn chuffed out a laugh before reaching up to run a hand over my head. "Well, damn." A rumbly groan escaped him as he pulled on my arm and dragged me into his lap, splayed across his jeans and breathing into his plain white tee. His lemon tea tree oil scent invaded me. "I don't see how I could possibly stay mad at you when you put it out there like that. Also—even if this makes me a sucker—I probably would have forgiven you for anything. I've missed you that fucking much. It's really just a cherry on the sundae that you have a better reason than just changing your mind or having second thoughts about us."

"Really?" It was almost too much to hope for.

"Yeah. It'll probably be a while before I'm totally over those eight fucking months of silence, but it means something to know it wasn't because you didn't want me."

"Trust me, wanting you is not an issue."

We sat there for a moment, breathing each other in before he asked, "Did you see him? Henri? After he sent the texts?"

"Fuck no. I changed my number a week later. That's why I never got your messages. Zach texted him from his phone to tell him to stay away, said he'd knock him out if Henri came anywhere near me. For a while I was nervous he'd show up at the apartment or Hal's, but it never happened. It's possible those birthday texts I got were just him being a dick, or drunk texting. He's also seen Zach easily break up several bar fights, so maybe he took those warnings to heart. Whatever happened, I'm glad."

"Damn. I'm sorry you had to go through that."

"No, Renn. I'm sorry. For not realizing how much pain I was causing you. For believing the whole time I was working my way back to you without considering how my actions would look from your perspective—"

"It's alright."

"No. Just because you understand why I did it, doesn't make it alright." A fresh wash of regret came over me. Renn had had too much blind faith in me before, and I was going to make sure he knew what he was getting into this time. "I want you, but you need to realize that I'm still healing. My behavior was careless, and I have no excuse other than to say that I'm still learning how to be in a healthy relationship. I'm learning how to have a conflict without shutting down or running away. How to express my emotions and not just swallow everything. To share my burdens with someone and take on theirs in a balanced way. I developed some terrible coping tactics being with Henri—"

"Sadie, stop." His face softened as he pulled me closer. "It's okay." He folded me in his embrace, rubbing my back.

After several minutes of silence, I dared to murmur into his shoulder. "I might have had my reasons, but it doesn't change the fact that I hurt you."

Renn's expression grew thoughtful, and I held my breath as he replied in his deep, steady voice.

"I was hurt. But it's my choice to give you the benefit of the doubt. Those things you're working on aren't all of *you*, Sadie. Who you also are is the woman who helped me stay calm when I found out some terrible things about my uncle. You're the survivor who has been doing everything in her power to move on from emotional abuse and reclaim her life and future. You're the friend who is always there for Zach, and the badass who stood up to the PTSA mean girls at the 5K. You're the person who reignited my creativity, got me to laugh, listened to me talk. For a few short months, I felt like the most complete version of myself and the man I want to be." He tipped my chin with his pointer finger. "I see you, Sadie," he whispered, kissing the top of my head. "You're the woman I want to be with."

As usual, he'd said the perfect thing. Laying against him, I felt hopeful. I'd done the work since those texts, been religious about my therapy. Henri didn't live in my head anymore. I wasn't the girl who wanted to run away. Sheryl might have given us a push by showing up at Hal's, but I wouldn't squander this opportunity. No more letting my fears keep me from being happy. I was giving this relationship with Renn a real shot.

WE SAT LIKE that, with my legs across his knees like he was Santa Claus, for about ten minutes, enjoying the proximity, moving past the worst hurts of our separation.

Our conversation moved toward filling in the details of what had been going on in our lives the past eight months. I told Renn about my classes and my new coffee shop gig, both of which I loved, and updated him on Zach and Teddy, including the wonderful news that they had moved in together and were expecting a baby via surrogate.

"Wow. That's amazing. Zach is going to make one heck of a dad."

"I know. Teddy too. They're not talking about it much yet, since it's early days. Just found out a few weeks ago that it took. So if you see him, don't mention it."

Renn filled me in on the studio, including how the insurance money from the burst pipe situation had helped in the long run since it gave them capital to tackle some deferred maintenance projects. I knew things still weren't great with his family, but at least the business was doing well. He told me he'd visited his dad's gravesite for the first time since the funeral, but shut the topic down quickly after mentioning it, apparently just as reluctant as before to talk about his grief. His mentioning his dad brought something else to my mind.

"Hey, Renn?"

"Yeah?"

"Why does your mom call you Tommy?"

"Because that's my name."

"What?"

"I'm actually Thomas Stoller Junior. Renn is my middle name, my mom's last name. As a kid, everyone called me Tommy. When I got older, and especially after my dad married Mary, I wanted to distance myself a bit. I asked everyone to call me Renn. But my mom can't ever remember. She, um, drinks a lot. That's why my dad had custody when I was a kid. I only see her every now and then because she mainly just crashes on people's couches and doesn't always live in Los Angeles. There used to be more times she'd be sober, but it's rare now. She's basically been on a permanent bender since my dad died. When she calls me Tommy, I don't have the heart to correct her."

I knew Renn's mom must care about him. After all, she'd taken the time to come spy on me at work, even if she hadn't approached me.

"I'm sorry about your mom. And I'm sorry it hasn't gotten easier with Pete."

"I don't want to talk about that dipshit right now," Renn uttered with a surprising amount of vitriol. Taken aback, I leaned away to stare at him as he caught himself. "Shit. I didn't mean it to come out like that. I know you meant well. It's just been tough with him."

"I understand." I looked at Renn, again detecting the hardness I'd first noticed on Halloween. The set of his jaw, the tightness radiating from his arms—they hadn't been there when I'd left in February.

He shook his head and ran a palm over his face. "It's as though finding that card opened Pandora's box and everything just keeps getting more jacked. We're all on edge. Even Gage can sense something's up."

"That doesn't surprise me. He's smarter than most of the coeds that come into Hal's." I could only imagine how difficult it was for Renn worrying Pete might be Gage's biological father. "I've also seen enough soap operas and TV movies to know that eventually Gage is going to get some rare disease, making it necessary to find out what his actual genetics are. Are you still set on not getting the answer to that?"

Renn huffed. "I told Pete over the summer I thought he and I should find out, just to know. We don't need to tell the boys. He said he'd think about it but hasn't brought it up since. Honestly, I haven't had too much time to worry about it because I've got my hands full with Robbie. There's no predicting when he's gonna go off." Renn's eyes looked away, and I could see the strain on his forehead as he continued. "I'm finding it difficult to forgive Pete and all his choices, especially seeing how this has affected my brothers. I mean it when I say that I don't blame him for my dad's death, and I could even look past the affair with Mary—chalk it up to being none of my business—but everything he's done since she died, that's on him."

"Poor Pete. He really thought he was doing the right thing."

"Why are you defending him?"

"I'm not defending him. I just see it from his side, having experienced what it's like when you know you should behave differently, but just can't. My grandma used to say to me, 'Sadie, if you're in a hole, for God's sake, stop digging.' It's brilliant advice, but hard to do."

Renn looked agitated, like he wanted to argue. But his better angels prevailed because he sighed and wrapped his arms tighter around my waist, pulling me back to his chest. He fit his head into my neck and nuzzled in. "I'm glad you're here. I've missed you."

He grazed his lips over me, and my body came to life under his ministrations. The den was on the other side of the house, but I could hear the faint sounds of Gage's laughter, still smell the greasy pizza scent wafting from that direction, but all that faded as Renn captured my complete attention. He positioned one hand on my lower back to press me closer. His other hand gripped my jeans at my waist as his thumb slid underneath my thin cotton sweater. Moving his lips from my neck to my face, he didn't hesitate as he kissed me greedily, capturing my mouth as his hand continued its exploration from hip to belly, inching up toward my breasts.

I shivered as his callused palm pressed on my bare skin. Renn was possessive, confident, and every ounce of his desire was on display as he progressed his hand over my ribs and bra, resting his fingers on the collarbone exposed by my V-neck. He moved his lips lower, kissing my jaw and pulling down the sweater to mouth every inch of skin he could touch.

The tentative flick of his tongue to the valley of my chest woke me from pleasure to participation. I groaned and pushed the top of his head into my breasts, and he made a throaty noise as I dug my fingers into his scalp, tugging on the soft waves of his hair to pull him even closer. I surrendered to the overheated sensations, twisting my hand in his shirt before moving my hold lower to grip the erection straining against his zipper.

"Damn." He pulled away from me and glanced toward the den, where an oblivious Gage was still laughing at whatever was on the screen. Renn's chest was heaving, but he took a few deep inhales to calm himself before calling out, "Hey buddy—you doing okay in there?" I smiled at him as he caught his breath. He returned the grin, reaching out to place my hand back on his cock, encouraging me to apply pressure.

"I'm good," Gage shouted. "I've seen this episode before, you know."

I almost giggled as I continued to grasp Renn, moving my palm back and forth over his jeans. Absently, I took note that he was rather large down there, and I had the briefest flash of panic because *ohmygodholyshitballs I was touching Renn's dick and this was really happening and it felt so good and jesusfuckingchrist was I going to see him naked!!??* Damn, I craved seeing him naked. I gave another squeeze. Yup, still real.

"Hey, Gage, would you mind shutting the door? Sadie and I are trying to talk."

"Sure." From the corner of my eye, I saw Gage get up to close the square-paned French doors leading to the den.

Renn pulled my other leg over him, so I was straddling his lap. The breath whooshed out of me when he stood up. I hooked my legs together instinctively against his back, lacing my fingers behind his neck to steady myself. He captured my gaze with serious eyes. All traces of boyishness vanished as he growled out, "Sadie, I let you go before and I don't want to do that ever again. If you need me to go slower, I will, but I know what I want."

I tightened my legs around his middle, clinging to him like a koala. "Renn?"

"I want you in my bed."

CHAPTER

Seventeen

RENN HAD A firm grip on my ass, locking our lips together as he carried me toward the hallway. It felt amazing, but I hadn't expected us to move so quickly. I thought maybe we should slow down.

I was just about to say so when I heard the front door open, followed by the sounds of shuffling feet and a bag being dropped on the tile. Archie's distinct New England accent drifted in from the kitchen. "Renn, where ya at, kid?"

The interruption was for the best. Before we jumped into bed, I needed to make sure Renn understood some things about that part of my life. I sighed and dipped my head into Renn's neck, chuckling as I slid down his body to my feet before leaning into his ear. "Foiled again, Batman."

He exhaled and peered at me regretfully before reaching down to adjust the bulge in his pants. Resigned, he twined our fingers together before leading me back toward the kitchen.

We hadn't gone three steps when Robbie appeared, presumably having scented out the pizza. He gave me a cursory glance before shrugging his shoulders and directing an upnod my way. Then he glared at Renn and muttered, "Gage better not have eaten all the pepperoni," before grabbing his backpack off the floor and heading to the den.

Renn watched him go before turning to me straight-faced. "Such a charmer, that one."

"Actually," Archie appeared in the hallway, speaking. "Robbie did okay today. I took him to the shop like we talked about and he watched me ink this lady's ankle. He also worked on some of his own stuff in his sketchbook and they're wicked good."

Archie was talking to Renn, but his eyes focused on our laced fingers as the three of us walked toward the living room. I steeled myself for his disapproval, even though his expression was in-decipherable. Renn must have also thought he'd need to run interference because he positioned himself between us. But the other man surprised us both.

"Good to see you, Sadie. Renn said you might be here."

Wait...what? That's it?

"It's good to see you too," somehow stumbled from my mouth.

I was bewildered as Archie pulled me in for a firm side hug before relaying his report that Robbie had behaved well at Studio Obscurum that afternoon. "He was excited in the shop, proud of his sketches, as un-pissy as I've seen him in a while."

Renn explained that he'd asked Archie to take his brother to the studio to hang out. "He seems to like it there if Pete's not around. Plus, since I ripped him a new one about staying out the other night, I thought he might enjoy a break from me."

"I was glad to bring him, Renny." Archie gave my shoulder a light squeeze before dropping his arm back to his side. "I wish you'd ask me to help more often. And you need to check out his drawings. I wasn't kidding when I said they're fantastic. Kid's got genuine talent."

There was a strong hint of suggestion in the older man's tone, causing Renn to ask, "You think I should do that right now? It's so rare for him to be in a good mood. He never lets me see his drawings or give him any encouragement." Renn turned to me. "Do you mind? It'll just be a few minutes and then I'm all yours again."

Archie raised his eyebrows and tilted his head at the den, imploring me to send Renn to the other room. *What was he up to?* Welp, if he wanted to get me alone to chew me out, I figured I might as well get it over with. "Go talk to Robbie. I'm fine here with Archie."

Renn looked between the two of us and, deciding no battle was imminent, gave me a peck on the cheek and went into the den.

As soon as Renn was out of earshot, I took the direct approach, turning to Archie. "Alright, we're alone now, like you wanted. Tell me the truth. Are you mad? I hurt him, and I know how protective you are."

Wariness stole across Archie's features. He took a step back and lowered himself to the couch, eyeballing me as he patted the cushion nearest him. I sat down delicately. He ran a hand roughly over his face before speaking.

"When Renn mentioned yesterday he'd reconnected with you, he acted the same way. Defensive." Archie sighed, and I noted a gray pallor in his cheeks that hadn't been there a year ago. "It's fair. When you took off in February, after everything happened with Pete, it pissed me off. But Renn told me what you said back then—that you were still dealing with things in your own life and weren't in the headspace to balance that with someone else's shit." Muffled laughter drifted in from the den and Archie's shoulders slumped as he melted further into the couch.

He looked so sincere, even a little lost. "That's exactly it, Archie. If we'd gotten together then, he would have had to do *all* the work. I wasn't in a place to offer Renn the support he needed. It would have broken me—"

"And hurting you would have sent Renn over the edge." He understood.

"Archie, I will always question walking away from Renn. But sometimes you just have to make the best decisions you can and hope they're the right ones. I'm in a better place now. I think I can give Renn what he needs. And…I've missed him."

"I'm glad to hear you say that because I'm worried." His voice was solemn.

"Worried? About what?"

He twisted his palms before wiping them on his pants and exhaling heavily. "You're already aware that Renn never truly dealt with losing Thomas." I nodded as Archie continued, "I figured he'd come around eventually, since other than turning into a catatonic statue anytime someone mentioned his dad without warning, he always seemed so happy and together. Then he met you, and it was like he couldn't stop that façade from cracking.

"Sadie, you made him feel more, create more, brought him into reality, into his grief. But after finding out about Pete and Mary, instead of letting that façade come down, he built it back up stronger than ever, except without the pretend good vibes. He insists he's fine and gets upset if anyone says different."

"And you don't think me walking away from him made things worse?"

"No. It wasn't you leaving that did that. It was finding out about his uncle. This only stops when he and Pete come to some sort of peace, and he deals with his dad's death." Archie leaned closer and looked meaningfully at me. "I think it will be easier for Renn to do that with you in his corner."

I'd only been back in Renn's life for a couple of days, but aside from a few brief flashes of temper, and his lack of kind words for Pete, I hadn't seen evidence of the man Archie was describing. "Is it really that bad?"

He glanced down the hall at the den's French doors. "I think I've said enough. Probably too much. I'm not trying to warn you off. No matter what he's going through, Renn is still the best person

I know." He produced a noise between a laugh and a grunt. "It's just been all about the grind for him lately—the boys, the shop. You should have seen him at the Halloween party I dragged him to. Even bought us matching skeleton onesies. I hoped he'd have a good time, but he just sat there looking like a melted popsicle. Today is the first time he's smiled in months. It's simple. Being with you makes him happy."

My cheek ticked up at the memory of Renn's costume. "For the record, you can't scare me away. I'm in this. I think we can make *each other* happy. Be real partners."

Archie nodded just as Renn came back into the room.

"I saw Robbie's drawings. You weren't kidding, Arch. They're excellent." He smiled at us. "There's plenty of pizza. You both could stay and eat with me and the boys if you wanted."

Renn and I had no firm plans for this evening other than talking. Hard to believe that an hour ago I wasn't sure if we could reconcile, fifteen minutes ago we were headed toward possible fun naked time in the bedroom, and one minute ago, his closest family friend had cautioned me this would be a tough road. So how else could I reply?

"Do you think there's any plain cheese left?"

THE NEXT DAY, I helped Zach with a project at Hal's. He was switching out some of the current décor with framed posters and jerseys he'd ordered online. Most of the wall real estate still showcased filmy mirrors and neon beer signs, but it was slowly progressing.

He was up on the ladder hanging a poster of three muscular dudes glaring daggers at the camera with the phrase "Legion of Boom" in bold beneath them while we caught up.

"How's school going?" he asked.

"Good. Some of the basic requirements are sort of kicking my butt. Ten years is definitely too long of a break between math classes, but I think I'll be okay."

He chuckled. "Did you decide on a major yet?"

"You know full well I'm keeping that to myself. I have a plan and you'll find out exactly when you need to." I smiled up at him as I held the ladder steady. My time with Renn last year had given me the idea for a new career path, but I liked the fact that I was the only person who knew what I'd be studying—at least for now. For so long, Henri had taken charge of my life, and even once I'd gotten back to Los Angeles, I'd run everything by Zach out of decision-making anxiety. But more and more, I was standing on my own and taking control without needing validation.

"Fine, keep your secrets about school." Zach pulled a level from his back pocket before continuing, "But what about work? Tell me, is Chester's still the bastion of amazing daytime schedules and free lattes you always hoped it would be?"

"C'mon, babe. Don't get spicy. I like the coffee shop. They're willing to work around my schedule and I have free employee parking. Can't ask for more than that."

Zach hmphed playfully before turning toward the subject I imagined he was most interested in all along. My love life. I filled him in on my conversations with Renn and Archie, including how I'd told Renn about Henri's messages.

"It's so crazy that I almost missed my chance with Renn because of those stupid texts on my birthday. Like Henri had just been waiting for the right moment to reach out and fuck everything up."

Zach checked the poster with the level, satisfied he had it centered, and descended the ladder. "In your defense, you were a mess after those texts. I saw you."

"But it still sucks that Henri had that power over me. To stop me in my tracks. I thought I'd done everything I was supposed to do after New Year's. I walked away and stopped communicating with him. I let myself get close to Renn. Then a few stupid messages come through and it's like I was back at square one."

"But your reaction showed you still had work to do, right? That you needed to deal with…" He trailed off.

"It's okay. You can mention the baby." Almost two years of therapy had paid off. I could now think about *all* the things Henri had done to me without worrying about backsliding. "So maybe those texts did help, in a sick, messed up way. Because they forced me to confront this huge pain that I'd pushed down so deep, I hadn't even realized how much it was affecting me, holding me back. And I'm doing so well now. But I don't like that Henri had the ability to wreck me."

Zach cocked his head. "What are you getting at, doll?"

"I'm saying maybe—at some point—I should just see him. Not to let him explain or forgive him, but just to prove he's not some bogeyman."

Zach seemed thoughtful for a moment. "I mean…you might have a point. I never would have advocated you seeing him last year, but I think you could handle it now."

"I think so too. He's been so in my head since I left Boston, but he's just a man. Not the antichrist. I'm tired of him having this hold over me."

"Whatever you decide, I've got your back."

I put down the tape measure I held and pulled Zach into a hug. "Dude, you're gonna make a great dad."

"I'm planning on it." He leaned back to look at me. "And for the record, I'm pretty sure there's a hot twenty-three-year-old who would like nothing more than for you to depend on him as well."

"Time moves on, babe. He's twenty-four now."

Zach cackled at that and headed toward the office, leaving me to think about our conversation. What would it be like to reach out to Henri? Did I want to fight with him? Congratulate him on his son? Let him try to explain the unexplainable? No. I just wanted to prove to myself he didn't have power over me anymore. I would keep thinking about it. In the meantime, I had something more important to focus on.

RENN AND I had agreed to have an actual date on Friday. In the four days between the impromptu family pizza party and then, we texted constantly, sometimes joking, sometimes serious, reacquainting ourselves, reminding me of just how good we could be.

Our plan was for him to come to my place for dinner. The implications of an intimate at-home date weren't subtle, and I intended to have that honest conversation with him about sex I'd almost started the other day. I wasn't worried anymore about Henri making unscheduled appearances in my brain, but the scars my ex had left me with would always be there to some degree. Renn needed to understand the depth of those issues. But it was a discussion we'd need to have in person, not over text.

Texts were for fluff.

And dirty talk.

TUESDAY

8:49 p.m.

RENN: A guy had me tattoo a fork and spoon on his inner arm today. Turned out good, but I thought it was a strange request. Do you remember when we traded our weirdest customer stories?

ME: Of course. I still shudder when I think about the guy with the shaved head that had you tattoo a picture of his eyes on the back of his skull, so he could stare at people from front and back. Creepy AF.

ME: Or the woman who had a list of her favorite foods on her inner arm. Like, why?

RENN: At least I spelled everything right. Would have sucked for her to be constantly looking at avacados or barbacue.

RENN: Seriously, if a person is set on a list running down their arm (more common than it probably should be), favorites from Trader Joe's is gonna be a regrettable choice. I'd try to talk them into a different one. Countries visited, favorite books, meaningful songs...

ME: ...people they want to kill.

RENN: ...

RENN: ...uh...

ME: Okay, I know you're young, but please tell me you've seen Billy Madison.

RENN: Sorry *sad face emoji*

ME: Jesus.

WEDNESDAY

7:27 a.m.

RENN: Good morning.

8:37 a.m.

RENN: You never replied. Was that text too early? Did I bother you when you're asleep?

RENN: And if that's the case, I'm sorry that I texted you again and potentially bothered you, again.

RENN: But I still hope you have a good morning.

2:05 p.m.

ME: Just now seeing these. I worked a super early shift and was trying to do homework at the same time. Didn't even look at my phone.

ME: Also, fun fact—you are not the only person in Los Angeles who thinks it's hilarious to put weird names on your drink order. I took a $5 tip to call out an iced mocha today for "Andy who loves his girlfriend and is very sorry about Sunday."

RENN: I wonder what happened Sunday.

ME: Hopefully nothing too serious. Otherwise Andy should have ordered the large size. And a muffin.

RENN: LOL. In other news...I'm really looking forward to Friday. We're still meeting at your apartment, right?

ME: I mean...I think it's the best chance we have of not being interrupted by Gage losing a tooth or Robbie looking at boobs.

ME: FML. I just read that back and it sounds like I don't like your brothers. That's not what I meant at all. I'm just looking forward to having you all to myself.

RENN: I know you like them. *happy face emoji*

RENN: And I am also looking forward to you having me all to yourself.

THURSDAY

1:00 p.m.

RENN: Archie can't stay with the boys tomorrow. Normally, I'd be okay with making Robbie watch Gage for a couple hours but not overnight.

ME: Overnight, huh?

RENN: I mean, not that this was necessarily gonna be an overnight date.

RENN: But I was sort of hoping it would be.

RENN: Unless that's not what you want.

RENN: In which case I'm totally fine with that.

RENN: Like, more than fine.

RENN: Totally fine.

ME: Hey Renn

RENN: Yeah

ME: What do you like for breakfast?

3:30 p.m.

RENN: So Lydia can't take the boys either. How bad would it be if I asked Pete to stay with them?

ME: Hard to say. I don't exactly know how it is with you guys these days. He sees them more now, right?

RENN: He sees them. Mostly Gage. Robbie just sulks in his room but Pete tries.

RENN: It's hard.

RENN: For him.

RENN: For me.

RENN: For the boys.

RENN: But I think he'll come over if I ask. Robbie can deal with it. Gage actually likes it because Pete will play board games. Kiddo is really into Stratego right now.

ME: Stratego is solid. Just don't pull the rookie move of putting your flag in the corner.

RENN: Nerd.

ME: If it really bothers you, we can postpone.

RENN: Fuck that.

ME: *smiley face emoji*

ME: Or...you know it is possible to do...ahem...overnight activities...without actually staying overnight.

ME: So, in theory, we could...um...do activities...and you could leave. If you didn't want to ask Pete for an overnight.

RENN: FUCK THAT!!!!!!

RENN: Let me make myself clear. Gimme a sec to get this out...

RENN: ...

RENN: In case you were wondering, there hasn't been anyone else. I've been dreaming about us being together for more than a year. With what I've been thinking of doing to you, the WHOLE night will barely be enough time.

RENN: I have spent months wanting to be near you, touch you and kiss you and put my hands on your skin. I want to run my tongue over that spot on your neck that drives you crazy. I want to touch the inside of your thighs and scrape my teeth on your hipbone.

RENN: I want to hold you all night. I want to put my arms around you in the dark and kiss the back of your head and run my fingers over the ink I put on your thigh. I want to wrap you up and hug your back to my chest and feel you pressed against me. And I want to wake up and have your beautiful eyes be the first thing I see.

RENN: Okay?

ME: Goddamn.

ME: Don't most guys your age just send like eggplant and watersquirt emojis?

RENN: I have PLANS, and they don't involve me tugging on my jeans at 11 p.m. and giving you a peck on the cheek and staying quiet for the neighbors while I tiptoe to my car.

RENN: I'm going to ask Pete to stay over.

ME: Please do.

CHAPTER
Eighteen

ON THE AFTERNOON of our date, I kept busy deep-cleaning my apartment and preparing a meal that would go off without a hitch. I'd seen enough kitchen disaster sequences in rom-coms to know I needed to avoid anything too elaborate. My nerves were jittery enough without having to worry Renn would arrive to find me covered in flour or holding a flaming potholder. I stuck with my tried-and-true homemade mac-n-cheese with broccoli and a green salad.

Dessert was Renn's request—homemade cookies. Through our texts, he'd reminded me of a story I'd told him while he was doing my tattoo.

When I'd run track in high school, my teammate Lindsey had been pissed because I always beat her in the 1600. For the team's bake sale junior year, everyone else's parents had made elaborate brownies, cupcakes, and cookies to sell. My grandma had just thrown Oreos at me. I'd attempted to bake my own and produced some very misshapen and sad-looking oatmeal peanut butter cookies. They tasted okay, but that didn't stop Lindsey from making fun of them and bestowing the nickname "Dumpy" on me for the rest of the year. Dumpy cookies, dumpy girl, I guess? It sucked at first, but as I kept running, the nickname took on an ironic life of its own. There was something hilarious about my teammates shouting, "Go Dumpy!" at the finish line. Later, when they apologized, I forgave them on the condition they keep using the nickname, at least on the field. And, when the bake sale happened again senior year, I produced five dozen yummy, perfectly-formed oatmeal peanut butter cookies that sold out quickly.

I liked that Renn had remembered. I thought it was his way of reminding me he knew I was more than the girl whose family had neglected her, or the woman Henri had manipulated. The Sadie he saw now had always been there, even if she'd been muted. When I opened the door for him at seven o'clock, the sweet scents of peanut butter and sugar—and victory in the 1600—lingered.

He was silhouetted against the silvery light of the early moon. Newer-build high rises dominated my three-story dingbat, making its outdoor walkways oddly dark even when the sun was out.

Some teenagers in the pool area pointed at us, likely because Renn was carrying a massive bouquet of roses, so ginormous it obscured his face, and a box of chocolates. He moved the flowers to the side to display a wide, shit-eating grin. His damp hair was up in its bun-pony, and I inhaled the tea tree scent of him as he walked into my apartment.

"Your smile looks suspicious." I teased.

"Because the flowers and chocolates might be over the top, but I couldn't resist." Renn put them down on the counter, along with another bag he'd brought, turning to devour me with his gaze. "I saw them when I was getting groceries at Vons. It hit me right in the middle of aisle seven that I've never dated anyone I really cared about before. Never bought flowers. I thought, 'Holy crap. I actually have a reason to buy these.' So of course I had to get the biggest ones. I hope that doesn't sound stupid."

"Definitely not stupid." I couldn't think of a time Henri had bought me flowers that weren't of the "I'm sorry" variety.

Renn reached out and folded me into his arms, looking down at my pink shorts and striped tee. "You look beyond amazing. I'm so happy we're finally doing this."

"Me too."

"It smells fantastic. You said you were making mac-n-cheese, so I brought Guinness." He pointed at the grocery bag on the counter.

"That's great. I also have water and soda."

I went into the kitchen to pull dinner out of the oven and throw the salad together, leaving Renn to poke through my record collection in the living room. Zach had taken most of the knick-knacks with him, so there were some bare spaces on the walls and shelves. But he'd left his couch, so the room was functional enough.

"I'd give you the grand tour," I joked as I brought the casserole dish to the table, "But you've essentially seen everything. The place is small. There's one bathroom down the hall, along with Zach's bedroom and mine."

"I thought Zach moved out."

"He did. But he kept his room, so he's got a place to chill if he needs it."

"That's...convenient."

I huffed. "He was just looking for an excuse to keep paying his half of the rent so he wouldn't leave me in the lurch when he moved in with Teddy. This way, I don't have to find a roommate and he doesn't have to feel guilty. It's kind of a win-win."

Zach and I had argued about it. Vehemently. But when it came down to it, I wasn't in a financial position to turn him down and I honestly didn't want to room with a stranger. So, we pretended he needed a space where he could get a break from Teddy, even though that had literally never happened.

But Renn didn't need the full explanation to understand where I was coming from. "It's cool how you and he take care of each other."

"Yeah. I insisted he keep the big room, though. Technically, my room isn't even a bedroom since it doesn't have a closet."

"I'm sure your bedroom is nice." His husky tone washed over me and I swallowed.

Thinking of bedrooms reminded me of the conversation we needed to have. But that was going to require at least a few fortifying cookies, so it could wait until after dinner.

We settled into the little dining table and ate leisurely. Both our phones sat on the table, facedown, and we remained blissfully uninterrupted. I saw no signs of the Renn Archie had described, although by tacit agreement we avoided the topic of Pete. I talked about Chester's Coffee Shop and my Advanced Sociology midterm. As with Zach, I was vague about where I thought my studies would take me career-wise, but Renn seemed happy just to hear about what it was like for me being back in school. He also had me laughing with stories about ridiculous tattoo clients and the *Game of Thrones*-level machinations of the PTSA.

"Seriously, Sadie, you really left me in the lurch with those ladies. After the 5K, they were practically feral with the need to gossip, trying to gather intel about what was going on with us. I finally had to tell them we weren't together."

"It's lame they're so pushy."

"You don't know the half of it. Do you remember that woman Hannah you met?" *High ponytail, size two, designer athletic apparel Barbie Hannah? Nah. Can't place her.*

"Um...I think so."

"Well, she straight up hit on me at the back-to-school drive in August. Like, super cliché, 'My husband is out of town, we should have some fun.' I turned her down, obviously, and I thought it would be awkward, but whenever I see her now, she acts like it never happened."

I grinned. "Sorry."

"You should be." Renn winked. "If you and I had been together, she probably wouldn't have been bold enough to do that. You left me alone with the wolves."

"Don't you mean the cougars?"

Renn chuckled. Halfway through dinner, he noticed the wooden lotus on a shelf in the kitchen and nodded toward it. "Did you get that before or after the tattoo?"

"Before. It was sort of the catalyst that got me thinking about the design."

"Well, doing your lotus got me thinking about…lots of things." He sat up in his chair and looked me straight in the eye.

I warmed at his words.

Renn dug back into his dinner and ate a healthy portion until finally declaring himself defeated by the carbs and dairy. "I gotta be honest…" He smiled as he pushed his chair back. "I was expecting blue soup."

I chortled. "Renn Stoller, did you just make a *Bridget Jones* reference?"

"You told me it was your favorite movie, so I watched it."

"That's so sweet."

"Well, it's your favorite. I can't guarantee I'm going to watch every movie you ever talk about."

"Noted…and, same." I grinned back. *Could it truly be this easy to be with someone?* I hated to spoil it by getting heavy, but I trusted Renn's willingness to listen.

I grabbed the cookies from the kitchen, and we sat on the couch with the plate on the coffee table between us.

"Do you want to watch a movie?" he asked.

"I do want to *watch a movie*…" I used air quotes. "But before we do that, I think we need to discuss some things."

Renn had been at the midpoint of bringing a cookie to his mouth, but he immediately put it down and turned toward me. "Okay."

I sucked in a breath. "I know it's not very sexy to talk about sex. But I think we need to. There are things you should hear before we do...that." I felt myself blushing but held his gaze.

"Who says it's not sexy? Sadie, you could be reading the instruction manual for a vacuum cleaner and it would be sexy. Because it's you. Whatever you need to tell me, I am here for it. Please."

I wrung my hands in my lap as I gathered my words, appreciating the openness of Renn's expression. "You need to understand why...being intimate...is hard for me, as much as I want to. In the past ten years, I haven't been with anyone other than Henri. And you know he was...unkind." Renn's features tightened, but he simply nodded as I continued.

"Throughout our relationship, he found ways to touch me—or sometimes to *not* touch me—and he used it to make me feel less than." I stopped to take a few deep breaths as Renn met my eyes quietly. "Henri would say things to me about my body. He would pinch my stomach and frown at me or stab my thighs to point out cellulite. He would withhold sex. Or demand it. It went from being something I remember enjoying to a weapon he used to hurt me. He never forced me. It wasn't about that. I think in his twisted way he thought he was making me better, like, molding me, or something.

"When we first got together, he gave me more love, more affection. And I craved it so much that in the end, he was getting off on how hard I tried to please him. So, he pulled back even more. That was our game. I kept doing things to make him love me and he took being a withholding asshole to the highest level.

"I'm nervous about being with you physically because I'm not sure if I know how to connect with someone in that way. But the other day, when we were kissing at your house, it was nice. Really nice." My face grew redder, but I wanted him to understand. "I trust you. And I think there's a chance we could be good together—in bed—but I need you to be patient with me. To go slow, okay?"

Renn seemed to consider my words and reached out to take my hands before speaking. "Thank you for telling me all that. I'm sorry Henri was such a bastard. And I think I've been clear about how much I want you. But there is no part of me that would push you to do anything you aren't ready for. If this…" He sort of waved his hands around the room. "If this is all you can do right now, hanging out, talking, eating together, then that is totally fine. I just want to be with you. In whatever way we can be. Being apart from you sucked balls."

I laughed. "We are a classy pair, aren't we?"

"Fuck yeah, we are. The fanciest." He squeezed my hands. "Us taking our time will not be a problem. It never has been." He looked at me searchingly. "I have been waiting to touch you for so long. No matter what you're able to give me, I'll still be the luckiest guy in the world."

I gave myself a few moments to digest the sincerity of his words before peering up at him shyly. I breathed out as I settled myself against his side.

Renn tilted my face, giving a hard press of his lips to mine. "I know we can figure this out. We might have to go slow, and it might be awkward. We might have to laugh at ourselves, but you know what?"

"Hmm?"

"I think you're right. We can be good together. However you'll have me, I'm yours."

I snuggled closer and we existed in the charged air, neither of us making a move to watch a movie. After a few minutes, Renn got up and went over to the credenza where he'd been looking at my vinyl collection earlier. He flipped through the fading cardboard as he took inventory of the only real insight I had into my mom and dad. The Carpenters, Carly Simon, Led Zeppelin, Stevie Wonder, James Taylor, Pink Floyd, The Rolling Stones. There were about two hundred records, a snapshot of my parents as young people. There was something peaceful about watching Renn touch things they had held.

He pulled an album from the collection and slid it out of its sleeve onto the record player. He reached his hand out to me as the sound of Seals & Croft's "Summer Breeze" came over the speakers. "Dance with me?"

In any other circumstance, I would have thought this move was corny as hell, but as I stood up into Renn's embrace, it seemed right. Neither of us knew what to do exactly, so we settled for the eighth-grade gym dance style of awkwardly rocking side to side with my hands behind his neck and his around my waist. Perfect.

As we moved, Renn traded off his atrocious singing with whispering in my ear, telling me how amazing I was, how happy he was to be with me. I was so incredibly grateful to the man in my arms. The one who had never given up on me, the one who had somehow found his way from the tattoo studio into my life, despite every roadblock. We danced for a while, next to the cookies, in the apartment I'd shared with Zach, listening to my parents' records. I lifted my face from where I'd rested it on his shoulder because in that moment I knew.

"Hey, Renn?"

"Yeah?"

"I love you."

He kissed the tip of my nose and pressed our foreheads together as he closed his eyes on the admission. "I love you too, Sadie. So much."

And I had never been surer of my next words.

"Will you come with me? To bed?"

He nodded solemnly as I took his hand, leading him down the hall.

MY BEDROOM WAS utilitarian. Considering its postage stamp-sized square footage, it had to be. I'd only been able to fit a hanging rack for clothes, a small dresser, and a queen-sized bed.

I couldn't tell if Renn noticed the cramped layout because the entirety of his focus was on touching every part of my body he could reach. Once inside the room, he spun us around and started kissing me, smashing our bodies together while running his hands feverishly up and down my back.

He pulled away to murmur, "Just tell me if I'm moving too fast or if you need me to stop." He ran his lips along my jaw and reached into his back pocket, taking out his wallet and throwing a condom on the dresser next to my bed. "No pressure." He palmed my waist reverently. "Just don't want to have to fumble around for it later."

Putting my hands on his, I reassured him. "I'm good. I promise I'll let you know if I'm not. Now please just carry on as usual."

"Usual?" Renn huffed. "Sadie, I don't exactly have go-to moves here. It's been more than a year since I've done this with anyone. There's a decent chance we won't even need that condom because I might come in my pants any minute."

I laughed. "Well, I guess that's the good part about dating a guy in his twenties, right? If that happens, we won't have to wait too long for round two...or three." I lifted my face up and bit down gently on his earlobe, feeling the immediate gooseflesh that spread across the back of his neck. "Because I would very much like to use that condom."

"Damn." Renn moved forward against me and my calves hit the bed. I sat down and gazed up at him, standing between my legs. He looked at me like a kid in a candy store, overwhelmed with options, emboldening me to reach for my top and pull it over my head, giving my hair what I hoped was a sexy toss as I threw my shirt to the floor.

Renn hesitated less than a second before leaning over me, pushing my back against the mattress as he palmed the silky black bra I had just revealed. He shifted us so we were both lying on the bed, and I felt the whole magnificent weight of him as he laid his body on top of mine and ground his erection against me.

"I want you so much," he said, rising on his hands and knees before working his way down my face and neck with his mouth. He didn't just kiss me, he devoured me, licking and sucking and tasting with abandon as he groaned into my body. He pulled my bra straps down to reveal my breasts, pushing them together so he could tongue both nipples in tandem. A shot of pleasure went straight down my spine as he grazed his teeth along the peaks. "Fuck, you are so beautiful."

As he continued his exploration further south, I waited to feel embarrassed at the slight jiggle in my midsection that no amount of running or dieting had been able to eliminate. But it never came. I only felt Renn worshiping my skin and stomach, eliciting a giggle from me as he swirled his tongue in and out of my belly button.

I grasped Renn's tee on his shoulder and tugged. He looked up at me briefly to confirm before pulling it off, and then went back to hungrily kissing my breasts, unhooking my bra to free them entirely.

From my vantage point, I could see the sinewy lines of his back, noting that the tattoos on his arm extended over one shoulder. His biceps strained as he braced himself on either side of me. I reached down to run my hands through his hair, tugging out the rubber band, arching my back as the ensuing waves tickled against my skin.

He looked up, resting his chin on my hipbone as he asked, "Can I take your shorts off?"

The mild twinge of panic in my gut gave me my answer. "Maybe...um...not just yet."

Renn smiled and nodded, nosing my belly before kissing his way back up until he was hovering above me, face-to-face. "What do you want? I just want to make you feel good."

What did I want? I wasn't sure I'd ever heard that question in bed before. I wasn't even sure I had been exposed to the whole scope of menu options. But as I gazed at Renn above me, nothing but honesty and love shining in his face, I knew one thing I very much wanted.

"I'd like to..." I stammered.

"To...?"

"Um...I want to..." I started blushing.

Renn leaned back on his haunches then, staring down at me and putting the full expanse of his muscular chest on display, before asking playfully, "Sadie, what can I do for you?"

My face burned as I answered, "I want to see you."

The glimmer in Renn's eyes turned to lava. He understood what I was asking for instantly and moved to stand up. I lifted myself, leaning back on my elbows to watch as he reached down to take off first one sock and then the other. I bit my bottom lip when he cupped himself over his jeans before undoing the button and lowering the zipper. The fit was loose enough to spare him any unsexy tugging. He simply let his pants fall to the floor and stepped out, kicking them away as he stood next to the bed in nothing but a pair of dark gray boxer briefs.

"At least you didn't come in your pants," I teased, noticing the dark wet spot of his precum through the fabric.

He smirked at me unabashedly as he put his thumbs into the waistband of his boxers and pulled them off.

The sensual spell broke in an instant.

"Jesus Christ!"

"What?"

I looked at Renn's cock, thickening even more under my gaze.

"You know what!" I accused.

I waved my wrist in a circle, indicating his general groin area. "You're so sweet and cuddly and puppies and rainbows and shit. And then you go and have a porn-star-sized package down there."

Renn chuckled and shrugged, like somehow he was oblivious to the fact that he had a big old pickle dick. "What were you expecting?"

"I don't know. Not like a pencil or anything, but just, like, a nice dick. Not a tree trunk. What the hell do you eat, anyway?"

"I'm pretty sure cock size has exactly zero to do with cheeseburger consumption."

"If you say so, but whatever you do, just know that if I'm gonna take that anaconda, you'd better be planning on lots of foreplay."

Renn's gaze turned hot again. "I can definitely be down with that."

Our interlude for levity was over as quickly as it had begun, but it had been exactly what I needed to bring me back from the edge. I reached out to touch Renn and the weight of him in my hand didn't seem like too much at all. His cock was pale with a thick vein along the underside, curved slightly upward, sticking out from a dark bush of hair he'd taken the time to manscape. He was uncut, the purple head pushing out prominently above the foreskin.

I'd never been with an uncut dude before, but I knew he'd be especially sensitive, a point proven when I gave him a few exploratory strokes, pulling the skin up over the head. When I did that, it looked a bit like the Sarlacc pit monster from *Star Wars*, but somehow still incredibly sexy. I was having some sort of surreal, out-of-body experience as I watched my hand slide along his foreskin, bringing the folds of it to the top, and I was continuing to float as I leaned forward without thinking to dip my tongue against the sensitive tip.

Renn pulled back immediately. "Fuuuuuuuuck, Sadie," he groaned. "This'll be over in five seconds if you do that."

I winked at him. "Remember what I said about round two... or three?"

"Come here," he growled, pulling me up to stand in front of him and pressing our bodies together as he delivered a demanding kiss. He reached his hands down to grab two very full handfuls of my ass. There was something so delightfully naughty about pushing my core against him while he was naked and I still had on my shorts.

Renn pulled one hand off my backside and brought it around to the front of me. "I don't have to take them off, but can I touch you? Please?"

I answered him by reaching my own hands down and unbuttoning my shorts, stepping away from him as I slid them languidly down my legs, leaving me in only a pair of tiny black panties. I stuck my fingers in the sides of them and energy coursed through me as I asked, "Do you want me to take these off, too?"

He shot his fingers through his hair before closing and opening his eyes. His chest heaved as he studied me from my toes to the top of my head. "You have no idea how much I want that."

I bent down to slide them off, revealing myself to Renn—and by revealing I meant *everything*, because I had gotten an extremely expensive Brazilian a few days prior—for the first time completely and utterly fine in my nakedness. He was looking at me with such unconcealed adoration. There was no need for any false bravado.

"I want you," I said.

That was all it took. He scooped me up and practically threw me on the bed, laying his body alongside mine. I touched him everywhere I could reach, from his neck to his spine to the squishy round globes of his perfect butt. He ran a hand down my side and trailed it past my belly button. He looked at me and I gave the slightest of nods. The next moment, his fingers ghosted along the inside of my thighs, up to my very center, before moving further to invade my folds.

He went in with two fingers, kissing my neck and declaring, "You're so wet."

He wasn't kidding. I couldn't remember ever being so turned on. And as Renn continued to use his fingers on me, scissoring and twisting them, no doubt getting me prepared for his monster cock, I'd never felt so taken care of in my life.

I was already squirming and ready to be filled when his thumb grazed along my clit, rubbing slow circles. In the back of my mind, I'd been wondering how he might be in bed since he was so young and hadn't had a ton of experience. But based on the way he was moving his fingers inside me, along with the attention he paid to my clit, I could tell he had a respectable understanding of a woman's body.

"This okay?" he asked, circling his thumb with more pressure. "Harder? Faster?"

I didn't think I'd ever legitimately been asked for sex directions. My general belief was that men asked things like that just so women could affirm how phenomenal their skills were. But I knew that wasn't Renn. "Um…it would actually be better if you moved more up and down, not circles."

Renn kissed me on the mouth, and his fingers made the turn I'd indicated. *Ohholyfuckingfucksticks.* That felt amazing. I whimpered and Renn took that correctly as his cue to move his thumb a little faster. My thighs began to shake as I closed my eyes, and when I came undone, Renn stuck three fingers inside, pressing his palm against me as I ground out the last of my pleasure against him.

I opened my eyes riding the wave of the best orgasm I'd ever had to see Renn propped up on his side next to me. He kissed my shoulder and brought his fingers to his mouth, licking them clean. That image was almost too much for my overheated senses to process, but it seemed to make him happy, so I figured I could deal with it. But then his face contorted, almost to the point he looked in pain.

"Renn?"

"Sorry, Sadie." He exhaled. "I'm just trying hard not to come. I almost did just now."

Me orgasming almost got him off? He really was a unicorn. I looked down and saw the angry purple head of his penis glowering at me. I reached down for it, but he put his hand on my wrist. "Don't. If you touch me, I'll come. I just...need a beat...to calm down."

I shook off Renn's hand. "I said I wanted *to see you*, Renn." Casting my eyes down again, I gestured with my eyebrows at his poor, neglected dick. "Please."

I saw the hesitation in his eyes. This made him feel exposed, and I knew how uncomfortable he was being vulnerable. I leaned over to whisper in his ear. "Please. I'd love to take the edge off. Remember, we'll always have round two...and three."

He laid down on his back in answer, hooking his elbow behind his head and resting it on the pillow as he closed his eyes. I ran my hand down his lightly furred chest, drawing circles over his nipples, fingers still buzzing from my orgasm. Mindful of his unease, I didn't linger, sliding my palm over his stomach to grasp his fat cock with one hand. I repeated the same strokes I had used before, but this time tested the pressure and the drag, monitoring his face to see what he liked. Running my pointer finger up and down the shaft, I paid particular attention to the sensitive spot beneath the head of his crown as his breathing hitched. I wanted to play more, but he was close. I clasped firmly and stroked, twisting my wrist a bit at the end to figure out if that worked for him. It did. In less than a minute Renn came, and I watched, fascinated, as thick ropes of white cum spurted and landed on his belly and chest. I squeezed two last strokes up, gathering the remainder of his spend on the tip of his cock, rubbing it between the folds of his foreskin.

He tapped my wrist to get me to stop. "Too sensitive," he choked out, finally opening his eyes. Followed immediately by, "So good."

I smiled and got up to grab a warm washcloth from the bathroom, proceeding to wipe him off while he lay there in a post-orgasmic haze. Renn might have been willing to lick me off his fingers, but I wasn't quite feline enough to clean him with my tongue.

"I'm a little embarrassed," Renn admitted. "I hope that was okay."

"It was perfect."

"It's overwhelming. There are so many things I want to do with you, so many ways I want to love you."

Forty minutes later, after we'd teased and touched and recovered, his fingers were back inside me, stretching me, before he finally rolled on the condom. I laid on my back and Renn came up and over me, entering in one sure stroke as he used his hands to pull my thighs apart and settle himself there. He pressed us tightly together, gently rocking our bodies as we both strained toward completion. His face above mine, he kept eye contact, pausing intermittently to kiss my lips.

I felt like a treasured gift, as though Renn was using every sure stroke to brand me and pull me further into him. He gazed at me with such affection, occasionally whispering my name or telling me he loved me, kissing me, running his hands along my face and sides as he kept our bodies sealed together. He pulled my hand up to lay delicate kisses across my fingertips and I realized that his body was doing most of the work. Stroke. Stroke. Stroke. Tunneling inside me. His strong back pushed up and down as I attempted to lean into him, but mostly just surrendered to the weight of him making love to me.

Renn knew how to work that slight curve of his dick and I was ready to come after a few minutes, but he kept edging me to make it last. Finally, I couldn't take it anymore, and I surged forward to claim my release, coming even harder than before. A moment later, Renn cried out and shuddered above me.

He said nothing after that, just got up and went to the bathroom to take off the condom. He came back with another warm washcloth and pressed it between my thighs, taking care even though there was no soreness, then tossed the cloth to the floor before gathering me in his arms. Laying a possessive hand over my waist, he claimed his place as the big spoon and trailed his fingers along my tattoo, murmuring a last, "I love you."

Round three happened just before dawn. Penetration wasn't an option as we didn't have a condom, so Renn merely held his position behind me, working his erection in and out of my thighs as I squeezed them together, using my own copious wetness as lube. He wrapped his arms around me and held me tight to him, just beneath my breasts, pressing his chest against my back as he reached one hand lower to touch me. It didn't take long. The erotic visual I had looking down to see the head of Renn's cock popping in and out between my legs as he worked himself to finish probably did more to get me there than his fingers did. I came with a cry, after which Renn pumped himself faster, reaching orgasm with a throaty moan even while remembering to hold his hand down to catch most of his cum, presumably in consideration of my bedsheets.

A few hours later, we got up to face the world. Three bouts of sex had both of us waking satisfied, and I watched with fascination as Renn moved about my room, naked, collecting his clothing and pulling his hair up into its bun-pony. The heavy weight of his soft cock and balls brushing against his inner thigh was a massive turn-on, as was the sight of his ass on display when he reached down to grab his jeans.

We both jumped at the telltale sounds of incoming texts. First one. Then another. And another.

I sighed. "I suppose we're lucky we got the one night. Any bets on what it is?"

"My money is on Robbie needing a lawyer."

I laughed. "Maybe he ran away to join a punk band."

"Or a cult."

Renn dug his phone out of his jeans and frowned at it. "There's nothing. Must be yours."

"Probably work trying to convince me to come in early." I stretched sleepily, keeping a greedy eye on his body as he dressed.

My phone had gotten knocked off the nightstand. Another text coming through sent me in the direction of underneath the bed, where I finally located it. Renn crawled behind me, brushing aside my rat's nest of sex-tossed hair to kiss me on the neck.

I unlocked my phone and stilled in his arms.

"Oh, no!"

"What's wrong?"

"Shit. Shit. Shit." I was powerless to stop the tears as I scrolled through my texts.

"Sadie, what is it? You're scaring me."

"Sorry." I took a deep breath. "There are a few missed calls and texts from Zach. He and Teddy...they...um..."

"What? Are they okay?" Renn squeezed me back into him.

"No. Not okay." Another deep breath. "They lost the baby."

CHAPTER
Nineteen

I T HAD BEEN almost a week since Zach told me about the baby, and I had reached the limit of my endurance for accepting his "I'm okay" texts.

Since I'd been back in LA, we'd never gone this long without talking. Deep down, I *knew* he needed me. The worst thing about cutting back my shifts at Hal's was not having a ready excuse to speak to him. He'd messaged to assure me he and Teddy were fine, that this was a contingency they'd prepared for. But when I spoke with Cyd, the new bartender, she said Zach had spent the bulk of his time in the back office this week. It wasn't like him to avoid people, to avoid *me*. I had to see in person how he was coping.

Having confirmed he wasn't working, I'd texted him to say I was on my way over. Then I'd turned my phone off, so I would be sure to miss any attempt he made to put me off.

When Zach opened the door, he simply gave me a wry look and stood back, gesturing toward the living room.

Teddy's house was a three-bedroom bungalow in the Holly-wood Hills. Not ostentatious by any means—probably a starter home in middle America—but easily a seven-figure property in Los Angeles. The first time I'd been here, before Zach had moved in, it looked like it'd been decorated out of a catalog, appearing less like a home and more like a mid-century modern museum.

Zach's influence had been immediate. Whoever had done Teddy's interiors would have been horrified as Zach's thrift store finds and duct-taped book spines started filling the shelves, along with his *Doctor Who* Funko Pop collection. "Pretty But Kind of a Bitch" now resided on a lavish custom-built sofa, which Zach and I sat down on.

"We're gonna be okay, Sades." He leaned forward to rest his elbows on his knees. "I mean, it totally sucks, but we got lucky getting pregnant on the first try. This was always a possibility."

That sounded rehearsed, but I was the last person to judge how other people coped with their pain. "I'll follow your lead here." I reached out to squeeze his hand. "But you know I had to come. If you're really okay, that's great, but if you're not, you don't have to pretend."

Zach nodded and asked if I wanted something to drink. Mr. Bingham, an undeservedly-named orange tabby cat that had been part of Teddy's household for ten years, made an appearance. The oddly subdued feline sat next to me, not purring, of course, but somehow sensing this wasn't the day for his usual hiss-and-show-me-his-butthole routine. I declined Zach's offer, but he got up to grab some water for himself. When he hadn't returned after a few minutes, I sought him out in the kitchen. I found him there, leaning against the fridge, water bottle in hand and staring into space. He looked over when he saw me.

"Sorry, doll. Sometimes it just sort of comes over me."

I wrapped him in my arms. "Of course! This isn't something you just get over."

He returned my hug and stepped away before taking a swig from the bottle. "The thing is, it's been completely weird for me this whole time dealing with this like it's a business arrangement." Releasing a breath, he ran his sleeve over his mouth before continuing. "When we found our surrogate, and we put all the contracts in place, we planned for what would happen in case of miscarriage. Not, like, how we would feel, but what our financial obligations would be and how we'd go about making medical decisions. Thank God this has been straightforward and didn't come to anything like that. Seriously, Sadie, you should have seen these documents. We had plans for every scenario. She had to have her own lawyer. We had to use our own. All we wanted was a baby, but everyone's interests had to be protected."

I recalled the research I'd done after I'd made my naïve offer to be Zach's surrogate. Some of this information was familiar. But it was one thing to read about the process, it was another to watch him navigate it.

"It seems inadequate to keep saying it, but I'm so sorry you and Teddy are going through this."

He huffed sadly. "The thing is, we really liked our surrogate. She seemed like the kind of person everyone gets along with. We met her husband and kids, her fucking Labrador. But then this happens, and it all just feels so transactional. Don't get me wrong—she's fantastic, but we don't even *know* her. Not really. We don't even know her and yet we have to go through the saddest thing in our lives with her. It just seems sort of effed up, right?"

I bent back against the counter and noted the green tinge of Zach's face, along with the fine lines of sleeplessness around his eyes. "Are you able to talk about this with Teddy?"

"Yeah. I've told him. He sort of feels the same way, but what choice do we have? We're listed with a couple of adoption agencies, too. We're planning on getting married sooner than later to help our chances. But God, it all seems so clinical." He crunched his hand around the bottle.

"What about trying again with the surrogate?"

"Teddy wants to. Money has never been an issue for him, so he always thinks of problems in those terms. Like, if we can throw enough cash at the situation, we'll end up with a baby."

"But..." I prompted. I could tell by his face it was there somewhere.

"But he doesn't understand that I might not be able to go through it again. Not like this. You know me. I don't operate this way, with lawyers and contracts and negotiations and ten people in suits all in a room. Teddy is so used to functioning in that world it doesn't faze him. He even told me we needed to come up with a marketing plan to make ourselves the most attractive option for couples looking for adoptive parents. A fucking marketing plan!"

"Oh, Zach." My heart ached for him.

"I love Teddy more than anything, but I don't want to talk about marketing plans and pre-decide what happens if there's a miscarriage. I don't want to deal with lawyers drawing up a contract about who's in charge of making decisions if the surrogate has an accident or gets gestational diabetes. I don't want to make a thirty-slide PowerPoint meant to convince people we'd be great fathers. I don't want to endlessly discuss money and negotiations and fine print. I hate that it's like this."

I moved toward him again, and this time he hugged me fiercely and murmured, almost confessing. "I just want to be a dad, doll." So soft I barely heard it. "I just want to be a dad."

And then Zach did something I realized with a shock I'd never seen him do before. He put his head in his hands and started crying.

LATER THAT NIGHT, Renn and I were on my couch making out. Having sex had deepened our relationship and I was learning new things every day. For instance, Renn had a particular habit of latching on to the sensitive spot at the top of my shoulder where it met my neck. He kept sucking and kissing it, not enough to leave a mark, but enough so I could tell it really turned him on. If this was a fetish of his, I'd decided I could happily live with it. Good thing he hadn't wanted to spend more of his time licking my armpits or sucking my toes. That would have been more of a conversation.

But even though it felt amazing, Renn could tell I was distracted, worrying about Zach. He pulled himself away from me reluctantly, so it would be easier to talk.

"It makes sense," I reasoned. "Zach is a total people person. Always has been. That's why he loves the bar. I mean, he can do the business side of things, but that's not what he's about. It's not where he shines."

"Poor Zach," Renn agreed.

"It's so unfair. My mom and dad were so cavalier about having a kid. They just dropped me off with Grandma and were all, 'Peace out. Off to save the world. Or at least improve its water supply.' And here you have Zach and Teddy, who would be fantastic parents, but can't catch a break."

"You really can't be their surrogate?" We'd discussed my previous offer to Zach several times—including my rationale behind doing it sooner than later—and the prospect of me performing this service didn't seem to faze Renn. All I saw on his face was compassion.

"I told you. No agency will let you do it if you've never had a kid before. I'm also just under the age limit for what they'd prefer. It's the kind of thing even Teddy's money can't solve."

"So no back-alley surrogacies?"

"Exactly."

Renn looked at me with the mildly constipated expression of

someone choosing their words carefully. "If you really want to help them, have you thought about doing it the old-fashioned way?"

"The old-fash—Wait...What!? What the hell, Renn!? I'm not having sex with Teddy!"

"No, no. That's not what I meant." He shook with laughter.

"Jesus! I know you don't think I'm having sex with Zach. That's disgusting!" I folded my arms.

"Also not what I meant." Renn put his hands on my shoulders and squeezed as he explained. "For the record, there will never be a time—ever—when I sanction you having sex with anybody else. What I meant was maybe you could get one of those kits where you do the whole thing at home."

"A kit? You mean like doing it turkey-baster style?"

He smiled as my arms slowly uncrossed. "Basically, yes. They make devices for this that are a few grades more technical than a turkey baster. I had a client a few years ago. She and her girlfriend were trying to get pregnant, but they didn't have the money for all those expensive doctors. They ordered this kit online, and it got delivered right to their house, and they did it there. She told me about it while she was on my table, because she was getting her son's name tattooed on her calf. They used her brother's sperm, and her girlfriend carried the baby." Renn took my hands in his. "If you really want to do this for Zach, it's something to consider."

"And you'd be okay with it if I did that? I mean, if I puke every morning and gain a hundred pounds, it's going to affect our relationship."

Renn looked thoughtful for a moment and then replied. "I wouldn't have brought it up if I didn't think we could handle it. I know it won't be easy. It's unconventional to have your girlfriend carry a baby for another couple right when you've started dating, but we're not exactly conventional, are we? I also know what Zach is to you, Sadie. That he's not just some dude you became friends with at work. He's your family. And if Robbie or Gage needed me to do something like this for them, I wouldn't hesitate." He leaned over to peck my forehead. "Besides, I love Zach too."

It was strange, sitting there talking this out with Renn. *We could handle it.* I was part of a couple again and my decisions affected both of us. I understood that being a surrogate would put a strain on our relationship. I wasn't totally naïve. But Renn and I were only a few months into officially dating. We hadn't discussed our long-term couple goals yet. It's not like it would be easier if I waited until we were even more deeply involved. And I needed to do this for Zach. To at least make the offer. Renn hadn't been exaggerating—Zach was my family, and I wanted to step up for him if he'd let me. He'd helped me reclaim my entire life, including encouraging me with Renn. I could give him nine months.

Decision tentatively made, I made a joking "ugh" face at Renn. "You realize that there is going to be some part of this that involves Zach or Teddy jizzing in a cup, right? Like, if we're not having sex, things have to, uh...happen...another way." I shuddered.

Renn laughed. "Let's not worry about those details right now. We can just get more information and ask them if this is something they'd even want to consider. It's a big decision, and a massive step to take without all those legal protections you mentioned earlier. I'm sure anyone that didn't know you and Zach as well as I do would start lecturing you about all the things that can go wrong, and particularly about if you're going to change your mind and get attached to the baby, but I have faith that you know your own capabilities."

Renn had always believed in me. And in this case, it was one hundred percent justified. I was definitely going to be attached to Zach's child. But not in the oh-my-God-I-said-I'd-be-your-surrogate-but-now-I've-seen-ten-tiny-toes-and-I've-totally-changed-my-mind type of way. More in the I-know-I-said-I'd-have-the-kid-in-bed-by-nine-but-*Napoleon-Dynamite*-was-on-and-you-had-Oreos-in-the-cupboard-and-Sadie-is-the-world's-best-auntie-slash-babysitter type of way.

The more I considered the idea, the more I liked it. Zach and I had been through so much, and our friendship was the closest thing to real family I'd ever had. I glanced at the tatted-up twenty-four-year-old holding my hand. Sometimes things that didn't seem right in theory could work amazingly well in practice.

Late December 2015

TEDDY WHISKED ZACH off to Mexico for the last two weeks of December. I'd agreed to pull a few shifts at Hal's—as well as check in daily with Cyd—so Zach could enjoy himself without worrying about the bar. I wanted to talk to him and Teddy about what Renn and I had discussed, but they were still reeling from the miscarriage, and it seemed too soon. Watching Zach cry in his kitchen had shaken me and I didn't want to inadvertently cause a repeat.

Since I was confident Teddy would take good care of Zach while they got their margaritas and salsa dancing on, I let myself relax and look forward to the holidays for the first time in over a decade. Renn had asked me to celebrate Christmas with him and the boys. We had been together for almost two months, and I could not remember being happier.

For so long, I'd jokingly accused Zach of being oversexed, but now I got it. Renn was a machine—a living, breathing sex god who could not get enough of me. We spent most nights at his house, but I slept at my apartment when I had the five a.m. shift at Chester's. One week this happened three nights in a row. On the third night, I'd woken to Renn knocking on my door at two in the morning. He'd rushed in, mumbling something about Archie showing up at the house unexpectedly to sleep off a hangover, providing adult supervision for the boys, and practically dragged me into the bedroom.

"We can't go three days ever again," he'd groaned out after, collapsing on top of me.

And we hadn't gone even two days without seeing each other since then.

It was blissful. It was easy.

Until it wasn't.

I showed up to the Stoller house on Christmas Eve carrying oatmeal peanut butter cookies, doctored with red and green M&M's, along with presents for the boys. Renn had given me the lowdown on an action figure Gage didn't already have. And even though a gift card to the Nintendo store wasn't exactly original, I figured Robbie would appreciate it. I also had something special for Renn. Thus equipped, I knocked with confidence.

But I could tell from the moment Gage swung open the door that something was wrong. His expression lacked its usual levity and there was a heavy silence behind him. A silence broken a few seconds later by Renn's shouted, "What the fuck, Pete!?"

I entered hesitantly. A quick glance down the hall showed my boyfriend pacing back and forth in the den. In the living room, Robbie sat on the couch, hands fisted across his chest, a lethal glare on his face. Archie sat in stony silence on the chair next to him. Gage hurled himself on the couch next to Robbie. He peered over at his brother and then adopted the same folded arms posture.

I looked at Archie and mouthed, "What's happening?" He hitched his neck to the left, indicating I should follow him into the kitchen. As I deposited the cookies on the counter, I heard Pete's voice drifting down the hallway. "I'm sorry, Renn, okay? I wasn't thinking of it like that."

Renn's reply of, "How can you be such a fucking dumbass!?" was clear before the click of the French doors closing reduced them to muffled shouting.

"What's going on, Archie?" Renn hadn't seen my arrival. I needed to figure out what was happening before I could plot my next move. Should I hide in the kitchen and just let this play out? Try to calm him down? How bad would it be if I stood by while my boyfriend murdered his uncle?

"Pete...that idiot." Archie leaned back against the stovetop, and I recognized he was upset because his Boston was coming out, the last word sounding more like *ijit*. He shook his head in disbelief as he continued. "He's been coming around more lately. And it's been quiet. Robbie still won't talk to him, of course, but he hasn't been trying to piss in his uncle's Cheerios or anything either. It almost felt like a truce."

I had gathered as much from my own frequent visits to the house, occasionally running into Renn's uncle watching TV or eating dinner with Gage. Pete had kept his word to try harder, but there was so much friction it was unclear if that was a good thing. I'd missed Thanksgiving since I'd agreed to cover the shift at Hal's, but Renn told me later it would have been a completely silent meal if not for Gage's chattering. The family did not know how to get past Robbie's discovery of Pete and Mary.

"What happened before I got here?"

Archie braced himself against the counter, knuckles going white as he explained what I'd walked in on. "So, Pete shows up not too long ago. Renn had asked him to come tonight so they could have less tension on Christmas tomorrow. Makes sense, right?"

"Sure." Archie wasn't telling me anything I didn't already know.

"Well, Pete gets here and puts presents under the tree for the boys. All good. But then he pulls out a gift bag and asks them to open it. Robbie just sniffs like it's made of horseshit, but Gage is game. In the bag, there's a snow globe. Gage shakes it up and sort of looks at his uncle like, 'Cool snow globe, dude.'"

This was all tracking so far. It was no surprise a nine-year-old wasn't interested in a snow globe. "Okay, so he didn't like the snow globe..." That couldn't be why Renn was so upset?

"No. The snow globe was fine. But then Pete opens his fool mouth and tells Gage to twist the little spinner thing to make it work. Gage does and 'It Came Upon a Midnight Clear' comes out. Pete starts going on about how that was Mary's favorite Christmas carol, how she used to rock Gage to sleep humming that song, and he wanted to give them a little memory of their mom for Christmas, blah, blah, blah."

Jesus. Was Pete the dumbest person on the planet? Archie gave me a knowing look as he saw me put it together.

He continued, "As you can guess, that whole scene blew up like a turd in a punchbowl with Robbie. He shoved his uncle and shouted something like 'don't you fucking talk about my mother,' and at that point Renn just grabbed Pete and pulled him into the den. I was trying to figure out what to say to little man Gage when you got here."

Thank goodness the den was on the opposite side of the house. We could all hear that a heated argument was happening, but couldn't make out the words. And I had a sudden awareness of my demons receding. I was no longer the Sadie who'd walked away from Renn—because those raised voices didn't cause me to seek the nearest exit.

"Archie, do you think I should go in there?" I looked at him. "Maybe I can help calm things down?"

He shrugged. "It's worth a try. These fights between them have been happening for months and it doesn't seem like it's getting better. It certainly can't hurt."

I slipped down the hall and rasped my knuckles lightly on the doors to the den before opening them. The two men were in a standoff, Renn tapping his boot and leaning forward in controlled rage. I couldn't remember ever seeing him so wound up. I was hesitant to approach, especially as he hadn't acknowledged my entrance yet. There was a console table between them, in the center of which was what I assumed to be the offending snow globe.

"Hey, um...I'm here. Archie sort of gave me the rundown on things."

Renn turned toward me with volcanic fury in his features. "So, then he told you this asshat decided to start Christmas Eve by upsetting Robbie and reminding him of everything we've spent a year trying to get past."

"Fuck, man! I said I'm sorry! I didn't mean it that way. I saw the snow globe, and I just figured it might be nice for the boys to have a bit of their mom on Christmas."

Renn's hands balled up at his sides. "How could you have possibly thought that was a good idea!?"

"We need to move on from never mentioning their names! We've got to start somewhere!"

"By bringing up Mary? By reminding Robbie exactly *how well* you knew his mother!?"

"I told you. I wasn't thinking about it like that!"

"That's just it, Pete. You never think! You just keep doing the wrong thing. You know how Robbie's been lately. He wasn't ready for this, and you should have fucking known that!"

I felt sorry for Pete. I understood where he was coming from, but Renn was right—he should have anticipated this would turn out badly.

Pete looked over at me and gave an awkward wave, attempting to break some of the tension. "Hey, Sadie. Nice to see you. Sorry about...all this."

I replied with a watery smile.

Renn's eyes darted back and forth between me and his uncle before he scrunched them into slits. He glared at the two of us as he pulled me closer. "What do you think, Sadie?" Acid laced his words. "You stuck up for Pete in the past. Should I forgive him for this?"

Whatthefuck? "Uh…You know I can't answer that. I just came in here to see if I could help cool things down."

"But you were so quick to tell me to see things his way before. To remind me *he's family*, that I should be forgiving. I suppose that's what you think I should do now—just ignore this shit?" Renn's quiet tone burned.

"Again, not my call." I looked him in the eye. "And I'm not sure what you're trying to get at here. I understand you're pissed, but there's no reason to be mad at me."

"I'm not mad." His voice rolled. "I'm just pointing out that a year ago you defended Pete, told me I should see things from his side. That he had his *reasons* for everything. But no matter what angle I look from, he's still a selfish dickwad who can't ever seem to do the right thing." Renn's chest heaved, hostility simmering. "Not to mention a jealous idiot. Who. Slept. With. His. Brother's. Wife." He directed that last bit of venom toward Pete.

I was stunned by the menace in Renn's tone. Archie had mentioned things weren't great between him and his uncle, but I hadn't realized his anger remained this intense.

"I thought—" Pete almost whined. "You said that…you agreed that the affair was…not your business. That we could leave it in the past."

"I know I said that. But it's hard." Renn stepped away from me and grabbed the snow globe from the table, shaking it and holding it up to eye level to look at the little Victorian village inside. "It's hard when you keep making it my business. Upsetting Robbie. When you keep bringing up Mary. And my dad. You keep making it so fucking easy to stay mad at you, Pete."

Renn continued looking at the globe, his eyeballs appearing exaggerated and oblong in the glass. Pete gripped a fist in his hand before taking a few quick strides.

"Yeah? Well, guess what, nephew—" Something seemed to break in Pete as he stepped toward Renn. "It's hard for me, too! To keep coming around here, knowing how much you and Robbie hate me, knowing how confused Gage is, but I keep doing it, I keep trying, because I know it's what Thomas would have—"

"*Fuck!*" At the mention of his father, Renn pulled his arm back and hurled the snow globe across the room, missing the large flat screen by a hair. Glass and water and little glittery snowflakes scattered everywhere as it shattered against the wall. "Don't tell me how hard this is *for you!*" he shouted.

At the crashing noise, Archie and the boys came running in from the living room, throwing the French doors wide. They stopped short at the entrance, taking in the scene, as Pete and Renn stared each other down. Gage barreled into my side, pushing his face against my hip. Robbie just stood there with his mouth in an O while Archie assessed the damage. I assumed that, like me, he was recalling the poor mason jar octopus Renn had smashed when he'd found out about Pete potentially being Gage's father.

Renn looked at all of us in turn before announcing, "Pete was just leaving."

He glared at his uncle, who looked like he might have something more to say but thought better of it. Instead, Pete muttered "Merry Christmas" and ran out the door to his car.

Renn stuck his hands in his pockets and marched toward his bedroom, declaring, "I just need ten minutes and I'll be fine."

Shockingly, Robbie and Gage seemed unsurprised by this turn of events, making it clear to me that they'd seen their brother and uncle butt heads many times. They headed to the kitchen after I reminded them I'd brought cookies, leaving me and Archie to deal with the aftermath in the den. I found cleaning supplies in the hall closet and pulled up most of the glass shards with a small sweeper. Archie produced a shop vac from the garage and suctioned up the rest of the mess. There were a few divots in the drywall from the force of the impact that would need to be filled in another day.

Archie spoke in hushed tones as we worked. "That's what it's been like, Sadie—it's just boiling in Renn, underneath. He doesn't know what to do with it."

"I know you warned me that he was still really mad at Pete, but...*goddamn.*"

He sighed. "Not just Pete, I suspect. Although I'm not a shrink." I eyed Archie, but he didn't explain his cryptic statement.

I felt like I'd just witnessed World War III, or at least something on a par with a Gordon Ramsey-hosted reality show. I'd sensed Renn had been concealing the depth of his anger with Pete from me. I was busy with school and work, balancing my own needs so much better in this relationship than I ever had with Henri. But that meant there were some things I could only know if Renn opened up and told me. And he wasn't talking.

"There've been other fights like that?" I asked Archie.

"Well, I'll admit this was worse than most. He hasn't broken shit since the studio that day. The snow globe must have been a bridge too far," Archie said. "It's usually fighting or silence. Pete tries. Pete fails. Renn blows up eventually. Rinse and repeat." Seemingly satisfied we were done, he lifted himself up to standing. Just before walking out of the room, he revealed, "Renny was having a bad morning, anyway. Sheryl called to wish him Merry Christmas, and he invited her over, but she said she already had plans. That's code for she ain't sober."

As I knelt alone on the soft gray carpet, stray pieces of glitter embedding themselves in my knee, I played the scene over in my mind. It had been the first time I'd seen such visceral evidence of Renn's pain and grief since we'd started officially dating. The instinct to comfort him was overwhelming.

The question of how to do that was even more so.

I WAITED THREE times the ten minutes Renn had asked for before heading to his bedroom, knocking softly. "Renn, I'm coming in."

He faced the door, sitting on his bed, appearing sheepish. "Sadie, I was just about to come find you. I'm really embarrassed. I'm sorry you had to see that. I feel so stupid, throwing things like a toddler."

I made sure my tone sounded concerned and not judgmental when I leaned against the doorway and replied, "It's kind of a go-to move for you, huh?"

He snorted. "I really miss that little octopus."

His remorse and embarrassment were genuine. I knew that. I understood having to cope. That's the thing about pain—when you let it live in you, eventually it has to find a way out. In Boston, Henri had always been critical in between bouts of kindness or indifference. But occasionally, he would go on hours-long benders of insulting me over how I looked, how I behaved, all the ways I failed to be a good girlfriend to him. Afterward, I'd go in the shower and sob it out. Not just stand under the spray, but literally curl up in a ball on top of the tiles and bawl while the water rained down on my face, drowning me and my noise.

It wasn't by accident that Renn hadn't thrown the octopus or the snow globe near anyone else. Even in the frenzy of the moment, he wasn't doing it to be violent. He did it because it was the most immediate form of catharsis. I wasn't saying it was healthy, but I did understand.

He rested his forehead into his fist. "I just wasn't prepared for all of this today."

I sat down beside him, leaning my head on his shoulder and grasping his hand in mine. "I know. Archie said you had a crap morning, too." He had control over himself, so I took a chance on venturing further. "Renn, I'm worried about you. I knew you were still carrying this anger, but I didn't know it was this bad. Like, eating you from the inside. If things aren't getting better and it's been this long, maybe you should consider trying something else. Maybe therapy—"

"No." He squeezed my hand gently, placating. "I am so glad it worked for you, but it's just not for me."

I tilted my chin down sadly. "Well, I think you need to do something, because I love you and it's difficult to just sit back and watch you go through this." Lifting my face to capture his gaze, I felt compelled to add, "And I know you're hurting, but it was really hard for me when you tried to blame me."

"When I what?"

"Renn, you basically implied this was my fault because I encouraged you to forgive Pete. I get you're mad, but none of this is on me."

"I know," he whispered. "I'm sorry if I did that. Honestly, I was so pissed, I don't even remember what I said."

"Even when you were saying it, I knew you didn't mean it. But it still hurt."

His face crumpled, as though he was holding back tears. He moved to rest his head in my lap, gripping the hem of my shirt. "I never want to do that to you, Sadie. I love you so much."

I ran my fingers through his messy curls, still somewhat unsettled, but also sure of his sincerity. And because it was Christmas, and had been a rough day, I didn't force the issue of him getting a better handle on things. I indulged him in his preferred coping method of avoiding the issue.

Renn came out of his room, a smile plastered on his face, and Robbie and Gage pretended their brother hadn't just smashed a snow globe and dismissed their uncle from the house. The boys were clearly used to the stuffing-things-down-and-not-discussing-them way of dealing with conflicts.

Archie and I shared a few meaningful glances as the brothers worked doggedly to maintain the façade all evening. They joked around, watching *A Christmas Story* in the den that had been a battle zone a few hours prior. Even Robbie had gotten the memo, smiling as Renn pulled me into his lap to share a mug of hot chocolate, tossing marshmallows into the air and catching them in his mouth.

Around eleven, Archie left, and we all went to bed. I startled when Renn reached for me almost immediately, but my initial hesitancy faded as I realized I was as eager as him to convince myself we were okay. When we woke in the morning, I felt able to put the previous day behind us. The boys were excited to open presents, including my humble offerings, and we ate breakfast. Besides a feast of eggs, toast, pancakes, and bacon, there were pop-top cinnamon rolls.

"Renn said we had to get these for you," Gage explained. "Because that's something you do on Christmas."

"My grandma used to make these for me." I pulled off a sticky piece and handed it to him, popping another in my mouth. The gesture reminded me why I fell in love with Renn.

We had agreed to exchange gifts privately, so later in the day Renn presented me with an oil painting he had done of me and Zach. It was the two of us, younger, heads together behind the bar at Hal's around the time we first met.

"I asked Zach for a photo, and he told me this was one of your favorites. I'm not a great painter, but I tried."

"It's beautiful, Renn." It wasn't a masterpiece, but it was certainly a solid rendering of the photograph. "I love you did this for me."

"I thought he could hang it up in the bar, you know, if it's good enough."

"I'll ask him. It would be nice next to the picture of Marshawn Lynch in a hoodie."

Renn laughed. "A solid pairing, for sure."

I handed him a little red gift bag. "It's not much," I warned. "I saw it at a swap meet in La Mirada and wanted you to have it."

Renn opened the bag to find a silver chain-link bracelet with an ouroboros charm.

"You gave me an ouroboros," I whispered, running a fingertip over my tattoo. "So, I wanted to give you one, too."

Renn undid the clasp and put it on his wrist, shaking his arm a bit until the charm rested in the middle. "I love it." He grabbed both my cheeks with his hands and kissed me solidly on the mouth. "And I love you."

It was a great ending to what had threatened to be a disaster of a holiday. I wouldn't soon forget Renn's outburst, but I'd also been around him long enough to appreciate it was a rarity, not indicative of the warm and loving man I knew him to be. We all lost our shit sometimes. Giving him grace was a no-brainer.

Still, the tension between Pete and Renn continued to fester.

I came home with Renn once to find Pete at the kitchen table playing a game with Gage, whereupon his uncle had simply stood up and left without a word. They had taken to working out most logistics and need-to-knows via text since in-person exchanges were so fraught. There was always an underlying combustive energy, the powder keg Archie had alluded to.

Yet, inexplicably, they still operated under the general principle that Pete was family, Renn unwilling to banish him complete-ly. Even with their utter inability to communicate. There were terse thank-yous when Pete agreed to babysit and more aggres-sive-than-passive arguments when plans had to change. Along with these mild everyday strains, I witnessed two more major blow-ups. One happened at Studio Obscurum when I came by to meet Renn. They were discussing purchasing new equipment, and Pete brought up Thomas's vision for the shop, refusing to stop talking about Renn's dad even after Renn exploded. Another happened at the house. During one of his ever-more-rare appearances for a family dinner, Pete asked Robbie to clear the table. This launched a shouting match over who had the right to boss who around, to which Pete added gasoline to the fire by stating that Thomas and Mary would have wanted Robbie to be more responsible.

Pete seemed more determined than ever to be his own worst enemy. But as I watched him navigate each interaction, I wondered if it was by design. No one could be this dense. *Was he bringing up Thomas on purpose? To what end?* I couldn't guess at his reasoning. What was undisputable was that the situation grew more untenable by the day. Something had to give.

CHAPTER
Twenty

T WAS A few days after my blessedly uneventful thirty-sixth birthday when I told Renn I wanted to approach Zach and Teddy about being their DIY surrogate. I had done a ton of research and finally felt prepared to have the conversation. I also had a renewed sense of urgency due to the fact that Zach and Teddy had surprised the hell out of us by coming back from Mexico married. They'd said there would be another ceremony for friends and family later, but their main objective hadn't been romance. It had been to make their relationship legally official, providing a better chance at adoption. Seeing them so laser-focused on the goal of parenthood made me even more sure of my decision.

The opportunity to discuss my offer arrived organically in the form of dinner plans we'd made weeks ago with Zach and Teddy to celebrate Renn's twenty-fifth birthday. I'd asked Renn if he minded having his celebration overshadowed by such a heavy conversation. He'd shaken his head with a wink, observing that all life-altering decisions were easier to make with Rosita's home-made salsa bar nearby.

As we prepared to head to the restaurant, I felt surprisingly relaxed, confident in both the veracity and practicality of my proposal.

"You told them to get me a present, right?" Renn joked as he changed into jeans and a black sweater. I'd met him at his house so we could go to dinner together. He was stretching out his hands and groaning a bit, the result of a six-hour tattoo session that day.

"Thank God it's your birthday." I reached out to massage his palm. "I'm glad to put an end to this one week where I'm *twelve* years older than you."

Renn extended his other hand behind me to zip up my powder blue mini dress, obviously pleased to see my tattoo on full display. He put his lips on the top of my shoulder. "Mmm...my sexy Mrs. Robinson. You are the best quarter-life crisis any guy ever had."

"Shut up. That's not funny," I said, laughing. But my laughter died as his hand continued up my thigh, drawing circles with his thumb and making me shiver as he scratched his nails lightly over my ink.

The buzz of Renn's phone in his pocket interrupted us just as he reached my hem. Rolling his eyes at the intrusion, he leaned back to check the message.

"Dammit! Robbie didn't make it for detention today. They're gonna add three more days."

"Robbie got detention?" I wasn't surprised Renn hadn't mentioned it. He rarely volunteered any issues with his brothers.

"Yeah. His science teacher caught him scratching his initials into the wood of his desk. When she gave him a few days of detention, he kept mouthing off, so it turned into two weeks."

"How very John Bender of him."

"Huh?"

"*The Breakfast Club*?"

"The what?"

"Jesus. Never mind."

"He's at Ryder's right now and I trust Lydia, so I guess I can wait to talk to him, but I wish he'd get it together. He's not exactly headed to juvie, and his grades are okay, but the backtalk to his teachers is new. I don't want things to escalate."

I'd gotten along well with Robbie so far. He was on the cross-country and track teams at school, so we went running together sometimes. It was great because we got to hang out without the pressure to talk. I wouldn't say we'd had any Hallmark moments, but he *had* once told me he liked me as Renn's girlfriend, and that I made good cookies. I pulled Renn into a hug. "If there's anything I can do to help, just let me know."

"Don't worry. I can handle my brothers." Renn kissed me and ran his hands down my back. "Right now, I want to focus on you and this dinner with Zach and Teddy." Renn loved to caretake. He *hated* being taken care of. He needed to understand it wasn't a burden for me to hear about his family. I sighed as we exited the bedroom.

We had one more obstacle to navigate before getting out the door. Pete was coming by to keep an eye on Gage while we were out. Renn's uncle let himself in, carrying a pizza.

"Hey, Pete," I greeted him as the two men stared at each other.

"Um...hi, Sadie." Pete took a chance on addressing his nephew directly. "I brought a pizza for dinner. Hope that's okay."

"There's actually something staying warm in the oven." Renn grew instantly irritated. "Chicken and broccoli."

"Oh. I just know Gage likes pizza."

"I'm sure he would love to have pizza for dinner. He'd also like ice cream for breakfast and to stay up and watch *The Daily Show*. But it's a school night." Renn's voice pitched higher.

Pete tried to thread the needle. "Okay then. Maybe I can just offer him a slice or two if he finishes his broccoli?"

"So you can be the hero and I can be the dick that denies him pizza?"

This was getting ridiculous. I put my hand on Renn's bicep. "Pete's compromise is okay, right?" I almost pointed out that there had been at least five school nights I could think of since we'd been dating when Renn had ordered pizza for dinner. He just refused to give Pete an inch. "It's just pizza, not heroin, and we need to leave."

Renn exhaled noisily as he gathered his hair into its bun-pony. "Fine. Gage's finishing up in the shower now." He grabbed my hand and pushed us past Pete. "We'll be home by ten."

I looked back to see Pete shaking his head in the universal motion for *what the fuck just happened*? He saw and gave me a tiny wave, mouthing, "Thank you."

OUR DINNER WITH Teddy and Zach went smoothly. I presented them with my idea before the chips and salsa were even on the table. By drinks and appetizers, I had answered the twenty different ways Teddy had found to ask me if I was very, very sure I wouldn't get too attached to the baby and change my mind. Three taco platters later, we'd agreed it would be prudent to contact a lawyer and get whatever legal protections we could, even if they wouldn't be standard practice. By the time we'd ordered dessert, all four of us agreed this was the best baby-making option for Zach and Teddy.

"You're positive you're okay with this?" Zach asked his husband for the tenth time. "I trust Sadie with my life, but that's because I know her almost as well as I know myself. I don't want to get too excited and then find out you'd still rather do it through an agency."

"Zach, if you tell me you like this idea, then I'm willing to put my trust in you. I realize that after the miscarriage you were really hesitating to go that route again. I saw how hard the process was on you." Teddy reached an arm across the table and grabbed my hand. "But now Sadie is offering us another way, and for that, I am so grateful. Even if it scares me."

I could see Teddy's love for Zach at war with his natural inclination to do things by the book. "Is there anything more I can do to put your mind at ease?" I asked. Renn reached under the table and squeezed my leg in support.

"No. Loving Zach has been an unpredictable adventure. I hadn't known how much color I was missing until he turned up the dial." Teddy let go of my hand and turned back to Zach. "I'm scared shitless. I am. But let's make this baby journey another adventure."

"It's gonna be great," I assured him, lacing my fingers with Renn's on my thigh. "And think of it this way—you'll never have to feel weird about touching my belly or asking me how I'm doing too many times. I have no shame, either. One hundred percent, I'll be calling you at three in the morning to bring me ice cream and hot sauce or whatever. And I will need near-constant foot rubs and pillow fluffing."

"Should I already be regretting this?" Zach deadpanned.

"Oh, no babe," I panned dead back at him. "You're committed now. Nine months of indentured servitude and pampering all for me."

Renn put our joined hands on the table. "I'm happy to help with that pampering, guys." He smiled at Zach and Teddy. "I'll even make sure Sadie eats her vegetables and gets sleep, doesn't stress too much. I'm okay leaving the foot rubs to Zach, though."

I slapped him playfully on the shoulder as Concerned Teddy reappeared, this time speaking to Renn. "And you're sure you're okay with this? Your girlfriend being a surrogate?"

"I love Sadie, and I think we understand each other. So much of our relationship is atypical, we've learned to trust our instincts." Renn continued slowly, so Teddy could imbibe his sincerity. "At the end of the day, she deserves to do amazing things, and I get why she wants to do this, why she needs to. The same way she understands why my brothers always come first for me. Because even if it's complicated, you show up for family." He brought our hands to his lips. "And Zach is her family."

Renn placed a chaste kiss on my knuckles as Zach caught my gaze. He glanced subtly toward my boyfriend and smiled at me with approval. Seeing Renn through my best friend's eyes made me love them both even more.

It seemed fairly settled after that. Zach and Teddy said they wanted to give my offer a few weeks to settle in their minds, so they could figure out if they had more questions, and then they'd start reaching out to their lawyer to see if they could anticipate any legal hurdles. Tentatively, we decided that we might be ready for Operation Fancy Turkey Baster—Zach's term—as soon as the spring. Assuming Teddy could make it through without letting his doomsday scenarios get the better of him, we were *doing this*. The evening felt truly celebratory, making me eager to get home and jump Renn's bones. But the daiquiris we'd had with dinner had left an impression. I excused myself to go to the restroom.

WHEN I EXITED the stall, three dolls decorating the shelf above the sink captured my attention as I washed my hands. They were supposed to be Day of the Dead-themed mariachis but looked more like creepy Beetlejuices wearing sombreros. The macabre little monsters were hypnotizing.

Which was the reason I didn't immediately notice her.

But then I saw.

I froze, feet stuck to the floor, as a woman I thought I'd never lay eyes on again stood at the other sink. She was busy holding a squirmy toddler, trying to coax the boy into putting his fingers under the faucet. When she peered up, her startled eyes met mine in the mirror.

"Sadie?"

Her expensively dyed hair was the same as ever, gathered in the type of fussy updo that only wealthy women in their sixties and seventies could get away with. The beige linen pants suit she wore had been tailored perfectly to her still-trim figure, and she'd apparently kept up with the procedures that softened the lines on her face. Nothing had changed—except instead of a designer purse, she carried a diaper bag.

"Mrs. Montgomery," I acknowledged Henri's mother flatly and glanced at the giggling toddler in her arms. The one with Henri's eyes. *Oh my God. This is him. This is Henri's son.*

She looked at me expectantly, like I was supposed to say more, but I had no words. If Henri's mother was here, if Henri's son was here, then he was probably here as well. I rushed past the woman as she stuttered, intent on reaching my table and telling Renn we had to get the hell out of there. Now. I could explain later.

But I wasn't one step out of the restroom, in a small nook that had once upon a time housed a pay phone, when I ran headfirst into Henri.

Head. First. Into. Henri.

Henri.

He was there. Somehow. Standing in front of me. Reaching to steady me.

Henri. Not a voice in my head. Not an apparition. In the flesh. In the alcove at Rosita's, gaping at me.

He startled as I bounced off his chest, both of us blinking hard and shaking our heads in disbelief as we realized who we were seeing.

"Holy shit...Sadie?"

I regarded him with his amazing suit and golden fake tan.

Put together as always. Meanwhile, I looked like precisely what I was—someone who'd spent the evening having fruity drinks and heavy conversation. My cheeks were red from the alcohol, not to mention I'd had to grab my decidedly unsexy Chester's Coffee Shop fleece from the car to fight the restaurant's arctic AC, so my cute little dress was covered.

My knee-jerk reaction was to wonder what Henri thought about my appearance.

Fuck that shit.

I straightened and made to bolt past Henri at the same moment he grasped my wrist. "Wait...please."

"Let go of me."

He dropped my arm instantly, but implored, "Please."

Mrs. Montgomery—her name was Cecelia, Cece to her friends, but in all eight years I'd known her, she'd always been Mrs. Montgomery to me—came out of the bathroom, hastily drying the boy's hands with a paper towel.

"Sadie, I'm so glad you're here. Henri said you might join us."

Huh? This woman had never had two kind words to say to me the whole time I'd lived with her son. She had sent me articles to "improve my fashion sense" and had once insisted I see her hairdresser because my highlights made me look like a "harlot." *And why would she think I'd be joining them?* I looked at Henri, who turned to his mother.

"Mother, can you take Liam to our table? I need to talk to Sadie, then I'll be right there."

"Of course, but why don't we all just go sit down?"

"Please, Mother."

She gave me a slight smile and eyed her son, confused, before patting me on the hand and offering, "So nice to see you, dear."

I couldn't stop myself from taking another peek at the toddler she held. Now I knew his name. Liam.

"Sadie, I think we should talk."

Henri wasn't touching me, but his commanding voice turned me to stone. I was still processing that he was here. Here and acting like it hadn't been a year since he'd last texted me, two years since I'd left him.

There was a part of me that yearned to give him the finger and walk away. But then I remembered my conversation with Zach about wanting to prove to myself I could handle letting Henri say whateverthefuck he thought he needed to. This reckoning was two years in the making, fate apparently deciding that today was the day. And I was safe. Renn, Zach, and Teddy weren't facing me, but I could see them from where I was standing.

I exhaled heavily, willing my arms to stay loose at my sides. Calming, I registered my surroundings—the Mexican pop music blaring from the bar, steaming fajitas being delivered to someone's table. I was good. I could do this.

"You think we should talk? Okay. What should we talk about?"

He appeared briefly flustered by the confident derision in my voice before his usual cockiness returned. "Darling, you know we need to discuss...us." He ran a hand over his face. "Let's find a quiet place where we can speak freely."

He was delusional. I watched him evenly, feeling the vice grip of his power over me loosening. He'd inflicted scars that would never fully fade, but as I continued to meet his gaze, I was sure of his inability to create new abrasions.

Henri mistook my silence for acquiescence, because of course he did.

"I'd love to spend some real quality time together," he said. "I'm in town on business, but my schedule's flexible."

His mouth kept moving as he spoke about his itinerary, but I didn't hear. Since I was feeling so steady, I figured I should take this opportunity to get answers to all my lingering questions. I'd made the mistake of leaving things open-ended before. Henri was trying to convince me to come sit with him at his table when I cut him off.

"You bring your son with you on business trips? He can't stay with his...mom?" I glanced over at the admittedly adorable little boy, recalling Henri's insane text suggesting that the three of us could somehow become a family.

Henri flinched at my abrupt inquiry but had an answer. "Liam's mom is not in the picture. It was her choice, and her loss, because he's a wonderful child. My mother helps. And I have a nanny."

Although he recited these facts with little inflection—a prepared statement—it was clear he loved his son. He continued in a warmer voice. "I brought them this time because it's been a tough year, so I was thinking maybe Disneyland was in order."

Cecelia still stared at us with abject interest. "Why does your mother think I'd join you for dinner? I haven't seen you in years. Plus, she always hated me."

"She never hated you, Sadie. She's just...particular. And ever since Liam came along, she's been after me to reconcile with you. I might have let her believe we're on our way toward getting back together."

I crossed my arms. "So, basically, you're just a stupid Liar Mc-Liarface." *Jesus. Smooth, Sadie. And you'd been doing so well.*

He smirked. "I see your language is still very...mature. Besides, it's not exactly a lie. You know I want you back. We belong together."

"Yeah, I got your texts." I needed closure, to know why he'd never followed up on them. After all, I'd been so affected by those messages I'd almost lost Renn for good. "Honestly, Henri, after you sent those, I thought I'd see you. I mean, I know Zach told you to stay away, but it surprised me you gave up so easily."

"You sound disappointed. I knew you missed me." He grinned like he'd won something. "I had every intention of seeing you after I sent those texts. I had planned to track you down and get you to talk. What I said stands—after eight years together, you owed me a conversation."

"Fuck you, Henri. After you knocked up someone else, I owed you nothing," I whisper-shouted to avoid making a scene, but my vehemence was unmistakable. And I was done with this little reunion. With perfect clarity, I realized that all the closure I needed lay in the fact that everything had turned out for the best. "My life has been a million percent better since we split up. And make no mistake—we *are* over. So we don't need to find a place to talk. There's nothing more to say. Please tell your mother I will definitely not be joining you." And because I was one hundred percent the bigger person, I added, "Cute baby. Excuse me."

As I made to walk by him, he commanded, "Wait."

I recognized that tone, the one I had responded to for so long. And maybe it was the years of history, the tentacles of hurts long since inflicted, but something made me stop and ground out, "What?"

"When I sent those texts on your birthday last year, I would have followed up, found you, talked to you, except..." Henri scratched his head, indecision tinging his face. "Except my father died." At that, I turned around and faced him again as he spoke. "Heart attack. And it's been a shitshow ever since, handling the estate, getting my mother set up, taking care of Liam, everything with the promotion. Losing him was...tough. I wanted you to take me back, but I also didn't want you to—"

"Didn't want me to what?"

He paused. "I didn't want you to see me like that."

I couldn't stop my eyes from widening momentarily. I knew how much seeking his father's approval had impacted his life. I recalled a dinner after father and son had played a round of golf with two of Henri Sr.'s buddies. Henri's father had spent the entire meal making fun of his son's game. Henri had taken the ribbing, seething next to me. Once we were alone later, he'd unleashed his mood, railing at how terrible I was at conversation and how I should strive to be as elegant as his mother. Henri had often framed his criticisms through the lens of "what would my parents think?" I could only imagine his father's death had been both liberating and terrifying.

And because I knew his pride, realized what this admission cost him, I squeezed his arm quickly. "I'm sorry about your dad, Henri. Truly."

I let go and began to head back to my table. He pouted after me. "That's it?"

"What's it? I feel bad about your father. But you can't use that to manipulate me into speaking with you further."

"That's not what I was trying to do."

He believed it. I sighed. "Go back to your mother. Go back to your son."

"Sadie, please. Talk to me. You owe me that. I *was* planning on trying to see you this trip, wishing you a happy birthday in person. I know you still need me, just like I need you!" His raised voice was attracting attention from the other diners.

"I don't need anything from you. Not anymore." I stepped away. "Henri, I wasn't just standing by this bathroom waiting for you to run into me. I'm here with my boyfriend." I gestured toward my table.

Henri looked over at where I was pointing and scoffed. "Zach is your boyfriend now?"

"Not Zach, idiot. The hot guy with the beanie."

With that, I again attempted an exit, but he followed me. "Sadie—"

I reached the table in five seconds. Zach's back was still to Henri, and I went to take my seat across from him, next to Renn, while Henri persisted.

"After everything, I deserve a chance."

Renn stared up in confusion at the man who had trailed me from the restroom. I grimaced at him just as Zach exclaimed, "What the fuck?!" grabbing the attention of every nearby table.

Looking between Zach and Henri, Renn put two and two together, realizing who the unknown man must be. Zach made to stand, but Renn reached across the table and pulled him down by the forearm with a firm, "I've got this."

"You need to leave," Renn spoke levelly to Henri.

Henri ignored him and gazed down at my head. "Darling, please. You can't expect me to walk away when we haven't even spoken."

Renn stood up then, the sound of his chair scratching across the floor echoing. "Don't fucking call her darling."

Henri sneered at Renn and looked back at me. "You left me for this...child?"

Renn made a move like he was about to put his hands on Henri, but I stopped him. "I didn't leave you *for* anyone, Henri. I left you. Just you." I held my ground, but it was beginning to be more of a struggle. Other diners gawked at us, and the hostess was whispering furiously to the manager, clearly debating an intervention.

"I can tell you still care, Sadie. I saw it in your eyes when I told you about my father."

"You need to go, man." Renn glared at Henri. "Right now."

With the eyes of everyone in the restaurant on him, Henri tipped his head at all of us in turn, including a stunned Teddy. Then Henri went to his table on the other side of the dining room. As he reached his mother, I saw him waving toward us. I didn't know what he was telling her, and I didn't care. I just wanted to be home and safe in Renn's arms.

A few hours later, that's exactly where I was, resting my chin on Renn's chest as I listened to the rhythm of his sleeping breaths. I reflected that I'd held my own with Henri, been firm in my assertions. But there had been something in the set of his shoulders as he'd stomped back toward his table at the restaurant that had me awake and on edge. Henri and I hadn't finished our conversation.

CHAPTER
Twenty-One

I HALFWAY EXPECTED TO get a text from Henri, or find him outside my apartment. He had the resources to track me down, even if he hadn't done so yet. But I wasn't necessarily dreading it. Now that I'd survived seeing him once, I was confident I could again. There was even a small part of me that *welcomed* the possibility, as I continued to feel like I had that night, that our story wasn't quite finished.

Renn was handling the situation less well. Henri had always been more of an abstract to him. Seeing my ex in the flesh, declaring he still wanted me, had rattled my boyfriend.

"Why not at least try to get a restraining order?" Renn and I were in his kitchen making homemade pizza. Well, as homemade as it could be when starting with readymade frozen crust.

"For what? Eating Mexican food?" I spread out tomato sauce on the rectangular dough. "C'mon, Renn. No court is going to issue a restraining order for some texts he sent over a year ago and an accidental run-in during dinner."

"I know." Renn hmphed as he came up behind me, pressing his chest to my back. "But I don't have to like it."

"Even if he showed up here tomorrow, there are no words he could say to change anything. I'm with you, and it's exactly where I want to be."

That seemed to reassure him. He continued to rest his chin on my shoulder, breath tickling my skin. "Sorry. I think I'm just pissed because Robbie is still acting up."

"Acting up?" Renn hadn't mentioned anything new regarding Robbie's behavior. "What's going on?"

"School called. He almost finished the detention from the desk thing, but apparently he made a scene at an assembly this morning so they're adding a few more days. If anything else happens, they'll suspend him." Renn moved back and leaned his elbows against the counter. Noticing the concerned look on my face, he hurried to add, "Don't worry. I'll figure it out."

I shook my head. Ever since Snowglobegate, I'd been hyperaware of Renn's behavior when it came to dealing with difficult situations or emotions. He only appeared to have two modes—pretend they didn't exist, versions of "nothing's wrong," or refuse to discuss them, versions of "I'm fine." Sometimes both. It was maddening.

Dammit with this going it alone horseshit. How come me being a surrogate was something for both of us to discuss and tackle together, but when the issue was about him or his family, it was for him to figure out on his own?

I was about to push the subject when the front door opened. Robbie and Ryder made their way into the kitchen, shedding coats and backpacks along the way.

"Hey, Sadie." Robbie seemed in a rare good mood as he turned to Renn. "Bro, is it okay if Ryder stays for dinner? We want to play Mario."

Renn exhaled thickly. "Funny thing, *bro*. I got a call from your school today. They said you made quite the impression during assembly."

Robbie and Ryder looked at each other, then started cracking up. "Those things are so dumb," Robbie said. "They brought in an *expert*..." He used air quotes. "To talk about mental health and suicide prevention." The tethers of the karmic universe must have been snapping as I recalled these presentations were funded by organizations like the one Renn had been supporting at the House Party of Hope so long ago.

Renn narrowed his eyes at his brother, and I was sure it was only Ryder's presence that kept him from unleashing. "And what's so bad about that?"

Robbie kept laughing, but in a forced way, almost hysterical. He shoved his hands in his pockets and refused to meet Renn's gaze. "It's just so lame when they try to tell you how special you are, how much everyone will miss you if you do something so...final." The laughter died on his face. "I don't need anyone to explain to me what it's like when someone commits suicide."

Poor Ryder did not register the temperature change in the room, continuing to chuckle as he added, "It was awesome. Robbie straight up walked out in the middle of the assembly and shouted, 'cool TED Talk dude' to the presenter. The whole school saw. So epic."

I looked at Robbie, standing stoically next to his friend. He reminded me of myself sometimes. I'd lived enough life to comprehend there were times when rule-breaking was necessary to one's mental health—because sometimes "the rules" were a suffocating, untenable box. People dismissed this as "acting out." Robbie chose not to be subjected to pain, on display for his entire school. He acted out instead. Running and anger and avoidance. Those were his coping mechanisms. As a kid, mine had been shutting down. I had considerable empathy for Robbie's pain. He needed help to manage it.

Renn's voice penetrated my thoughts as he spoke gently to his brother. "I get why you left."

I couldn't stop the thought from forming in my brain. *Of course Renn got it—he modeled the practice of turning away from his emotions every day.*

Renn turned to his brother. "Ryder can stay. But Robbie...?"

"Yeah?"

"You need to do the detention. Without complaint. I understand the reason you took off, but you have to face the consequences. Otherwise, they'll suspend you."

Robbie nodded and grabbed Ryder's arm, tugging him toward the den.

Renn started chopping up romaine for a salad while I went back to scattering bell peppers on the dough. I wanted to talk to him about finding better ways to deal with his own grief and anger, that I didn't think Robbie could get better until he did.

I was still ruminating on how best to broach that discussion when Pete and Gage came in from Little League. Considering Gage's team had two or three games per week—many with the extremely-unfriendly-to-working-parents start time of 4:30—we'd agreed that attending them would require a group effort between Renn, Pete, Archie, and myself.

Pete's schedule was the most flexible, so he had been covering the lion's share. He and Gage continued to spend more time together. Pete hadn't made progress with Robbie, but I'd often found him playing games or building Lego sets with Gage. His uncle's presence still put Renn on edge, even though he'd resigned himself to its frequency.

We'd been expecting them back a little earlier, but the reason for the delay became clear when Pete hefted a grocery tote full of ice cream sundae supplies.

He saw Renn glaring at the bag. "Don't worry, Renn. I already told Gage you had to agree, but we wanted to celebrate that little man hit his first home run today!"

"A home run!" Renn gave Gage a fist bump. "Awesome job buddy!"

"It was so cool!" This was the first year Gage was in the division where players pitched to each other, and he'd been struggling more than when he'd played T-Ball or coach toss. "I think I'm finally getting the swing of it! Get it—the *swing* of it." Gage laughed as he bounced up and down on his heels. "Uncle Pete told me that one."

"That's great. Hey, listen—your brother is in the den with Ryder playing *Mario Kart*. Go in and tell them I said you get to take a turn, to celebrate your hit."

Gage took off like a shot down the hallway.

Renn turned to his uncle as he pinched the bridge of his nose. "Pete, telling Gage I have to agree to the ice cream doesn't help. I'm still the bad guy if I say no."

Was this *Groundhog Day*? Hadn't they just had this argument? Before Renn could get even more worked up, I intervened, putting my hand on his. "I think sundaes would be a great way to celebrate Gage's big game. After dinner, of course."

Pete put the ice cream in the freezer before heading into the den to say hello to Robbie. He had zero chance of getting a reply, and every chance of getting told off, but seemed to view this ritual as obligatory every time he came to the house. Renn volleyed his eyes between me and Pete's retreating form. "I can't say no if both of you are against me," he grumbled.

"Hey, that's not fair." I stood in front of him and put my hands on his shoulders. "I'm never against you. Tonight just isn't a good time to have another big fight. It's already been a rough day with Robbie—"

"And I missed Gage's big hit," Renn spoke so quietly, I almost couldn't make out the words.

I felt terrible for him. He took so much pride in always being there for his brothers. I gave his shoulder a gentle squeeze before running my hands up and down his arms. "Don't be so hard on yourself. You had to work. Gage understands. There'll be other games. Other hits."

Renn shook his head sadly. He reached out to wrap me in his arms, and I sighed internally as he held me close. He was already feeling guilty. Talking to him about setting a better example for the boys was a no-go, at least for tonight.

Pete came back in the kitchen, his expression showing he had something more serious on his mind than ice cream. I widened my eyes at him and frowned, trying to signal that this was not a good time to bring up anything substantive with Renn. He didn't get the message.

"Renn?"

"What is it, Pete?" Renn pulled back from me, instantly on alert.

"I think you were right."

Renn let out an exasperated sound before glaring at him. "Am I supposed to read your mind? What was I right about?"

Pete released a whoosh of his own and took an extra fortifying breath for good measure. "We should find out about Gage. If he's mine."

"Ooooh-kaaaaay." Renn's posture grew less rigid. "I've already told you I think it's something we need to know. Why are you acting so cagey?"

"Because..." Pete coughed and blew out more air like Darth Vader had just released him from a chokehold. "Because...if it turns out that he is my son..." He paused and cleared his throat again. "I want to tell him."

There was stunned silence as Renn and I processed what Pete was saying.

It didn't last.

"What?!" Renn clenched his fists as he shouted, and for an

instant I thought he was going to advance on Pete. "No fuck-ing way!"

At his intensity, I whipped my head around to check the hallway and the closed doors to the den, confirming the boys hadn't heard. I surreptitiously glanced around the kitchen for any small items Renn might decide to hurl against the wall, keeping a protective eye on the turtle-shaped sugar bowl I had developed a particular fondness for.

Pete made his case. "Look, Renn. I realize this isn't what we discussed earlier, but I've been thinking a lot about it. Keeping this secret, not finding out, made sense when Thomas was alive, but now it doesn't. I love Gage. We've been getting along great. I want to be a real father to him."

"No. Fucking. Way. He's already lost Dad once. I won't put him through that again."

"Gage doesn't even remember Thomas! He was practically a toddler. It's not the same for him as it is for the rest of us."

"No! You can't just waltz in here and expect me to go along with this. What happens to Gage when you decide to fuck off again, huh?"

"I'm not going anywhere, Renn. Christ, I've been sticking it out this whole past year, trying to make amends, with you and Robbie treating me like a flaming pile of shit the whole time, not giving an inch. But I'm still fucking *here*, aren't I?"

"But for how long?"

"For. Ever. You can keep spitting and fighting and putting all your crap on me, but I meant what I said. I'm here and I love you and your brothers and I want to make this right."

"Fuck you!" Renn snarled at his uncle, all instinct now, running off adrenaline and years of pent-up resentment.

Pete ran his fingers through his hair and paced back and forth. De-escalation seemed called for, but he clearly had no idea how to facilitate it. Neither did I.

"What do you think?" Renn turned my way abruptly, fury blackening his features.

"Me?" I stammered.

"Yes. You. Should I let him potentially implode Gage's entire life?" Renn shifted back to Pete. "You realize this is going to hurt Robbie, right, if it comes out? His brother becomes his half-brother-slash-cousin? He's already on the edge. Or does that even matter to you?"

"Of course it matters," Pete gritted out. "I get that the whole situation is messed up, but you know as well as I do it'll all come out eventually. Didn't we learn last year that secrets don't stay hidden forever?"

Renn looked at me again. "Well?"

I knew Renn wasn't asking for my honest opinion. He just wanted me to validate his way of thinking. I didn't want to tell Renn the truth, that I agreed with Pete. Secrets always came out, and ultimately, it would be better for them to make a conscious decision to inform the boys, to control the narrative, rather than risk a repeat of the red envelope fiasco. It would hurt, sure, but this family was already hurting. What would cause the least pain?

My silence gave Renn his answer. "You fucking agree with him!" I looked down at my feet. "I can't believe this. You're siding with Pete...again!" Renn looked around and I felt a momentary panic for the sugar bowl turtle, but he settled for banging his fist against the wall and fleeing to his bedroom, slamming the door so hard the frame shook.

The oven timer dinged. Still slightly shocked by Renn's intensity, I pulled the pizza out while Pete leaned on the counter. "Sadie, thank you so much for—"

"Don't, Pete." I held up a hand. "It's not to help you. I just happen to think you have a point. I hate that Renn feels this way, like he's being ganged up on."

"You probably don't believe me, but I hate it, too."

A curt nod was my only reply.

Ten minutes later, I made my way down the hall to Renn's room, rapping on his door twice before opening it. Déjà vu assaulted me. Christmas Eve. Renn was in the same position on his bed, facing the door. He appeared controlled, but nowhere near ready to have a conversation about how he needed to get a hold of his anger and stop *literally shutting the door on me*. I thought some distance might be called for. A change of script.

"I think I'm going to sleep at my apartment tonight," I said. "Give you some space."

"That's a good idea."

Well, okay then. I turned around, intent on leaving the house before I started crying.

"Wait!" Renn reached out to grab the hem of my shirt. "Sadie, I...I want you here. I always do. But I don't want to say something I'll regret. I just need to think this through on my own without being distracted by whether you and Pete are on the same side."

"You know that's not how it is. I'm always on your side." I sighed. "When are you gonna figure out that you don't have to be an island?"

Renn looked up at me with red-rimmed eyes, calmer. "You actually think we should tell Gage?"

I sat down next to him on the edge of the bed, laying my hand over his. "I think the first thing you should do is get the test done. Find out. It may all be a moot point." I rested my head on his shoulder. "If it turns out Pete is Gage's father, I agree it's best not to hide it."

"Really?"

"Look at it this way—Gage will get to have a dad. You and Robbie and I don't have our fathers anymore. Would you deny Gage if he has that chance?"

Renn seemed pensive for a moment and then groaned into my neck. "No." He placed a kiss on my clavicle. "I just don't want my brothers to get hurt." I reached up to run a hand through his hair, holding his head close. After a minute, he whispered, "And I want us to be okay, Sadie."

"Me too." He clung to me a little while longer in the silence—not exactly fraught, but uncertain nonetheless.

I wished Renn realized that having a serious relationship meant that he had someone in his corner for the hard stuff. He seemed to understand it from the other side. Hadn't he done everything in his power to make me feel safe and cared for when I first laid down on his tattoo table? Been patient with me as I worked to banish Henri-in-my-head? I wanted him to know that I could do more for him, for his family, than just help cook dinner and cheer at his brothers' extracurriculars. But he wasn't in the right frame of mind for that discussion. No way would he hear me after that fight with Pete. He'd see it as another attack.

I waited until after ice cream sundaes before I took off. Throughout dessert, Renn and Pete competed in the game of which man could be more aggressively silent, and I left feeling unsettled. It was weird coming back to my apartment after spending almost every night in Pasadena. The white walls seemed lifeless, and I admitted to myself it was time to think about moving. I loved the neighborhood, but Zach had been home. This place was just drywall and cheap carpet.

I spent the rest of the night cleaning, watching TV, and reading through a subreddit on surrogacy. Worries about Renn and Pete and Robbie sat in my stomach like boulders, and the fact we'd chosen to spend the night apart wasn't relieving my anxiety. I'd come into this relationship because I was ready to be a genuine partner for Renn. But if he wouldn't let me support him—or even admit the depth of his emotions—then we were at an impasse.

I woke up still nursing my fears. An overnight text from Renn saying he'd ordered a DNA testing kit online compounded them. If FedEx cooperated, they could know Gage's paternity in a week or two.

Ten days later, the results hadn't arrived, and it didn't seem like mine and Renn's relationship was back on track. We were doing the same things we'd done before, but it felt different. On a scale of "what's for dinner?" to "what's going to happen if my littlest brother turns out to be my cousin?" our conversations remained locked at level one.

His insistence on normalcy bordered on manic. Cute little love notes sent via text, sometimes more than one per day. "I love you more than I ever thought possible," and "I'm so happy you're mine," all interspersed with fun dad jokes and GIFs that I was certain were meant to evoke memories of the time we first met—a time when I was still careful about what I asked him, how much I probed. They didn't give me fond fuzzies. They made me a little nauseous.

I wanted to pre-game what we might do if the test came back as a match. But he wouldn't. We sat next to each other at two of Gage's practices. I helped him repaint a wall at the studio. Renn quizzed me for my Advanced Communications final. Showed up unannounced at Chester's with a bouquet of lilies. Surprised me with takeout after a shift at Hal's. Made love to me like a man on a mission.

I attempted to speak to him about my concerns, but he shut me down every time, assuring me everything was fine. He had it under control. No need for me to worry. I should focus on being a surrogate. On my classes. On anything other than the fact that my boyfriend was possibly unraveling.

CHAPTER

Twenty-Two

March 22, 2016

AFTER TWO WEEKS of tension masked behind routine, I woke up resolute in my decision to force a discussion with Renn. From the bedroom, I heard Gage pouring cereal into a bowl. A stench reminiscent of a day-old gas station burrito wafting down the hall indicated Robbie was still on his kick of eating microwaved sausage for breakfast. Renn cursed softly as he stomped around by the closet, searching for a belt that had mysteriously vanished.

"Renn, I want you to talk to me. It's hard to just do nothing when you're clearly burning from the inside." It was my second attempt this morning to engage him.

He took a pause in his belt hunt to roll his eyes. "Can we not have this conversation and say we did? You keep insisting something's wrong, but I'm fine. It's in your head."

Ugh. I hated when Renn reminded me of Henri. Not exactly gaslighting but in the same variety pack. At least I'd gotten to the point in my life where the trick didn't work anymore.

"It's not in my head. You're pissed about meeting with the school today." He had an appointment with Robbie's counselor that morning. There had been no other detention-worthy incidents, but they'd asked him to come in to talk about Robbie's behavior. "And because the DNA results still aren't back."

"You know what, you're right. I do have that bullshit meeting today, and I *am* annoyed that the results aren't in. So maybe lay off, okay?"

I was so tired of pushing everything aside. But he did have a rough day ahead. "Alright, Renn. But we need to discuss what's been going on with you and Pete, and Robbie. I'm concerned about you."

He scoffed dismissively and I felt a stab of frustration in my gut.

I recalled those few times he'd opened up to me about losing his dad. But ever since finding out about Pete and Mary, he'd been almost completely buttoned-up. And as the tension within his family had escalated, he seemed less and less like the Renn I thought I knew.

We'd achieved part of what Archie had hoped for when he'd spoken to me about Renn's state of mind in November, why he'd thought I'd be good for him. Renn was undeniably happier. Our relationship had fulfilled him enough to relieve some of his burdens. I'd provided a buffer for Pete to forge a good relationship with Gage. As a couple, we were fun and creative and easy. But how strong of a partnership could we achieve if Renn couldn't be honest with me about his feelings? His darker thoughts? I hated watching the way he powered through his pain. It was breaking him.

I produced the belt Renn was seeking from a basket of folded laundry. Some of his strain eased when he took it from me, chuckling. "You really hate putting things in drawers, don't you?"

"It's a character flaw. Sue me." I raised an eyebrow and smiled. We still had our moments.

"Nah. I'm getting used to the new world order—clean clothes live in the laundry basket, clean dishes stay in the dishwasher."

"I knew you'd see it my way, eventually."

He came over and gave me a quick kiss, squeezing my hip as he walked out. "I'll text you after I'm done with Robbie's counselor."

I nodded at his back.

WHEN I SHOWED up at Chester's half an hour later, my manager offered me the option to go home, since she'd overstaffed the day shift. Free from making lattes, I headed to Robbie's school, hoping Renn would accept a shoulder to lean on after his meeting. I realized he might see the gesture as overstepping, but I needed reassurance that he thought of us as partners. His stonewalling that morning still stung. If this relationship was truly going to work, he couldn't relegate me to the sidelines while he dealt with his more difficult family issues alone. Tapping in to provide snacks for Gage's practices or going on the occasional run with Robbie wasn't enough.

Renn and I both had volunteer clearance at the school since I'd helped during the track meets, so when I signed in at the front desk, they said I could go ahead to the counselor's office. The admin told me they must still be meeting since Renn hadn't brought back his visitor badge. It was already 10:37, and the meeting had been scheduled for 9:45. It surprised me it was still going on.

As it turned out, it had been over for a while.

Heading down the hall, I passed by the family resource center, stopping short when I heard Renn's voice.

"...it was frustrating. Mr. Marshall thinks he needs to see a therapist."

Darn. That must be about Robbie. I had a feeling the school might recommend something like that, and also that Renn wouldn't like it. But who was he talking to?

I peeked in and saw Renn sitting on a desk, resting back on his arms. Just as I was about to enter, a manicured red fingernail reached out to rest on his chest, and I blinked hard as a female voice purred, "I'm so sorry. I understand how difficult these things can be."

I froze. If Renn had turned toward the door, he would have noticed me, but he was still leaning back, head aimed skyward as he spoke. "I hate the school getting involved like this. I try to be there for him, let him know how much I care, but apparently it's not enough."

That red claw slid across Renn's collar, coming to rest on his shoulder. I waited for him to recoil from the intimate gesture, but he didn't. He didn't look like he was enjoying the touching, but he was certainly...tolerating it. And because he'd failed to discourage that fingertip, other fingertips soon appeared, until finally, two over-moisturized palms were squeezing his biceps. I watched in disbelief as High Ponytail Hannah came into my field of vision, wedging her way between Renn's legs.

"This is a hard age, Renn. If you ever need to talk, I'm here. I sympathize with what you're going through in a way other people can't." That was a direct jab at me. Hannah had seen me with Renn at school events, knew we were together. But that didn't stop her as she began slowly kneading Renn's arms.

That motion seemed to alert him to her proximity. He pulled her hands off his body and scooted back to put more space between them, shaking his head. With that, I realized I didn't have to add "Renn might be cheating" to my list of worries, but his inability to immediately push her away brought back memories of Henri's indiscretion. Was the potential there? Perhaps he considered her a friend and was just talking to her the way I talked to Zach. Then again, Zach didn't rub my shoulders like a seductive massage chair, and he'd never once propositioned me for a booty call when his husband was out of town.

Which was another reason it made me sick when Renn said, "Thank you for listening. I appreciate you're so easy to talk to."

What the fuck?

She was easy to talk to?

And that was when he looked over and saw me. Just as his words registered. Just as my jaw dropped and my knees threatened to buckle. Electricity shot through my nerves, gremlins dancing on my insides as my heart tried to thump its way out of my body. I quickly shut my mouth and turned, fleetingly catching Renn's stunned expression. Not wanting to satisfy Hannah with a confrontation, I returned to the office, dropping off my badge before sprinting to my car.

I assumed Renn would follow me. Offer some sort of explanation. Or apology. Even as I left Robbie's school, unsure of what else to do, I figured I'd hear from him soon. But he didn't reach out. He didn't come after me. He didn't text me. I had to endure hours of alternating between humiliated and furious. Renn's bullshit was starting to *hurt*.

I could have tried to text or call him, but we already had plans to meet at Studio Obscurum and attend Gage's game, so I figured I could wait until I saw him in person that afternoon. I intended to *have* that conversation. No more waiting. We had lots of things to talk about, and this morning's performance with Hannah was just one more addition to the list.

RATHER THAN GO home to stew and stress, I called my manager and asked if I could still work the second half of the day shift. She was grateful since the coffee shop was busier than usual, so I headed in. It was hectic enough to keep my mind off Renn. In fact, I was so busy pulling shots and subbing almond milk for two percent that I didn't notice when Henri came in.

One minute, I was putting new napkins in the dispenser at the condiment bar, and the next, I was looking up at Henri across the shop, smiling eagerly at me with his hands in his pockets. I didn't want to cause a scene, and I was almost off shift anyway, so I gave an aggressive head tilt toward a corner table and he got the message, coming to sit down across from me.

"How did you find me?" I was calm. I'd been expecting this.

"I noticed your jacket at the restaurant. I figured there was a connection. I tried coming in Sunday and you weren't here. When I mentioned your name, the barista said you were scheduled for today." My Chester's Coffee Shop fleece had given me away. Not a surprise. Henri had always loved to nitpick my clothes.

He'd deduced where I worked since I'd literally been advertising the company's logo on my person. And I realized that—despite all his texts and talk—solving an easy puzzle was about the extent of the effort Henri would put in to force this reunion. When I'd left Boston, I'd worried he might have true stalkerish tendencies, his voice so consuming in my head. Some part of me had expected threatening letters crafted out of cut up bits of magazines, or dead roses on my doorstep. At the very least, I'd worried he'd easily be able to reel me back in if I let him near me, let him speak to me.

But now I saw him through the lens of someone who wasn't in his thrall. I understood that all his "I'll never stop loving yous" were mostly hyperbole. I was sure he wanted me. But I was also sure he wasn't about to wreck his life to have me. At the restaurant, he'd confirmed as much when he'd said that he'd intended to come after me—except his son, his mother, his job, and his overall situation had to be taken care of first. Our supposedly all-consuming love had been pretty darn low on the priority list. In the end, I'd been forced to conclude that Henri wasn't a diabolical Bond villain. He was just a terrible human being. An emotional abuser who'd used my aching desire to be loved to his advantage. A petulant man-baby who'd tied us both in knots trying to attain his parents' vision of success, taking it out on me when those unrealistic expectations went unfulfilled.

I stuck out my bottom lip so my breath would blow upward, moving the stray hairs off my forehead.

"Okay. You found me. Congratulations. But I'm not sure what you're hoping to accomplish here. I meant what I said. We have nothing left to say to each other." He looked different, smaller somehow. I leaned back in my chair and flattened my lips.

He flinched at my defiant expression but soldiered on. "Darling, when I saw you at the restaurant, I felt that pull again, and there was a moment where you seemed unsure...like you felt it too, that you remembered how good it was between us." He inched closer but at my continued grimace his voice faltered. "I thought, now that you've had some time to think about it, you might have...realized."

Looking at him across from me, with his stupid face, I berated myself for my brief bout of compassion in the restaurant, offering support when he told me about his father's passing.

"Henri, you are just...wrong. There wasn't one thing I said or did that should have given you that impression. Truly, your ego knows no bounds."

"Darling—"

"Don't 'darling' me. I've always hated it. Whatever you thought you sensed at the restaurant, you were mistaken. You should leave." He leaned closer, but I held my ground.

"Sadie, I understand you needed a break. Time to think. But are you really going to throw away the eight years we spent together? We can make it good again. Have our second chance."

"That's just it, Henri—it was never good. Not for me, at least." I debated whether it was worth it to say more. I didn't think he had the capacity to comprehend what he had done. And I knew that had a lot to do with his father. But I didn't care what the root cause of his ugliness was. I just didn't want it near me any longer.

"C'mon, Sadie, we had some great times together. We can again." At the hint of true emotion—possibly even confusion—in his voice, I figured I could give it one shot. *Okay, Henri, ready or not, gigantic truth bomb coming your way.* I clasped my hands together in front of me and took a deep breath.

"No. We didn't have great times. You're remembering things only from your fucked up perspective." Emboldened, I moved my chair closer to him. "Every supposedly good memory I might have is tainted by all the crappy ones around it. Every time you took me out and told me I should have worn different clothes. Every time you made fun of my cooking or complained about how I didn't take care of the apartment. Every time you reminded me I owed you for everything, from my money to my living situation to my appearance. Every time you hinted that I'd somehow embarrassed you because I offered an opinion on anything. Every time you would belittle me in front of your friends, just hurtful enough to keep me quiet for the night, but subtle enough that no one could say you were a total dick. Every time you woke up and left the house without giving me a kiss goodbye, or came home and went straight to the couch without acknowledging my presence. Every time you refused to tell me you loved me, but then talked about how needy I was. Should I go on?"

He looked genuinely affronted. "Sadie…it wasn't…like that." He spoke quietly, with a conviction that didn't carry over into his expression. "You make everything sound terrible, but I was there. We had a life together, and you just walked out on me. All I wanted was for you to be the best version of yourself. For us to be the best version of us! Maybe there were bad days, but there were also good times. There were! I'm sorry about Marlene. That was a mistake. I'll own it. But you didn't even try to let me make it right." He ran a palm aggressively from chin to forehead, pulling on his hair as he bent his fingers over his scalp.

"This isn't about you putting your dick in Marlene, Henri. Even if that was the last straw. It was everything that happened before that." Every pent-up emotion in me rose to the surface. "I tried for years, Henri. Years! That's what staying through all that shit was—that was me *trying*. I kept trying to make you happy, trying to make you act like you even liked me, let alone loved me. The more I tried, the more you made me feel like garbage—"

"I *did* love you. I still do."

I sat there with my arms crossed, unspeaking. I'd said my piece. He undid the top two buttons of his navy polo, shaking the collar to fan himself. His mouth opened and closed a few times with no sound coming out until finally he rasped, "I'm...sorry." He'd said those words before, but the timber of his voice was new. The faintest whisper bubbled from his lips as he conceded, "I didn't... appreciate you."

There was some satisfaction in hearing him admit it. "No. You didn't. You almost destroyed me. If it hadn't been for Zach, I probably would have kept making excuses for you and faded away to nothing."

"Always golden boy Zach," Henri said angrily.

"Yeah, golden boy Zach—the best friend anyone ever had. But he could only get me so far. Just to Los Angeles. The rest of the break-up I had to do on my own. And it hasn't been easy getting past us, Henri, getting past you. You fucked me up good. But I didn't break completely."

Henri appeared to be listening, but not understanding, because he continued pleading his case. "So you won't even give me a chance to make it right?"

It was wild. His hubris. Even though we'd been apart for years. Even though he'd had a baby with someone else. Even though I'd introduced him to my boyfriend. He just couldn't wrap his head around not being in control.

"Henri, seriously, it's been over a long time. Just go. Lose my number. Have a nice life or whatever."

"Do you honestly believe that pony-tailed kid will be enough for you? That he can give you what you need?" Henri must have been sensing his defeat if he was acknowledging meeting Renn.

"That *kid* is twice the man you'll ever be."

Henri was still sputtering nonsense about how I needed to hear him out when I stood up and pushed past him toward the door. I was done. He didn't merit one more nanosecond of my time or energy. As I stepped out onto the sidewalk, I looked back at him. "Don't come here again. Don't call. Don't email. This should be the last time I see you."

"Sadie—"

"Bye."

Exhilaration raced through me as I walked to the parking lot. I supposed Henri coming in today of all days was a good thing. It had given me some much-needed perspective, and I wanted nothing more than to get to Renn, to tell him that—even though it was difficult between us right now—I knew the difference between him and my ex. Renn loved me the right way.

Chester's was in Hollywood, about halfway between my apartment and Studio Obscurum. Gage usually played close to home, but today's game was in Encino, closer to Westwood, which is why we'd planned to meet at the shop. But I ended up having to backtrack because, just as I was leaving, I got a text from Pete asking if I could swing by the house and pick up Gage's new catcher's mitt.

PETE: I tried to get a hold of Renn to ask him but he isn't answering.

ME: He's not at the studio with you?

PETE: I haven't seen him all day.

PETE: You might even run into him in the house, in which case I'm sorry for sending you on a fool's errand.

ME: NP. I'll swing by and grab it.

That was strange. The appointment at Robbie's school had been over hours ago. Where had Renn been? I hoped he wouldn't blow off Gage's game just to avoid talking to me. *Why was he acting like I'd done something wrong, anyway? He was the one who'd had Hannah's paws on him.* I'd been feeling so good about dealing with Henri. Now apprehension replaced that triumph.

THE LOS ANGELES traffic demons were asleep at the wheel because I made it to Pasadena in record time. As I pulled up to the now-familiar bend in the curb, I thought to myself how much I was already connected to this house. Renn had given me a bronze front door key, attached to a coffee cup keychain made by Gage out of modeling clay. I knew the combination to the security system—1991, Renn's birth year, unchanged since Thomas set it up so long ago. My running shoes were lined up inside the front door, next to the basket where the boys tossed their backpacks.

I went into Gage's room and found the catcher's mitt underneath his bed. As I turned to leave, I ran into Robbie coming out of his room. He seemed startled to see me, but not in an oh-no-I've-been-caught-doing-something-naughty way.

"Uh...hey, Sadie." He looked over my shoulder. "Is Renn here?"

"No. Just me. I came to pick this up for Gage." I held up the mitt. "Renn and Pete are meeting me at the studio."

"Oh right. The game."

Robbie shuffled his feet. He had a generally antagonistic relationship with Gage, but perhaps he was feeling left out? "Do you want to come with me?" I asked.

"Huh?" The question clearly surprised him, so the fun of spending two hours watching nine-year-olds mostly walk or strike out wasn't what was on his mind. "Um...no. I hope the game's okay, but I have plans with Ryder."

Robbie still seemed distracted, but I had to leave. I was already cutting it close. "Okay, well...see you later."

I started moving past him when he stopped me. "Sadie?"

"Hmm?"

"I have something for you, to show you. I've had it a few days, but I didn't want to give it to you in front of my brothers."

I nodded. "Alright."

Robbie shrugged off his backpack and undid the big zipper pocket. He slid his pointer finger between two sheets of sturdy cardboard and pulled out a thick piece of paper. "I made it in art class. It's not very good, but I thought maybe...you would like it."

I took the paper and held it away to get the full effect. It was a stunning watercolor painting of a blue lotus, impressionistic with a brilliantly chaotic style. I had known Robbie was artistic, but since he didn't like to show his work or talk much about it, I'd only seen glimpses of a few things. But this was more accomplished than any of Renn's paintings. Robbie wasn't just good. He was a rare talent.

"You made this for me?"

"Our teacher said we could do whatever, and for some reason, I thought of your tattoo. But can you, um, like, not make a big thing? Renn and Archie are always trying to talk to me about my drawings, but I was hoping you could just take it and not make a whole huge deal about it."

He squared his shoulders, almost daring me to acknowledge the significance of his creative gifts.

"We don't need to have a big sloppy discussion, if that's what you want." I reached over and ruffled his hair like I normally only would with Gage.

"Thanks."

"But can I just say one thing?"

He looked at me suspiciously but nodded.

"Since you don't want me to go on and on about how good you are, I just want to tell you that it means a lot that you're giving this to me. That's all."

"Cool." He zipped his backpack up and slung it over one shoulder. "I'm glad you like it. It's been...better...since you came back."

I could have said so much more. How I was falling in love with Renn's family as much as him, how special I thought Robbie was, and how much I wanted him to know it. I wanted him to know that I cared about his pain, and didn't judge him for his mistakes, that I understood what it felt like to worry about disappointing people. I wanted to tell him it was okay for him to feel things, to be sad and then find happiness again, to be angry and then forgive. But I kept my word and stayed quiet.

CHAPTER
Twenty-Three

March 22, 2016

T RAFFIC WAS ON my side again and I reached the studio before
our agreed-upon time, even with the unplanned side trip to
the house. I went inside and scanned the stations for Renn but
the main room was empty. Even though he hadn't texted me all
day, and had apparently been dodging Pete's messages as well,
I'd still hoped he'd be there. I was upset he'd let Hannah maul
him, but especially for dismissing me this morning, as well as
every other time I'd tried to talk to him recently. Still, between
my take-down of Henri and the beautiful painting Robbie had
gifted me, the day was looking up, so I wanted to be optimistic.
Renn still had five minutes before he was officially late.

Pete came in from the back room. I held up the mitt.
"Where's Gage?"

"At the ballfield with Archie. Players go early for warm-ups."

"Okay." I sighed. "I guess I'll give Renn a few minutes and then
just go."

"Actually, I was hoping we could talk." He leaned against the wall near me, crossing one ankle over the other.

"About what?"

"I wanted to thank you."

I wasn't in the mindset to have this conversation. Not today. I intentionally mistook his meaning, attempting to sidestep the elephant. "It was no problem to grab the mitt."

Pete huffed out a laugh. "You know full well I'm not talking about the glove. Although I do appreciate that. I wanted to thank you for having my back these past few months. With Renn—"

I put up my hand. "No, Pete. Let me be perfectly clear here. Whatever I've said or done has nothing to do with you. I've only ever acted in the way I thought was best for him. If it helped you in the process, that was unintentional."

"That's exactly what I'm saying. We both want what's best for Renn."

What was he driving at? I reflected on the past year, everything Renn had told me and things I'd seen for myself. The months of Pete attempting to make amends. School pickups. Family dinners. Holidays. Detached text exchanges and even icier in-person attempts at conversation. Always insistent on trying. Leaving Renn very little room to breathe or process his actions, keeping him on edge. Pete had kept his word to be more present in their lives, but seemed to be on a mission to make his presence as provoking as possible.

"Do you really?" I questioned. "Want the best for Renn?"

Pete uncrossed his ankles and stood tall in front of me. "Sadie, I'm not an idiot. I know I've been pushing him."

I hadn't expected him to just own it like that. I paused before finally asking, "Then why are you doing it?"

"Because I love him."

I scrunched my face from cheeks to eyebrows. "Huh?"

He exhaled loudly. "I love him. I realize it doesn't always seem like it, and I'm not very good at it sometimes, but I love him, and he needs to deal with his shit. And if he hates me for forcing him to confront his grief and resentment, so be it."

What the hell? That was his game? All the constant pecking at Renn was intentional? "So, like, that stunt you pulled on Christmas—with the snow globe. That was on purpose?"

"I realize I could be more careful. I could just never mention Thomas or Mary and we would probably get to a better place."

"And don't you want that—to have peace with your nephews?"

"Be real, Sadie. You know that's not what Renn needs. You see how much pretending everything is fine costs him. The way he holds himself back. He needs to come to terms with all that's happened to him since his dad died. He never has. I know you see it, too."

"You can't make him do that." *Believe me, Pete. I have been failing at it for months.*

"Maybe not. But I can keep him from that place of cheerful fakery and bullshit he existed in for the four years before he met you, before he found out about me and his stepmom. If I can keep him angry enough, he can't go back there, and then he can finally move forward." It wasn't terrible logic, except...

"But can't you see you're making him crazy?"

"At least it's honest! Think about it. He took on his dad's whole life. He's raising Thomas's kids, running Thomas's shop, living in Thomas's house, and yet he can hardly mention his dad's name. He's still so bitter. Something he won't admit to. And I know it's partly my fault. I could have made better choices after Mary died. But what's done is done and I'm fucking trying now!"

I could see that he was. And when he put it like that, it almost made sense. It had been clear to me for a while, brought into stark relief when I saw Renn with Hannah this morning, that my boyfriend was on the edge of a cliff. He had to acknowledge he couldn't do everything on his own, that he was hurting. He needed a push, and that's what Pete was trying to do.

If I had used Renn's method of just shoving my feelings in a corner, I never would have reclaimed my life. Zach had helped, therapy had been a lifesaver, and meeting Renn had been the icing on the brownie of my recovery. Letting people in mattered. My victory over Henri this afternoon could never have happened if I had just plopped my ass on Zach's couch two years ago and refused to talk about anything.

Pete was still standing in front of me, letting me digest his motivations, until I responded with tight lips. "I guess it's better knowing you're being so pushy on purpose. I'd hate to think you were oblivious to Renn's pain. Robbie's too."

Slumping back against the wall, keeping his head bowed, he whispered, "I'm not oblivious. Never think that." He pressed a palm to his temple. "I loved my brother, and knowing I can't make this better for his boys...it's killing me." He kicked away from the wall and walked a few feet past me, giving me his back.

As I watched his shoulders shake, I felt Pete's helplessness like a physical force. It was a mirror of what I'd been experiencing with Renn for weeks now. I reached out a tentative hand to him. "It's going to be okay, Pete."

He turned around. "You sure about that?"

"Renn is one of the best men I've ever met, and I know for sure he can be rational and kind and focused on what's important." I grasped for his hand. "I think he's capable of forgiving you, even if it's taking longer than you'd like."

"I hope you're right." Pete draped his other hand over my shoulder and brought me in for a hug, silently commiserating. As we embraced, I realized it did comfort me to understand where Pete had been coming from these past few months.

"What...The...Actual...Fuck!"

Aaaaaaaaaaaargh.

Dammit.

FML.

Renn stood in the doorway, veins popping from his neck.

"Relax, Renn." Pete pulled away and held up his hands. "Our conversation got kind of heavy and Sadie was just being a friend." I nodded in affirmation.

Renn stalked over to where we were standing. He glanced sideways at me before turning red-hazed eyes on his uncle. "And why were you having a serious conversation with *my* girlfriend? What were you talking about?"

Pete sighed. "It's just been a bit of a day is all." He stepped farther away from me. "Nothing to worry about."

"Well, that's convenient, isn't it?"

Pete looked mildly exasperated. "What the hell is that supposed to mean?"

"It means maybe you were just waiting for your opportunity. Moving in on other people's girls is sort of your thing, right asshole?"

"Hey now—" Pete objected at the same moment I gasped out, "Renn!"

At my voice, he turned his glare on me. "Is this to get me back for this morning?"

Renn's demeanor grew lava hot in seconds as his chest heaved. He couldn't be this upset over me hugging Pete. Was this just the result of the pressure cooker he'd been living in the past few months? Had something else happened? He'd been ready to blow for a while now, but this was next level. He was absolutely seething.

Twilight spilled in from the still-open door, streaking across the hard lines of Renn's face as his jaw ticked.

"What happened this morning?" Pete broke our standoff as he stepped between us.

I started to answer, but Renn cut me off. "I went to the school and the counselor basically informed me Robbie is messed up in the head. So that fucking sucked. When I came out, I ran into one of the PTSA moms. And I guess I got caught up in finally having someone listen and just let me exist without demanding I overanalyze everything with them." Renn exhaled as he looked between both of us and sing-songed: "*You should talk more. We need to talk this out...* Why the fuck does everyone always want to talk all the fucking time?"

Okay, we all had bad days, but this was beyond. Renn needed to get a grip. I hadn't stood up to Henri today only to fail at standing up to the man I truly loved when he needed me. I squared my shoulders.

"First, she had her hands all over you, and you took your sweet-ass time pushing her away. Second, you then spent the entire day ignoring me. You had to have known how it hurt me to see her groping you, to see you opening up to her, but you didn't even bother to text. Third, I only want you to talk because it's clear your anger and grief are tearing you apart." I waved my hand up and down in front of him, willing him to see his own outburst as evidence.

He took a step away from me, pressing a fist to his forehead.

The Renn I knew was in there somewhere because I could see him forcing himself to calm down. It was like watching a human balloon deflate. He closed his eyes and breathed out, moving his hands to his hips and stretching his fingers. After a few more deep breaths, he rolled his neck and shoulders before replying. "The thing with Hannah—I can't explain it. At first, I didn't realize she was touching me. I was so zoned out, but then I just...I guess it was nice to feel like someone wanted me without wanting something from me, you know?"

"Oh, she wanted something from you." I looked down pointedly at his crotch.

He huffed. "Okay, I mean, I know she wanted *that*. But lately, you've just been... It hasn't been as easy as it used to be."

"Well, duh. We're sharing our lives together. It isn't all going to be good times."

"I get that. At least, I hope I do. But all the things you want from me—like, I know you want me to talk about my dad—and I just don't think I can. I don't want to."

Me being in Renn's life was supposed to help ease his burdens, but if he insisted on keeping me at arm's length, that wouldn't work. Having a girlfriend he hid his feelings from would actually add to his difficulties.

Since the snow globe incident, I'd been thinking the change in Renn had stemmed from his interactions with Pete, but he was clearly unnerved that I kept catching him in vulnerable moments. Before we were together, he had shared some of his feelings with me, even about his dad, but always on his terms, controlled. Now, he saw concern on my face every time he had a fight with his uncle or a worrying interaction with Robbie. I pressed him to confide in me because I loved him and needed him to know I had his back. But he didn't seem to want that.

Pete had stood there awkwardly through our exchange but attempted his escape. "Uh...guess I'll meet you at the game." He reached over to grab the mitt I'd put on the table.

"Wait!"

Pete and I both turned at Renn's shout. "Hang on, Pete. You need to hear this." Conversation with me temporarily paused, Renn gestured for us to sit. I could only assume he was about to tell us why he'd come in so bothered. They sat down on two pleather waiting area chairs while I grabbed a nearby rolling stool. Renn stumbled over his next words. "When I got here and saw you guys...hugging...I...um...I had another thing..." He pressed his lips together.

At his expression, I put aside that he'd just said he didn't ever want to *really* talk to me and focused on the fact that something else was obviously upsetting him. "What's wrong?"

He looked at me. "I was going to text you. I just needed a minute to cool off. Plus, I had to tell Hannah it was never gonna happen."

I smiled at that, and it was enough to get him speaking more confidently. "I saw you drive off. I was about to text, but I got a call from my mom. She was in Riverside and needed me to come pick her up. Her call cut off abruptly, and I got worried. I guess texting you sort of slipped my mind. Anyway, when I found her, she was wasted, told me some guy she's been dating got pissed and just left her there. I drove her back to the city and the whole time she's just going on and on about how sorry she is for bothering me, how grateful she is that I came. And all I can think is 'I can't believe this person is my mom.'" Renn stopped himself from saying more. Stopping himself from saying too much was one of his superpowers. "In the end she was fine."

"But why didn't you text Sadie once you knew Sheryl was okay? Or reply to any of the dozen texts I sent you?" Pete asked. "You had to have dropped your mom off hours ago."

"Because I got your texts, Pete. And I stopped by the house to check for the mitt, but I didn't get three feet inside before I saw the mail in the slot by the door." Renn reached into his back pocket and pulled out a folded white envelope with a ragged edge, obviously opened in haste with a finger. He handed it to his uncle.

"Congratulations. It's a boy."

The LZN Laboratories logo was clear in the corner of the envelope as Pete took it from Renn's fingers. Pete appeared confused at first, and then his features slowly brightened with something bordering on elation. He leaned back in the chair and pulled the thin white paper from its sleeve. His eyes scanned the page and his lips moved as he read under his breath, "...99.9% accurate..." He looked at his nephew in awe before reverently and quietly affirming, "He's really mine."

"I know they addressed it to you, but I won't apologize for opening it," Renn declared. "I saw it at the top of the pile and there was no way I wasn't going to."

"I understand, Renn. It's fine." Pete's hand trembled as he held the letter. The shivering seemed to catch over his whole body, knees bouncing in front of him as he blinked repeatedly. Despite obvious efforts to hold himself in check, he emitted a shuddering breath as tears started falling down his cheeks.

Renn seemed uncomfortable with Pete's display of emotion. He kept talking. "Once I saw what it said, I just got in my car and started driving. I had to get my thoughts together. That's why I didn't text, and I forgot about the mitt until I got here. It's just...a lot."

Pete sat heavily in his chair, head in his hands. From beneath the cocoon of his fingers, he murmured, "I realize the situation is totally fucked, but I am so happy right now." He peered up, eyes wet and shiny. "I didn't want to admit how much I wanted him to be mine." He looked at Renn imploringly. "I know how hard it'll be to tell him and we'll need to make a plan and come up with the best way and all that, and I'll do it however you decide, because I get you've been the boss, and I don't even know if we should change our arrangements, at least not yet, and—"

"Pete!" Renn frowned at his uncle. "I'm not ready to think about any of this right now. Obviously, we'll need to...decide things. But I can't wrap my head around any of it today."

"Of course, of course. That makes total sense. We'll do whatever you think is best." Pete wiped his eyes with his sleeve before glancing at Renn, who looked disoriented and rigid in his chair, a far cry from the berserker madman who'd come blazing in fifteen minutes ago. The ecstatic new father looked at me. I gestured to the exit with my neck, and Pete got the message to give us some space.

"Just let me know when you're ready, Renn." He grabbed Gage's mitt—his son's mitt—and headed out. "I'll see you at the game. If you decide not to come, just text, and I'll make an excuse." His nephew still appeared lost, so he appealed to me for confirmation, and I nodded.

I waited until Pete had shut the door firmly behind him before kneeling in front of Renn. I placed my palms on his thighs. "What do you need, baby?" We hardly ever used pet names, and it did the trick of waking him up.

"I don't know."

As I rested my hands on Renn, I thought to myself that this crisis could not have come at a worse time. He was already on edge and had been volatile for months. Pushing things to the back burner and putting on a cheerful face would not work here, especially since Pete wanted to tell Gage the truth.

"It's weird." Renn shook his head. "For the past few hours, I've been trying to wrap my head around the fact that my brother is actually my cousin."

I didn't know what to say to him. I'd learned these past few weeks that I had no idea how to talk to Renn. Not about something like this.

I approached cautiously. "I know you probably don't want to hear this right now, when this is so fresh, but it's just biology. Gage is your brother in every way that counts. Not to mention you've been more like a father to him the past six years. So much of this is semantics."

Renn put his hands on top of mine. "I appreciate you saying that, trying to make it better, but I think I should be alone for a while. To process everything."

I frowned at Renn's code for *I'm feeling very emotional and I hate it when you see me like that.*

"If you want some space right now, I'll respect it, but we're going to need to talk about all this eventually." I tried to keep my voice level but got a little feisty at the end.

Renn stood up at the same moment I did. "Sadie, it's fine. I just need time to figure out my next move."

"Yeah. But sometimes there is no next move. You can't always deal with your shit by attempting to stay one step ahead of it. After a while, that stops working."

"I think I've done okay so far."

This had gone on long enough. We couldn't keep going in circles, having this same fight. Pete was right. Renn needed a push. To face actual reality, not just exist in the reality he carefully curated. Even if it hurt. Something had to change.

"Really?" I countered. "You think it's okay you feel tortured every time someone mentions your dad, or that you can't be in the same room with your uncle without the threat of war? I don't think you realize how much bottling everything up makes it all worse. Believe me, I learned with Henri that you can't just get over things by ignoring them."

"Can we please, please, please—*just for fucking once*—not compare everything bad that happens to your time with Henri!? I get it. That guy sucked. But not everything is about that!"

I recoiled like he'd slapped me. I had been so eager to tell Renn about my takedown of Henri earlier. Instead, I felt Renn flipping all the switches Henri had installed. The ones that would always be there, as long as I had my memories. That's what Renn didn't seem to understand—there was no moving on from your past. There was just trying to find a better way to live with it as you moved forward.

"That was a low blow." I pivoted in an attempt to salvage the situation. "But I'm telling you, as someone who loves you, that you are not okay. I've been worried about you for months."

"Well, I'm fine. Just stop worrying. Problem solved." Renn crossed his arms, and it was the first time in a long while I felt every one of those eleven years I had on him.

I tried a different tactic. "Even if that were true—and it definitely isn't—what about Robbie? He isn't dealing with his stuff either, and he's learning that from you."

"Don't bring Robbie into this! Or how I'm handling him. Talk about a low blow."

"Are you kidding me?" I waved my arms in the air, practically spinning in frustration. "I'm supposed to be your girlfriend. We see each other every day. Don't I deserve to have an opinion on the boys, especially now?"

He seemed to contemplate my question, distracting him from his anger. "I don't know," he ground out, running a hand through his loose hair. "I hadn't thought about it."

"Renn, do you want to be with me, like, for real?"

"What is that supposed to mean? You know how much I love you."

"I do. These past months have been magical, the best time of my life. But we are sort of at a crossroads here." I was afraid to utter the next words, but they needed to be spoken out loud. "You have to see that we shouldn't be together if you can't let me support you, or even admit when you're hurting. And if you're just going to dismiss my concerns when I have them or try to convince me I'm not seeing what is obvious to literally everyone around you, I can't accept that."

He looked at me, anger in his eyes battling with fear. I knew he didn't want to lose me, but did he want that enough to let me in?

"I love you, Sadie. I want to be with you."

I tried yet another angle. "Archie told me you were pretty angry before we got together, ever since you found out about Pete and Mary."

"I kind of wish Archie would keep his fat nose out of our business, but that's a fair statement. It's why we belong together. I was miserable without you, but you've brought so much happiness into my life...not to mention mind-blowing sex."

He waggled his eyebrows at me, trying to bring levity into the situation, but I knew his tricks by now. I frowned. "That's just it. Being with me helps you fool yourself into playing pretend, into convincing yourself everything is fine."

He pinched the bridge of his nose, shaking his head. "You're overthinking, Sadie. What does that even mean?"

"It means that if you won't talk to me, then I'm just distracting you from dealing with the actual issues in your life."

Since we'd started dating, Renn had compulsively supported

me—accepting why I'd run away the first time, being patient with my sexual hesitancy, advocating for the surrogacy, protecting me when we'd run into Henri. With each turn, he'd done everything in his power to safeguard my heart and feelings. But when it was his turn to be exposed and need help, he would not go there.

I toyed with the idea of giving Renn more time. But then I thought of the beautiful lotus Robbie had given me, my keychain from Gage, all the memories I'd already made with the boys. It wasn't fair to them for me to enable Renn's destructive behavior. One of us had to stop playacting, and the more we dragged it out, the harder it would be for everyone.

"Are you breaking up with me?" Renn sounded incredulous.

"I think I have to," I whispered. "I love you so much, but I might not be good for you. At least not right now." Henri had made a game of shutting me out. Renn had made an art of not letting me in. The situations were diametrically different, and yet the same truth remained.

"Renn, it's not okay for me to accept so little of you."

"Are you serious?" He turned toward me and started waving his arms. "Today of all days!? When I had that shit meeting with Robbie's counselor, dealt with my mom, and found out about Gage?"

The accusation in his voice washed over me like acid. I was sure we were both remembering the last time I'd left him, the day a faded red envelope had blown up his family. This situation felt eerily similar, and I realized with sadness that we hadn't come nearly as far as I'd thought we had.

I sighed and looked around Studio Obscurum, nostalgic for those first easy months of knowing him. "It's a strange day for me too, Renn. This doesn't compare to what you've been through, but Henri actually came to Chester's this afternoon looking for me."

As though we weren't on the verge of ending our relationship, Renn reached for me. I put up my hand and stepped back. "No. I'm okay. I let Henri talk and then I said some things before I told him to go away and never come back. And I'm glad I got a chance to say those things to him. They needed to be said."

"I wish I could have seen you. I bet it was impressive...And I'm sorry for what I said earlier...about you making everything about Henri." He reached for me again, and this time I let him clasp my fingers. "Fuck, Sadie. You know I didn't mean it."

"I do. And I want you to know that all I could think about after speaking to him was getting to you, to tell you all about it, mostly because I realized how good of a man you are, and how lucky I am that you love me."

"But you don't want to be with me?"

"More than anything, Renn. But not like this. Not when you can't talk to me. When I'm holding you back. I know you don't see it that way, but I feel it. I'd rather walk away from you now than get to a point where you resent me for needing more than you're willing to give—because that's where we're headed. It just took me a minute to see it."

"Shit." I thought Renn might have said more, but he was clearly overwhelmed with everything that had happened. "Today of all days." He dropped my hand, shaking his head.

"It's better that it's today, Renn. With everything else going on, with the heavy stuff you need to tell the boys, this will be the least of your worries."

"I fought for you so hard the last time. But I just...can't right now," he said. "It's too much."

"This is different. Last time was about me, how I wasn't in a place to be with someone. This time it's about you. I hope someday you'll be ready—truly ready—to share all the parts of yourself. I hope you'll let someone love you enough to lean on them, especially if you're hurting. I wanted to be that girl. Because that's the way I love you. Enough to let you love me back."

He didn't have an answer for that. There wasn't one. I grabbed my bag and walked out.

CHAPTER
Twenty-Four

March 23, 2016

From: SadieFrom1980@gmail.com
To: Archie@studioobscurum.com

Hey Archie,

I had to do it.

I know you were hoping I could help Renn be happy again. And I really tried. But I'm not what he needs right now. He needs to confront his demons, and I hope with me gone he'll be forced to acknowledge that. I understand what it's like to live half a life, to be stuck in place. I don't want that for Renn. And I've come too far since Boston to settle for it in my own relationship.

Walking away this time was the hardest thing I've ever done. Knowing I'm taking one more precious thing away from Renn. But I'm betting that losing me will shake him, and he'll decide to fight harder for everything else.

Take care of him, Archie. Because I'm going to love him forever.

Thank you for being a friend, *hum *Golden Girls* theme song here*

Sadie

From: Archie@studioobscurum.com
To: SadieFrom1980@gmail.com

Sadie,

I understand. I saw the same things you did. He's getting worse.

For what it's worth, I think there's a good chance your sacrifice will be worth it. It's only been a day and I've already seen some signs losing you will be the reckoning he's needed.

Since Thomas died, you're really the only thing Renn has ever wanted for himself. Every other important piece of his life was basically inherited or thrust upon him. I remember the first time he told me about you, that he had a potential new client who was so funny and snarky and cool in her DMs. You lit him up from the start. He might have been half in love with you before he'd even seen your face. I'm glad he had you, if only for a short while.

Take care of yourself. And when it comes to Renn—maybe keep the door open?

With Respect,
Archie

From: SadieFrom1980@gmail.com
To: Archie@studioobscurum.com

I'll try.

Late April 2016

A MONTH HAD GONE by since I'd walked away from Renn. I remained entrenched in the post-breakup limbo state, second-guessing my decision, remembering the good times and crushed by the knowledge there would be no new memories. I couldn't go any significant stretch of time without thinking about him, and even though those thoughts were torture, it was the only way I had him in my life right now, so I couldn't give them up.

I considered Archie's email as well. Should I keep the door open for Renn? Archie was optimistic that my leaving would be Renn's wake-up call. Maybe I could just wait until he was in a better place. I loved him, and he had essentially waited for me before. But if I pined with no expiration date, was I just wasting away and putting myself in a new sort of holding pattern?

Four weeks after I walked out of Studio Obscurum, still unsure, I found myself in the place where so many of my choices got hashed out. Across from Zach.

He'd insisted we meet at a coffee shop near his house. When I arrived, he'd already ordered for both of us, and I barely avoided a spit take when I sipped from my cup.

"Dude, are you mad at me? What is this nastiness?" Zach knew full well I liked a plain black coffee with stevia.

"What?" He shrugged. "It's a salted caramel cream espresso flat foam extra hot something or other. The house specialty."

I sniffed the cup and made a face. "Just...why?"

"Sorry, doll. I asked the barista to give me two of whatever her favorite is. I'm still getting to know the area. It'll never truly be my neighborhood until I'm in with the local coffee shop crew."

It was weird to see Zach insecure about anything, let alone something so inconsequential as befriending the nearby baristas. The fits and starts in his quest toward fatherhood and lasting domesticity with Teddy had exposed a side to him that hadn't been there when he was just a single bartender living his best unencumbered life. But I'd also never seen him happier, so I was determined to ease his mind. "Babe, they're gonna love you no matter what you order. Just don't wear that shiny green leather harness thingy you bought at Pride last year until they know you better." I winked. "It makes you look like a leprechaun Dom."

"I only bought that because you dared me. Also, a leprechaun Dom sounds awesome."

"You know what—you're right." I laughed. "Definitely wear the harness next time."

He smirked. "Duly noted. Now please tell me why we had to meet so urgently. Are you still stuck on Archie's email?"

He understood me so well. "Yep. I'm at a crossroads. My heart wants to be with Renn, which means I should give him time, but my brain tells me I've worked too hard to put my life on pause again."

Zach considered my words, rotating his cup absently in front of him as he leaned back in his chair. "You know...if you waited, you wouldn't be putting your whole life on pause. Just one part of it."

"I know...I know..."

"I'm guessing there's a 'but' at the end of that..."

I nodded. "*But* I can't help thinking Renn and I weren't ever on a path to having a real future together. Not truly. It's possible we were meant to be together just for a time."

"Why would you say that?"

I squared my shoulders and put the abomination coffee down on the table. "Almost from the moment you met Teddy, you were thinking of forever. Renn and I knew each other for almost two years, dated seriously for five months, and never talked about where our relationship was headed."

"Never?" He seemed genuinely surprised.

"Not in any meaningful way, only in the near term, like who was going to Gage's games, what we'd eat for lunch or do on the weekends. The farthest in the future we ever got was discussing the possibility of me having a baby—*for you and Teddy*. It never seemed to faze him that everything we planned for was day-to-day. Even though we were falling in love, he was so consumed by his burdens that planning ahead wasn't in the cards. His mind wouldn't allow him to take on more. I let go of my past, but he never has. He carries around his grief and his secrets like bowling balls hidden in his jacket. They weigh him down and make it difficult to move forward, and no one else is allowed to see them."

I'd had these epiphanies over the past few weeks. Verbalizing them to Zach relieved me of some of their heaviness. I had been so secure in Renn's love. He'd done such a good job of caring for me, I hadn't realized until the end how little of him I'd actually had.

"You're wondering if you should wait for him to come to terms with things?"

I nodded. "It's hard to walk away knowing there's a possibility Renn will be ready to share his life with someone someday. Selfishly, I can't stand the thought of some other woman getting to be that person."

"But you're also worried he'll never be ready."

I snorted. "You know, you really missed your calling as a mind reader."

"My powers only work on brains fueled by Cap'n Crunch, the Doobie Brothers, and anxiety. So, basically, just you."

My cheek ticked up and I sighed. "I just don't want to waste any more time in my life. I've lost so much already."

"I get it, doll. You want the kind of future with someone that is mapped out slightly beyond the lifespan of a season of *The Bachelor*."

I looked at him wearily. "I can't accept less than that. Not anymore."

He paused and took a sip of his drink. "Can I ask you something, sort of unrelated but also…not?" He looked around as though to ensure no one was listening.

"'Course."

"Don't you think helping me and Teddy, being our surrogate, might also delay your ability to plan a future?" He looked abashed as he asked me, bringing his hands to the table.

I reached across to grab them. "Hey, you. Look at me." He turned, and I glanced up, holding his gaze steady. "I know you're scared, but don't go putting words in my mouth. You've already put enough filthy things in my mouth today." I glanced down and made a face at the coffee cup on the table. "Being able to help you with this is amazing. I can't thank you enough for the opportunity you're giving me, for the faith and trust you've shown in our friendship. This thing we're doing..." I lifted one hand and moved my pointer finger back and forth between the two of us. "Isn't interrupting my future. It is my future. And yours."

Zach's eyes shone with unshed tears. "Thanks for that, doll. And whatever happens, you and I will always be each other's family."

"Just you try to get rid of me." I straightened in my chair. "Now that we've settled that, can we get back to the real issue? Tell me what to do about Renn."

"You know I can't tell you that." I stuck my tongue out at him, and he chortled. "Alright. I can't decide for you, but the good news is, you don't have to choose right now. You just broke up, so your decision-making instrument is probably faulty, anyway. Give it time."

It was good advice.

But as it turned out, I didn't need Zach's sage wisdom. Because the decision was removed from my hands by a letter I received three days later.

April 20, 2016

Dear Sadie,

I hope it's not too weird I'm writing a letter, but you deserve better than an email or some lame text. I've struggled so much to get my thoughts on paper. By the time you read this, please understand it's probably draft 1000, but I really wanted to get it right.

First and most importantly, I want to say that you weren't wrong. It took me a month to admit that...well, a month on top of six years...but there it is.

After you left, I went to Gage's game, and I lied. I told my family you weren't feeling well. When I woke up the next morning, I realized I was going to have to tell the truth—that you were gone. I also realized I needed to tell Gage and Robbie about Pete and the DNA results. I knew I could prolong it, but the story was going to come out eventually. And that's when it hit me. No matter what I told people, no matter how much I put things off, the truth was going to catch up to me.

So that's what I wanted you to know—you were right. About lots of things. I see that now.

Robbie needs more support than I've been willing to admit.

Gage has a right to learn about his father because that kind of secret can't stay hidden.

I need to forgive Pete and give him a real chance to make amends.

In a way, I was using our relationship as a Band-Aid to avoid those truths.

And this truth—I'm NOT okay.

The hardest part is that the person I am most angry with is not around anymore for me to yell at. I know it's not rational for me to be upset with my dad for dying. But there it is. I feel so guilty for being mad at him, but he left me right when I was supposed to be starting MY life. Instead, I got stuck holding the bag and living HIS. Before Mary died, I was starting to process my grief, and I think if she would have lived, things might have gone down differently. But that's not what happened, and right up until the moment you walked out of the studio, it never made sense to me to do anything other than simply plow ahead.

But once you were gone, I felt it—that anger burning inside of me. It's always been there, and I've always been able to push it down. Except now I can't.

Because it cost me you.

There is so much I shoved down. Did I ever tell you I was thinking about going to art school? That I wanted to travel? That I considered apprenticing under someone other than my dad? I didn't even let myself think about all the plans I never got to make.

I don't regret my choices. Raising my brothers has been the making of me in so many ways and I wouldn't have wanted to be away from them after my dad died. But just because I made what I believe was the right decision doesn't mean that all those darker thoughts don't still live inside me.

What's crazy is I could fool myself until you left. I thought I was okay, that I must be fine because I was surviving and because people thought I was doing so well. Everyone, from Archie to the boys' teachers to neighbors to clients, has told me what a great job I'm doing, how amazing it is that I took on all these responsibilities. I couldn't give myself any wiggle room to fail. I couldn't let anyone see my bad days.

But they were there, Sadie. You called me out on them. I haven't dealt with my grief, and it's consumed so much of me and what I'm willing to show the world. I have been taking my anger and bitterness out on other people, especially Pete. And to my shame, you.

And the thing is, I can't guarantee I'm going to fix it. Right now, even knowing what I do, I still don't want to talk. I don't want to ask for help. I want to put myself back together again, but I don't have a clue where to start.

So you're right—we can't be together. I can't take the risk of hurting you, taking my anger out on you again. I think we found each other at the exact right time. I needed someone to wake me up, to show me what was really going on inside of me. And God, did you ever do that, Sadie. I was never more creative or alive than when I was with you. You made me feel challenged and special, and so fucking wanted.

But it's not enough, is it? It's not enough that we love each other and bring out the good in each other if I can't treat you the way you deserve. When you walked away from me last year, I didn't understand why you did it. But now I do. You couldn't love me the right way. I understand because I feel like that now.

Don't wait for me.

I can't make you any promises or honestly say that I'll be able to deal with my issues. I think we did what we were supposed to do for each other—we opened each other's eyes to the possibility of a different future. The difference is that you're ready to face that future, and I'm so proud of you for that. But I'm not. And I can't risk hurting you again, so please don't ask me to.

This has to be the end, the real end. I want to imagine you out there living your dreams, knowing I helped you get there. Because I want to keep loving you. And letting you go is the best way I can do that. Right now, it's the only way I can.

Renn

Early May 2016

DON'T WAIT FOR ME.

I read the letter dozens of times over the next few weeks. Part of me *was* waiting for Renn to reach out again. Even though his words sounded definitive, my heart was not on board with the idea this was the end. It was hard to close the door. I checked my phone a lot, found reasons to open my email in the middle of the day.

But nothing ever came, and I eventually accepted that I needed to honor Renn's words. By loving me, he had given me an incredible gift, and it was time to use that gift to full advantage and move on. It wasn't easy, but he had made a sacrifice in letting me go. We both had.

I kept the memories of Renn like a treasure chest in my soul, and whenever the melancholy hit, I would pull one out and think about it. Renn singing Steely Dan's "Dirty Work" while doing my tattoo. Renn taking me and the boys bowling and proceeding to roll a gutter ball every time Gage did, until finally asking for the bumpers. Renn learning the Seahawks roster so he'd have more to talk about with Zach. Renn waking me up in bed with a sexy smirk and a "good morning" in his Mater voice. There was pain there, too. But unlike the memories of Henri that had paralyzed me, my time with Renn had made me better.

I moved on because I could. To be sure, I wanted love in my life. I wanted Renn. But with that option off the table, I focused on other things I wanted, things that would make me happy. I was a thirty-six-year-old woman reveling in finally having my own aspirations. I missed Renn, but I was going to be okay without him. My memories were there. I had a beautiful, colorful reminder of our time together on the back of my thigh, one that I could run my finger over and smile at. And life still had a lot of happiness in store for me, a lot of surprises. For the first time since Boston, I felt sure of it. I was excited to find out what happened next.

April 2018

"**D**OLL, YOU NEED to push that bowl away from the edge of the table. Mr. Bingham is going to knock it off if you give him half a chance."

I looked over at the evil-eyed tabby in question. He glowered at me with his old man cat face, and I shivered as my soul protected itself from his attempts to collect it. "I still can't believe Teddy named that demon feline Mr. Bingham. Jane Austen would not approve."

"It's ironic, obvs."

I hmphed. "Well, you should ironically return him to whatever section of hell's front porch he's supposed to be guarding." I looked down at Charlotte, sleeping peacefully in my arms, and whispered, "I'm sorry Daddy and Papa make you live with that mean beast."

"Hey now!" Zach made googly eyes at his daughter. "Mr. Bingham is just miffed because he had Teddy all to himself before I moved in, and now that Kit's come along, he's exercising his cat prerogative to be bitchy. Also, Teddy decided not to go with 'Papa' anymore. It didn't feel right."

"Way to bury the lead. What are we calling him?" Charlotte, Kit for short, was only six months old, but I assumed she was picking up on names.

"Baba. His family is Turkish and I think becoming a father made him want to create a connection with them, at least symbolically, since his parents passed away a while ago."

"Baba." I tested the word on my tongue. "That's nice."

The baby stirred and Zach took her from me, having warmed a bottle. After much discussion, we'd concluded that me pumping breast milk was the best solution for Charlotte's feedings. It allowed her to get all the benefits without me having to nurse her. I didn't mind pumping, and Zach and Teddy weren't rigid about it. They supplemented with formula as needed since I didn't make it to their house every day.

As planned, we'd made it work on our own terms, through constant communication between the three of us. Zach and Teddy were the parents, and I was an extremely doting and involved auntie. From the moment she'd been born and I'd placed her in my best friend's arms, I had never once doubted we'd made the right decision. If anything, bleary-eyed and sleep deprived as they were, I imagined the guys wanted me in their lives more, not less. But I felt it was important to keep the line clear. As much as I loved her, Charlotte had two parents, not three. Still, I had moved closer to Teddy's house during my second trimester, and often popped in for dinner or, as on this day, breakfast. I'd been by Teddy's side for walks in the park and had laughed hysterically when Zach tried to configure the baby wrap around his chest for the first time. I had enjoyed every moment of growing Kit in my belly, but the part I liked best was having the husbands with me for every appointment, watching Zach light up as he listened to the heartbeat, seeing Teddy clutch invisible pearls when they found out they were having a girl.

I could see a future ahead of us where I helped plan a few birthday parties or accompanied them to Disneyland. Zach and Teddy would defer to me when the time came to talk to Kit about using tampons. We would continue to maneuver as we saw fit, knowing that our bond was strong enough to anchor this unconventional situation.

Zach got his daughter settled with her breakfast. And even though she was a dead ringer for her baba, it seemed certain she would be mischievous like Daddy. Arms free of baby duty, I dug into my Cap'n Crunch. It was already soggy, but I wasn't picky. I was excited to head into work. I had a feeling it was going to be an interesting day.

"Are you nervous?" Zach asked.

"A little. But it's a school I've never been in before and the potential for catastrophes isn't as high when you're just filling in. Hopefully, it will help me get a full-time position somewhere next year."

The timing of my pregnancy had worked out well. My dream of helping people—especially making sure kids felt seen, heard, and loved—had kept me going during the accelerated program I'd used to get my credentials and student teaching completed. I may not have wanted to be a biologist, but I loved teaching biology to kids. I'd finished the requirements before I'd needed to quit working, and filling in as a substitute since Kit's birth had been a great way to stay in the game. Still, I itched to have my own classroom in the fall.

"I know you'll knock 'em dead." Zach reached over to pat my hand. "And thanks for coming by with more bottles. I hope it's not too difficult to keep pumping."

"Meh. I just sort of hook myself up and read. That industrial pump Teddy rented does the job. I'll text you about how it goes today."

Zach smiled at me as he snuggled his daughter, who proceeded to spit up on the Seahawks onesie she was wearing. I got up to put my bowl in the sink and Mr. Bingham watched as I dumped the milk down the drain. I rinsed the bowl, so he wouldn't get even a smidge of a taste of it. He showed me his butthole.

I USUALLY WORKED on the northeast side of the city, but that day I was at a high school closer to downtown. My assigned classroom was a bit of a mess because I wasn't substituting for the regular biology teacher. I was filling in for another long-term sub who had gotten a bad flu. I'd be here four days, executing some straight-forward lesson plans. Making things even easier, the school was on half-days this week due to parent-teacher conferences in the afternoons. Since I wasn't part of those, I planned to spend my free time after lunch prepping for the next morning.

The class was working with microscopes desperately in need of cleaning. After I did that, I assessed the room, frowning at the lifeless space. The out-of-date informational posters and bare bulletin boards were probably not doing much to inspire students. Since I had time, I located butcher paper and replaced the white bulletin boards with a deep purple color. I googled some interesting pictures of magnified human body parts—students were always fascinated by the idea of eyelash mites living their best microscopic lives on people's faces—and printed them out to post.

As I hung the images, the cheap printer paper barely survived the stapler, so I feared the boards wouldn't last the week with rowdy teenagers coming and going. I recalled seeing a laminating machine in the flex space between the classrooms.

I was turning on the machine to warm up when I heard Ms. Leong next door talking to one of her conference attendees. "...

have seen tremendous improvement since he got here. It was iffy for a while, but he seems to have turned a corner."

That sounded good. I guessed it was easier to have conferences when you could give the family a positive report.

"That's a relief. He's been working hard, and it's good to hear it's paying off..."

Oh. My. God.

I froze, a stack of laminating pouches sliding through my fingers, scattering onto the floor as every hair on my arms stood rigidly at attention. I shrank back and my breath hitched at the continued sound of his voice. His words whirred together, drowned out by the ringing growing louder and hotter in my ears.

"He's also been speaking up more in class." Ms. Leong still hadn't seen me, hadn't noticed me drop the stack of plastic sheets.

"Great. I was worried he wasn't making friends. It's been slow, but he's finally met some new people."

My innate sense of self-preservation kicked in. I bent down and tried to pick up my mess as quietly as possible, intending to sneak back into my classroom. Why wasn't he in Pasadena? One sheet had somehow scattered underneath the table, so I had to reach for it. And because my arm was shaking, and because Murphy's Law is absolutely a thing, I accidentally swiped the cord with my hand and the laminator came crashing down to the floor.

Crack!

The machine was still intact—thankfully, I hadn't broken expensive equipment on my first day here—but the noise of it colliding with the floor was deafening, echoing in the small space between classrooms. The other teacher was immediately in the doorway. "Ms. Baxter, are you alright?!"

"I'm fine." I raised my arms up as if to prove it. "Just a minor mishap with the laminator." I put the machine and the pouches back on the table, hoisting myself up. I had just enough time to turn around and dust off my elbows before he came in behind Ms. Leong.

"Is everything—Oh, shit. Sadie?"

"Hey, Pete."

He simply stared at me for a moment, and I stared back. So many emotions came rushing up to the surface. The last time I'd seen him, when he'd just found out about Gage. And before that, when we'd both admitted to feeling helpless when it came to Renn.

Satisfied I was okay, and that the laminator was still operational, Ms. Leong looked back at Pete. "You two know each other?"

"Um...yeah. Sadie is a, uh, family friend." Pete swallowed thickly and turned to me. "I can't believe I'm running into you right now."

That was the understatement of the century. I straightened up and attempted to neaten my pants and shirt. "Same. It's been a minute."

"It's been too long." Pete looked a little thicker around the middle, and there were flecks of gray in his hair, but then he smiled and it was exactly the same. He turned to Ms. Leong. "We were done with our conference, right? I'd love the chance to catch up with Sadie—I mean, Ms. Baxter—if I can."

"We're done. I'm glad I could give you an excellent report on Robert. But I'm not sure about Ms. Baxter's schedule." Ms. Leong, a very sweet veteran teacher in her fifties, gave me a sympathetic look that clearly said the ball was in my court—she'd be happy to make my excuses to Pete if that's what I wanted.

"I'm actually free right now." I nodded at her in gratitude. "I'd love to catch up."

My shock was wearing off as I motioned for Pete to follow me into my temporary classroom. The echoing snick of the door shutting behind him drove home that we were standing together, only a few feet apart for the first time in two years. It felt unreal.

"I can't believe you teach here," he marveled. "Robbie never said anything."

"I'm just substituting. This is my first day, so he probably didn't know."

I was still wrapping my brain around the fact that I was talking to Pete. I'd imagined what it might be like to run into him or Renn or Archie again, even Robbie or Gage. But it was one thing to suppose how it might go down, and another to experience the mind-bending reality. I collected myself, leaning my knuckles against one of the chest-height lab tables.

"Well, you're a sight for sore eyes. You look amazing."

I peered down at my well-fitting charcoal gray slacks, black button down and black heels. My hair was longer than the last time he'd seen it, recently highlighted, and braided in a loose rope down my back to show off the silver statement earrings that had been a birthday gift from Teddy two months ago. I guess if you had to run into a ghost from your past, it was lucky if it happened when you looked your best.

As I spun to face Pete, I saw his fingers hovering over his phone. "Sorry," he said sheepishly, putting it back in his pocket. "Just sending a text telling them I'll be in a little later than planned." I couldn't help but wonder if *them* included Renn.

My mind raced with questions I was too afraid to ask. "I've gotta be honest, Pete. I'm kind of in shock here. I don't even know what to say."

He laughed. "Yeah. This was not how I was thinking this afternoon would go down when I came to talk about Robbie's chemistry grade."

His nephew seemed like a safe enough topic. I could talk about Robbie without being tempted to ask about...anything else. "I'm curious about why he's in school here. Did you leave Pasadena?"

He shook his head. "Nah. We all usually live in the house still, me included. But I kept my apartment downtown. After everything that happened, Re—Um, we decided it would be best for Robbie to have a fresh start. We used the address for my place to get him enrolled here."

"Ah. Cool. And it sounds like it's going well." Things had to be improving if Pete was the one covering teacher conferences.

"Thank God." Pete chuffed. "Robbie seems to be through the worst of his teenage asshole phase. He's even talking about apprenticing in the shop next year."

"That's great." I left it there, painfully. With Pete standing right in front of me, it was difficult not to interrogate him. Were he and his nephews getting along? How did Gage take the news about his paternity? Was Renn okay? Did he miss me?

Pete gave me a sideways smirk, like he could read my mind but had no intention of satisfying my curiosity. He knew as well as I did who should answer those questions.

"How have you been, Sadie?"

Like Pete, I hesitated to fill in the blanks. I had a career I loved. I'd been Zach and Teddy's surrogate. I was still running. I was happy, healthy, and thriving. *And missing Renn every second of every day.*

"I've been good. I moved to North Hollywood, but I'm enjoying the chance to teach in this part of the city."

I sounded ridiculous, even to myself. "Should we talk about the weather next?" Pete asked, and I laughed, some of the tension finally broken.

"It really is good to see you," I reiterated. "But I meant it that I have no idea what to say. I know I left kind of...abruptly. I hope you understood."

He nodded. "Completely. I was there, remember? I don't want to say too much, but the truth is we are all in a better place now, and I doubt we would have gotten there if you hadn't come into our lives, into *his* life."

A better place. It wasn't much, but it was enough to fill me with a keen sense of relief. I sat down on the corner of the desk and took a breath. He didn't allude to Renn again, instead keeping to lighter subjects such as Gage's improved fastball and Robbie's new art classes.

"Thanks for telling me about the boys, Pete. I'm so glad you're all doing well."

"Don't thank me yet. In fact, you might be pretty upset with me in a minute."

"Huh?"

Ten seconds later I heard purposeful footsteps stomping down the hallway. With so few people in the school this late in the afternoon, I knew it couldn't be a coincidence. At the knock on my classroom door a moment later, I looked at Pete wide-eyed.

"What did you do?"

He shrugged. "It felt too much like fate. What can I say? I'm a romantic."

Pete walked over to my closed classroom door and opened it like he had every right to do so. I held my breath.

"What's this about, Pete? Is Robbie okay?" Renn's deep voice sounded frantic. "What the hell is this text? '911. Robbie's school. Room 206.' What is going on?"

"Robbie is fine. As far as I know, he's with Ryder at the house." Pete stepped aside and Renn came barreling through the doorway, still looking down at his phone.

I was leaning against the desk, bracing myself with my hands. I conjured a shy smile that was somehow in place by the time Renn finally glanced up at me. He did a double take, an actual double take like the kind you see in cartoons—blinking his eyes a few times, before shaking his head as though to clear his vision. His eyeballs then made a valiant effort to pop out of his face. His reaction turned my timid smile into a huge one.

"Holy fuck. Sadie," he stuttered only a beat, and then walked my way fiercely. I thought for a moment he was going to launch himself at me, so intent was his stride, but he stopped a foot away, before finally reaching to take my hands.

The two years had been kind to him, the last traces of boyish-ness gone from his face, replaced with more defined angles under a short scruffy beard. His standard daywear was the same—long-sleeved Studio Obscurum t-shirt and gray pants—but the bun-pony was larger, his hair longer and captured in a full coil. The lone tendril hanging loose against his cheek evoked images of running my fingers through his curls. I blinked the memories away.

He continued to hold my hands and gaze at me mutely, as though he couldn't believe this was happening. *Same, Renn, same.*

A throat-clearing noise sounded across the room. "Well, uh, I think my work here is done." Pete let himself out, shutting the door firmly behind him. Neither of us broke our stare to acknowledge his departure.

Renn glanced down at our hands before looking up at me again. "This is so crazy. I can't even believe this is happening."

"I know—"

"And I realize we need to talk, and I have so much to say, but I just...I..." His eyes were shiny as he stumbled. "I've thought of this so many times... Can I...hug you?"

"I want that so much." *Pride? Self-preservation? Never heard of 'em.* I leaned forward into his embrace as his arms tightened around me. I wrapped mine around his shoulders and plastered myself to him, burying my nose in his neck. He started swaying our bodies to a silent rhythm, as though he still couldn't get close enough. I understood the sensation. It was like that first drop of water after a grueling run. Like my body wanted to make up for every time over the past two years I'd wanted him and he wasn't there. Every time I'd reached for his warmth and come up empty.

His lips snaked out to skim against my neck before he forced himself to pull back. He laughed and grinned at me. "I'm not sure I could have stopped myself, honestly, but hugging was probably a bad idea because it makes me think about...other things." He leaned back further. "Shit. I hope it's okay I said that."

"More than okay." I laughed, leaning back in his arms without letting go. "How are you, Renn?"

He huffed. "The short version of that answer is I'm good. But the long version is that I have so much I want to tell you. And ask you. So much that I don't even know where to start." He exhaled, shaking his head. "I wasn't expecting to do this today...fucking Pete." I startled when he said that, mainly because he said it with fondness rather than vitriol.

"Fucking Pete," I concurred, smiling, finally pulling away completely to catch my breath.

He looked around and began putting the pieces together. "So, teaching? That tracks."

"Yeah. I got a vision of it when we were together. Helping people, kids especially, that's what gets me out of bed in the morning." I pointed to the picture of the eyelash mites. "Plus, biology is a pretty cool subject to teach."

"I'm sure your parents would be proud. Saving the world just like they did, but in a different way."

"Something like that."

"No more making lattes, then?"

"No. I quit Chester's right before I had Char—" I caught myself just in time. *Wait, should I just tell him?* "Uh, before I finished student teaching. Zach still pulls me in for shifts at Hal's sometimes, when he's short-handed."

"I'm weirdly glad to hear that. How is Zach doing?"

"He's good." *In for a penny, in for a pound.* "He and Teddy, they have a daughter now. Charlotte—Kit—is about six months."

Renn eyeballed me with an inscrutable expression before glancing down at the floor. He spoke quietly. "I thought that might be the case. I was almost afraid to ask, though."

"What do you mean?"

He exhaled on a woosh and took another step back, shoving his hands in his pockets before peering up sheepishly. "I mean, I saw you—at Chester's—about eight months ago. And you were obviously pregnant. And I was pretty sure it was Zach and Teddy's.

I mean, that was what you wanted to do. But I was also terrified that maybe you fell in love with someone else, that you were having some other guy's baby, and I just was too chickenshit to find out."

There was so much to unpack in that statement. *He had come to see me? But then he'd changed his mind?* I wasn't sure if I wanted to kiss him or shake him. He attempted to explain.

"Look, Sadie. I don't know how much you want to hear about what's gone on with me these past two years. I don't know where your mind is—"

"Everything, Renn. I want to hear everything."

He backed up against one of the student desks before sitting on it. "It was only a few months after I sent you that letter I knew I had made the biggest mistake of my life. Once my perspective was less...cloudy, I realized letting you go was the dumbest move I could have made. I should have asked you to wait, should have known that I was going to ask for help eventually. Once I could see things as they truly were, I felt incomplete. I wanted you there. Badly. But by the time I figured that out, months had gone by and it seemed like I owed it to you to work on myself, to make it all mean something."

I understood what he was saying since I'd had similar reasoning when I'd walked away from him. I nodded encouragingly, but said nothing as he continued.

"I finally got it through my thick skull that everyone was basically dying to support me. Archie told me he had always wanted to do more for us. My dad was his best friend, after all. I just hadn't been willing to let him. And even before I found out about him and Mary, I'd been keeping Pete at arm's length. Anything to stop the memories from coming. But once I realized how much pushing people away was holding me back, hurting my brothers—that it fucking cost me a relationship with the most amazing woman on the planet..." He took a moment to look me up and down with volcanic heat in his eyes before breathing out, "God, you're so beautiful." Then he shook his head, willing himself back to the story he'd been telling. "Anyway, I just got tired of it. I made some changes. Started going to therapy and working through my shit."

He'd actually gone to therapy? If I'd had any lingering doubts that leaving him had been the wrong move, they evaporated instantly.

Renn rested his hands on his knees, pushing on them lightly as he continued. "I talked to Pete about art school and considered it seriously. He and Archie were both encouraging, offering to cover for me at the shop. Ultimately, I decided it wasn't for me, but I've been spending a lot more time drawing and painting. About a year ago, I decided to do some traveling. It worked out because Pete wanted a chance to be on his own with the boys for a while. Archie agreed to keep an eye on things, and I went to Europe, Central America, Mexico, did the whole backpacking and hosteling thing for a few months, got to put some ink on a few of the locals. It turns out I'm the kind of person who likes to travel, but I don't necessarily want to do it all the time. I missed being in one place for a while, so I headed back to the States. I met up with an old friend of my dad's in Las Vegas, another tattoo artist, and I worked in his shop for about three months. Learned a bunch of new techniques and also more about the business side of things. What's crazy is that I could still keep up with my therapist through all of this. You can use Skype for those things now. Eight months ago, she helped me recognize I was ready to come home to Los Angeles. I realized that this is where I need to be—with my family, especially Robbie and Gage. And I want to work at Studio Obscurum. I want to be around people who knew my dad, now that I'm finally able to talk about him without feeling like it's a knife to the gut."

"I'm thrilled for you, Renn. I'm so glad you've found some peace." I frowned at myself. "God, that sounds so trite. I hope you know how sincere I am. I guess I just wish...I dunno...I wish I could have been there for you, too. Helped you."

He barked out a laugh. "You absolutely helped me. None of this would have happened without you. You told me once, after we had to be apart the first time, that it made you stronger just knowing that I was out there. Well, hear me now when I say… likewise." He twined his fingers together and stretched them out in front of himself. "Which sort of brings me to what happened when I got back and decided to try and see you. I couldn't kid myself anymore that there was a single good reason we shouldn't be together. I was in such a different place than when I'd written the letter, and even though I asked you not to wait for me, I had to find out…for sure."

He pushed away from the desk and came over to me, putting his warm palm against my cheek. "I wanted to find out because I never stopped loving you, Sadie. There was never anyone else for me…not even once."

I leaned my cheek into his hand. "Me neither," I whispered.

He circled his thumb against my cheek before dropping his hand, stepping away but staying near.

"It seemed wrong to text you, and I wanted to see you right away, so I took a chance and went to Chester's. I saw you through the window. At first, you were behind the counter and all I could see was how beautiful you were, but then you stepped out and I saw your belly." He got a faraway look as he spoke. "Like I said, I figured it was probably the surrogacy, but I couldn't bring myself to come in, to find out. I had been so mean to you. Whatever was happening, it was clear you'd moved on from our breakup. It didn't seem right to intrude."

"So you were never planning to talk to me?"

"It's funny you should mention that, because I've been thinking about it a lot lately. Archie and Pete have both been bitching at me that I needed to get over myself and contact you. Apparently, I'm a stupid fucking idiot or a wicked dumbass, depending on which one of them you talk to."

I laughed. I could picture the scene. When I'd seen Pete earlier, I realized I'd missed him, and now it hit home that I missed having Archie in my life as well. And I ached with how much I'd missed Robbie and Gage.

"Pete told me it felt like fate," I said.

"Pete can occasionally be a smart man."

Again, Renn's voice was fond. A lot had clearly changed. I didn't want to open up the gates to a potential minefield, but it compelled me to ask, "How is that going, you and Pete?"

He paused before answering. "Surprisingly well. It started getting better after we told Gage the truth."

"You told Gage?"

"Uh-huh."

"And it wasn't the explosion you were worried about?"

"I think it very well could have been. I mean, thank God it wasn't happening to Robbie. But what is there to say other than Gage is a great kid with a gentle soul. We ended up pulling both boys into the living room and having a big confab. This happened pretty soon after you split. I was still barely speaking to Pete at the time, but we thought it was better to get it over with. We decided to lay out the truth for them, minus the more salacious bits, and Gage just sort of says 'okay' and asks to watch TV."

"What? Really?"

"Yep. At first, we thought he was just in shock, but that wasn't the case. You know how he is—all sunshiny and chill. He just digested what we were telling him and then said he basically already knew, like he'd always felt it deep down."

"I'm not sure if that's fantastic or creepy." I reached over to tuck the errant strand of hair behind Renn's ear. "But I do know where he gets his sunshiny chill from."

He grinned. "All four of us ended up going to my therapist together for a while, and the boys went on their own too. Robbie couldn't really stay mad when Gage was so cool about everything.

Dr. Maddox helped us get better at talking to each other. It turns out I wasn't the only one who was mad at my dad."

"Do you still go?"

"Sometimes. But not as often. Things still aren't perfect. That's one reason Robbie had to switch schools. And now that Gage is eleven, he's asking more questions. I appreciate having the assist in answering them."

"That's great, Renn."

He took my hands in his again. "It's still so surreal to see you. And I want to talk to you about so many things. I want to hear all about teaching and Charlotte. But it's hard to do that when I also want to touch you so badly." He stopped and glanced regretfully around the classroom. "And this isn't the time or place."

He was right. Even though the school was basically empty, this classroom was not the ideal location for our reunion. "Agreed. Even if I am just a substitute, I'd like to keep my reputation intact, and it's already bad enough that I hurled the laminator onto the floor."

"What?"

"Nevermind." I inhaled heavily. I wasn't so foolish as to believe we were doing anything other than working our way back to each other. He'd made his feelings clear. And even if I had a few remaining doubts, it was what I wanted as well. "Why don't you come by my place tonight? I'm in NoHo now. I can text you the address."

"I'd love that. Seven o'clock?"

"That works. Your number still the same?"

"Sadie, you don't honestly think I would have changed my number when there was a chance you might have texted me, did you?"

CHAPTER

Twenty-Six

April 2018

FOUR HOURS LATER I was sitting nervously on my couch, waiting for Renn to arrive. I'd cleaned every imaginable surface in the apartment, gone for a lengthy run, and hooked myself up to the pump for twenty minutes, long enough to prevent any leaky breast emergencies.

He arrived right on time with flowers and chocolates, a clear callback to our first proper date. My new apartment looked similar to the one I'd shared with Zach, other than it only had one bedroom. I'd taken the time to add more personal touches to this space, including purchasing a retro-style credenza to house my vinyl collection in a place of honor. The blue and green color scheme was also more my style than the purple and gray Zach had preferred.

"It's nice," Renn said approvingly. "Plus, you're even closer to me now."

He put his offerings on the kitchen counter, and I motioned for him to sit on the couch with me. He looked amazing in dark jeans and a plain black V-neck sweater, hair gathered beneath the olive-green beanie I remembered so well.

"Sadie—"

"Renn—"

I smiled as we interrupted each other, before gesturing for him to continue.

"Sadie, I'm just going to come right out and say this." He leaned toward me and I marveled at how comfortable I already felt with him again. It was hard to imagine it had been two years. Hard to imagine I'd finished my education, moved apartments, and grown and birthed another human being in the time we'd been apart. He must have sensed the same level of rightness because he wasted no words. "I've had hours to think about this now, along with months and years before that, and I just want to tell you that nothing has changed for me. If anything, I'm even more sure. No one makes me feel the way you do, and I want to be with you. Always. I want my future to be with you."

I opened my mouth to speak, but he grabbed my hands to quiet me, touching his knees to mine. "Please, just let me get this out. All of it. I've thought about how so many people in your life failed you—your parents, your grandma, Henri. So many people failed to love you the way you deserved. When we finally got together after Halloween, you told me you'd stayed away because you'd felt unworthy, that finding out about Henri's son made you feel unlovable. When you came back, you said you were finally ready to be loved...and I felt so lucky because I would be the one to do that. And then...after we broke up...I realized I hadn't. You gave me the chance to be the first person to really love you the right way—and I didn't."

He rubbed his thumbs in circles over the backs of my hands, and I lit up with awareness as he continued.

"Sadie, I thought we were okay back then because I loved everything about you. I didn't understand what you were trying to show me all along, that it's not enough just to love someone. You have to let them love you in return, let them see all of you. I didn't allow you in. But I am ready now. I want everything with you, Sadie. If you let me, I'll do whatever it takes to prove to you we belong together."

I'd had a feeling he would say something like this, and I already had my answer prepared. "You don't need to prove anything to me, Renn. I want to be with you, too. I'm not interested in forcing you to work harder for it or making it more difficult than it needs to be. I think we've paid our penance and then some. We've already lost two years together because things got complicated."

My words were all the invitation he needed. He reached over to grab me and hoisted me into his lap, pulling me close for a long, drugging kiss. And it didn't matter that he'd just come through my doorway five minutes ago, been absent from my life for years before that. We'd been working our way toward this moment since the first time I'd walked into Studio Obscurum. At long last, both of us were ready. We'd simply run out of time to waste.

His tongue snaked into my mouth and it felt like coming home. He pulled away just long enough to murmur, "I love you," before diving in again. After running his lips along my neck, he added, "I know we have a lot to talk about, but I couldn't wait any longer to tell you, or to kiss you." He proved his point by sealing our lips together again.

We barely made it to the bedroom before our clothes were in a heap on the floor. I took one second to wonder if Renn would notice how full my breasts were or that I had new little stretch marks along my sides, but with the reverent way he was touching me, I didn't worry for long. Once we were fully undressed, standing next to my bed, I dropped to my knees to take him in my mouth.

He groaned. "Sadie, the only action my dick has gotten has been with my right hand. I'm already close."

"Good." I returned to my task.

Renn came in less than two minutes and then practically growled as he threw me on the bed, using his magic fingers to bring about one of the most intense orgasms I'd ever had. As we both lay there panting afterward, he chuckled. "Well, now that we've gotten that first one out of the way, I'd like to take my time."

So we did. Renn used his hands and mouth and tongue to reacquaint himself thoroughly with every part of my body, and I did the same. When he pushed himself inside me, I almost cried. I'd missed this more than I'd realized—being this close, him filling up my body and my soul. He gazed down at me steadily as he branded me with his confident movements, remembering every trick and turn of my body. A few hours later, he was lying on his side behind me when he lifted my leg up to enter me from behind. The position didn't allow for deep penetration, but the intimacy of being lined up that way was incredible. He gripped his arm across my chest, pulling me as close as possible, pumping into me with short strokes as he used his fingers to help get me there.

"I'm so lucky you're mine. I'm never letting you go again," he whispered into the dark.

We were still awake at two a.m. I laid my head on Renn's chest and listened to his heartbeat as he ran a lazy hand up and down my back. I let my fingers tangle in his happy trail before reaching down to execute a few slow strokes of his semi-hard cock. He looked over at me and raised an eyebrow.

"I know I'm young, Sadie, but I don't think a fourth orgasm is happening right now."

I laughed and kept my hand exactly where it was. "Sshhhh. Just think of it as a dick massage then. Your barnacle penis and I are getting reacquainted."

"My what?"

"Your massive monster cock, Renn," I said without inflection. "When I was looking up biology factoids and pictures to print out for the classroom today, one website highlighted that a barnacle's penis is eight to nine times its body size, the largest in the animal kingdom."

"Wait a minute. You mean to tell me you had that little gem in your pocket and you decided to go with the eyelash mites?"

"What can I say? Dick pics just don't belong on classroom walls. Even marine peen."

He squeezed me tightly to him and kissed my forehead. "God, I missed you."

"Me too."

I rolled off him and we landed on our sides, sharing my pillow, nose-to-nose as we spoke in hushed tones.

"Tell me about Charlotte." The moonlight was peeking through the blinds just enough for me to catch him smiling.

"She's perfect. The center of her daddies' existence." I reached out to tug gently on a strand of his hair. "After I got your letter, I gave myself a few months to get my head on straight, but then Zach, Teddy, and I started drilling down on timing and logistics."

Unsure how much Renn wanted to hear, I gave him the condensed version of events, leaving out some of the more awkward details about the actual...ahem...insemination. I talked about how we tried for two months, succeeding on the third cycle. I mentioned how I loved being pregnant and had none of the symptoms you heard about in TV and movies—no weird cravings, no particular nausea or fatigue, no backaches. When it came time to give birth, I turned out to be one of the rare women who had things relatively easy, laboring for less than four hours and producing a healthy baby with no drugs or other interventions necessary.

I knew Renn would be curious about the biology of things. Everybody was—it was shocking, the number of nosy questions I'd received about how we'd "made" Charlotte and who her "real" father was—so gross. But Renn was someone I planned to share my life with, so it seemed right for him to know that, with the way we'd done things, there had been a fifty-fifty chance for either

Zach or Teddy to be the biological father, and Teddy's swimmers had won the day.

"And it doesn't matter to either of them one bit," I said.

"I hear that. If anyone understands that blood and biology don't decide family, it's me."

With that opening, I asked Renn to catch me up on his life. Apparently, it was a constant series of negotiations. Pete had moved into the house full-time, but Renn was still the main decision maker for the boys, even Gage, although Pete was highly present in their lives. They hadn't written a blood oath about it or anything, so circumstances could still change, but they weren't planning to do anything legal or official to acknowledge Pete as Gage's father. Gage had started calling him "Pete" instead of "Uncle Pete," but Renn said he'd only recently let a few "Dads" slip. And things would certainly evolve. Now that Robbie was fifteen and Gage eleven, they had their own opinions.

I rolled onto my back and put my hands behind my head. Renn crooked his elbow and rested his head in his hand, looking down at me from his side. He ran a tentative finger between my breasts and continued until he had his full palm resting on my belly.

"I don't want to scare you, Sadie," he began, roaming slow circles across my torso. "But hearing you talk about Charlotte makes me think about babies. In particular, it makes me think about *my* babies...with you."

My eyes grew wide looking at him and I caught my breath. By every conceivable measure, this was moving insanely fast, but there were four years of history pushing the pedals.

"Sadie, you are it for me. We can go at whatever pace you're comfortable with—race car or stoned sloth—but I want my future to be with you. Kids, sharing a life, marriage if that's something you're into, raising my brothers together, getting to be Charlotte's Uncle Renn, bringing you coffee while you grade papers—all of it. I meant what I said." He put the flat of his hand on my belly, sliding it over to palm my hip as he declared, "I want everything with you."

I grinned in the darkness, almost pinching myself as the words I'd been hoping to hear for years washed over me. I wanted to shout to the heavens in elation, open the door and scream my joy to the neighborhood—but restraint seemed called for. "Let's be together tomorrow, Renn. And we'll see about the rest."

"Okay," he whispered, kissing my shoulder.

I would tell him soon, tell him how much I loved him and wanted a future. But in that moment, I just wanted to be greedy, surrounded by his desire and vulnerability, to take what he was finally willing to give me.

In the morning, we woke up in no hurry to leave the bed. I glanced over as Renn took an assessing look around my room. His gaze landed on a floating shelf above my dresser which housed the wooden lotus Zach had given me, next to the framed lotus Robbie had painted.

"I think of them as my bookends," I said.

"Bookends?"

"Uh-huh. When I first came from Boston, I was a mess. Zach gave me the wooden lotus at the beginning of my healing journey. Robbie gave me the drawing on the day I knew I would be okay." *The day I was strong enough to leave you because you refused to give me what I needed.* I didn't have to voice the thought out loud. Renn understood. "And of course I have the lotus you tattooed on me carrying through the whole thing."

I'd put the shelf up just before Charlotte was born, appreciating the symbolism, wanting to make peace with losing the love of my life.

"But aren't you forgetting something?" Renn asked.

"What?"

"You have your lotuses, and you say they symbolize the beginning, middle, and end of your journey, but what about the ouroboros?"

I squinted at him. "What about it?"

"Well, the ouroboros is the snake eating itself, right? It's infinity. Right there in the middle of your lotus. They're both symbols of your strength."

My cheek ticked up. He was being philosophical now, and I loved it. I loved him. "What are you getting at?"

"I'm saying the ouroboros is a reminder that our journeys are never truly over. We're always at the beginning of something, or the end of it. The strength you earned leaving Henri didn't end. You carried that strength into your next journey."

He was right. I honestly hadn't thought about it that way. But then again, he was the one who had designed this tattoo. I'd told him I wanted the lotus. Somehow, he'd known I also needed the ouroboros.

"Sadie, just because we had to be apart to work on different journeys doesn't mean we don't belong together. We're also the ouroboros. We're meant to go on more journeys together." He rolled over on top of me and pinned my arms above my head as he leaned down to kiss along my jaw and neck, whispering, "Lots and lots of journeys."

Renn pushed up onto his fists and braced himself above me. He lifted his left arm up and showed me something I hadn't noticed yesterday.

"Hey!" I grabbed it to look closer. On Renn's wrist, perfectly inked, was the fourth panel of my tattoo, my lotus and ouroboros with the broken chains beneath them.

"I still have the ouroboros charm you gave me for Christmas in a drawer at home, but I got worried when a few links on it broke. I had Archie do this when I got back from Las Vegas because no matter what happened, I wanted you with me."

I didn't know what to say. It was so intimate and yet so understandable. How many times had I touched the back of my leg and been grateful to have that permanent mark from Renn? I couldn't blame him for wanting one of his own. To always be with each other.

"It's beautiful." *Fuck waiting and reveling.* Time was a construct. And a luxury. "I want everything with you, too, Renn. All the things. As soon as possible."

He leaned down and kissed my nose. "Okay."

EPILOGUE

I WAS STILL WIPING down the kitchen counters when the doorbell rang at four o'clock. I wasn't sure I'd done more than just smear grease around, but at least I'd tamed the mountain of dishes and scrubbed off the weird rings that always seemed to pop up around the electric burners. I'd had visions of cleaning the house from top to bottom before our friends arrived to celebrate Renn's thirty-first birthday, but that had been a fool's bet from the start. With three toddlers to keep alive, I'd had to settle for cleaning the guest bathroom and picking up just well enough to prevent most trip hazards. Anyone looking past the surface would find piles of unfolded clothes in the laundry room, and a refrigerator I'd not wiped down properly since the holidays. Not to mention exactly zero beds in the house had been made that morning—just pull the blanket up and call it a day, amiright? Plans usually went awry with tiny tyrants running the show.

As if on cue, Harper came toddling into the kitchen and wrapped herself around my ankle. "Doh-bell," she announced triumphantly.

"I know, baby girl. I heard it." Then I heard Gage swing the door open and say hello to Zach, Teddy, and Kit, who wandered into the kitchen. I frowned at Zach when I saw he was carrying a massive birthday cake.

He laughed at my expression and bopped me on the nose. "Don't worry. I also have brownies, cupcakes, and ice cream in there." He pointed at the grocery bag Teddy was carrying.

"That's good you brought peace offerings, because I'm still pissed at you about earlier."

That morning, I'd run a half marathon in Santa Monica. My time wasn't great, but I'd completed the race. It was the first competitive event I'd done since the twins were born. The only bad part happened at the finish line. My cheering section—comprised of Renn, our three daughters, Robbie, Gage, Pete, Archie, Teddy, Zach and Kit—were all wearing royal blue shirts with green lettering reading "Team Dumpy." To make matters worse, they had my picture on the back, just in case there was any confusion about who Dumpy was. There was a reason I'd never told Zach about that, and Renn was certainly going to pay one day for letting it slip.

"I have no idea what you're talking about, doll. Those shirts were gold." Zach cackled like a cartoon villain. "In fact, I was so grateful to Renn for telling me that story, it inspired me to put extra thought into his gift. Spoiler alert—it's a weekend away in Santa Barbara for the two of you. We'll babysit. Just say when."

I looked at the envelope he held out to me.

"For real?"

"Sure. You guys deserve it. You never got a honeymoon, and since you've done nothing but pop out babies during this pandemic, I'd say you've both earned a break."

I thumbed through the brochure. There were pictures of ocean views and gorgeous food I wouldn't have to prepare or cut into bite-size pieces for small people. "Okay. This almost makes up for Dumpy."

"I'm glad you said that since those t-shirts will definitely be making a reappearance."

I snapped my head up and slitted my eyes at my supposed best friend, until Teddy finally put an arm between us, smiling fondly at his husband. "Leave her alone, Zach. We all know you're hilarious." He turned to me. "Don't worry. I'll make sure we burn the shirts."

"Thank you."

"No problem…Dumpy." I startled for a moment before bursting out a laugh. Teddy's humor was sharp, but rarely seen.

"Hey, Baba!" Kit was no longer content to be quiet. "Don't call Suro dumpy! That's not nice!"

I bent down toward Kit and held my arms out. She came over and made a show of nosing her way in next to Harper. Now that she was four, her dads had explained the lightened-up version of our unconventional family ties. We weren't totally clear on how much she understood, but one thing that came out of it was that she started calling me Suro. I preferred it to Aunt Sadie, and the guys liked it too, so it stuck. "It's okay, sweet buns. Daddy and Baba were just teasing me. Sometimes friends do that."

Kit gave me a hug as she cast one more suspicious glare at her parents. Harper sort of petted Kit on her head and then squirmed for me to release them both. Hand-in-hand, they wandered into the living room to investigate the contents of the toy basket. I sighed when I realized how much time I'd spent collecting all the toys from some very unusual places around the house—how the hell did Mega Blocks always end up in the shoes?—and every single one of them would be strewn about the floor in thirty seconds.

I knew Zach and Teddy were thinking the same thing as they helped me put out chips and salsa and pop some pre-made apps in the oven. Renn had requested we keep things low-key. Apparently, his idea of the perfect birthday was cheering me on at a run in the morning and then going on a mysterious errand all afternoon.

"Where is the birthday boy?" Zach asked.

"He should be here soon with Robbie and Archie. Said he had a surprise but had to stop by the studio to get it. He was super vague."

The baby monitor crackled, and I heard the telltale signs the twins had woken up. They generally kept each other entertained for a few minutes and I smiled at their happy babbling.

"They are so good with their naps," Teddy commented. "Charlotte was such a beast to get down, and we always had to pick her up immediately when she got up."

"It's because there's two of them. Built-in playmates."

I hadn't always been so sanguine about the twins. Renn and I had gotten married only two months after getting back together, just a courthouse affair with a backyard party. I finished out a year of pumping for Charlotte, which made it difficult for me to get pregnant, but we were both eager to try. After Harper was born in August 2019, we were on the fence about having another. At the time, I'd really wanted to get back in the classroom since I'd never been able to do more than work as a long-term substitute. But then the pandemic broke out. It seemed like the universe was trying to tell us something. Since the world was going to be shut down for a while, Renn and I decided to just go for it and have one more baby to complete our family. Except one baby ended up being twins—because when the universe speaks to you, sometimes she is sarcastic—and in December 2020 I gave birth to Simone and Sawyer. Harper and her sisters were only fourteen months apart, and we had our hands full for a while, but sanity had been making a slow return to our lives.

Gage went to see what Harper and Kit were up to and quickly found himself dressed in a tiger costume with a firefighter's helmet on top. Pete had moved into his downtown apartment full-time after Harper arrived, and at first, Gage shuffled between our two places, but he'd been spending more time with us lately. It wasn't surprising since he'd grown up here and was close with the girls. He patiently indulged his cousins, whom the world thought were his nieces, whom he thought of as sisters. I knew it made Pete sad, but he let his son be the arbiter of his time and did everything he could to stay close.

I was debating going to get the twins out of the bedroom when Renn came in—Pete, Archie, and Robbie on his heels. Shouts of "Happy birthday" came from our friends, even though they'd already said it that morning. I figured everyone wanted to celebrate after a long period of barely-managed chaos. For Renn's thirtieth last year, we'd not even acknowledged the occasion. No one had been vaccinated yet, so it hadn't been feasible to have people over. Our household had included two teenagers and three children under the age of two. Between the boys' online classes, managing the babies, and trying to keep Studio Obscurum afloat through the shutdown, most days had ended with me and Renn in a puddle on the floor.

Everything was easier now. I finally had a permanent job at a high school within reasonable driving distance. My career had solidified a few years later than expected, but I found it just as fulfilling as I'd imagined. Childcare had been a worry, but we'd ended up doing a nanny share with Zach and Teddy. They'd been adamant that all four girls grow up together, and we agreed.

It was important to me that Kit get to know Robbie and Gage, especially now that Robbie was grown and flown. After a pandemic-inspired gap year, he had started at Cal State Long Beach and was living in student housing. As proud as we were, we missed him terribly. At least he was apprenticing at the studio.

Renn came in and gave me a kiss, looking at his phone.

"Something up?" I asked.

"Just a happy birthday text from my mom." He shrugged. "Meh—at least she remembered." If there was one gray cloud in our lives, it was that Sheryl's drinking seemed to keep getting worse. Renn had put some firm boundaries in place so she had only the barest interaction with her granddaughters. It wasn't a simple situation. Maybe it would change, maybe it wouldn't, but we could only do so much.

"Thanks for giving me the afternoon," he continued, swiping his finger through the top of a cupcake. "I'm really excited to show you the surprise."

"I think it's funny that it's your birthday, but I'm getting a surprise."

"Trust me, this was mostly for me."

With that vague pronouncement, he glanced at the baby monitor and unleashed the soft smile he reserved exclusively for his daughters. "I'll go get them."

Everyone else found their way into the living room and I noticed Robbie seemed especially amped up. "You okay?"

"Yeah. It's just been a good day." He was grinning, and I wrapped my arm around his shoulders. Robbie leaned into my hug and reminded me we had a date to go running later that week.

Renn came in, Simone in one arm and Sawyer in the other, and my breath caught with love. Harper was having no part in sharing her daddy's attention and launched her little body around his legs. "I'm trapped," Renn feigned distress, handing one twin to Teddy and the other to Archie as he allowed Harper to tackle him to the sofa. Kit jumped on his back to complete the cuddle huddle.

"Alright, alright." I tried to calm everyone down before they destroyed the living room. "Enough suspense. What's the big surprise?"

Renn stood up. "I have to take my pants off." He reached for the string tie on the waistband of his sweats, giving me a wink.

Zach leaned forward on his elbows and declared, "Well, I like where this is going so far." He gave a playful leer until Teddy swatted at him to quit it. I looked at Zach, mouthing, "You are so predictable," and rolled my eyes. He blew me a kiss.

Renn pulled his sweats off to reveal he was wearing shorts underneath. He gestured to his leg. I looked down and saw that the tattoo outlined on his calf, the one Thomas had started, was now finished and colored in. Beautiful shades of purple, blue, and green filled in the Earth, while the melting heart had the color scheme of a sunrise.

"I did it!" Robbie burst out. "I mean, Archie watched the whole time, but it was me."

"It was all you, kid," Archie confirmed.

"You did great," Pete concurred. "Definitely inherited Thomas's artistic gift."

Renn looked at me with glassy eyes and I knew we were both remembering the day he told me about this outline. "I've been thinking about filling it in for a while now. I wanted to surprise you because I know you'll understand. The blank space didn't feel right anymore. Thank fuck."

I stepped into his arms and whispered into his ear, "I'm so glad. Happy birthday."

He murmured back. "You've given me the best present ever. This life we have. I hope you know that."

"I do know that. I feel it every day."

"What are you guys whispering about?" Zach broke in. "Either share it with the class or expect the Team Dumpy shirts to be on Etsy very soon."

I flipped him the bird as I turned back to kiss my husband. When I pulled away, Harper, Sawyer, and Simone were all practicing with their middle fingers. Kit attempted to chastise them while Robbie and Gage cracked up. Renn was right. All our empty spaces were not just full, they were overflowing.

ACKNOWLEDGEMENTS

I first got the idea to write a book after a fraught 2020. In addition to Covid ravaging the world, both my best friend's husband and my own ex-husband passed away unexpectedly. I had been a voracious reader of romance novels in my early twenties and had gotten away from it. Coming back to reading was like medicine amid so much real-life sadness. After a time, I became compelled to write. I wanted emotionally complicated characters—flawed characters—to find their HEAs. The stability Sadie finds within her found family after so much upheaval, as well as the experience Renn has with complicated grief, were both drawn from my own life. These characters had work to do, but in the end, they deserved to find happiness with each other. I hope you agree!

Of course, I was only able to go from reader to writer with a mountain of support and encouragement.

First and foremost, to the GLA Crew: Aviva, Chun, Erin, Leann, Madison and Woody. I can never thank you enough for the two years of love, laughter, questions, critiques, guidance, and constant reassurance that it was okay for me to want this.

To the Monday people (still need that name!): Alexander, Judy, Marc, Russ, Veronica and especially Alicia for the emergency re-reads. I couldn't have reached the finish line without your honest analysis and thoughtful suggestions.

To Scott—no classes, no book. Thank you.

For all of the alpha readers, beta readers, friends, and classmates who shared their experiences, read chapters, offered critiques and advice, or simply encouraged me—thank you. Special thanks to Sara, for being my first cheerleader, and Connie, for being the last, most meticulous set of eyes.

To Stephanie Anderson at Alt 19 Creative: Thank you so much for working with me, never being annoyed by my many emails, and taking this book as seriously as I do. All of the creative collateral—especially the cover—makes my heart happy, but I am just as appreciative of your kind words and sage advice in the home stretch of this process.

Angela O'Connell did amazing work editing this book. I promise that next time I will do better on the style guide, so she won't have to fix five hundred ellipses.

To my best friends: Britt, Adam, Eric, Niki, and Joanne. One of my main objectives for this book was to honor the idea that you can, in fact, choose your family. Sadie's bond with Zach was inspired by my own experience of found family, of loving and being loved by you all.

And of course, to my amazing husband and son, who had to live with me through all this. Sorry we had to have so much take out for dinner, and for bringing my laptop to baseball games, and because I was too busy writing to finish *The Mandalorian*, and for that time I had to explain "barnacle penis" in our browser history after some weird ads popped up, and for so many other things I could list. Thank you for supporting me in spite of everything, and for telling me how happy it made *you* to see *my* joy. There will never be enough words to express how blessed I am.

My biggest and most sincere thanks goes to any reader who takes a chance on this book. I truly hope you enjoy it.

ABOUT THE AUTHOR

Rory London is a writer of contemporary romance who lives in the delightfully gray Pacific Northwest, who is too into football and holidays, and who would probably write a lot more if there weren't so many books to read. When not writing or reading, Rory is probably drinking large quantities of coffee or diet soda, or taking long walks around the neighborhood, muttering about the characters that need to make it out of their brain and onto the page.

Other interests include outdoorsy things—as long as there is a real bathroom nearby—and indoorsy things—especially the kind that include good friends hanging out.

Rory lives with two other humans who bring laughter and joy into each and every day, as well as the world's most lovable dog, and three cats who are secretly plotting their revenge.

Connect with me via email at rorylondonauthor@gmail.com
Website: www.rorylondonauthor.com
Facebook: Rory London, Author
Instagram: @rory_london_author